ENCHANTRESS OF NUMBERS

This Large Print Book carries the
Seal of Approval of N.A.V.H.

ENCHANTRESS OF NUMBERS

A NOVEL OF ADA LOVELACE

JENNIFER CHIAVERINI

LARGE PRINT PRESS
A part of Gale, a Cengage Company

Farmington Hills, Mich • San Francisco • New York • Waterville, Maine
Meriden, Conn • Mason, Ohio • Chicago

LIBRARY OF CONGRESS CIP DATA ON FILE.
CATALOGUING IN PUBLICATION FOR THIS BOOK
IS AVAILABLE FROM THE LIBRARY OF CONGRESS.

ISBN-13: 978-1-4328-4366-3 (hardcover)
ISBN-10: 1-4328-4366-4 (hardcover)

ISBN 13: 978-1-4328-4367-0 (pbk.)

Published in 2018 by arrangement with Dutton, an imprint of Penguin Publishing Group, a division of Penguin Random House LLC

Printed in Mexico
1 2 3 4 5 6 7 22 21 20 19 18

To my mother,
Geraldine Neidenbach,
my favorite mathematician

The
BYRON, MILBANKE,
and KING FAMILIES

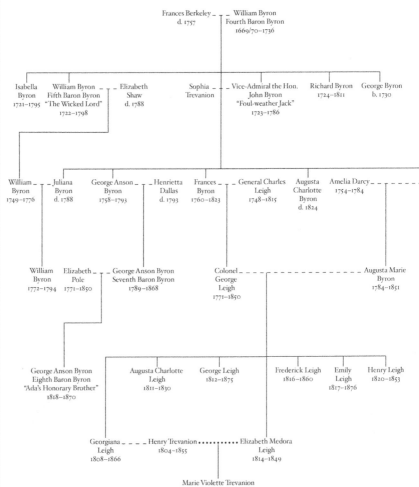

Frances Berkeley – – William Byron
d. 1757 Fourth Baron Byron
1669/70–1736

Isabella | William Byron – – Elizabeth | Sophia – – Vice-Admiral the Hon. | Richard Byron | George Byron
Byron | Fifth Baron Byron | Shaw | Trevanion | John Byron | 1724–1811 | b. 1730
1721–1795 | "The Wicked Lord" | d. 1788 | | "Foul-weather Jack" |
| 1722–1798 | | | 1723–1786 |

William – – Juliana | George Anson – – Henrietta | Frances – – General Charles | Augusta | Amelia Darcy – – – – – – –
Byron | Byron | Byron | Dallas | Byron | Leigh | Charlotte | 1754–1784
1749–1776 | d. 1788 | 1758–1793 | d. 1793 | 1760–1823 | 1748–1815 | Byron |
| | | | | | d. 1824 |

William | Elizabeth – – George Anson Byron | Colonel – – – – – – – – – – – – – – – – – Augusta Marie
Byron | Pole | Seventh Baron Byron | George | Byron
1772–1794 | 1771–1850 | 1789–1868 | Leigh | 1784–1851
| | | 1771–1850 |

George Anson Byron | Augusta Charlotte | George Leigh | Frederick Leigh | Emily | Henry Leigh
Eighth Baron Byron | Leigh | 1812–1875 | 1816–1860 | Leigh | 1820–1853
"Ada's Honorary Brother" | 1811–1830 | | | 1817–1876 |
1818–1870 | | | | |

Georgiana – – – Henry Trevanion • • • • • • • • • • Elizabeth Medora
Leigh | 1804–1855 | Leigh
1808–1866 | | 1814–1849

Marie Violette Trevanion
1834–1873

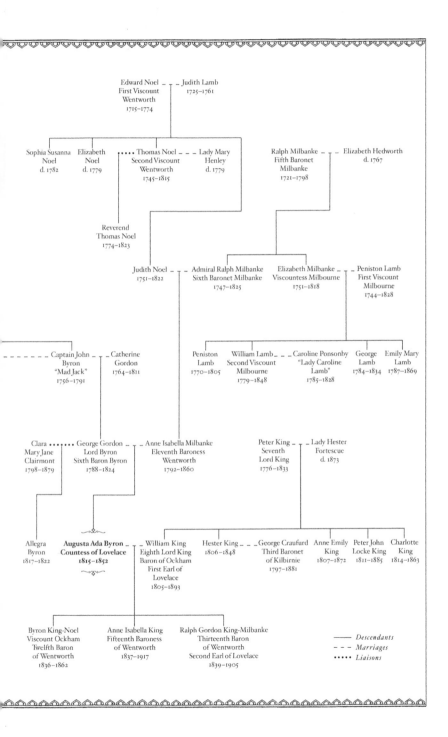

Edward Noel – ⌐ – Judith Lamb
First Viscount   1725–1761
Wentworth
1715–1774

Sophia Susanna   Elizabeth   •••• Thomas Noel – – – Lady Mary   Ralph Milbanke – ⌐ – Elizabeth Hedworth
Noel   Noel   Second Viscount   Henley   Fifth Baronet   d. 1767
d. 1782   d. 1779   Wentworth   d. 1779   Milbanke
                                1745–1815   1721–1798

Reverend
Thomas Noel
1774–1823

Judith Noel – ⌐ – Admiral Ralph Milbanke   Elizabeth Milbanke – ⌐ – Peniston Lamb
1751–1822   Sixth Baronet Milbanke   Viscountess Milbourne   First Viscount
                1747–1825   1751–1818   Milbourne
                                                                      1744–1828

– – – – – – Captain John – ⌐ – Catherine   Peniston   William Lamb – – – Caroline Ponsonby   George   Emily Mary
          Byron   Gordon   Lamb   Second Viscount   "Lady Caroline   Lamb   Lamb
          "Mad Jack"   1764–1811   1770–1805   Milbourne   Lamb"   1784–1834   1787–1869
          1756–1791   1779–1848   1785–1828

Clara ••••••• George Gordon – ⌐ – Anne Isabella Milbanke   Peter King – ⌐ – Lady Hester
Mary Jane   Lord Byron   Eleventh Baroness   Seventh   Fortescue
Clairmont   Sixth Baron Byron Wentworth   Lord King   d. 1873
1798–1879   1788–1824   1792–1860   1776–1833

Allegra   Augusta Ada Byron – ⌐ – William King   Hester King – – – George Craufurd   Anne Emily   Peter John   Charlotte
Byron   Countess of Lovelace   Eighth Lord King   1806–1848   Third Baronet   King   Locke King   King
1817–1822   1815–1852   Baron of Ockham   of Kilbirnie   1807–1872   1811–1885   1814–1863
                                    First Earl of   1797–1881
                                    Lovelace
                                    1805–1893

Byron King-Noel   Anne Isabella King   Ralph Gordon King-Milbanke
Viscount Ockham   Fifteenth Baroness   Thirteenth Baron   ——— Descendants
Twelfth Baron   of Wentworth   of Wentworth   – – – Marriages
of Wentworth   1837–1917   Second Earl of Lovelace   ••••• Liaisons
1836–1862   1839–1905

PROLOGUE:
MY WAY IS TO BEGIN
WITH THE BEGINNING

1816

A piteous mewling jolts Lady Annabella Byron from her melancholy contemplation of the fire fading to embers though the evening is still young. With a start she straightens in her chair, tumbling the dispiriting medical journal from her lap to the train of her pale green silk gown. Instinctively she clutches her skirts, crumpling the letter from Dr. Baillie, which she has momentarily forgotten she holds. She wishes she could forget it entirely, this dreadful missive that confirms her worst fears about her husband's erratic behavior, his inexplicable cruelty.

Another plaintive cry, and Annabella's thoughts fly to her daughter, an infant scarcely seven weeks old. Images of the child's soft cap of dark hair and sweet rosebud mouth fill her mind's eye, and she feels her milk come down. She scrambles to gather up the fallen journal, tucks the letter inside, and sets both carefully upon her chair before hurrying down the corridor to the nursery.

She finds the nurse already there, cradling the fretful babe in her arms, gently rocking from side to side, murmuring tender endearments that fail to appease. Annabella loosens her gown, seats herself in the rocking chair, and gestures for her daughter; Mrs. Grimes quickly places the baby in her arms, and immediately the ravenous child latches on and begins to nurse, sucking greedily.

When the baby's hunger is sated, Annabella gently passes her, already half-asleep, into Mrs. Grimes's capable embrace. After whispering a few instructions, she inhales deeply, straightens her gown, and steps out into the corridor to confront what can no longer be avoided.

As she descends the stairs, her small, delicate hand grasping the banister for support, laughter drifts upward from her husband's quarters — his own voice, rich and rolling, and his half sister's, light and happy and eager. Augusta, whom Annabella once considered a friend and ally in the management of her fractious, impetuous husband, has proven to be a rival for his affections instead. Although Byron and Augusta grew up in separate households, the offspring of Captain John "Mad Jack" Byron by his two consecutive wives, and they did not meet until they were quite grown, they share a bond of intense affection that Annabella, an

10

only child, knows she cannot fathom.

She reaches her husband's chamber and raises her hand to knock upon the door, but she cannot quite bring herself to do it, and at the sound of their voices — impassioned, intertwining, harmonious — her hand falls to her side. Remorse takes her breath away. She loved Byron devotedly, loves him still, but a fierce schism has torn them apart, and for all her vaunted reason and powers of calculation, she cannot figure out how to rectify it. Nor indeed should she, as Dr. Baillie has confirmed.

If only she could take her younger self in hand and convince her to pay attention to the signs all around her, the sudden tempests and long absences and misunderstandings that revealed with all the subtly of a thunderclap that Byron would make a very poor husband. But even if she could, she knows her words would be a waste of breath. From the earliest days of their courtship, caught up in the heady intoxication of a blossoming romance with the greatest poet of the age, that self-possessed, precociously intellectual heiress had willfully ignored anything that warned of impending doom.

And there had been many such warnings.

She first observed George Gordon, sixth Lord Byron, in March 1812, at a party given by Lady Caroline Lamb, the beautiful, erratic daughter-in-law of her aunt Lady Melbourne. Within days of embarking upon her first London Season, Annabella had learned that Byron was the most sought after guest at any gathering thanks to the sudden, excessive fame that had followed the unprecedented success of his poem *Childe Harold's Pilgrimage,* two brilliant cantos published with the tantalizing hint that he might compose more if they were well received. All eyes followed him when he entered a room, and murmurs of anticipation swept along in his wake. He was a genius, some whispered in awe. He was a libertine, said others, looking scandalized, but often no less admiring.

Annabella observed all this commotion with the same studious detachment she applied to any natural science. She was quite the fashion herself that spring, graceful and pretty at nineteen, with long, glossy brown hair, clear blue eyes, creamy fair skin, and a petite, well-shaped figure. She had received an excellent classical education, and in mathematics, science, and languages she was regarded as a prodigy, and not only by her doting parents, who cherished her as an only daughter born long after they had given up hope of children. In her manner she was frank and articulate, without any of the flighty airs other young ladies assumed, and she was known for being calm, strong-minded, pious, and concerned about the plight of the working poor. The

12

fact that she was descended from Henry VII and stood to inherit a substantial fortune only added to her charms, and she was not surprised to find herself attracting the attention of many worthy suitors.

That fateful morning at Melbourne House, Annabella studied Lord Byron from across the drawing room as one would examine any wild, exotic, and possibly dangerous beast, but she did not seek out his acquaintance. "I felt no need to make an offering at the shrine of *Childe Harold,*" she told her mother afterward, her voice rippling with disdain for the silly young ladies who flung themselves into his path.

But it was not only the ladies who venerated him. Young gentlemen glowered, tousled their hair, knotted their neck handkerchiefs at their throats, and left their shirt collars unbuttoned in imitation of their idol. In conversation, when they lacked clever observations of their own, they quoted Byron's evocative phrases, nodded sagely, and exchanged significant glances as if in agreement that nothing more needed to be said. Some who Annabella knew could not tell the difference between an iamb and a dactyl went about with ink-stained fingers and a distracted air as if privately conversing with their poetical muse. Byron ignored them, which seemed only to intensify their admiration.

Annabella, who had composed verses long

before she had ever heard the name Byron, became so annoyed and disgusted with the way they carried on that when she returned home she took pen in hand and let her feelings burst forth in a poem. "The Byromania" was both a rebuke and a lament, chiding those who went about "smiling, sighing, o'er his face / In hopes to imitate each strange grimace," and mocking "his magic sway" which "Compels all hearts to love him and obey." Very satisfied with her work, she read the poem aloud to her most trusted friends, but although they giggled and praised her and begged her to let them copy it, she refused. She dared not risk letting the poem fall into Byron's hands. Although she might disparage him in secret, she did not want him to dislike her.

One might have expected a young lady so determined not to succumb to Byromania to avoid him at all costs, but as the Season progressed, Annabella instead took advantage of every occasion to study him. "There passes the comet of the year, shining with his customary glory," she murmured acidly into an acquaintance's ear as he walked by at a party without glancing their way, his deformed foot rendering his gait awkward.

"Just ignore him if he vexes you so much," the young lady whispered back, her gaze fixed on the poet so ardently that Annabella knew she was not inclined to ignore him herself.

Annabella prided herself on her indifference to his masculine beauty, his strong jaw and flashing dark eyes, and she whispered little jokes to her friends about how his hair seemed perpetually windswept, as if he had just finished racing a horse across the moors instead of perambulating from the hall to the drawing room. "He must arrange it that way on purpose," she said, evoking shocked giggles from her friends. "What an affectation! He must think himself the hero of one of his own poems."

Then, in April, at a party given by her friend Lady Gosford, her curiosity and exasperation finally got the better of her. She could not simply ignore Byron, as her smitten acquaintance advised, just as one could not ignore a sharp pebble in one's shoe. It was time to shake him out and be done with him.

She resigned herself to contriving an introduction, and when she crossed paths with her cousin William Lamb in the hall, she decided to get it over with. "My dear cousin," she greeted him, smiling. "How good it is to see you."

"Annabella," he exclaimed, taking her hand and kissing her on the cheek. At thirty-three, he was tall, dark-haired, and strikingly handsome. "How lovely you look. How are my aunt and uncle? Is your father feeling better?"

"He's much recovered, thank you. He'll be pleased that you asked." She glanced about for his wife. "Is Lady Caroline here?"

His smile faded. "No. I regret that she is . . . indisposed."

"Oh, dear. Nothing serious, I hope."

"Just Caro being Caro."

"I see." She knew he meant that Lady Caroline had had one of her infamous rows, either with her husband or with his imperious mother, Lady Melbourne. "A pity. I had hoped to ask her to introduce me to Lord Byron."

"Why would you want to meet him?" her cousin asked sharply. "Why would you think Caro should make the introduction?"

"I don't *want* to meet him, but I think I *should*," Annabella replied, taken aback. "Lady Caroline told me that they were quite intimate friends, so naturally I thought of her when I decided the deed must be done. She does know him, does she not? Or was she merely boasting?"

"She knows him, but I don't think you should. I beg your pardon" — he offered her a quick, abrupt bow — "if you'll excuse me —"

"Cousin?" said Annabella, bewildered, but it was too late. He had hurried off down the hall.

"Men and their jealousies," a woman remarked behind her. Turning, Annabella discovered her aunt Lady Melbourne — tall and regal, elegantly attired in a gown of rich mauve silk, her brown hair adorned with strings of pearls and elaborately arranged to add several inches to her stature.

"William is jealous of Lord Byron?" Annabella's cousin had served as a member of Parliament for seven years and he stood to inherit a substantial fortune as well as the title of Viscount Melbourne. By all accounts he had a brilliant political career ahead of him. Why should he be jealous of a poet who possessed literary laurels, a title, and fame, but no fortune to speak of except a decrepit ancestral estate? At least that was what the rumors said. "William doesn't wish to write poetry, does he?"

"Certainly not," said Lady Melbourne, laughing dryly. "Never mind him, or Lady Caroline. I'll introduce you to Lord Byron myself."

Annabella's heart thumped, but before she could demur, Lady Melbourne took her arm and steered her down the hall and into a small salon made to seem even smaller by the dark paper hangings on the walls, a pattern of gold ogees and flowers on a vermillion ground. The crowd gathered around Lord Byron added to the claustrophobic atmosphere, but as Lady Melbourne sailed toward him, the throng parted and dispersed like a flock of startled gulls before a schooner.

In a voice touched with a hint of amused irony, Lady Melbourne introduced Annabella and Lord Byron, and after exchanging a few perfunctory inquiries with the poet about the health of various mutual acquaintances, she sailed off again, leaving Annabella somehow both pleased and inwardly fuming.

"I found much to admire in your *Childe Harold,*" Annabella told Byron when they were alone, almost indifferently, so he would not mistake her for one of his fawning fanatics. "In particular, its deep feeling, and its call for the liberation of enslaved nations. On the whole, it was quite good."

"I thank you." He inclined his head courteously, but his penetrating gray eyes never left hers, and the corners of his mouth curved in a way that made a curious shiver of anticipation run up her spine. "Until you said so, I wasn't quite sure."

She almost smiled, but she realized just in time that he was mocking her. "I'm sure your next work will be much improved for the practice," she said sweetly, hiding her indignation.

"Improved or not, better or worse, it will still be vastly superior to anything else published this year," he said darkly, casting a challenging glare about the room as if confronting a host of mediocre poets. "At least it will say something. At least it will be *new.*"

She understood implicitly that this was not

a boast so much as a lamentation over the state of English poetry, and she bristled. "Indeed, your opinion of your fellow poets precedes you," she said, a trifle sharply. "I've read your *English Bards and Scotch Reviewers.* It was quite scathing, one might even say unkind."

"It was not meant to be kind."

"In that case, it was a resounding success, but I cannot understand what would have compelled a gentleman in your position to so mercilessly caricature a man like Mr. Blackett."

"Ah, yes." He nodded. "Joseph Blackett, the cobbler."

"The poet," she corrected him. Though a cobbler by trade, Mr. Blackett had shown superior genius that belied his humble origins. Annabella and her mother had become his patrons, providing him with a cottage on their estate and an income so that he might devote himself to composing poetry. His promise was cut short by his untimely death at the age of twenty-three, a loss Annabella still mourned.

"The cobbler with higher aspirations," Lord Byron corrected her in return.

"You dismissed Mr. Blackett as a peasant and a fool," she accused, surprised by how much the memory of his satirical barbs still stung. "Why shouldn't a shoemaker aspire to write poetry?"

"I intended no harm."

"You called him 'the tenant of a stall' who 'employs a pen less pointed than his awl.' How could that do no harm?"

Byron shrugged, amused by her outrage. "Insightful criticism can spur a poet to improve his craft. You may recall that Mr. Blackett was not the only man I called out in that work."

"No, but he was certainly the lowest in rank. Unlike the great lord of Newstead Abbey, Mr. Blackett depended for his livelihood upon the generosity of patrons. It was unkind of you to push a man so far beneath you even further down, especially when he had only a year to live."

Byron's sensuous mouth curved in a mocking smile. "In my defense, Miss Milbanke, I could not have known he was going to die."

"But you persisted in belittling him even after his death! What possible good did you hope to accomplish with that dreadful epitaph you wrote last spring?"

He winced at the word "dreadful" but said, "Most readers, I am told, found it amusing."

"Readers with a spiteful sense of humor, perhaps," she countered. " 'Poor Joe is gone, but left his all: You'll find his relics in a stall.' And then, 'Yet is he happy in his hole, With verse immortal as his sole.' Charming pun."

"How flattering. You learned it by heart."

She felt heat rise in her cheeks. "Only those

phrases that most offended my sense of justice."

"If your Mr. Blackett wanted to be regarded as a proper poet, shouldn't I have criticized his work as I would that of the greatest duke in the land? Wouldn't it be more insulting to hold his verses to a lower standard solely because of his rank?"

"Perhaps you shouldn't criticize his work at all."

"A bad poem foisted upon the defenseless public deserves whatever criticism it receives. I've done him a favor. His fame is greater for my criticism than it ever was for his poetry." Before she could protest, he added, "Nonetheless, you're kind to defend his memory and legacy, just as you and your mother were very good to support Mr. Blackett in life."

His sudden turnabout so astonished Annabella that she was rendered speechless, but she inclined her head in acknowledgment of the compliment. It seemed sincerely meant, but she did not know him well enough to be certain.

Intrigued in spite of herself, she set aside her indignation and twice more that week sought out his company in Society. On both occasions they discussed poetry and literature, debating which was the best novel written in the English language and whether a poem could ever evoke strong emotions from a reader if the poet himself had never experi-

21

enced them. These conversations were animated and witty, and Annabella could not mistake the curious sidelong glances they drew — and no wonder, for they were an unlikely pair, the passionate, headstrong, irreverent poet and the prim young woman for whom virtue, reason, and self-control were guiding principles.

As she came to know Byron better, Annabella gradually felt her icy disdain thawing. She decided that he was rather more handsome than she had first believed, and more modest and courteous than his reputation allowed. And he was undeniably gifted, a genius, one of the few people of her acquaintance whose intellectual powers equaled her own. Despite the troubling gossip about his character, she glimpsed flashes of true goodness behind his caustic condemnation of society and any hapless fellow who annoyed him, until at last, convinced that she had discovered a kindred spirit, she decided to bare her soul by showing him her poetry.

She enlisted Lady Caroline Lamb as her intermediary, for she doubted her cousin William would be willing. Soon thereafter, when they met at a dinner party, Lady Caroline seized her arm and led her off to an empty salon and withdrew a letter from her reticule. "Byron's response," she announced with a curious gleam in her eye as she unfolded it.

The broken seal told Annabella that Lady

Caroline had already read it. "What does he say?" she asked, suddenly anxious.

"I'll tell you. 'I have read over the few poems of Miss Milbanke with attention.' That's good. 'They display fancy, feeling, and a little practice would very soon induce facility of expression.' "

Her heart sank. "He does not think I have that already?"

"Apparently not. Let me give you the best bits. 'I like the lines on Dermody so much that I wish they were in rhyme. . . . The line in the cave at Seaham had a turn of thought which I cannot sufficiently commend. . . . The first stanza is very good indeed, and the others with a few slight alterations might be rendered equally excellent. The last are smooth and pretty.' High praise indeed from a man disinclined to give it."

Annabella felt a thrill of pride. "Does he say anything more?"

"He seems sorry that you did not have anything more to show him. Then he writes, 'She certainly is a very extraordinary girl; who would imagine so much strength and variety of thought under that placid countenance?' Then he says — oh, dear."

Her heart thumped. "What's wrong?"

"I hope this won't upset you, but he showed your poems to a friend."

"Why? What friend?"

"He doesn't give his name but says only

that he is an author fifty years old. Ah, but the friend was 'much more enthusiastic in his praises than I have been. He thinks them beautiful; I shall content myself with observing that they are much better than anything of Miss M's protégé Blackett.' "

It was unnecessary to slight Mr. Blackett, but Annabella would forgive Byron this time. "Let me read the whole of it myself," she said, reaching for the letter.

Quickly Lady Caroline snatched it out of reach. "No, no, my dear. Byron said I should share with you only as much as I think proper, and I have done that."

"But I want to know what else he wrote."

"No, you don't," said Lady Caroline emphatically, shaking her head as she folded the letter and tucked it out of sight down her bodice.

Annabella cajoled and teased, but Lady Caroline laughingly refused to divulge anything more, so Annabella thanked her and contented herself with Byron's praise and Lady Caroline's promises to tell her immediately if he offered any more.

Thus she was quite taken aback a few weeks later when Lady Caroline wrote to urge her to avoid Byron at her peril. In a letter so disjointed and rambling that Annabella suspected it had been written under the influence of alcohol, Lady Caroline warned that Annabella was in grave danger from the corrupting influence of London society, of whom Byron was its most sinister and dangerous representative. "You must shun friendships with those whose practice ill accords with your Principles," Lady Caroline insisted, urging her not to be tempted by Christian charity to tolerate evil in those she loved. "At all costs avoid befriending & protecting those falling angels" — it was obvious she meant Byron — "who are ever too happy to twine themselves round the young Saplings they can reach — but if they are falling you cannot save them — depend on that."

It was a strange and unsettling letter, and although Annabella scoffed at the image of herself as an imperiled shrubbery and Byron as a predatory, choking vine, Lady Caroline's words nonetheless took root. Annabella knew Byron had a reputation for depravity, which, along with madness, seemed to be the Byron family misfortune, passed from one generation to the next like land, debt, and title. These warnings cooled her admiration, and when Byron left London for his ancestral estate in Nottinghamshire, she was relieved to see him go. In September, when he wrote to halfheartedly propose marriage, she gently refused. He almost too happily promised never to raise the subject again, although he hoped they would remain friends.

That should have been the end of it. If only she had heeded Lady Caroline's warnings, that *would* have been the end of it.

But by the early days of the 1813 Season, Annabella's thoughts lingered upon the celebrated poet with disconcerting frequency. At parties, her cheeks flushed and she remained silent when other young ladies gossiped about his latest sexual conquests, confessed their longing to take him to bed themselves, and whispered rumors that he was extraordinarily well-endowed. On another occasion, her heart beat in sympathy for his pained frankness when she overheard him ask a circle of admirers, "Do you think there is one person here who dares look into himself?" Soon thereafter, he declared, "I have not a friend in the world."

His listeners talked over one another in their eagerness to contradict him, but he glowered and brushed them aside. Annabella knew what he meant. Sycophants and awestruck admirers surrounded him, attracted like dull, fluttering moths to the flame of his talent. She yearned to be the true friend he longed for and clearly needed — his true, devoted friend and nothing more. But when she tried to exorcise her rekindled affections by writing down all the reasons why she must not marry Byron, she found herself composing a long list of all there was to admire about him instead.

As spring passed into summer, Annabella and Byron crossed paths as they made their rounds of the London Season, but they did not speak. She received another proposal of marriage from Frederick Douglas, the heir of Lord Glenbervie and member of Parliament for Banbury in Oxfordshire, which she summarily rejected. As if to prove that Fate had a wicked sense of humor, it was at a party hosted by Lady Glenbervie, mother of her most recently spurned suitor, where she turned a corner and discovered Byron with a pretty, dark-haired woman on his arm.

Silently Annabella withdrew before they noticed her, but not before taking in the woman's rosy cheeks and shining eyes, her soft, merry laugh and her gaze of unabashed affection. Nor did she miss Byron's utterly rapt expression, or the unfamiliar gentleness in his smile, or his obvious delight with whatever his companion was murmuring in his ear. As she stole quietly away, Annabella felt a sting of jealousy so acute that she was obliged to admit that absence had made her much fonder of him. And the relief she felt later that evening upon learning that the woman whom Byron regarded with such tender affection was not a new sweetheart but his half sister, Mrs. Augusta Byron Leigh, convinced Annabella that she was, in all probability, thoroughly in love with him.

It was a delicate matter to renew their acquaintance, but Annabella found an excuse to write to him, and before long they were

27

corresponding regularly. Confessing none of her new feelings, she offered to be Byron's friend, a strong moral influence to guide him away from vice and toward redemption. His reply was slow in coming and irreverent: He considered himself incorrigible, devoted to passion, sensation, levity, and imagination, but she was welcome to try.

In the letters that flew back and forth between them, she argued the merits of logic and reason, he the sublime beauty and thrilling power of imagination. She quoted great philosophers like Locke and Bacon; he refuted almost every line with quotes from the great poets. When she insisted that rational thought offered the path to salvation, he fired back, "I care very little for logic and arithmetic. If you tell me that two and two make four, you merely provoke me to find a way to make them five. I am a poet, and poetry has little to do with reason. It is rather the lava of the imagination whose eruption prevents an earthquake."

His tempestuous words, her increasing sense of him as an overpowering, uncontrollable force of nature, made her pulse race and her head grow light. Sometimes the physical stirrings his letters provoked obliged her to set the pages aside and go for a brisk walk in the garden until the unfamiliar sensations receded. But she was determined to redeem him, for the sake of his soul, his genius, and his core of goodness and generosity, which he only occasionally allowed her to see, precious glimpses of the better man she knew he could become with her moral guidance.

Once, after complimenting her on her most recent, "very pretty" letter, he remarked, "What an odd situation and friendship is ours! — without one spark of love on either side, and produced by circumstances which in general lead to coldness on one side, and aversion on the other."

In her reply she agreed that their friendship was indeed rather unusual, but she would not say that she felt no spark.

"You are a very superior woman," he told her warmly a few weeks later, "and very little spoiled, which is strange in an heiress — a girl of twenty — a peeress that is to be, in your own right — an only child, and a *savante,* who has always had her own way."

When she protested that he scattered slander amid his praise, for she was not at all spoiled and certainly had not always had her own way, his reply suggested that she had provoked his amusement — but also unexpected tenderness. "You are a poetess — a mathematician — a metaphysician, and yet, withal, very kind, generous, and gentle, with very little pretension," he wrote, bringing a blush to her cheeks. "Any other head would be turned with half your acquisitions, and a tenth of your advantages."

But her head had been turned, although for far different reasons.

The months passed, but even as Annabella argued the case for religion, rationality, and restraint, she found herself struggling to convince Byron that she was not without feeling, that she was not as somber and didactic as her letters suggested, that there was more to her than virtue and piety. Had he not inferred as much from her poems, through which she had revealed her innermost self to him? "Come and visit me at Seaham," she invited, scarcely believing her audacity. "You will find new inspiration in our windswept shores, the craggy bluffs overlooking the North Sea. I will introduce you to my parents, and I will reveal all to you."

She was disappointed when he laughingly replied that whatever she might say, he knew her to be fonder of numbers and geometry than passion and poems. She was more disappointed yet when he evaded not only that first invitation to visit Seaham, but several others she sent after it. But that was nothing compared to how absolutely crushed she felt when a friend shared a rumor that Byron was about to be engaged to another lady.

Rumors were not betrothals, but there it was. Then, just as Annabella resigned herself to losing Byron forever, she received his fervent letter asking for her hand in marriage.

Bewildered and overjoyed in equal measure, she promptly accepted, sending a cascade of astonishment throughout England. Ignoring speculation that Byron had proposed to her only after the other lady had refused him, Annabella set herself to the task of convincing her astonished friends that she had not made a terrible mistake. Byron made that task all the more difficult by finding one reason after another not to come to Seaham to meet her parents, but since his letters were as warm and affectionate as ever, she convinced herself that his delay was nothing to worry about. "I am very much in love," he wrote reassuringly, "and as silly as all single gentlemen must be in that sentimental situation."

They had been engaged for almost two months when Byron at long last made the journey from London to County Durham. By that time Annabella's mother had worked herself into such a state of nerves that when her future son-in-law arrived, she was too overcome with anxiety to leave her room to meet him.

Lady Judith emerged the next morning and was introduced to her famous future son-in-law, but the damage was done, and the entire visit was fraught with tension and uncomfortable silences. Yet it was not all unmitigated misery. Byron got along well with her genial, unpretentious father, Sir Ralph Milbanke,

and in stolen private moments Byron introduced Annabella to the pleasure of kisses and
caresses, evoking thrilling sensations that she
had never dreamed possible — but otherwise
he was restless and taciturn, she uncertain,
hesitant, and overwrought.

"You seem neither silly nor sentimental,"
she observed as they took a stroll around the
garden one afternoon. She dared not add that
he did not seem very much in love, either.
"Have I offended you?"

"Darling, your only fault is that you are a
great deal too good for me," he replied lightly,
"and *that* I must pardon, if nobody else
should. I must, of course, reform thoroughly."

"See that you do," she teased, smiling up at
him, but his gaze was fixed on the path ahead
of them, and he replied with a somber nod.

One evening, after she had spent hours in
forlorn contemplation in a solitary walk along
the seashore, Annabella waited until she
could catch him alone, then summoned up
her courage. "My dearest, have your feelings
about our marriage changed?" she asked
tentatively. "Because if they have, as your true
friend — which is what I have always wanted
most to be — I am prepared to break off our
engagement if that is what you want."

He stared at her. "What I want?" he echoed,
his face mottled with emotion. "My God,
Annabella." Trembling, he staggered to the
sofa, and to her horror, he fainted upon it.

With a gasp, she snatched up a handkerchief, dipped it in a pitcher of water, and hurried to his side to lay the cool cloth upon his brow. Her heart thudded as she watched the color drain from his face, and she considered calling for help, but soon his eyelashes fluttered and he stared balefully up at her.

"Are you all right?" she asked. "Shall I summon the doctor?"

"No, don't bother anyone." He tried to sit up, but he fell back upon the cushions, and when he spoke again, his voice was thick with anger and reproach. "Marriage was to be my salvation. You don't know what you've done. You don't know."

"I haven't done anything. We're still engaged, if that's truly what you want." When he only shook his head, she clasped his hand and held it to her heart. "I only meant to release you, if you wished to be released. Please, forgive me."

She yearned for him to assure her that he wanted with all his heart to marry her, but he merely nodded.

Afterward, he made no attempt to explain his alarming collapse, nor did he apologize for his odd behavior. Instead he cut his visit short by several days. On the morning of his departure he bade her parents a curt farewell and offered no kind words or assurances to his bewildered fiancée. Annabella followed him outside to his carriage wringing her hands, afraid to speak rather than say something that would make the dreadful parting even worse.

At the last moment, he turned about on his good leg and glowered at her. "I have grave doubts about our marriage," he said brusquely. He took her hand, bowed stiffly over it, and climbed aboard the carriage, leaving Annabella breathless from shock and confusion. She mulled over his words as the carriage disappeared down the drive behind a stand of trees, but she could make no sense of them. Were they still engaged? Had he broken it off? She hardly knew what to think, and she *always* knew what to think.

Her renowned confidence shaken, she sent letters after him to London, apologies, explanations, declarations of love. "I would rather share distress with you than escape it without you," she confessed in one last, desperate plea for reconciliation.

He broke his silence with a letter sent from Boroughbridge. "My heart," he addressed her, raising her hopes only to dash them immediately after. "We are thus far separated — but after all one mile is as bad as a thousand — which is a great consolation to one who must travel six hundred before he meets you again. If it will give you any satisfaction — I am as comfortless as a pilgrim with peas in his shoes — and as cold as Charity — Chastity or any other Virtue."

34

The thought of his suffering comforted her only very little.

"I expect to reach Newstead tomorrow and Augusta the day after," he continued. "Present to our parents as much of my love as you like to part with — & dispose with the rest as you please."

His tone was wearily acerbic as he spoke of her disposing of his love — but his reference to her mother and father as "*our* parents" surely meant he intended to marry her.

Their correspondence resumed its former regularity, their letters increasingly warm and affectionate, as by unspoken agreement they said nothing of the calamitous weeks at Seaham.

As the year drew to a close, Annabella became increasingly worried about Byron's reluctance to set a date for their nuptials. "It would be very difficult under these circumstances to fix a precise date for my return," he insisted, reminding her of his determination to sell his ancestral estate and clear his debts before taking a wife.

"We need not delay until you sell Newstead Abbey," she replied. "We will have my marriage settlement, and we can get by on a very small income, making do with only one horse and one carriage, and receiving only that quiet society which I think we both prefer." She meant that he *ought* to prefer it, as she did. She knew he loved revelry, the theatre, drinking parties, flirtations, but she hoped to teach him better habits. "I will be content, darling, as long as we live within our means, for as you know I abhor debt."

She refuted every argument for delay, and so at last the date of the wedding was set for the second of January 1815. Impatiently Annabella awaited Byron's return to Seaham, knowing from his last letter that he had set out from London on 24 December accompanied by Sir John Cam Hobhouse, his best man and closest friend since his years at Trinity College. Five days later the gentlemen still had not arrived, compelling Annabella to refer to Byron's letter several times to verify the date, and provoking an anxious Lady Judith to again take to her bed.

At last, late in the evening of 30 December, a coach pulled up the drive and surrendered its passengers at the front door. Annabella had already retired to her bedchamber when a maid announced their arrival, but she hastily dressed and hurried downstairs to meet them. Turning swiftly down the hallway, she nearly crashed into Byron, standing alone in the foyer, pale and unsmiling, as if he had forgotten the errand that had brought him there.

"Byron, at last," she cried, flinging her arms around him.

"What's all this?" he asked, patting her on the back, frowning in bemusement. "You almost make me wish I'd stayed in the carriage."

Quickly she composed herself and escorted him to the drawing room, where they interrupted her father affably querying another man about how a simple journey from London in decent weather should have taken nearly a week.

"Darling," said Byron, indicating the gentleman, "allow me to introduce my great friend, Sir John Hobhouse, without whom I would not be standing before you tonight, but rather drinking my cares away in some tavern along the Great North Road. Damn you," he added to Hobhouse affectionately.

His friend grinned back, but one glance at Annabella and his smile quickly faded. He was not as handsome as Byron, his brown hair thinner, his cheeks fuller, his features less regular. He had a Roman nose and a small, pursed mouth, and as they quickly sized each other up, she detected puzzlement in the slight furrow of his brow. She could only guess what Byron had told his friend about her, but evidently she was not what he had expected.

She invited them to sit and offered tea but called for brandy when Byron requested it. They chatted politely while the men drank, but not even her father's genial remarks could dispel the tension in the room. Annabella said little rather than risk blurting the question she most wanted answered: If Hobhouse deserved the credit for delivering Byron to Seaham, did he also merit censure for their absurdly leisurely pace?

Perhaps sensing her indignation, Hobhouse downed the last of his brandy and rose. "I beg you to excuse me," he said, bowing to her and to her father, "but I'm exhausted from the journey, and I must retire."

"Of course, of course." Stiff from the late hour and the cold, Sir Ralph hauled himself up from his armchair. "I'll show you to your room."

"Good night, Sir John," Annabella added, managing a thin smile.

As Sir Ralph led Hobhouse from the room, Byron suddenly bolted from his chair and wrapped his friend in a fierce embrace. Annabella looked away, muffling a sigh and pretending to ignore Hobhouse's murmurs, which had a tone of steeling a comrade for battle.

Reluctantly Byron released his friend and watched him go. "Well, my dear," he said when they were alone, offering Annabella a crooked smile, "now it is only we two."

His words would have evoked a thrill of anticipation if they had not been weighed down with resignation.

Annabella badly wanted an explanation and an apology, but she refused to nag Byron for them, so when it became apparent that none was forthcoming, she bade him good night, hoping that a good night's sleep would improve his mood. To her relief, the next morning she found that some of the tension had indeed eased overnight, and thanks to the jovial Sir Ralph, breakfast was a cheerful affair. As her father regaled their guests with amusing stories, Annabella felt the muscles of her neck and shoulders relaxing, the dull headache that had plagued her for days easing. She laughed aloud at a joke Byron made, and after breakfast, she and Hobhouse shared a pleasant, unaffected conversation as she escorted him on a tour of Seaham.

That evening the wedding party rehearsed the ceremony in the drawing room, with a few friends and family providing an affectionate audience. A mischievous impulse inspired Annabella and Hobhouse to switch places, so that Byron pledged his troth to his best friend, who wore a lace shawl over his head in place of a veil, and simpered and feigned reluctance until the room echoed with laughter. At midnight, they all wished one another a happy New Year, drank toasts, sang fond old tunes, and agreed that the holiday was an auspicious occasion indeed to embark upon the seas of matrimony.

But the following day, the eve of the wedding, all frivolity vanished and apprehension descended upon the household like a heavy fog, chill and obscuring. At dinner, conversation was forced and abrupt, and when they retired for the night, Byron embraced Hobhouse and clung to him as he had on the night of his arrival, and when he finally tore himself away, he bade his friend such a mournful good night, it was as if he never expected to see him again.

The following morning, Annabella woke at dawn to the sound of distant gunshots. "Were there poachers in the woods this morning?" she asked Mrs. Clermont when she bustled in to help her wash and dress.

"Not that I know of, dear," she replied, shaking out Annabella's chemise and avoiding her gaze.

"I heard a pistol fire, not once but several times." Annabella threw her former governess a quizzical look as she went to the basin to wash her face. "What happened?"

"I couldn't say," Mrs. Clermont replied, which didn't mean that she didn't know.

Annabella pried the story out of her mother at breakfast. When she asked why Byron and Hobhouse had not joined them at the table, she learned that Byron had risen before dawn and had gone out to stalk around the grounds, and at the sound of gunshots Hobhouse had gone after him. He had found Byron wandering idly about, setting his glove upon stumps, fence posts, and tree branches and firing his pistol at the makeshift target.

"They're taking breakfast in Lord Byron's

room," her mother said, "after which they'll dress for the wedding."

"I see," said Annabella, although she was still trying to make sense of it.

"My dear," her father said, peering at her from the head of the table, "you do realize that you don't have to go through with this?"

"Ralph," Lady Judith exclaimed.

"You don't, Annabella."

"Of course I must go through with it." She inhaled deeply, glanced at her plate, and pushed it away, her appetite fled. "Think of the scandal. I offered to release him once, but he was overcome with distress and made it clear that I should not suggest it again. And I *want* to marry Byron. I love him. Everything will be fine once we're married and he learns to conform to my wishes, as he has promised."

Her parents exchanged a long, wordless glance, her mother sighed, and they went on with breakfast as if the disconcerting suggestion had never been made.

Soon thereafter she and her mother and Mrs. Clermont withdrew to her bedchamber, where they arranged her hair and dressed her in a simple lace-trimmed gown with a white muslin jacket. "You look lovely, my darling girl," her mother proclaimed, her voice trembling. Dabbing her eyes with her handkerchief, she took Annabella by the hand and steadily told her what she might expect from her husband that night in the marriage bed. Annabella listened carefully, for it was all quite astonishing and she had much to learn if she did not want to disappoint him.

"Lord Byron is a man of the world," Lady Judith concluded. "He won't expect you to know what to do, and he'll take pleasure in instructing you."

Annabella nodded, her mouth suddenly dry. Her mother gave her one last, lingering embrace and hurried off to take her place in the drawing room.

"Let's give them another quarter of an hour," Mrs. Clermont proposed, and Annabella nodded again. She dared not sit and wrinkle her gown, so she went to the window, her heart thudding hollowly in her chest. A thin layer of icy snow shrouded the lawn, and a fine carriage waited in the drive to whisk the newlyweds off on their honeymoon, which they would spend at Halnaby Hall, her father's country house near Darlington in North Yorkshire. Secluded and comfortable, far from the prying eyes of curious folk craving glimpses of the famous couple, Halnaby would offer them a private sanctuary in which to begin their married life in happiness, harmony, and peace.

Just then a pair of footmen emerged from the house carrying her trunk to the carriage, and suddenly their resemblance to undertakers carrying a coffin to a hearse struck her with such force that her throat constricted until she almost could not breathe. "Water, please," she rasped, shaken, and Mrs. Clermont hastened to bring her a glass.

At the appointed time, Mrs. Clermont escorted Annabella downstairs to the drawing room, where a small circle of close friends and family had gathered for the ceremony. Annabella's gaze fell first upon her parents, who smiled back with shining eyes, and then upon the Reverend Thomas Noel, nodding encouragingly at the far end of the room, and lastly upon her bridegroom, breathtakingly handsome and elegantly attired in a morning suit of charcoal gray and a white silk cravat. He was not looking in her direction when she entered, his head bowed close to Hobhouse's ear until Hobhouse spotted her and gave Byron a little nudge. He turned his head her way, straightened, and offered her something between a fond smile and a rueful grimace.

Two kneeling mats had been placed upon the floor before Reverend Noel, and remembering the comical rehearsal, Annabella half expected Hobhouse to take her place upon one of them. But he stepped back as Mrs. Clermont led her forward, and before Annabella knew it, she was reciting her vows in a clear, steady voice, her eyes locked on Byron's. He spoke in his turn, more hesitantly.

By eleven o'clock, it was done. They exchanged a chaste kiss, and outside, just within the front gate, a six-gun salute announced the news to the world.

As tears of relief and joy filled Annabella's eyes, Byron squeezed her hands and gave her a look that she had seen once before, in the eyes of a bear pacing in its cage. "You have me now," the look said, "but you had better pray these iron bars hold."

Overcome, she fled the room, only to remember with a start that she must return to sign the register. Byron wordlessly passed her the pen, and miraculously her hand did not tremble as she wrote her name. She was Lady Byron now, she thought distantly, and it seemed she could feel the blood draining from her face.

After a subdued wedding luncheon, where the toasts rang hollow and the carefully prepared delicacies tasted like sawdust in her mouth, Mrs. Clermont accompanied her upstairs to change into her traveling clothes — a warm dove-gray dress of fine wool and a slate-gray cape. When she descended, her father escorted her outside to the carriage, too heartily proclaiming her the loveliest bride he had ever seen and declaring that her future was certain to be joyful and prosperous. Thick flakes of snow had begun to fall, so her parents quickly returned inside, leaving her alone in the carriage to examine the wedding gift Hobhouse had left on the seat, a volume of Byron's poems bound in yellow morocco leather.

The carriage rocked as Byron climbed in, and after seating himself across from her, he put his hand out the window to seize Hobhouse's. With a lurch the carriage set off, but Byron would not release his friend's hand, so Hobhouse ran alongside the carriage as it moved down the drive. Just as Annabella was about to urge Byron to let go, their grasp was broken, and Byron sank back into his seat, disconsolate.

Mortified by his profound lack of joy, Annabella turned her gaze to the window, where heavy flakes were falling thick and fast, obscuring the landscape. As they passed through the town of Durham, a few miles west of home, the rich, glorious bells of the Durham Cathedral rang out in celebration and greeting.

"Ringing for our happiness, I suppose?" said Byron, his voice acid. They were the first words he had spoken since he had climbed into the carriage.

"They surely are," said Annabella. "The people know which carriage to watch for."

He fixed her with a malignant stare. "You do understand that I married you only because I must marry someone, and you have a fortune?"

Her heart thudded, but she kept her voice even. "I hope my fortune was only one of many appealing virtues."

"Ah! Virtue! Yes, you are the very Viceroy of Virtue, the Princess of Parallelograms." He peeled off his gloves, clenched them in a fist, and slapped them against his knee. "If you had married me when I first asked, two years ago, you might have saved me. You could have molded me into a paragon of righteousness in your own image. But now —" He shook his head, frowning. "Those two years have ruined me."

"Ruined you?" she exclaimed, shocked. "How so? You've never been more successful or, I daresay, more beloved."

"It is enough that they have, and it is all your fault, for refusing me."

"I didn't believe your first proposal was in earnest, and . . . I felt differently then." She could not bring herself to mention Lady Caroline Lamb or her dire warnings, for after they were engaged Byron had confessed, or perhaps boasted was a better word for it, that he and her cousin's wife had been lovers — explaining, too late, William's reluctance to introduce her to Byron. "What does that matter now? I did accept, we are now married, we love each other —"

"We most assuredly do not."

For a moment she could not breathe. "Don't be unkind, not today. Don't fall into one of your dark moods."

"All of my moods are dark." He fixed her with a look of bleak despair. "I'm afraid you'll soon discover that you've married a devil."

She clasped her hands together beneath her cape and held herself as still as marble. "I don't believe it, despite your devilish behavior now, which I blame on the excitement of the day and shall forgive. Surely you haven't forgotten that I did offer to release you from our engagement. You have no one but yourself to blame for your current predicament."

He barked out a laugh, and for the rest of the forty-mile journey, he shifted between brooding in silence, muttering caustic remarks, and wildly singing Albanian folk songs he had learned on his travels. She replied with cool, reproachful glances, knowing that anything she said would only inflame his temper.

At last they turned onto the road to Halnaby Hall. A thick blanket of snow covered the grounds, and the carriage slowed as the driver steered around or pushed through the drifts. As they approached the house, Annabella's spirits rose to glimpse lights shining in the windows through the false twilight of the storm. In front of the house, all of her parents' servants and tenants had lined up to greet them. She had known most of them since she was a girl, and their faces, proud and cheerful and full of expectation, warmed her heart.

When the carriage halted, Byron tore open the door, jumped down, and strode into the house without a word for anyone. Shocked, Annabella composed herself and waited for the footman to help her descend. Fighting to conceal her dismay, she made her way down the receiving line alone, forcing a pleasant smile through her tears and thanking each servant and tenant for the kind welcome. With a grateful cry she embraced Jane Minns, a girl from a local farm with whom she had practically grown up, a newlywed herself and trusted confidante who served as her lady's maid whenever Annabella resided at Halnaby Hall. When she came to Mrs. Milligan just outside the front door, she asked the unflappable housekeeper to prepare dinner, and sighed in relief to hear that it was nearly ready and would be served within the hour.

Crossing the threshold alone, she removed her cape, wiped the snow from her shoes, and followed her husband's wet footprints through the foyer until they faded down a corridor. The door to the drawing room stood open, so she peered inside and discovered Byron pouring himself a brandy.

"Dinner will be served soon. I'm sure you must be famished." As for herself, she had no appetite. "My mother instructed the housekeeper to prepare the master suite for us to share. I hope that pleases you."

He shrugged and gulped his brandy. "I've always preferred to sleep alone, or with one of my dogs, but do as you please. One animal is as good as any other, as long as she is young."

Annabella took a deep, shaky breath. "I can't imagine what I've done to offend you, but this is my wedding day. Please, if you can't be affectionate, at least be civil."

His eyebrows rose. "Affectionate?" He set down his glass and extended his hand to her. "Will affection appease you? I can be affectionate. Close the door and come here."

She took his hand, and before she had quite figured out his intentions, they quickly consummated the marriage on the couch. The act gave her only a little of the pain her mother had warned her about and some of the pleasure Annabella had anticipated, so it was not unpleasant. Afterward, as she lay in his embrace and he kissed her brow and fondly called her his "dear philosopher-wife," she dared hope that after the initial shock of their irrevocable vows faded, he might become content.

Her hopes suffered a blow early the next morning. They shared a bed, as she had hoped they would, although the custom of separate bedrooms was more popular among people of their rank. The room was cold despite the fire on the hearth, so upon retiring they had drawn the heavy bed-curtains closed to ward off the chill. A few hours before dawn, Annabella was jolted awake by a rough shake of the mattress and Byron's cry, "Good God, I am surely in hell!" Blinking, she sat up and glanced frantically about, her pulse racing until she discovered what had disturbed her husband — the flickering light from the fireplace seen through the scarlet bed-curtains gave the illusion that the room was engulfed in menacing flames. Reason required that she take no offense at his outburst, so she murmured a few soothing phrases until he fell back against his pillow and sank into sleep.

After dawn they woke again, and upon rising they discovered at least a foot of snow blanketing the grounds outside their window, and in the distance, ice sparkling like crystal on the lake. It was a beautiful scene, but the room was frigid despite the fresh fire the chambermaid had started while they slept. As they washed and dressed, Annabella drew closer to the fire to warm her hands. Her new wedding ring, gleaming softly in the firelight, slipped loosely on her finger, so she bound it with a piece of black ribbon until it fit more securely.

"What are you doing?" asked Byron sharply. "What an omen of horror and death you've created! Remove that ribbon immediately."

"It's only a ribbon," she murmured, but she obeyed. They finished dressing in silence, and then, as they stood side by side warming themselves by the fire before they descended to breakfast, Annabella's ring suddenly slipped from her finger and tumbled into the grate.

"What have you done?" exclaimed Byron, seizing the poker and dragging the ring from the ashes. Snatching his handkerchief from his pocket, he picked up the ring with it, wiped off the soot, and waited for the ring to cool before thrusting it at Annabella. "Put it back on — or don't. It matters not. The damage is done."

"What on earth do you mean?" Annabella examined the ring, which had survived its ordeal unblemished. "There's not even the tiniest scratch."

"It's an omen," he said, agitated. "This marriage is cursed."

"Nonsense." She had no patience for superstition. "This signifies nothing except that my hands are too cold. I'll wrap a *white* ribbon around my finger and fit the ring over it. It will not fall off again."

He nodded brusquely, but she could tell he was not satisfied.

Later that day, when a letter arrived from Augusta, Byron became strangely perturbed. He paced the length of the drawing room as he read, his expression fierce and exultant, his eyes fixed on the pages in his hand. "Listen to this," he commanded. "My sister addresses me, 'Dearest, first and best of human beings.' What do you think of that?"

"I think . . . I think that Augusta is a very

51

loving and generous sister. She clearly thinks the world of you."

"You aren't jealous?"

"Why should I be?"

"What if I told you I love her equally in return?"

She laughed uncertainly. "I would feel very sad and worried if you *didn't* love so devoted a sister."

"I miss her. I miss her even more than I miss Hobhouse."

"So do I." Annabella could think of few people she missed less than Hobhouse.

"I miss Augusta so much it tears my heart to bloody shreds. I long for her love, like I crave air to breathe and food and drink."

"I believe you have her love whether she is with you or not," Annabella pointed out, "but if it would comfort you, we could invite her to visit."

He whirled about and strode toward her, and instinctively she stepped back when he thrust his face close to hers. "You would do that? You wouldn't object to her intrusion on our honeymoon?"

"Of course not. We have three weeks here at Halnaby and a lifetime ahead of us to be alone. We can surely spare your sister a few days." Tentatively, she laid a hand on his arm. "I love Augusta too. I don't begrudge the two of you time together."

For a moment his despondent scowl gave

way to hope, but then he made a sharp, cutting gesture and shook his head. "No. No. That would be a disaster."

Bewildered, Annabella attempted levity. "Only if she brings the five children along."

"Ah. The children." His expression softened. "I adore the children. Maybe that would be all right, if she brought them and their host of nannies and nurses."

Annabella had not intended to invite the entire Leigh household, but if it would lift Byron out of his miserable mood and salvage their honeymoon, she would not object. But as the days passed, Byron seemed to think better of the idea, and the invitation was never sent.

Except when they came together for meals and for bed, the newlyweds were most often apart, he writing furiously in Sir Ralph's study, she reading philosophical and religious works she hoped would help her better understand her mercurial husband. Byron's moods shifted erratically from contrition to despair, and when he interrupted his writing to spend time with her, he rambled on and on about the history of madness in his family, unspecified crimes he had committed — terrible, unspeakable crimes — and the curse that shadowed their marriage.

Annabella listened with increasing dread and apprehension, wishing that he would unburden his conscience to her if it would relieve his torment, deeply frightened by what he might reveal if he did. God had abandoned him long ago, he declared, and his deformed foot marked him as cursed and fated for hell from the moment of his birth. He claimed that he had two natural children and another wife, but when she asked the name of the woman and where she resided, he would not say, so she did not believe him. He confessed seductions, not only of Lady Caroline Lamb but of another married woman, Lady Frances Webster, with whom he had dallied while he and Annabella were exchanging letters about his path to redemption. She recoiled from that admission as if he had struck her, but she reminded herself that they had not been engaged then, so he had not betrayed her, not really.

One night as they lay together in bed, he told her that there was yet another seduction in his past, one far worse than those he had already confessed, so terrible and wrong that he dared not speak of it.

"Does Augusta know about this?" she asked.

"Oh, for God's sake, don't mention this to her."

"You must confide in someone," she persisted. "I'm your wife, and your secrets are safe with me. Let me help you. Let me share the burden of your conscience."

"No. No one must know."

Annabella refrained from pointing out that at least one other person already knew. Muffling a sigh, she drew closer to him and rested her head on his chest.

"You deserve a softer pillow than my heart," Byron murmured, and sank into sleep.

In the morning when they sat down to breakfast, she repeated her offer to be his confidante.

"You mean my confessor," he retorted. "You can't absolve my sins if we don't practice the same faith." He spread butter on toast, then gestured with the knife. "Go on, convert me. I dare you to try."

"I will not. Your own dispassionate reflection on the state of your soul would accomplish that more effectively than anything I could say."

"You feel no Christian charity for me, then, only contempt."

"That's not true," she protested. "I feel . . . sorry for you."

He almost choked on his bread, and he gulped tea to wash it down. "Sorry for me?" he spluttered. "Because I'm beyond salvation? Because my sins are unforgivable?"

"I don't believe they are, but no, not because of that." She steeled herself. "Because you married a woman you do not love. I never would have married you if I had known that you did not love me. Be that as it may, *I* love *you,* and I will always be what

55

I've long promised to be — your true friend."

He studied her across the table, a smirk playing in the corners of his mouth. "Then if I were unfaithful, you would not resent it?"

She would indeed, but carefully she replied, "I have been taught that a wife should not notice . . . deviation."

"Then you would let me be unfaithful?"

"As your true friend, I love you too much to let you do anything that would injure you."

"You don't truly love me, then. A woman cannot truly love a man unless she also loves his crimes. No other love is worthy of the name."

Annabella strongly disagreed, and she told him so, but she would not let him see how deeply it pained her to think that he might already be contemplating an illicit affair.

She was close to despair — scarcely able to eat, unable to compose her thoughts enough to write reassuring letters to her parents, exhausted from being jolted awake from restless slumbers by imagined noises.

Then, as if his fragmentary confessions had relieved an equal measure of his torment, Byron's tempests began to subside. He still referred bitterly to his mysterious crimes, but he was calmer and less vicious when he did, and his old courtesy and spontaneous generosity, which she had badly missed, returned from wherever he had banished them. By day he and Annabella strolled together on snowy paths through the dormant gardens or enjoyed spirited discussions about literature and poetry by the fireside, and at night a new tenderness brought a glorious warmth to their lovemaking. The hours Annabella cherished most of all were spent in the library, Byron laboring upon the last few poems of his new work, *Hebrew Melodies,* she seated nearby, copying the earlier verses in her neatest hand and preparing the manuscript for submission to his publisher.

Although she would not break his concentration by rapturously praising his new poems as she copied them, Annabella marveled anew at his prodigious talent, and she glowed to read the transcendent lines she was certain she had inspired.

She walks in beauty, like the night
Of cloudless climes and starry skies;
And all that's best of dark and bright
Meet in her aspect and her eyes:
Thus mellow'd to that tender light
Which heaven to gaudy day denies.

Annabella had raven tresses, like the woman in the poem, and her brow was definitely "so soft, so calm, yet eloquent." How could Byron compose such a paean to her beauty if he did not love her?

Those happy, industrious moments when they were united in purpose were to Annabella fresh springs in a desert — precious, rare, and essential to life.

When their honeymoon at Halnaby ended, Annabella and Byron returned to Seaham more cheerful and optimistic than when they had departed three weeks before. Annabella was delighted to see her parents and Mrs. Clermont again, but her greatest happiness came from her husband. There were occasional dark moods, but they were rare and swiftly subsiding. Together they enjoyed the outdoors, climbing craggy bluffs and walking along the shore. And more than ever they enjoyed the sensual pleasures of the bedchamber, where there was no more talk of hellfire or unforgivable crimes.

Eventually, however, Byron grew restless for London. He offered to go alone and have her join him later, so she could spend more time with her family while he attended to business matters, but Annabella, mindful of his sardonic inquiry about her stance on adultery, insisted upon accompanying him.

Since it was along the way, Byron proposed to visit Augusta and her children at Six Mile Bottom, the Leigh family country house near Cambridge. Her husband, Colonel George Leigh, was absent on duties for the prince, Byron said, and his sister desperately wanted company.

For Annabella, the visit proved to be a

fortnight of misery, an unmitigated disaster from the moment their carriage halted in front of the house.

The furious outbursts, excessive drinking, caustic accusations, despairing moods, and bleak allusions to unforgivable crimes that she thought Byron had left behind in Halnaby seized hold of him again. She practiced stoicism and patience, unwilling to engage in the furious arguments he seemed eager to provoke. When he raised his voice, she lowered hers to a murmur. When he kicked over chairs, she busied herself with a book or sewing, waited for him to storm from the room, and set them upright again. If he hoped for a fiery explosion from her, he would have to settle for a slow, cool burn.

He showed kindness and gentleness to his sister and her children, especially the baby, Elizabeth Medora, but to his wife he offered only spite and contempt. When the children and servants were elsewhere, Byron would humiliate Annabella by telling Augusta about his escapades with Lady Frances Webster and other women, making no effort to conceal that many of his trysts had taken place while they were engaged. At night after the children went to bed, he asked the women to play "kissing games," as he playfully called them, in which they took turns kissing him while he reclined upon the sofa.

When he tired of the game, he would turn

to Annabella with a sardonic smile and say, "We can amuse ourselves without you, my dear. Go up to bed." Having dismissed her, he would linger with his sister while Annabella retired alone, and though she would cover her ears with a pillow, their distant laughter and merry conversation mocked her as she dutifully tried to sleep. Byron would join her eventually, jolting her awake long after midnight, drunk and irascible, but as he was disinterested in making love to her, she was usually able to drift back to sleep. Only once, near the end of their visit, were they intimate, but it was a hasty coupling, and Byron spoiled it by saying, "Now that I have *her,* you will find I can do without you."

"Except in this," she murmured defiantly, but he had already fallen asleep.

His cruelty grieved and bewildered her, but it was some comfort that Augusta was unfailingly kind, that she gently defended Annabella when Byron's malevolence flared. But although Byron conformed to his beloved sister's wishes more readily than to his wife's, even Augusta could not tame him completely.

It was a relief when the fortnight passed and the newlyweds continued on to London, leaving Augusta and the rambunctious children and the beloved baby Medora behind. With Lady Melbourne's help, Byron had leased a gracious residence at 13 Piccadilly Terrace, the home of the widowed Duchess of Devonshire, currently residing in France. It was beautifully furnished and boasted splendid views of Green Park, and Annabella had only just settled in when she learned that she was pregnant.

Byron rejoiced at the news, and for a time Annabella dared hope that the happiness they had enjoyed during their six weeks at Seaham might be renewed. But it was not to be. Misfortunes descended upon them as thickly and heavily as the snow that had fallen on their wedding day. Annabella's dear uncle Wentworth died, but the substantial inheritance Byron had hoped would go to Annabella went instead to her mother. When he resorted to putting Newstead Abbey and another property, Rochdale, up for auction, they failed to meet the reserve price, denying him sorely needed income. Creditors harassed him mercilessly, and finally a bailiff was quartered in their luxurious home to ensure that he did not flee to the Continent without paying his debts.

Byron drowned his troubles in brandy and distracted himself with his work at the Drury Lane Theatre — with work, and with particular members of the company. Annabella was eight months pregnant when Byron staggered home late one night thoroughly drunk, and when confronted by his wife's indignant anger, he declared that he was sleeping with a bit player named Susan Boyce, and he intended to continue seeing her, and he might even bring her to Piccadilly Terrace to amuse him while Annabella was giving birth.

For all her understanding that a wife should not notice deviation, Annabella was devastated, but there was little she could do. As her time approached, even the servants loyal to Byron closed ranks to protect their mistress. Fletcher, Byron's longtime faithful valet, guarded his master's door at night so that he would not stumble into his wife's chamber in a drunken rage. Summoned from Annabella's parents' household, Mrs. Clermont settled into the room next to Annabella's, watchful and protective. A nurse had been hired, but with no baby yet to care for, Mrs. Grimes took charge of the expectant mother instead, seeing to her every comfort and making sure she was never left alone.

Annabella contemplated the impossible — leaving her husband and delivering her child at her parents' new home. Upon the death of her brother, Lord Wentworth, Lady Judith had inherited an annual income of seven thousand pounds; the Wentworth family name, Noel; and the ancestral estate of Kirkby Mallory in Leicestershire, where Annabella thought to take refuge. But as he was her husband, Byron's will was law, and she would have no rights to her child unless she proceeded with utmost caution.

Women were permitted to leave their husbands in only a few circumstances — and there were even fewer conditions under which Annabella would be willing to leave Byron, whom despite everything she still loved, for whose salvation she tirelessly prayed. Byron's secret crime, his unforgivable sin — was it sodomy? He had alluded to such behavior in his rare confidences about his school days and his travels in Turkey. Was it murder? Or something worse? What could possibly be worse?

Annabella did not know, and she hardly dared imagine. What she did understand all too well was that if Byron's cruelty resulted from mental derangement due to insanity, then he was ill and it was not his fault, and she must endure and forgive. If, however, his behavior sprang not from illness but from evil, then she had no choice but to flee with her child before they were irredeemably corrupted by his sin.

Racing against time, Annabella studied medical journals and secretly consulted doctors. She had read a paper published in the *Edinburgh Medical and Surgical Journal* that attributed certain kinds of mental derangement to the final stages of hydrocephalus, water on the brain, signifying that death was imminent. She wrote to Dr. Matthew Baillie, a distinguished physician renowned for his study of the nervous system, and asked if he thought that ailment might explain her husband's symptoms. Dr. Baillie was unwilling to diagnose Byron without examining him, but he advised her to leave her husband for her own safety until he could be thoroughly examined.

Annabella dared not risk such irrevocable measures unless she was absolutely certain, but before she could gather enough evidence, nature intervened.

On Saturday, 9 December, Annabella felt ill and fatigued all day, but when sergeant-at-law Samuel Heywood, a old friend of her parents, called, she roused herself to meet with him. She entrusted to him the secret of her medical investigation and asked him to share what she had learned with Lord and Lady Noel. "Do you think," she ventured, "that I should join them at Kirkby Mallory before the birth of my child, or should I wait until I hold irrefutable proof?"

They discussed the matter in hushed voices without reaching a conclusion, for she felt too nauseous and light-headed and uncomfortable to think clearly. Eventually Sergeant Heywood wished her well and reluctantly departed with only her message for her parents.

Later that evening, she realized that she was in labor.

She made her way downstairs to the drawing room, where Byron sat drinking brandy with Hobhouse, his favorite drinking companion. Studiously ignoring Hobhouse, she rested a hand on her abdomen and said to Byron, "I wanted to tell you that my time is imminent."

He did not leap up and send a servant for the doctor. He did not ask how she felt and escort her upstairs to bed. Instead he fixed her with a baleful look and said, almost casually, "After the child is born, do you want to continue living here with me or not?"

He must have overheard her speaking to Sergeant Heywood, for the servants would not have betrayed her. A contraction seized her; she grasped the back of the nearest armchair for support. "Did you not hear me?" she asked, voice strained, tears filling her eyes. "Your child is coming."

Hobhouse had the decency to look concerned, but Byron merely rose and poured himself another drink. With a sob, Annabella fled the room as quickly as she could and started carefully up the steep staircase. Mrs. Clermont must have heard her cry out, for she hurried to meet her and assisted her to her room. Soon thereafter, the front door slammed, and she knew that Byron had left for the theatre.

Her labor was long and slow in building. Dr. Le Mann arrived at eleven o'clock, examined her, and advised her to rest as much as she could, while she could. She dozed intermittently, awakened by contractions that steadily increased in frequency and strength. Hours passed, and she knew Byron had returned home when her cries of pain were answered by loud thumps and crashes coming from the floor beneath her bed — her husband, flinging bottles of soda against the ceiling of the room two flights below. He had done so on other occasions to warn her to be quiet while he worked. She doubted he was writing now. In his inscrutable malice, he only wanted to disturb her rest.

On the morning of Sunday, 10 December 1815, Annabella gave birth to a healthy baby girl with a strong chin and dark hair like her father's. Exhausted and weeping and longing for her mother, Annabella prayed those would prove to be the only characteristics her daughter inherited from him.

It was not until the following morning that Byron appeared at her door. "The child was born dead, wasn't it?" he asked, his face ashen.

"She's very much alive," said Annabella, incredulous. How could he not know?

As she gingerly sat up in bed, Mrs. Grimes entered the room carrying their daughter, swaddled in a soft blanket and apparently sleeping. "Let me have a good look at her," Byron said. After a wary glance to Annabella, and her answering nod, the nurse placed the baby in his arms. "Such a pretty child," he exclaimed softly, rocking slightly back and forth. He glanced up at Annabella, grinning. "You know, if she resembles my sister, it's probably because she was conceived at Six Mile Bottom."

Annabella doubted that would have anything to do with it, but she was too tired to argue. "Perhaps."

Byron's gaze returned to his daughter. "Oh, what an implement of torture I have acquired in you," he cheerfully told her, in the high, singsong voice reserved for speaking to young children.

Annabella's heart sank. She could easily guess whom he meant to torture.

Byron glanced up again, his eyes bright with inspiration. "We should name her Augusta, after my sister."

"I would prefer Judith, after my mother."

"Absolutely not. I despise that old bird." He bent his head to kiss the baby's smooth brow. "Augusta it shall be."

Annabella resigned herself to it. Perhaps the beloved name would encourage Byron to adore his daughter as much as he loved his sister.

In the days that followed, Byron plucked a middle name from some high branch of his family tree last used during the reign of King John, and the child was christened Augusta Ada. In a simple act of defiance and possession, Annabella always slightly emphasized the second of the two names, as if "Augusta"

67

were merely an honorific — a synonym for "Miss," perhaps.

Out of concern for her health, Dr. Le Mann confined Annabella to her room for two weeks following the birth. After that respite, Hobhouse was among the first visitors who called to pay his respects. Watching him as he admired little Augusta Ada, Annabella was reminded of her suspicions that Byron and Hobhouse were implicated in some terrible crime, and that perhaps guilt rather than illness provoked her husband's violent outbursts.

Although she had hoped that the presence of a child in the household would mitigate Byron's dreadful tempers, the fact that he was now a father affected him not at all. He still drank heavily and stayed out until all hours. He still consorted with his actress, and he boasted of his trysts to Annabella, indifferent to the misery he inflicted.

Once more she secretly consulted doctors and studied medical texts, desperately hoping to find some physical cause for his madness, a diagnosis that would lead her to a remedy. As a last resort, in his absence she stole into his bedchamber to search his papers and belongings for something, anything, that would enlighten her. The most telling items she discovered were a vial of laudanum and an edition of the Marquis de Sade's *Justine.* She had not read the novel, but the marquis's reputation for obscenity was known everywhere.

One night in early January Byron woke her with a kiss, sat down on the edge of her bed, and with brandy heavy on his breath, told her that he intended to live exactly as he pleased, not only with the actress but in every other way a man could live. Almost as an afterthought, he reminded her that a wife had no legal right to object to her husband's behavior unless he beat her or confined her, neither of which he intended to do.

"Then it is not illness but evil that compels you," said Annabella, resigned.

Byron shrugged and looked almost gleeful. "I certainly don't feel ill."

He gave her a merry peck on the cheek, rose, and left her to mourn him — for it did almost feel as if he had died. The good man she thought she had married certainly was no more.

Byron had willfully chosen the path to damnation and was striding cheerfully down it, away from her, away from Ada.

She had no choice but to heed Dr. Baillie's advice and leave him.

That decision brings her to his chamber door on the evening of 14 January 1816, while Byron and Augusta laugh merrily within and Ada slumbers peacefully in her cradle upstairs. If Annabella delays any longer, she will only prolong her misery.

She knocks on the door and opens it before they respond, assuming that they will ignore her. They sit so closely on the sofa that Byron's left leg pins Augusta's dress to the cushions. Byron smiles at his wife lazily, Augusta more brightly. "Annabella," she cries, trying to rise but finding herself held fast, giggling when she discovers why she cannot stand. "I'm so sorry. Did we wake you?"

"No, little Ada did." She crosses the room and stands before them, hands folded at her waist, perfectly serene.

"Augusta Ada, my precious child," says Byron, sipping his brandy. "As lovely as her namesake."

His sister blushes, flattered, but she gives him a playful shove. "A good husband would say, 'As lovely as her mother.' "

"I never claimed to be a good husband."

"Perhaps not, but you should aspire to it."

Annabella cannot endure another word of their silly banter. "I'm leaving for Kirkby Mallory in the morning, and I shall take Ada with me."

"Lord and Lady Noel will be thrilled to meet their granddaughter," says Augusta, "but are you sure you're up to the journey so soon?"

"I'm perfectly recovered, thank you." Annabella does not disabuse her of the notion that she only intends to visit. "I wanted to bid you both good night, and farewell."

Augusta looks as if she wants to rise and embrace her, but she does not ask her brother to free her gown. "Good night and safe travels."

From Byron's appraising look, Annabella suspects he understands her intentions. "When shall we three meet again?" he asks, and from his intonation she knows he quotes from *Macbeth,* posing the First Witch's question to her sisters gathered around the cauldron.

In thunder, lightning, or in rain? Annabella thinks, remembering those precious happy hours at Halnaby when they discussed literature and poetry. Her heart aches, but she manages to keep her voice from trembling when she replies, "In heaven, I hope."

Augusta's smile falters. Annabella swiftly turns before they see her tears gathering and hurries back to her room. Summoning the servants, she puts them to work packing trunks and cases for her and the baby, and she instructs Mrs. Grimes to prepare to accompany them. Neither Byron nor Augusta comes after her and attempts to persuade her to stay — as far as she knows, they will remain exactly where she left them throughout the night. Augusta definitely does not emerge from her brother's chamber before Annabella finishes packing and has the footmen take her luggage downstairs so it may be loaded onto the carriage at first light.

She checks on the baby one last time and silently weeps over her for a moment, but then she dries her tears and retires to her own bed. Exhausted by deep sorrow, she falls asleep as soon as her head touches the pillow, but she wakes just before dawn feeling no better rested than when she lay down.

In the thin light of the gray midwinter morning, she rises, washes, and puts on her warmest dress. Next she quietly steals to the nursery, where she finds Mrs. Grimes changing Ada, her own satchel packed and waiting by the door. Annabella bundles her daughter warmly against the cold and carries her downstairs, the nurse following close behind. Annabella quakes at the sound of their footfalls, for it is impossible to be perfectly silent even with the greatest care.

They pass Byron's chamber door, and Annabella hesitates. She holds her breath and strains her ears, wondering if she will hear Byron lamenting their departure, Augusta soothing him, but all is silent within. Her gaze falls upon the rug outside the door, preserved in memory of Byron's favorite Newfoundland, Boatswain, who had often slept upon it. For a moment she is tempted to hand the baby to Mrs. Grimes, fling herself upon the carpet, and wait there until he wakes and opens the door — but what then? If she begs him for mercy, for reconciliation, for fidelity, he will glare at her, full of contempt, and vehemently refuse.

She turns away and passes on to the foyer, where Mrs. Clermont gives the nurse a hamper of food she has packed for their journey. As Annabella and Mrs. Grimes put on their warmest wraps, a footman appears and in a voice barely above a whisper announces that the carriage is loaded, the driver and team ready to depart.

"Good-bye, my dear," Mrs. Clermont says to Annabella, a tear glimmering in her eye. "Be safe. Be well."

"Look after him," Annabella beseeches her, in spite of herself, in spite of everything.

Mrs. Clermont sniffs and throws a look of disdain over her shoulder. "As you wish — as far as he will allow it."

Annabella thanks her with a nod. She carries her daughter outside to the carriage, which quickly speeds its three passengers off to Kirkby Mallory, where they will find sanctuary and love. Annabella and Byron will never meet again, nor will Byron ever again see his daughter.

I know this because I was there, a small, innocent witness to the last days of my parents' shared lives. I know this because although today the world knows me best as Ada Byron King, Countess of Lovelace, mathematician and scientist, I was once a tiny child whisked away at dawn from my first home by a mother desperate to save us from my father's corruption and sin.

I was there, and I will tell you all that followed after.

CHAPTER ONE:
SOLE DAUGHTER OF
MY HOUSE AND HEART

January–April 1816

You may well wonder how I, no more than seven weeks old when my mother left my father and launched the great scandal that came to be known throughout England as the Separation, can claim to have witnessed the tumultuous events that provoked so much curiosity and gossip. It is a fair question, since some of the incidents I have described occurred before my birth. Certainly, I have always possessed uncanny powers of perception, understanding, and synthesis, but not even I can see beyond the frame that encloses my own life.

Obviously I have no firsthand experience of the years that preceded my birth, and I will not pretend to remember the contentious events of my infancy. Instead this account of my parents' courtship, marriage, and separation and my own earliest years is comprised of facts I learned later: tantalizing details revealed by my mother, Lady Byron; glimpses of unattended papers not meant for my eyes; servants' gossip overheard in the corridors of my grandparents' palatial home of Kirkby Mallory; and detailed accounts Lady Byron painstakingly composed for her lawyers.

There were an exhausting number of the latter.

You may say I have borrowed other people's memories, and I will not deny it. I will see your challenge and raise you one confession: Sometimes it is difficult for me to distinguish between memories that are truly my own and stories that were inculcated by Lady Byron, her parents, and her friends, who perpetually hovered around me like a swarm of judgmental wasps.

Can you honestly say that you are any more certain of the origin of your own memories?

Though you may question their provenance, these are my memories, recorded here for posterity. And why should I not write my life? My father did so, although as far as I know, the only manuscript of his carefully crafted memoir was destroyed at my mother's command. Not that I claim my life merits memorializing as his did. Indeed, at this moment, my pride has been so battered that I believe the list of those who might wish to read my memoirs will be very short indeed. Perhaps admirers of my Great Work would be interested in learning about my life and education. Someday my children, if they are in a forgiving mood, might be curious about my youth and my consuming passions. They have shown little interest thus far, but someday, when they are much older and have learned firsthand that loving one's children does not guarantee that one will never fail them, they may want to know me better.

I confess to a stirring of superstitious fear that I tempt Fate by setting down this memoir now, as if the story of my life is nearing its conclusion. I am but thirty-five; surely I have years left to fill with accomplishments and reflection. My health has not been particularly worse than usual, and yet something compels me to take pen in hand now rather than wait until I am white-haired and wizened. In recent months, I have been plagued by disturbing suspicions that I may draw my last breath sooner than my doctors will admit — but the future is even less certain than the past, so I will say nothing more of that here.

Instead I will return to my story, for it is unkind to leave my heroine and her child suspended in peril so long.

After my mother spirited me from my father's home at 13 Piccadilly Terrace on that cold winter morning, we stopped to change horses in Woborn and continued on to Leicestershire, arriving at Kirkby Mallory quite late at night. The servants, who had never met us, were perhaps confused by the late hour or by Lady Byron's exhaustion, for they led her to the kitchen rather than the drawing room, as would have befit her rank. Before long the mistake was corrected, Lord and Lady Noel were awakened, and there was, I imagine, a tearful reunion in the drawing room. My grandparents were shocked, no doubt, by their lovely daughter's gaunt frame and haggard features. Knowing my grandmother as I later would, I'm sure she wept at first, then dried her eyes, strengthened her resolve, and began planning how to restore her precious daughter to health — and how to punish her wicked son-in-law.

Until then, Lady Byron had been able to conceal the worst of her sufferings from her parents, but once she moved us into their home, the truth in all its horror came out. They were devastated, outraged, and filled with righteous indignation, and since strangling my father was out of the question, Lady Noel promptly contacted her lawyer. Even as my mother continued her correspondence with doctors and arranged from afar for my father to have a complete medical examination, my grandparents were consulting with Colonel Francis Doyle, a lawyer renowned as a mediator in marital affairs, to arrange for a legal separation, if Byron could be persuaded to consent to it.

But of course, I knew nothing of this. I knew only that the unpleasant scenes of shouting and weeping that had played in the background of my earliest days had faded, replaced by gentle laughter and tender endearments. I discovered that my mother's milk was sweeter, richer, and more abundant than ever, and as she regained her strength, I, too, flourished. Every day I sensed that I was warm and safe and loved.

As the months passed, I was happily ignorant of all that went on behind the scenes, of the meetings with lawyers, of the exhaustive measures taken to reach a just settlement and to keep the conflict out of the courts. I could not have understood that I had become a point of contention in the negotiations, as my mother wanted sole custody of me and my father refused to give up his rights.

As my mother traveled to and from London to meet with her legal advisors, or to various spas seeking remedies for her persistent illnesses, Colonel Doyle wrote to my grandparents warning them that Byron or his agents might attempt to abduct me. "It is of the utmost importance that Lord and Lady Noel never lose possession of their grandchild," he emphasized. "You must guard the infant with every possible vigilance."

Alarmed, Lady Noel purchased two pistols for defense and informed the groundskeepers that they would serve as my guards, patrolling the estate as they went about their usual duties and keeping a sharp watch for intruders. Her orders sent a thrill of excitement through the household staff, for nothing added interest to the tedious duty of looking after an elderly lord and lady than the threat of a kidnapping.

I have said that I have no memory of these events, and yet, perhaps an impression of my circumstances was etched upon my mind. When I was a very young child, I often felt a faint, persistent dread, as if I were being watched by a malicious intelligence. When I was a bit older, walking and talking and questioning everything, I was vaguely certain that at any moment, my wicked father might burst into Kirkby Mallory, snatch me up in a rough embrace, and spirit me off to parts unknown, far from everything I knew and everyone I loved. Now, with the benefit of hindsight, I understand that although my father wanted to see me, he had no intention of burdening himself with a small child and making himself an outlaw in the process. Yet the whispers that he might do so and the preparations to stop him surely left their mark upon my fertile imagination.

Despite their best attempts, my mother and grandparents could not keep the scandal out of the press, especially after my father published two poems about the Separation, "Fare Thee Well" and "A Sketch from Private Life." He published them privately, intending to circulate them only among his most intimate friends, but the printer leaked a copy to a newspaper editor, and one morning my mother was shocked to discover them featured prominently in the paper beneath the headline "Lord Byron's Poems on His Own Domestic Circumstances."

You may recall that soon after my birth my father declared me "an instrument of torture," and in this he proved prescient, for he wielded me against my mother to win sympathy for himself. "Fare Thee Well" offered the sort of romantic overtures that never failed to make the ladies swoon, for although my father lamented his estrangement from my mother, he reminded her and all the world of their eternal bond, which would endure beyond all suffering. I made my poetic debut in the ninth stanza when he appealed to my mother to reconcile for my sake:

And when thou would solace gather,
When our child's first accents flow,
Wilt thou teach her to say 'Father!'
Though his care she must forgo?

Any sympathy he might have won from the public with those tender lines was likely ruined by the second poem. In nasty, satirical strokes, "A Sketch from Private Life" unkindly skewered Mrs. Clermont, my mother's erstwhile governess and longtime faithful servant, and blamed her for turning my mother against him. The poem was brilliantly

81

wicked, but it was an unwarranted attack on a woman utterly unable to defend herself, and a gentleman simply did not treat a loyal member of his household that way. He called her the "hag of hatred," for heaven's sake. The poem also included an unflattering portrait of my mother as a pure, pious, unfeeling, unforgiving, heartless machine — a figment, I regret to say, that made an impression on the public that lingers to this day, despite her many accomplishments and charitable endeavors in all the years since.

Even so, the publication of the poems ultimately served Lady Byron well, for they portrayed my father as vicious and hypocritical, deserving of the strong condemnation that soon bombarded him. The press vilified him, and as the scandal grew and increased its frenzy, he received the worst punishment London society could inflict upon a man: the cut direct.

The cut took place in early April at the home of Sarah Villiers, Countess of Jersey, one of the few women of fashion who sympathized with Byron in his ordeal. Perhaps because her own illicit affairs — appropriately discreet and tolerated by her husband — were numerous, she had invited her besieged friend to attend her ball, a daring act of kindness and loyalty. Lady Jersey could not compel her guests to embrace him, however, and when my father entered the ball with my aunt Augusta on his arm, they were met with cold glares and hostile silence. Gentlemen whom Byron knew well met his greetings with wordless, stony looks before deliberately turning their backs; ladies who had once simpered and swooned held his gaze for a moment to acknowledge they had seen him, then turned their heads and pretended not to know him; well-matched couples left the room when the siblings entered, as if Byron's marital discord were contagious. Even Lady Jersey, who treated Byron with the utmost courtesy up to the moment his sister's distress compelled him to escort her home from the ball early, later called on my mother to assure her that my father's presence at the gathering had been "most unexpected."

Then, as now, the cut direct was an established social custom with specific rules of etiquette and one unmistakable purpose: It announced that all ties of friendship between the parties had been irrevocably severed. Lord Byron was no longer welcome in London society.

Ten days after his public humiliation, my father, who thus far had adamantly resisted my mother's appeals for a legal separation, finally acquiesced. He did not relinquish his paternal rights, but he insisted upon, and was granted, a stipulation that my mother could not take me abroad out of fear that we would settle in a foreign land where absent fathers had no legal rights whatsoever. He wrote to Augusta to ask her to serve as an intermediary between him and his estranged wife, watching out for me and writing to him often about my health and looks and habits, but never to mention my mother's name to him or to allude to her "in any shape — or on any occasion — except indispensable business." He then composed one last letter to my mother, entreating her to be kind to his sister and to permit her to visit me, and he enclosed a small emerald ring, a family heirloom, which he begged her to give to me. She complied, but not until many years later, when I was of an age to be safely entrusted with it. The ring became one of my most treasured possessions, and I intend to pass it on to my own daughter upon my death.

With the bitter legal squabbling of the Separation complete, my father decided to go abroad, but although he was hounded by creditors and ostracized from society, he was determined to leave England with a grand, defiant flourish that his enemies would never forget. He ordered an extravagant new carriage fashioned after one belonging to Napoléon Bonaparte, who the year before had escaped exile on the island of Elba and had been welcomed by cheering crowds in Paris only to face defeat three months later at the Battle of Waterloo. I suppose if one must go into exile like a deposed emperor, one might as well depart in imperial style. What parallels, if any, my father wanted observers to draw between his own downfall and that of the erstwhile French emperor, we can only imagine.

Into that spectacular carriage Byron loaded his beloved Newfoundlands, his pet peacock, his personal physician, his friends Hobhouse and Scrope Davies, and what clothing and possessions he had managed to fling into trunks before the avaricious bailiffs and creditors descended upon 13 Piccadilly Terrace. Early in the morning on 23 April, he and his companions set out for Dover, where the carriage was immediately loaded onto the ship out of fear that the bailiffs might attempt to seize it too.

Capricious winds and foul weather kept my father on British soil for another two days, but on 25 April, he bade Hobhouse farewell at the pier, boarded the ship, and set sail for Ostend, Belgium, a seventy-five-mile crossing that ordinarily took about eight hours. Instead the rough seas made it a horrible, stomach-churning, sixteen-hour ordeal, but my father distracted himself from the wretched conditions and bouts of seasickness by working on the third canto of *Childe Harold's Pilgrimage*. I know I was in his thoughts then, and that he grieved to part from me, for he preserved his thoughts in timeless verses, perhaps hoping that someday I would read them.

Is thy face like thy mother's, my fair child!
ADA! sole daughter of my house and
   heart?
When last I saw thy young blue eyes they
   smiled,
And then we parted, — not as now we
   part,
But with a hope. —
   Awaking with a start,
The waters heave around me; and on high
The winds lift up their voices: I depart,
Whither I know not; but the hour's gone by,
When Albion's lessening shores could
   grieve or glad mine eye.

My father never returned to England.

CHAPTER TWO:
I KNOW THAT
THOU WILT LOVE ME

April–December 1816

As fiercely as my mother had fought for custody, it may surprise you to learn that after we fled London, she spent very little time with me at Kirkby Mallory Hall. There were legal matters she was obliged to attend to in the city, of course, but much of her time was spent visiting friends or resting at favorite spas. My mother has complained of fragile health for as long as I can remember, her worst symptoms never failing to appear at the least opportune moments — when an unpleasant duty required her attention, for example, or when I fell ill and badly wanted her to care for me. This remarkable and unfortunate coincidence has persisted throughout my life.

Fortunately, my beloved grandparents and devoted nurse Mrs. Grimes looked after me so well that I hardly noticed my mother's absence. Indeed, whenever she breezed through Leicestershire on a visit, I did not recognize her, and when she swept into the nursery and tried to pick me up, I shrieked and wailed and reached desperately for Grandmama or Mrs. Grimes. The first time I behaved so thoughtlessly, Lady Byron laughed and said, "She is angry that I've weaned her, and she wants to punish me." The second time, however, she became very much displeased, and before she set off on her next trip, she ordered my nurse to have me kiss her portrait every night before I went to bed so I would better remember her. The dutiful Mrs. Grimes obliged, but I reached four months of age, and then five, without learning any better.

Then it happened that my mother's visit home coincided with an exhausting few days when I was teething, and I frequently disturbed the restful peace of Kirkby Mallory with my wails of pain. Resolving to speed the process along, my mother sliced my inflamed gums with a lancet, so briskly and unsentimentally that Mrs. Grimes flinched.

"I don't disagree with your theory, my dear," my grandmother said over my screams, lifting me from my cradle as Mrs. Grimes hurried off for a wet cloth for me to gnaw on to staunch the bleeding, "but perhaps this would be better done by a surgeon or apothecary. A particular dexterity is required, I think."

"Nonsense. She'll be fine in a moment."

My mother reached for me, but when I shrieked and hid my face on my grandmother's shoulder, she let her hands fall to her sides. "She would thank me, if she understood."

Regrettably, I did not understand, and for a time after she went away again I refused to kiss her portrait unless my grandparents became quite stern with me, for I associated the woman in the picture with the lancet cutting open my tender gums.

Although my mother was often obliged to be away from me due to her health, you mustn't think that she lacked affection for me. Despite the distractions of whatever seaside resort or gracious country house she inhabited, she always found time to send my grandparents sweetly anxious letters inquiring about my health, growth, and comfort. She even took the extra time to include a cover note instructing my grandmother to save her letters in case she was ever required to submit evidence of her maternal devotion to the courts. I like to think, however, that my mother really wanted them kept for *me*, as a sort of diary that I would enjoy someday when I was old enough to read them on my own.

When I was a trifle older and had become a more agreeable companion, my mother occasionally allowed me to accompany her on her travels, with my nurse and my mother's maid completing our little entourage. Although you may protest that at six months of age I would have been too young to recall it, my earliest memory is of one of our trips together in early June of 1816. My mother had taken me to Ely, in Cambridgeshire, to tour the magnificent cathedral there. The dean's wife herself showed us from the Galilee Porch inside to the West Tower, and oh, how my young eyes widened as I marveled at the glorious Octagon, with its vast stone tower, eight high archways, and glazed timber lantern suspended high above. Our tour moved on to the beautiful, light, airy Lady Chapel, where we admired the multiple bays of tall, traceried windows and marble pillars; the graceful ogees and seating booths of the arcade; and even the intriguing evidence of damage carried out during the Reformation, when faces and other images were hacked out of the relief carvings along the walls, which provoked my curiosity about the people who had been depicted in the once finely detailed scenes. Even the luxuries of Kirkby Mallory Hall had not prepared me for such splendor.

It was when we were returning to the cathedral proper, passing along the covered walkway from the Lady Chapel to the north aisle of the chancel, that I first became aware of the bold, curious stares of other visitors. Unnoticed until then, clusters of onlookers had gathered not far from us, murmuring excitedly as they watched, some nodding toward us, others impertinently pointing. My mother had been recognized, and it was easy to guess the identity of the infant she carried. I heard my name spoken here and there in unfamiliar voices; intrigued, I turned my head this way and that, trying to discover who had spoken of me with such excitement. My interest turned to alarm as the crowd closed in on us from both ends of the walkway — curious, no doubt, to see whether the offspring of the notorious Byron had sprouted horns and a tail. My mother murmured urgently to the dean's wife, who quickly ushered us past the onlookers down a side corridor to solitude and safety.

My mother was too disconcerted to wait until the gawkers dispersed, so we cut short our visit and left the cathedral. We spent the night at a nearby inn, and in the morning when we rose and went down to breakfast, the innkeeper showed us to a private dining room. Before we could be seated, he wrung his hands and said, "I'm terribly sorry, Lady Byron, but I thought it best you know that your carriage has attracted quite a crowd in front of the inn."

My mother grew very still for a moment, but then she went to a window, drew back the curtain, and looked outside. A dozen or more men and women surrounded our carriage at a respectful distance, noting the coat of arms painted on the door, rising on tiptoe to peer through the windows, drawing back in disappointment when they spied no passengers within.

Sighing, my mother let the curtain fall and settled us down to breakfast, her face bearing a slight frown that showed she was thinking intently. When we finished eating — she swallowed barely a mouthful herself — she summoned the innkeeper and announced the plan she had devised: She would send out her maid, Merle, to board the carriage, cloaked to conceal her identity and carrying a bundle about the size of a large, healthy baby. After the carriage sped her away and the crowd dispersed, my mother, my nurse, and I, similarly cloaked and disguised, would depart the inn in a borrowed carriage and meet our own parked at a designated spot out of sight a half mile down the road.

The plan worked perfectly, and soon we were seated comfortably in our own carriage on our way to the next destination on our itinerary. Unfortunately, our carriage attracted a swarm of impertinent sightseers at our inn at Peterborough too, and several eager folk hurried after us into the lobby. One apple-cheeked matron rushed forward, arms outstretched, begging to give "poor fatherless Augusta Ada" a wee kiss. A young gentleman, declaring himself an aspiring poet, requested a lock of my hair "for luck," calling it a relic of my genius parent. As Mrs. Grimes sheltered me in her arms and turned her back to the crowd, Lady Byron bristled, drew herself up, and beckoned to the innkeeper. Her haughty frowns kept the would-be well-wishers at bay until a pair of footmen could escort us to safety.

We stayed two days in Peterborough, calling on the young Marquess of Exeter at Burghley House and strolling along the river Nene. The next day we moved on to Bury, where we paid our respects to the Earl of Derby and toured the gardens of Knowsley Hall. We were strolling along the water gardens when suddenly a woman, perhaps thirty years old and clad in plain but respectable attire, approached us. "This is for you, my lady," the woman said, thrusting something small and rectangular at my mother. When she did not take it, the woman came forward in a rush and pressed it into her hands. "You must read it. Read it for the sake of little Augusta Ada. If you do, even your frozen, unforgiving heart must melt."

Stunned by the stranger's nerve, my mother stared at her wordlessly.

"Get along with you," Merle ordered, incredulous. "Who do you think you are, accosting her ladyship so impertinently? Leave us alone before we call the authorities." The maid swept forward and waved the strange woman away, and only after she ran off in the opposite direction from the house did Merle return to my mother's side, breathless. "What did she give you?" she asked, gesturing to the object in my mother's grasp.

"A book." My mother opened the cover and read the title page aloud. "*Lord Byron's Farewell to England; with Three Other Poems, viz. Ode to St. Helena, To My Daughter, on the Morning of Her Birth* — Oh, for heaven's sake." Impatiently, she passed the book to Merle. "The nonsense I must suffer courtesy of his loyal readers."

"What shall I do with it?" Merle asked, pinching the book between her thumb and forefinger and holding it at arm's length as if she carried a dead rat.

"Throw it in the pond. Burn it. I don't care."

Merle and Mrs. Grimes exchanged a look as my mother stalked away, frowning with great intensity as she studied the lilies and water reeds. It was evident that neither servant thought it would be wise to destroy something their mistress might want to examine later.

Sure enough, when we were safely en-sconced at our inn, my mother did indeed request the book and sat near the window reading it while Mrs. Grimes and Merle worked quietly, keeping me amused or sewing. "This is a fraud," my mother finally said, tossing the book on a nearby table. "Lord Byron did not write this trash. This did not come from his pen, or from John Murray's publishing house. This is the work of some barely literate charlatan who hopes to profit from the Separation, from our unhappiness. Put it on the fire."

This time Merle obeyed, and poems the strange woman had hoped would reconcile my parents turned to ash and smoke.

If my mother needed more evidence that the drama of the Separation still held the nation in its thrall, she certainly had it then. These unpleasant encounters ruined the trip for her, and that evening, from the blessed solitude of our rooms, she wrote to my grandparents to announce that we would be moving on from Peterborough earlier than expected. "Everywhere we go, we are stared at as fearsome, exotic beasts," she complained wearily, "like *lionesses.*" It was impossible for her to travel incognito with me, she noted, adding that from now on I was to be called *Ada,* only Ada. She underlined the name with a dark, emphatic stroke so there could be no misunderstanding.

By the middle of June, my mother had settled our party in a charming little cottage in Lowestoft, a lovely resort town on the North Sea coast in Suffolk. Happily I played with Mrs. Grimes on the broad sandy beaches, I watched the gulls soar and keen high above the pier, and I took eager, toddling steps on the shore just out of reach of the waves, my arms raised above my head, each hand holding fast to one of my mother's. Here we may have been recognized, but we were left to ourselves. Here, more than one hundred miles northeast of London, no one disturbed our holiday with bold stares or demands for kisses and locks of hair.

Those were lovely days, but my restless mother could not linger, and so we eventually moved on. From Lowestoft we returned to Kirkby Mallory to visit my grandparents, but my mother did not enjoy my grandmother's company as much as I did, so we were soon off again, this time to London. My mother settled us in lodgings somewhere between Knightsbridge and Green Street and was quickly caught up in such a whirlwind of social gatherings, lectures, and business that I scarcely saw her. "Lady B might as well have left the bairn at Kirkby rather than drag her from pillar to post only to ignore her once we got there," Mrs. Grimes said with a sniff to my mother's maid, but Merle was loyal to her mistress and my nurse found no sympathy there.

One event in particular stands out in my memory of those weeks, although perhaps it is only the retelling of the event that I recall. It was autumn, I know, for the trees in the back garden had begun to turn, and on this notable day, my mother had instructed Mrs. Grimes to put me in my warm dress of soft blue wool and my cloak with a hood, for we were going out to meet someone.

I could tell by the firm set to my mother's mouth that this was an errand she undertook out of duty rather than affection. She said little as the coach took us through the city to a neighborhood less fashionable than our own, and through the front door of a residence that, while comfortable and tastefully furnished, was a trifle worn and faded compared to our rented rooms. A doll and a wooden ship had been propped up and forgotten against one wall of the foyer, and I heard the busy hum of children's voices somewhere overhead. Although I craned my neck and reached both hands toward the stairs, I was carried instead into a parlor, where a plumply pretty, dark-haired woman sat on the edge of the sofa watching the doorway.

My mother led the way into the room, and Mrs. Grimes followed close behind with me in her arms. A quick intake of breath and a slight straightening of the strange woman's spine betrayed the intensity of her emotion, and I knew it took every ounce of her will to refrain from bounding out of her chair to embrace us. "Is this she?" the woman said, a tremor in her voice.

"Of course," said Lady Byron, somewhat curtly. "Who else would she be?"

The woman uttered a small, apologetic laugh as she rose and met us in the center of the room. "She could be no one else," the woman said, gazing into my face almost reverently. "She has her father's eyes, and his chin. Does she show any signs of my brother's poetical genius?"

"She's only a baby," my mother replied, a frosty rebuff to the woman's warm enthusiasm.

"Yes, yes, of course." The woman smiled down upon me, and as I smiled tentatively back, her eyes glistened. "Oh, if only he could be here now! He speaks so tenderly of her in his letters, if only —" She broke off, quite overcome, as tears spilled down her cheeks.

"Augusta, do contain yourself," my mother ordered. "You'll upset the child."

The woman nodded, squeezed her eyes shut, and raised a handkerchief to her mouth. In a moment, she had regained her composure enough to smile at me again. "I am your auntie and namesake, dear Augusta Ada," she said, and my mother kindly did not correct her regarding my new designation. "I am your father's elder sister, and I love you very, very much, as does he." She glanced to my mother. "May I hold her?"

My mother hesitated before agreeing, but as soon as Augusta took me in her arms, a sob escaped her throat, and she began trembling from the effort to contain her weeping. At a gesture from my mother, Mrs. Grimes took me back again.

"I'm sorry," Augusta said tremulously. "In her sweet face I glimpse my brother, and I miss him so terribly —"

"You must control yourself in front of the child," my mother said, reaching out to stroke my back, although I was not at all upset, merely a little bewildered.

"I will." Augusta took a deep, shaky breath. "I will be calm hereafter, I promise you."

What my mother said to that I do not recall, but I remember stilted conversation, more tears from my aunt, more firm reproofs from my mother to compose herself. We did not linger long, departing before tea could be served, before I could meet the children — my cousins, surely — I had heard playing upstairs.

"Mrs. Leigh is too flighty, too easily upset," my mother said to Mrs. Grimes as we rode home. "Who knows what she might say in front of the child, what untruths and exaggerations she might blurt out in a moment of distress?"

"She does seem somewhat fragile," my nurse agreed.

"Ada must never be left alone with her."

"Yes, Lady Byron. I'll see to it."

My mother nodded and fell into a pensive

silence, studying the scenes of London passing by outside her window. "Mrs. Leigh hopes that Ada will inherit her father's genius," she murmured, as if thinking aloud. "What a terrible fate to wish on an innocent child." Suddenly she fixed my nurse with a sharp, commanding look. "Nothing of the poetical must be permitted to take root in Ada's mind or character. She must be brought up with structure and discipline, with rigorous attention to developing her faculties for logic and reason."

Mrs. Grimes shifted me in her arms, dubious. "Do you mean that I should not allow her to play, Lady Byron?"

"Not at all. She shall play, but with suitable toys in well-regulated games. Blocks and such, for learning geometry. Balls, also for geometry, and to study motion." My mother nodded, warming to her idea. "She must never be exposed to Lord Byron's poetry — little danger of that at Kirkby Mallory, as Lady Noel has disposed of all her copies of his books — and absolutely no fairy stories."

My nurse's brow furrowed. "None at all? But children love fairy stories."

"Children often love what is not good for them. Adults do also, more's the pity." For a moment her gaze turned inward, but the moment swiftly passed. "No fairy stories, no poetry. She has too much of the Byron blood in her, and it may lead to her ruin as it has to his. Her salvation depends upon developing her moral and intellectual powers and suppressing everything of the imagination."

My nurse murmured agreement, undoubtedly relieved that when my formal education began, a governess would take over those duties. It would be difficult enough to forgo fairy stories without taking responsibility for entirely subduing a bright, active little girl's imagination.

The interview with my aunt Augusta so vexed my mother that soon afterward she took me back to Kirkby Mallory Hall. A few days in her mother's company inspired her to set out for Bath, taking her maid as her only companion. My mother and I had spent so much time together that summer and fall that, unlike before, her absence left me feeling bereft, and I did not need to kiss her portrait at bedtime to remind myself that I loved and missed her.

And yet I was happy to be home, embraced by the warmth of my grandparents' boundless affection. My grandmother often excused Mrs. Grimes for the day so that we could spend the hours together — bright, happy mornings followed by long, tranquil afternoons. I took my first careful steps alone in their spacious library, and despite the pervasive fear that my father might send masked marauders to breach the walls and make off with me, I felt a sense of belonging and contentment that I never knew at any of the lovely places my mother took me in our peripatetic season. I had free run of the place, cherished by my grandparents, indulged by the servants, denied only my parents' presence — and imagination.

Only one room in Kirkby Mallory Hall seemed to me to lie ever in shadow.

On the ground floor my grandfather kept a smoking and billiards room for the amusement of himself and his gentlemen friends. The smell of whiskey and cigar smoke made me wrinkle my nose in distaste, but what transfixed me with curiosity and apprehension was the great portrait that hung above the chimneypiece. A dark green curtain shrouded it and was never drawn back, nor was its presence acknowledged by anyone in the room. From my grandmother's disparaging comments and servants' gossip, I had learned that the portrait was a famous and quite valuable painting of my father.

Whenever I was feeling especially brave, I would steal into the room alone and gaze up at the covered portrait, wondering what lay behind the dark green curtain. What did my father look like? Of course I did not remember, although in later years it brought me some comfort to think that I had seen him, and he had seen me, though I had no memory of our brief time together. Was he handsome? Was he malformed? There must be something truly terrible about his appearance or my grandmother would not have hidden him from view. He must be very important or she would have gotten rid of the portrait altogether. In my imagination — that wicked, persistent faculty — he became a chimera of the magnificent and the monstrous. I could not gaze upon his covered portrait without a stirring of apprehension about my father, certain that he was sinister, dangerous, and malformed, and that since I was his child, something sinister and dangerous lurked within me too.

In November my mother returned to Kirkby Mallory Hall for my christening, but she neglected to inform my aunt Augusta that the solemn event had taken place, or that my grandmother had replaced her as my godmother. Nor was Augusta invited for the party on 10 December my grandparents arranged to mark my first birthday, perhaps because it was an appropriately modest affair, just my mother, my grandparents, and the household staff. We had a pudding and a few gifts, and I wore a new yellow dress.

Much later I discovered that my first birthday was a melancholy occasion for my mother, as she recorded in a poem she titled, "To Ada." The poem began,

Thine is the smile and thine the bloom
When Hope might image ripened Charms

But mine is fraught with memory's gloom
Thou art not in a Father's arms!

Three stanzas later, she lamented,

Thou Dove! who may'st not find a rest
Save in one frail and shattered bark!
A lonely Mother's bleeding breast —
May Heaven provide a surer ark!

My mother must have thought well of her poem, for soon thereafter, she sent a copy to her friend Theresa Villiers. "It has occurred to me," she mused in an accompanying note, "that the verses may be misunderstood, as if they expressed a wish that she were with her father, such as he is; when on the contrary, I consider her as *fatherless.*"

I suppose I might as well have been, for all that I was allowed to know of him.

My father was in Venice at the time, and I know not whether he marked my birthday in verse or fond remembrance. I like to think that I crossed his mind as he was poled along a canal in a gondola, beneath an arched bridge, past an open window through which he heard someone singing *bel canto.*

CHAPTER THREE:
DULL HATE AS DUTY
SHOULD BE TAUGHT

December 1816–September 1817

In that same season, the publisher John Murray produced irrefutable evidence that my father had thought of me, if not on my first birthday, then at other times throughout the preceding year. In November, my father's sublime third canto of *Childe Harold's Pilgrimage* was published to great acclaim and tremendous sales. If my father had not thought it unbecoming a gentleman to accept money for his poetry, I have no doubt that his financial troubles would have been resolved immediately.

Since my mother and grandparents refused to seek out news of the poem's reception, it took a few weeks for word to wend its way to Kirkby Mallory. When it finally did come, it struck with such force that one might have supposed the very stones of Mallory Hall trembled from the impact. Naturally my mother and grandparents could not resist obtaining a copy of the poem to see for themselves if the whispers were true, and that Byron had addressed his personal affairs in this poem just as he had in "Fare Thee Well" and "A Sketch from Private Life." To their chagrin, just as my mother had dreaded, my father had again used his poetry, which he must have known would be read throughout the country and in many foreign lands, to express his feelings about the Separation, and about me.

I have told you how the canto began, with Byron's wistful musings about the infant daughter he had left behind in England. After narrating Childe Harold's travels from Dover to Waterloo and along the Rhine into Switzerland for one hundred fourteen stanzas, the narrator returns to me in the one hundred fifteenth.

My Daughter! with thy name this song
    begun —
My Daughter! with thy name thus much
    shall end —
I see thee not — I hear thee not — but
    None
Can be so wrapt in thee; Thou art the
    Friend
To whom the Shadows of far years extend:
Albeit my brow thou never should'st
    behold,
My voice shall with thy future visions blend,

And reach into thy heart — when mine is
  cold —
A token and a tone, even from thy father's
  mould.

The idea that my father had thought of me
more often and more deeply than anyone else
had, including the loving family that had
cared for me so devotedly throughout my first
year, did not sit well with my mother. My
grandmother was even more indignant, and
she rebuked him in absentia for abandoning
me, never mind that it was my mother who
had left my father, and that neither she nor
my mother and grandfather wanted him
anywhere near me.

Unmoved were they by my father's tangible
longing to see me again, which my family
dismissed as poetic artifice meant to arouse
the sympathy of the public and the courts.
" 'To hold thee lightly on a gentle knee,' "
my grandmother read aloud, with unusual
bitterness, " 'And print on thy soft cheek a
parent's kiss — / This, it should seem, was
not reserved for me.' And whose fault is that,
I ask you?"

"Mother, please," said my mother wearily,
rubbing the headache out of her temples.
"Read no more, I beg you."

My grandmother pursed her mouth. "Oh,
yes, we must not hear again the most offensive lines —"

"Indeed we must not —"

" 'Yet, though dull Hate as duty should be taught, / I know that thou wilt love me.' "

"And so we shall hear the lines regardless," my mother said acidly, to no one in particular.

My grandmother gestured to the pages littering the sofa between her and my mother. "This is highly offensive. I shall speak to my lawyers about this — this *slander,* these bold, outrageous lies. We are not teaching Ada to hate her father. We scarcely speak of him."

"Although how Byron believes Ada will learn to love him when they are separated by hundreds of miles . . ." From his favorite armchair near the fireplace, my grandfather frowned at the pages and shook his head with genuine regret. "Well, I daresay he hopes in vain."

"And how dare he slander you, Annabella, with this title he bestows upon your daughter — 'The Child of Love — though born in bitterness, / And nurtured in Convulsion.' " My grandmother's eyes sparked with righteous indignation. "How dare he? Ada was born into a mother's loving embrace, and has been nurtured here, with us, her family, we who cherish her and care for her with most tender affection. 'Convulsion' indeed!"

"Makes a man want to thrash him," my grandfather muttered. "I'll show *him* a convulsion."

"Mother, Father, please calm yourselves,"

my mother commanded. "None of this does us any good. It certainly does no good for Ada." She gathered up the poem, folded the pages crisply, and tucked them into the book she had been reading, Francis Bacon's treatise *The Advancement of Learning.* "Let me be perfectly clear: Ada shall not read Byron's poems when she is able, they shall not be read to her, and they will not be discussed in front of her. It's obvious that her father's words upset her, and little wonder."

My grandparents glanced to where I sat on the floor surrounded by my favorite wooden blocks — watching them, trembling with anxious bewilderment, my play forgotten. They let the matter drop, then and thereafter, at least in my presence, but a shadow hung over our Christmas merriment in the weeks that followed. Once I caught my grandmother glaring up at the covered portrait hanging in the smoking and billiards room as if she would rather set fire to it than allow it to grace the chimneypiece one day more.

Even though Lady Noel was outraged *for* my mother, not *at* her, my mother still found her complaints and constant indignation unbearable. Although I'm sure my grandmother did not intend it that way, perhaps my mother heard implicit criticism in her mother's bitter words, as if Lady Noel were berating her for choosing from among her many suitors the one least likely to bring her happiness. In any case, my mother decided that even a mansion as spacious as Kirkby Mallory was too small for both her and my grandmother, and so she told my grandparents that her fragile health obliged her to move to a place where she could find more restful sleep and good fresh air to improve her strength and vitality. She decided to take a house in Frognal, Hampstead, and I was to go with her, as would her maid and my nurse. On the day of our departure, the first of April, my grandmother hugged me tightly and wept, and as our carriage pulled away and I waved good-bye through the window, it looked to me as if her heart had truly broken.

I missed my grandparents terribly, but my mother was relieved to be free of their constant worry and unceasing scrutiny, and that pleased her, which in turn pleased me. Soon after our arrival, though, my mother received an official document declaring that although she would retain sole custody of me, due to the ongoing dispute, I had been named a ward in chancery. From afar my father was asserting his rights under English law, and apparently he still feared that my mother would take me abroad and settle in a foreign land where he would be allowed no parental rights. In January a letter came from my father, through the usual intermediary, my aunt Augusta. "I require an explicit answer that Ada shall not be taken out of the country on any pretext whatever," he wrote to his sister. "I repeat that I have no desire to take the child from her, while she remains in England, but I demand that the infant shall not be removed." My mother had no desire to take me abroad at that time, but my father's demands, which she deemed "needless interference," affronted her greatly. If not for the legal ruling that granted him his request, I think my mother might have taken me across the Channel for a holiday in France just to spite him.

My mother did not know then, and I would not discover for many years afterward, that it was in this same month that my father's illegitimate daughter was born in Bath, about one hundred twenty-five miles west of our lodgings in Hampstead. Called Allegra Byron, she was the daughter of Claire Clairmont, the stepsister of Mary Godwin Shelley. Mrs. Shelley, of course, was the wife of the poet Percy Bysshe Shelley, the daughter of the writer Mary Wollstonecraft and the philosopher William Godwin, and the author of a remarkable novel, *Frankenstein,* which would be published the following year. I am unaware of any of Miss Clairmont's accomplishments, and I never did meet her daughter, my half sister, who died in Italy of an illness when she was only five years old. Throughout my childhood I always longed for a sibling. Perhaps somehow I sensed that I had lost a sister and unwittingly grieved.

Hampstead was pleasant and pretty, and our house was cozy and comfortable. We had all the fresh country air my mother required, and we often went for long rambles, or so they seemed to me, my stout little legs working at a quick march so I would not fall behind my swift, graceful mother. Sadly, there were no little children for me to play with, for I was not permitted to consort with just any youngsters, but my mother steadily built herself a coterie of friends. Though her rank and wealth assured her a place among the most elite ladies and gentlemen of the aristocracy, she chose her companions not for their status in Society but for their accomplishments — intellectual, artistic, or spiritual. She preferred the company of reverends and vicars, Dissenters and reformers, the spinster playwright Joanna Baillie and the celebrated actress Sarah Siddons. A few of her friends clearly liked children and were kind to me, but most were too preoccupied with serious matters and important ideas to waste precious time playing pat-a-cake with a precocious little girl. They came to tea and dinner parties to impress Lady Byron and to be impressed by her, and since she was invariably the highest-ranking lady at these gatherings, everyone deferred to her in all things, an arrangement I trust she quite enjoyed.

Whenever I beheld my mother holding

court with her circle of friends, I felt my own loneliness more keenly, and when suitable playmates failed to appear, I asked my mother if I might have a puppy instead.

"Certainly not," my mother said. "I could not bear the noise and the mess. Hounds I can tolerate, because they are necessary for the hunt and they remain outside, but I will permit no beasts to crowd my hearth and soil my carpets."

"Could I have a kitten? They're much quieter."

"But no less destructive, with their claws and their mess. Certainly not."

"Maybe a bunny —"

"No, Ada," my mother said firmly. "I cannot abide animals in the house."

Or anywhere else, I thought glumly. She forbade me to ask her again, but she could not prevent me from imagining how lovely it would be to have a pet to cuddle and love and whisper my secrets to. The scenes I envisioned were so delightful that I soon began to pretend that I had a puppy all my own, a brown-and-white springer spaniel I called Freddy. What a charming companion he was too, always eager to play and to accompany me on my rambles around the garden. If it was not quite as wonderful as having a real puppy, that was not Freddy's fault.

One spring afternoon, my mother and her

friend Miss Montgomery came upon me and Mrs. Grimes in the garden, where I was amusing myself by pretending to teach Freddy how to roll over and shake hands. "To whom are you speaking?" my mother asked sharply, while Miss Montgomery glanced around suspiciously as if expecting to discover a black-cloaked villain crouched behind a pear tree.

"Nobody," I replied.

"I distinctly heard your voice." She looked to Mrs. Grimes, who had hastily risen from her seat on a nearby bench, still clutching her knitting needless and a skein of yarn. "It was a strange tone indeed with which to address your nurse."

"She was only playing, Lady Byron," said Mrs. Grimes. "She likes to pretend she has a puppy for a playmate. It's only a game."

"He's brown and white and has the softest fur," I chimed in, smiling.

A strange apprehension filled my mother's eyes as she swiftly approached, startling me into silence. "You see a dog here, now?" she asked, kneeling beside me and snatching up my hand.

I shrank beneath her penetrating gaze. "I don't *see* him. He's not real — but sometimes he seems real —"

When she recoiled in horror, I knew I had said the wrong thing. "How often do you see this dog? Do you see other things too?"

"I —" I glanced helplessly to Mrs. Grimes, but my mother shifted to block her from my view. "I hear you, and Mrs. Grimes, and —"

"It's just a child's game," said my nurse. "I thought it harmless —"

"You forget who her father is," my mother said curtly. Abruptly she released my hand and stood, but her eyes never left my face. "Ada, if you ever see animals or people who aren't there, or hear voices when no one else is in the room, you must tell me or your nurse immediately. Do you understand?"

Frightened, I gulped and nodded.

Mrs. Grimes hurried to me and rested her hands on my shoulders. "It's nothing, really, my lady. It was all in fun."

I had seen grown men grow pale beneath the frigid look my mother fixed upon Mrs. Grimes at that. "I have told you before, and I will not warn you a second time. You endanger this child's life and sanity when you indulge her imagination. Do not let it happen again."

As Mrs. Grimes bobbed a curtsey and murmured apologies and promises, my mother threw me one last look of warning before she strode off toward the house, with Miss Montgomery scurrying to keep up with her.

"I'm sorry," I told Mrs. Grimes, fighting back tears.

"It's all right, little one."

"Does this mean —" I took a deep breath. "Does this mean I can't play with Freddy anymore?"

Her only reply was to sigh and kiss the top of my head. In my mind's eye I watched Freddy bound away with a stick in his mouth, far away and out of sight.

A stray thought came to me then, the vague awareness that my father loved dogs, especially Newfoundlands. If he had raised me, surely I would have been permitted to keep as many dogs as I wished. A faint anger like a wisp of smoke rising from embers unfurled in my heart, and I wondered how else my life might have been different had my father absconded with me to the Continent as my mother and grandparents had feared.

In the summer of 1817 my mother wanted to travel with her friend Miss Frances Carr to Scotland, and since Miss Carr was not encumbered with young children, my mother decided to set down her own young burden at Kirkby Mallory. My grandparents were thrilled to have me back, and although I missed my mother more than I had at any previous parting, my grandmother and my nurse swiftly filled the sudden emptiness of my days with play and songs and hugs, and filled my tummy with sweet delicacies from the kitchen that my mother denied herself and thus never allowed on our own table.

I considered Kirkby Mallory my home, and I adored its spacious halls and well-lit galleries, and the way it smelled of fresh-cut flowers in spring and summer, well-tended fireplaces in autumn and winters, and warm oak, clean linen, and old books in every season. The exception was the kitchen, which smelled exactly as you would hope the domain of a generous, bustling cook who loved to stew, roast, and bake would smell. Even so, the longer I stayed away while traveling with my mother, the more time I needed upon my return to feel as if I were truly at home and not merely visiting. I had been home almost a fortnight before I felt bold enough to steal away to the smoking and billiards room, where I intended to test my bravery by staring up at the mysterious covered portrait and reflecting upon what terrors the curtain might conceal.

To my astonishment, I discovered that the portrait was gone, curtain and all. Several smaller portraits filled the space upon the chimneypiece, one of Lord Wentworth, my grandmother's brother, who had died unmarried and had left her Kirkby Mallory Hall; another of my grandmother herself as a young woman before her marriage; and a few more of my mother's aunts, as bright and fresh as spring blossoms. The family portraits had a fixed, complacent look, as if they had always been there and could not imagine their pride of place ever belonging to another. For an unsettling moment, I wondered if I had only imagined the large cloaked portrait that had hung there in shrouded solitude before, but I quickly seized my imagination in a firm grip and reassured myself that I was not mistaken.

My father's portrait had been taken down, but why, and what had become of it? I longed to know, but I understood that I must not ask.

The summer months passed happily, interrupted by sudden, sharp, painful bouts of loneliness and longing for my mother. A few playmates my own age would have been a great consolation, but the only potential friends were the servants' offspring or children from the village, and they had been deemed unsuitable companions for Lady Byron's daughter.

Although I saw other children only very rarely, and usually from a distance, in August I somehow managed to contract that most ordinary of childhood ailments, chicken pox. It was a misery. I itched and cried and burned with fever. I begged for my mother, and she and my grandmother exchanged frequent letters, so I knew that she was aware of my illness, but still she did not appear.

"When is Mama coming?" I asked my grandmother one night as she tucked me into bed, thoroughly miserable, feverish and uncomfortable, and feeling utterly abandoned. "Did you not tell her I need her?"

"I'm sorry, my little love," said my grandmother, smoothing my sweaty hair off my brow. "Your mother thinks that it would be imprudent for her to return at this time, while there is any chance of her taking the pox. We would not want your mother to fall ill too, would we?"

"No," I said in a small voice. I had not thought of the danger to my mother at all, which surely proved that I was a very wicked and selfish child.

I don't know what I thought my mother could have done for me that my grandmother and nurse were not already doing. Even the best of children can be little tyrants, believing themselves absolutely entitled to every bit of the love and servitude bestowed upon them by the adults entrusted with their care, and I was certainly not the best of children. Even so, Mrs. Grimes was so tireless in her efforts to ease my suffering — going without sleep, barely pausing to eat or drink, leaving the sickroom only reluctantly — that I was deeply moved. Her impetus was not duty but true affection, and I was so thunderstruck by this astonishing realization that once, as she bent over me to refresh the cloth upon my brow, I seized her hand, pulled her close, and flung my arms around her neck. "I love you, Mrs. Grimes," I said, with every ounce of feeling in my fever-wracked body.

"I love you too, my precious little lamb." Mrs. Grimes eased me back upon my pillow, smiled, and kissed my forehead. "Now, you must be a good little girl and sleep, so you can get well, and we can play in the garden again. Will you do that for me?"

I nodded and obediently closed my eyes, my heart full, and I soon fell deeply asleep.

After that, I got better little by little, day by day, until at last my fever cooled and my angry red rash faded. In late September, assured that the danger of contagion had passed, my mother at last returned to Kirkby Mallory. As delighted as I was to see her again, I could not help noticing that she seemed different — sadder, quieter, more apprehensive about the future. At first I assumed, with a child's certainty of residing in the center of the universe, that my illness had frightened her, that she feared it might yet return to claim me. Perhaps I had been closer to death than anyone had let me believe.

I was much mistaken, as I learned when I overheard my mother confiding in my grandmother one evening when they paused outside my doorway on their way to their own bedchambers. Knowing that they would be displeased to find me still awake, I had feigned sleep, and I heard my mother sigh heavily. When my grandmother asked the reason for her melancholy, she confessed that the grim reality of the Separation had only recently dawned upon her. "At first I was so relieved to be free that I did not think of the loneliness that would follow," she told my grandmother, her voice so low that I almost could not make out her words. "Then I was preoccupied with securing custody of Ada, and that struggle allowed no time for introspection or brooding over the future. It has only been since midsummer that the burden of my solitude has begun to weigh heavily upon my shoulders. I feel as if I am crossing a desert in the dark, loaded down with anger and disappointment and sorrow, and I do not like to face this journey alone."

At that, I almost sat up in bed and declared that she was not alone, that she had me, and that I would gladly accompany her anywhere. But I restrained the impulse, and so it was my grandmother who assured my mother that she was not alone, that her parents loved her deeply and would gladly carry as many of her burdens as she allowed.

"Thank you, Mother," she replied. "I am grateful, but I'm mourning the death of my marriage and of all the dreams and hopes of my youth."

"Surely not all your hopes for the future are lost," protested my grandmother. "You're still very young, and you have Ada."

In the silence that followed, I pictured my mother shaking her head. "My hold on Ada is tenuous at best, and it is challenged on all sides."

"Challenged? By whom?"

"By Mrs. Grimes, for one, from what you've told me. Ada loves her."

"Of course she does, as well she should. That doesn't mean she loves you any less. No one can replace a mother in a child's heart. Do you love me any less for loving your father too, for loving Ada?"

"Certainly not." My mother inhaled deeply. "Of course you're right. In Ada I find a great deal of hope and promise, if those Byronic branches and shoots can be pruned back. I don't mean to wallow in melancholy. I'll find a way forward, some noble endeavor to occupy my thoughts and fill my hours."

They moved on, leaving me to ponder their unexpected exchange, for they rarely conversed so spontaneously and frankly. As my thoughts churned, my curiosity soon transformed into worry, but I eventually drifted off to sleep.

The next morning, I waited for Mrs. Grimes to come dress me. My tummy rumbled with hunger, and the day had quite begun, and I thought it very strange that she should be delayed. Then a terrible thought struck: Perhaps she had come down with the chicken pox. I threw back the covers, scrambled from my bed, and padded down the hall, not far, to my nurse's little chamber.

There I found her folding the contents of her wardrobe into neat piles upon her bed near a tapestry satchel. As I watched from the doorway, as silent as a shadow, she placed a bundle of stockings into the satchel, followed by a muslin petticoat.

"What are you doing?" I asked, alarmed.

She gasped and whirled about to face me, a hand pressed to her heart. I noticed then that she was not attired in her customary uniform, but in the navy dress with mother-of-pearl buttons she wore on her days off. "Goodness, child," she said, catching her breath. "You gave me quite a start. Did no one come to help you dress or take you down to breakfast?"

I stared at her, perplexed. Why should anyone else do the tasks that she performed every morning without fail? My gaze went to the satchel and from there to the piles of clothes on her comforter. "Are you going on a trip?"

Mrs. Grimes pressed her lips together and nodded.

"Where are you going?"

She smiled as she resumed packing, but her mouth trembled as if she had to struggle to keep in it place. "To my younger sister's home in Manchester."

"Can I come too?"

"I'm sorry, little lamb, but no. Your family would miss you too much."

"When are you coming back?"

She regarded me sadly for a moment. "Perhaps you should go find your mother or grandmother and ask one of them to dress you for breakfast."

My heart plummeted. "I'm not hungry." Something was very, very wrong. "Will you dress me, please?"

I heard footsteps in the hall behind me, and I turned to discover my mother approaching. "Ada, darling, what are you doing out of bed?"

"It's time to get up," I replied, surprised. I had expected a reprimand for lying so long abed, but my mother seemed unaware of the broken rule. I was not about to enlighten her.

"Come, then." She held out her hand. "Let's get you dressed."

Dubious, I glanced over my shoulder to Mrs. Grimes, and when she nodded, I seized my mother's hand and tripped along happily beside her back to my bedroom. My mother almost never dressed me or took me down to breakfast, so this was quite a treat.

At the table, she sat adjacent to me while I ate porridge and bread with jam and butter, taking nothing herself but nodding absently while I chattered on about how much I would like to have a kitten, perhaps for my birthday, and if that was too soon then perhaps Christmas. Not once did she mention her disdain for pets, which I took as an encouraging sign.

Afterward, she washed my face and hands and let me join her in the study, where I practiced making letters on scrap paper, which were little more than wavering, indecipherable marks with a pencil, though drawn with great effort and concentration. I enjoyed myself so immensely that it was not until I began to grow hungry for luncheon that I remembered Mrs. Grimes and her upcoming trip.

Certain that she would not have left without saying good-bye, I raced upstairs and burst into her room only to find her gone, the piles of clothes gone too, as well as the satchel and the few cherished possessions she had kept out of my reach on the top of her bureau — a small glass vase that she regularly replenished with fragrant blossoms, a prayer book that had belonged to her grandfather, a china teapot painted with bright scenes of the gardens at Windsor Castle, which she had won in a spelling contest as a schoolgirl.

I darted to the window and peered outside, but I did not see her. "Mrs. Grimes?" I called, and when no reply came I raced back downstairs to the front entrance, tugged the door open, ran outside a few paces, and looked wildly up and down the drive. There was no carriage to be found, not even a cloud of dust to show that one had recently departed.

A footman discovered me there and persuaded me to return inside and shut the door, and since I did not want to get either of us in trouble, I complied. My mother met me in the foyer, but before she could scold me, I demanded, "Has Mrs. Grimes left?"

"Yes, Ada, she has."

"Well, she didn't say good-bye to me before she went and that's not very nice. I will scold her when she comes back." I glared unhappily at my mother. "When is she coming back?"

"It is not your place to scold your nurse."

"I won't scold. I'll just *tell* her." I took a deep breath, fighting back tears. "When is she coming back?"

My mother inhaled deeply and extended a hand to me, but I would not be fooled twice in the same morning, and I did not take it. "Mrs. Grimes will no longer be your nurse," she said, letting her hand fall to her side. "You shall have a new nurse beginning tomorrow. She is very nice, and kind and pretty, and I think you shall like her very much."

"I shall hate her," I shouted, balling my hands into fists. "I want Mrs. Grimes!"

At the time, Mrs. Grimes's dismissal seemed to me a purely arbitrary decision, made in the moment, a blow struck from out of nowhere. What I did not learn until years later, when I discovered the letters my mother and grandmother had exchanged that summer, was that my mother had been planning to give Mrs. Grimes notice for months. From Scotland she had written to my grandmother complaining that Mrs. Grimes had "a selfish way of assuming authority directly opposite to my wishes" and had failed in her attempts "to regulate the Child's temper." She had already engaged another nurse who came very highly recommended, and she wanted my grandmother to break the news to Mrs. Grimes while she herself was traveling, so that she might avoid any unpleasantness. "Really, I hardly dare return till this matter is settled," she added.

My grandmother objected to firing Mrs. Grimes, who had been promised a two-year engagement, and she was no more willing to level the blow than my mother was. "My dear daughter, if you wish Grimes discharged then you should do it yourself," she had written in reply. "She has been an exemplary nurse and I hardly know what reason to give."

"We need give no reason except that I am not satisfied with her service," my mother countered. "Ada is too willful and disobedient; a better nurse would have rid her of those habits. Offer that as a reason if you must. I will write a good character for her and she shall be able to use that to find another post. Will that satisfy you?"

It did not, but my grandmother eventually capitulated to the inevitable. She still pled the case for retaining Mrs. Grimes, describing in fervent detail the nurse's tireless ministrations to me on my sickbed. When that effort failed, she argued for softening the blow, and she even offered to pay Mrs. Grimes the entire sum of her wages for the two-year engagement she and my mother had agreed upon. My mother would have none of it, and since my grandmother refused to be the bearer of such bad and unjust news, they had reached an impasse.

"I am sorry that I must take the apparently harsh measure of dismissing the Nurse immediately on my return," my mother wrote, her exasperation unmistakable. "I am deeply impressed with the painful and pernicious consequence of presenting myself to Ada in the role that I have too often been obliged to play to her, that of the Villain. It is a fact too well-known, and too bitterly felt by myself, that for a long time Ada never saw me without beginning to cry — No wonder when Mama was made the constant bugbear. It nearly made me mad — and would do so again. It is my fixed determination not to remain a week in the house with Grimes present."

In that, my mother kept her word. She gave Mrs. Grimes only a day's notice to leave the house, and she deliberately distracted me that morning to avoid a ghastly tearful parting scene.

I am older now than my mother was then,

and I know her too well to believe that she was obliged to dismiss my beloved nurse because she had failed to carry out her duties, although I admit that it is possible my mother truly believed that. Mrs. Grimes was not let go because she failed to curb my willfulness, but because she had taught me to love her, and I could not be allowed to love anyone more than I loved my mother. It was a pattern that was to be repeated throughout my childhood: Whenever I became too fond of a nurse or a governess, that unlucky woman would be peremptorily shown to the exit.

But although I did not possess in childhood the evidence I would discover as a woman grown, I did learn one important lesson through these recurring heartbreaks: If I loved anyone too much, they would be taken from me.

CHAPTER FOUR:
SMILES FORM THE CHANNEL OF A FUTURE TEAR

September 1817–July 1818

I resolved to hate my new nurse and to make her hate me, or at least to hate her situation so much that she would resign. Since I must have a nurse, if I drove this interloper away, my mother would have to invite Mrs. Grimes to return. And so I became a virtuoso of naughtiness, refusing to leave my bed unless dragged from it, fighting tooth and claw when the nurse tried to wash or dress me, kicking the rungs of my chair at mealtimes, refusing to eat, running away when it was time for lessons, hiding when it was time for bed, and just generally being an absolute terror to live with.

The new nurse resigned after a week. I went to bed happily that night, looking forward to welcoming Mrs. Grimes back to Kirkby Mallory the following day. But the next morning after breakfast, which I enjoyed with perfect manners, I was summoned to my mother's study to meet a new nurse, a frowning matron who might as well have been named Mrs. No Nonsense, for that was all that she was about.

She lasted two days. I was not exaggerating when I called myself a virtuoso.

On the day after the frowning matron's departure, I was ordered to spend the day alone in my room to contemplate my sins. I sulked, but quietly, hoping to earn a reprieve for good behavior, for the first snow of winter had draped a soft blanket of white over the estate, and I longed to go play in it before it melted. Shortly before luncheon, I was summoned downstairs to meet a dignified older woman with pale hair, pale skin, and pale eyes. Apparently she had once been a nurse in the household of a cousin of Queen Charlotte, and she wanted to meet me before consenting to take charge of me.

She lasted an hour.

That night my mother sent me to bed without supper, and as an even worse punishment, she departed for a week in London without bidding me good-bye. Angry, despondent, doubly abandoned, I strengthened my resolve and silently vowed that this battle, my mother would not win.

But I had overestimated the subtlety of my scheme, and after my mother had been gone two days, my grandmother drew me onto her lap, kissed me, and said, "I miss Mrs. Grimes too, and I am certain she misses you, but your mother has decided, and that is that, so you

131

might as well stop terrorizing these poor nurses."

It was then I realized that Great Britain was apparently inhabited by a vast multitude of unmarried women willing to nurse resentful, disobedient children who dwelt in fine houses, and I could not possibly exhaust the supply. Mrs. Grimes would not return to me.

When this inescapable truth finally sank in, some of the fire went out of my rebellion, and I became almost tolerable again. My mother remained with us at Kirkby Mallory most of the time, which helped lessen the pain of my mourning. Nurses came and went, old and young, cheerful and grim. Once I overheard my mother preparing one to meet me, or perhaps warning her what lay in store, saying, "Ada's intellect is so far advanced beyond her age that she is already capable of receiving impressions that might influence her — to what extent I cannot say. Therefore you must take great care what you do and say in her presence." The nurse stammered that she would be very careful to provide me with only the most wholesome influences, but she was sacked within a fortnight for offenses I no longer recall.

My second birthday arrived, and a few of my mother's friends visited to celebrate the occasion, but no friends of mine came, for no such creatures existed. While I played with a wooden Noah's ark full of cunning little carved animals I had received from my grandparents, I overheard my mother remark to a visiting friend, "Ada loves me as well as I wish, and better than I expected, for I had a strange prepossession that she never would be fond of me." I could not protest that of course I loved her and always would, or I would have given away that I had been eavesdropping. Nor could I tell anyone how miserable I felt when she told another friend, "As she grows older, my heart uncloses to the kindly influence of her smiles." I had never guessed that her heart had ever been closed to me, but I consoled myself with the thought that at least it was opening now.

About a week after my birthday, my mother received word that my father had sold his ancestral estate, Newstead Abbey, for the astonishing amount of ninety-four thousand five hundred pounds to Colonel Thomas Wildman, a former classmate of my father's at Harrow. Although the mansion had fallen into near ruin, I'm sure my father regretted parting with it, but he also must have felt tremendous relief at being able to settle his debts and provide for his living expenses abroad. The estate would have passed from our immediate family anyway, since as a mere girl I could not inherit it and the Separation made it increasingly improbable that my father would ever have a legitimate male heir. Even so my mother felt the loss of Newstead

Abbey keenly, more for the romantic ideal of what it had represented than for the property itself.

This regret compounded her unhappiness over the wretched turn her marriage had taken, but my indomitable mother refused to give in to despair. She had told my grandmother that she would escape melancholy by devoting herself to a noble endeavor, and she found it in a new ambition to educate the children of the working poor. During her travels in Scotland, she had visited the Infant School the socialist Robert Owen had established near Glasgow, as well as the school her friend Harriet Siddons had founded in Edinburgh. There, the old, outdated system that demanded learning by rote and humiliating a child in front of his classmates if he failed to learn a lesson had been jettisoned. Their new, progressive form of schooling emphasized "cheerfulness" — appealing to children's natural curiosity about the world to inspire them to learn. Bright pictures of animals and specimens from fields and forests were displayed in the classroom; walks in the countryside were encouraged; music, art, dancing, and drawing as well as reading and writing were essential elements of the curriculum. No pupil was ever beaten or threatened, not in word and never in deed.

My mother agreed that through thoughtful education, the children of the working poor would improve their character, increase their competence, and benefit not only themselves, but society as a whole. She decided to establish an Infant School at Seaham, paying the expenses herself, dispensing with conventional lessons in favor of a pleasant, happy environment where learning was play and children grew to love it.

I was not to attend this school, of course; girls of my rank, if they were educated at all, were tutored at home, and though I was bright, I was still a trifle too young for formal schooling. I'm sure my mother's evolving philosophy of education influenced her, however, in the ongoing struggle to find a suitable nurse for me. After a brief interim with no nurse at all — a dull yet welcome respite, to me — throughout which my mother lamented that she had already hired and fired the only suitable candidates within a hundred miles, she had found someone very promising indeed, thanks to a recommendation from her friend Selina Doyle. My mother sang Miss Clara Thorne's praises at dinner the evening before her first day in our household, but I expected she would enjoy no greater success than her predecessors.

The following morning, I woke to a sense of impending doom, and when I was obliged to report downstairs to meet Miss Thorne, I was so unhappy that I could not even lift my head to cast an appraising look her way when my mother introduced us. Almost any nurse could survive a few days with a thoroughly unresponsive child, but eventually they all grew bored and either quit or did something not "cheerful" in an attempt to provoke me into action, earning my mother's displeasure and a swift carriage ride away from Kirkby Mallory. Miss Thorne seemed more tolerant of dullness than most. Listless, I cooperated when she wanted to dress me, I ate my meals dutifully but in silence, and though I did not have the heart to pay attention when she read to me or invited me to sing with her, at least I did not throw tantrums.

One morning, she came to my room, where I lay staring dolefully up at the ceiling, and instead of greeting me or ordering me out of bed, she said, "Do you mind if I look out your window?"

I didn't want to answer, but the oddness of the question compelled a reply. "Please yourself."

"Thank you," she said brightly, as if I had welcomed her graciously, as a young lady ought. From the corner of my eye, I watched as she crossed the room with the usual bounce in her step and peered out the window, rising on tiptoe to see better. Miss Clara Thorne was quite small, with glossy, dark brown hair arranged in an elegant coil at the nape of her neck, sparkling brown eyes, a pert nose, and ruby lips that usually curved in a

136

smile. I had overheard my mother's maid tell a footman that she was the natural daughter of a grand Scottish laird and an actress, and after her mother died of consumption when she was only two years old, her father had arranged for her to be brought up as the ward of a respected minister. In time, when she proved to be clever, her father had arranged for her to be educated as well. Although the laird apparently found her delightful and made no secret of her relation to him, she would not inherit his fortune, nor could she marry well because she was illegitimate, so she was obliged to earn her living as a nurse or governess.

"Hmm," Miss Thorne mused, drawing back from the window.

She said nothing more, so after a long silence, I prompted, "What?"

"Oh, nothing. It's just that I thought I heard Puff singing outside, but I suppose I was mistaken."

I frowned, curious. "Who is Puff?"

"Why, *Puff*, of course. Everyone knows of Puff." When I merely blinked at her, bewildered, her eyes went wide. "You mean to say you've never heard of Puff, favorite lady-in-waiting to the Queen of Fairies?"

"I know what a queen is," I said carefully, reluctant to appear ignorant. "And I have eaten fairy cakes."

Miss Thorne put her hands on her hips and

regarded me with astonishment. "Do you mean to say that not only have you never heard of Puff, but you also don't know what fairies are?"

I shook my head, embarrassed.

"Oh, dear me. We shall have to do something about this shocking lapse in your education." She held out her hand, and when I did nothing, she gestured for me to get out of bed. "Come along, now. We haven't a moment to waste."

I promptly scrambled out of bed and washed and dressed, and as I ate breakfast, Miss Thorne enlightened me about the mysterious, magical folk who inhabited the most beautiful, enchanted places in England and Scotland, as well as Ireland and Wales and certain regions of France. Most were tiny, beautiful, delicate winged creatures, although others were burly, furred, and horned. Most were merry, whimsical, and kind, but some were temperamental and jealous and even savage when provoked. All were magical.

Puff was a very special fairy, kind and beautiful, gentle and generous. She wore a gown of silver thistledown, and her wings were shaped like a dragonfly's, in iridescent shades of silver, rose pink, and sky blue. She loved to sing and to play a tiny silver lute, and the magic of her melodious voice could comfort the bereaved, encourage the despondent, and inspire the timid.

In the weeks that followed, I learned a great deal about fairies, about their curious ways, their magic and mischief, their habits and habitats, their trickery and tempers, and magical charms to protect oneself from their wicked brethren. Miss Thorne offered her enthralling tales sparingly, as rewards for good behavior or lessons learned, and I quickly transformed from a sullen, disobedient, angry little wretch into the most well-behaved, respectful child in Leicestershire. I learned the alphabet and the numbers from one to twenty, and when I saw how my progress pleased my mother, I worked even harder to be an obedient child and diligent pupil. If I did well enough, I hoped with no little resentment, she might pay as much attention to me as she did to the children of the working poor.

As the winter passed, I grew to adore Miss Thorne. I still missed Mrs. Grimes, but with a wistful fondness rather than a painful ache of grief. We welcomed spring together, and Miss Thorne showed me birds building nests with twigs and vines and bits of string, and we found a wren's nest nestled in the nook between two branches of an elm, low enough that I could see into it when she lifted me. Week after week we returned, once to discover three eggs resting inside, and before long, three hatchlings. For hours we would sit side by side on the long, soft grass and watch, entranced, as the mother bird flew back and forth bringing food to her babies. "One day they'll be grown, and they'll fly off on their own," Miss Thorne told me, giving me a smile and a little nudge. "Just like you will someday."

I laughed, because the notion that I would ever be grown enough to fly free of my mother, or that I would ever want to, was too silly to be believed.

Miss Thorne taught me about seeds, too, and about how they were made and how they sprouted, but she also made up delightful tales about Puff, and the queen she served, and all the other fairies of her court, which were friends and which quarreled, who did good deeds and who fell into one amusing mishap after another. There was always a perceptible shift from science to story, a lightening or deepening of her tone as the subject required, a musical lilt to her voice that was present, and then absent. I found one endlessly fascinating and the other thoroughly amusing, and as spring turned to summer, I thrived on a wholesome diet of both.

My mother was very busy with the Infant School, so I saw her less frequently than I would have liked, but one fine midsummer day when she had come for a brief visit, she gave Miss Thorne the afternoon off and suggested I lead her on a walk through the forest and show her what I had learned about the natural sciences. Thrilled and proud, I cheerfully pointed out the birds' nest, the tiny oak seedlings, the concentric dark and light rings in the trunk of a fallen tree, and so on. Then we strolled deeper into the wood, and without thinking, I pointed at a wide ring of mushrooms nearly three feet across. "Look, Mama," I exclaimed. "A fairy ring!"

She gave me an odd look. "Those are mushrooms. They are fungi, connected underground."

"Yes, I meant to say mushrooms," I quickly replied.

She frowned, bent closer to me, and searched my expression. "Where did you learn about fairy rings?"

"I don't remember. I think I saw it in a book."

As soon as I spoke the lie, I realized it was as damning as a confession. I knew my letters but could not yet read more than my own name, and even if I had seen a drawing of a fairy ring in a book, I would have needed someone to read the caption to me.

Our pleasant nature walk came to an abrupt end. We returned to the house, where I was fed my luncheon — my mother sat with me, sipping her tea in silence, eating nothing, studying me carefully — and afterward I was sent to my room to practice writing numbers.

I heard Miss Thorne return, heard her summoned to my mother's study, and, with my little heart beating like a baby wren's, I waited with my ear pressed to the door for the sound of her footsteps on the stairs.

When I heard her pass by my room on her way to her own, I gathered my courage and followed. The scene before me was sickeningly reminiscent of the last time I had seen Mrs. Grimes — the wardrobe with the doors flung open, an empty satchel, a beloved nurse folding clothes into neat piles.

"I'm sorry," I blurted tearfully. "It's my fault. I forgot not to talk about fairies."

"Oh, sweet Ada, don't blame yourself." Miss Thorne smiled fondly and held out her arms to me, and I ran into her embrace. "It was I who flouted the prohibition against fairy tales. That I had no idea they were banned and was unaware I was breaking a rule does not change that fact." Her voice took on an edge as she spoke, sharp and yet amused. "It's best that I go, because I cannot promise never to tell you another fairy tale, for you seem to enjoy them and I quite like telling them."

"It's *not* best that you go," I said, my voice muffled. "Please stay. I can do without fairy tales."

"You shouldn't have to." Miss Thorne knelt so our faces were almost the same height, and she took out a handkerchief and wiped my eyes. "Now that you're an expert on fairies yourself, you may make up your own stories, in your own mind, where they will trouble no one."

I sniffed and blinked at her, uncertain. "May I?"

She put her head to one side, considering. "My understanding is the rule is against *telling* fairy tales, or reading them. The directive says nothing about *thinking* them." She smiled and stroked my hair away from my face. "The imagination is not a dangerous thing, Ada darling — but that is as close as I shall come to speaking ill of your mother to you."

It was a testament to my mother's esteem for Miss Thorne despite her failure to suppress my imagination that she allowed us to say good-bye. Once she was gone, I was so miserable I could not leave my room for two days. My mother arranged for my meals to be brought to me on a tray, a surprising indulgence that I suppose could have been a sort of apology, though not an admission of wrongdoing, because my mother was never wrong.

I don't know why my mother neglected to tell Miss Thorne that fairy tales, ghost stories, and the like were forbidden, when it was a matter of such grave importance. Perhaps she was so busy with the Infant School that she simply forgot. Perhaps she assumed that Miss Thorne was so well educated and intellectually advanced that she would know better than to inculcate me with silly fancies. Another mother would have explained the rationale behind the rule and instructed the otherwise exemplary nurse to heed it in the future. But it was not in Lady Byron's nature to forgive a transgression or to offer an opportunity for the transgressor to commit the same error a second time.

This I would eventually learn better than anyone.

CHAPTER FIVE:
WISHING EACH OTHER, NOT DIVORCED, BUT DEAD

July 1818–January 1822

In the aftermath of Miss Thorne's departure, I was heartbroken and lonely, which exasperated my mother but moved my grandmother to pity. Lady Noel had been a constant loving presence in my life for as long as I could remember, and I relied upon her steadfast affection as never before. She taught me how to sew and knit, and I never felt more useful than when she allowed me to help her hem handkerchiefs for my grandfather or embroider a pretty floral design in the border of a new tablecloth. Although I still longed for friends my own age, I was grateful for the comfortable, serene, undemanding companionship my grandmother offered. She was not always striving to improve my character, only the quality of my stitches.

I suppose that could be precisely the reason my mother did *not* enjoy her company very much, for my mother seemed to believe that an hour not spent in self-improvement or the forcible improvement of others was an hour wasted.

I have called my grandmother serene, but it is true that around this time, I began to notice that my mother had a particular gift for setting my grandmother's nerves on edge, with a pointed barb of criticism here and an artfully placed silence there. The only person who agitated my grandmother more was my father, with whom she shared a mutual antipathy.

A year after Miss Thorne left me, Byron again disrupted our household from afar with the publication of the first two cantos of another poem, *Don Juan,* which was considered a brilliant comic masterpiece everywhere but Kirkby Mallory. He had again sharpened his satirical knives and carved a portion of his estranged wife to serve up to his worshipful readers and a public hungry for gossip about the Separation. This time, my mother had been transformed into Donna Inez, Don Juan's mother, "a learned lady, famed

For every branch of every science known.
In every Christian language ever named,
With virtues equall'd by her wit alone,
She made the cleverest people quite
    ashamed,
And even the good with inward envy groan,
Finding themselves so very much
    exceeded

In their own way by all the things that she did.

Donna Inez had a prodigious memory, her favorite science was "the mathematical," and "Her wit (she sometimes tried at wit) was Attic all, / Her serious sayings darken'd to sublimity." She dabbled in various languages, but "Her thoughts were theorems, her words a problem, / As if she deem'd that mystery would ennoble 'em." But she did not need words, for "Some women use their tongues — she look'd a lecture, / Each eye a sermon, and her brow a homily." In short, my father wrote, Donna Inez was "a walking calculation; / Morality's prim personification . . . perfect past all parallel."

My father's poetic genius captured my mother's likeness so perfectly that even the exaggerations were spot-on. Anyone who read the poem — and everyone would — could not possibly fail to recognize Donna Inez's living, breathing counterpart, with all her flaws, perfection apparently being one of them.

My usually serene grandmother spluttered with outrage and threatened to contact her lawyers, but my grandfather discouraged her, noting that litigation would only draw attention to the poem. It might also serve as a tacit admission that my mother saw herself in

Donna Inez, which she would perhaps prefer to deny.

To her credit, my mother tried to evaluate the poem on its artistic merits alone, noting that it was witty and eloquent, and quite entertaining, if a trifle indelicate in some places and dangerously close to vulgar in others. "Indeed, after *Childe Harold,* I am quite relieved," she admitted. "It is not nearly so disagreeable as I had expected. Here, for example" — she pointed to a page — "while it's true he belittles my sense of humor, at least he admits that I have one. And in these stanzas, the quizzing is so good as to make me smile at myself — therefore, others are heartily welcome to laugh."

Thus she spoke to my grandparents to settle their agitation, but a few weeks later, I overheard her confiding to a friend that although the character of Donna Inez did not trouble her, the description of the lady's marriage did:

Don Jóse and the Donna Inez led
For some time an unhappy sort of life,
Wishing each other, not divorced, but dead;
They lived respectably as man and wife,
Their conduct was exceedingly well-bred,
And gave no outward signs of inward strife,
Until at length the smother'd fire broke out,
And put the business past all kind of doubt.

My mother felt the sting of my father's rebuke in another stanza in which Donna Inez "call'd some druggists and physicians, / And tried to prove her loving lord was mad;" but since he was sometimes lucid, "She next decided he was only bad." No explanation for her behavior was offered, the narrator noted, "Save that her duty both to man and God / Required this conduct — which seem'd very odd."

"I have never wished Byron dead," my mother protested to her friend in a strangled sort of voice. It sounded as if she wept, but I was listening from the hallway and dared not peek into the room to verify. "Do you suppose he wishes me dead? How could he write such a terrible thing? And I had no choice but to investigate whether he was mad. How else could I help him?"

"Perhaps it is all a fiction. If you are Donna Inez, then Lord Byron must be Don *Jóse.*" My mother's friend scornfully mispronounced the name as my father had written it, deliberately altering the emphasis to suit his poem's meter. "That cannot be. Before the Separation his conduct was certainly not 'well-bred,' and there were many 'signs of inward strife.' "

"The poem may not be a perfect reflection of us and our marriage," my mother admitted, "but it's so very close to the truth that I cannot know what *he* believes to be true, and what he has embellished for comic effect."

"It is *all* embellishment," her friend declared, and my mother seemed to take comfort from her certainty. Even so, she sighed and wished aloud that he would cease writing about her altogether if he could not be kind.

Eventually the storm subsided, at least in my hearing, but soon after we celebrated the New Year of 1820, another tempest struck. Although my family were taking greater care not to speak on certain sensitive topics in my presence, I gleaned from fragments of conversations that abruptly ended when I entered the room that my father, currently residing in Venice, was writing or had written his memoirs. Although he did not want the manuscript published until after his death, he had sent one copy to his publisher, John Murray, and a second to my mother, along with a letter warning her that although he had omitted certain "important and decisive events and passions" to avoid compromising other friends and family, he had not taken such precautions with her.

"I could wish you to see, read and mark any part or parts that do not appear to coincide with the truth," he told her. "The truth I have always stated, but there are two ways of looking at it and your way may not be mine." She would find no flattery within the pages, he warned, "nothing to lead you to the most remote supposition that we could ever have been, or be happy together. But I do not choose to give to another generation statements which we cannot arise from the dust to prove or disprove without letting you see fairly and fully what I look upon you to have been, and what I depict you as being."

"It is his account of our marriage that will endure," my mother lamented to her maid soon after the manuscript arrived. "It is bad enough that he derides me in verse, which I can dismiss as parody. A memoir, however — that is supposed to be fact, and that is how readers will view it, although I know it to be a highly subjective fiction."

"Can't you do as he asks, and mark the parts you think are false?" Merle asked.

"Surely I would need to mark every line," my mother exclaimed, "and there is no certainty that he would revise his pages according to my wishes. It is far more likely that he would mock my marginalia. No. No. I shall not give him anything else to satirize. The only possible response to this outrage is silence."

I heard them coming toward the door then, so I quickly scampered into the room, panting as if I had only just then arrived from somewhere else. They abruptly ceased their conversation, so I was left to wonder how my mother decided to respond to my father's offer, if she made any reply at all.

I confess I searched for the manuscript the next time my mother traveled, but I did not find it, only the letter I described above. I had learned to read quite well by then, thanks to my endlessly changing cast of nurses, who were increasingly hired for their value as tutors. I had long ago abandoned my scheme of driving away nurses so that Mrs. Grimes would be rehired, but none of my mother's new hires stayed for long, for sooner or later she found reason to be dissatisfied with each and every one of them. And not only my nurses suffered her wrath. Too much salt in the soup meant the dismissal of a cook, a scorch mark on a freshly pressed petticoat sent a lady's maid packing, an annoying laugh was the downfall of a driver, a woebegone manner banished a footman from the premises. My mother went through household staff the way other ladies used up stockings.

A series of nurses led me through a rather rigorous curriculum for a child of four: arithmetic, geography, French, music, drawing, exercise, and outdoor play. My lessons were brief, only about fifteen minutes each, with mandatory rests in between. I yearned to run and skip and dance in those intervals rather than rest — after sitting still through my lessons, lying down made me only more restless — and when I found it impossible to obey, I was made to recline on a hard wooden board, which made fidgeting painful. When I did manage to be good, I was rewarded with tickets, and when I had collected enough, I could redeem them for gifts — new building blocks, a wooden puzzle, a book on botany. I easily won tickets for learning my lessons, for I gobbled up knowledge as fast as it could be fed to me. Just as easily, I lost tickets for naughty behavior, for fidgeting, and for refusing to lie still during rest time. The ticket system was also employed outside of classes, if I was having an especially difficult time complying with my mother's wishes. I remember a spring day in 1820 when I lost fourteen tickets in a single hour because I wriggled and squirmed in my chair instead of holding my pose when an artist came to Kirkby Mallory to take sketches of me. "If *he* didn't persist in demanding her portrait, I would have sent the artist home and let the child run and play instead," my mother complained to my grandmother when the exasperated artist politely requested a pause of a quarter hour so he might search for his lost patience in a walk about the grounds. "What trouble and expense to go through to make a portrait of a four-year-old child!"

"You will be glad to have it for yourself, when it is finished," said my grandmother, smiling. "We had your portrait made when you were nearly the same age."

"I was ten, as I recall, and I sat perfectly

still as instructed so the artist could do his work."

"Yes, I'm quite certain you did," my grandmother acknowledged.

I didn't know at the time who the imperious *he* was who required me to sit still in that chair on a beautiful spring day. I assumed my mother referred to my grandpapa, whom I loved and did not wish to offend, so when the artist returned, I held perfectly still so he could complete his sketches. I found out later that it was my father who had demanded my portrait, and that he had made numerous requests for it, persisting despite my mother's repeated demurrals. I did not earn any tickets for sitting so perfectly still, and when I asked my mother why, she said I should not expect rewards for finally consenting to do what I should have done without complaint in the first place.

In early 1821, a few weeks after my fifth birthday, my mother engaged a governess for me and my formal education began. It resembled in many ways the instruction I had received over the previous year, but the lessons were longer and the discipline more rigorously enforced. Unfortunately, my new governess, Miss Lamont, was as bland and uninspiring as cod in milk sauce. She was a few years younger than my mother, with none of her self-possession. She had a long, thin nose; large, startled blue eyes; and the weakest chin I had ever seen on a woman. Her hair was not blond, nor was it brown, but some indeterminate shade in between, and throughout the day, wiry locks sprang free from her chignon and trembled as she moved as if searching frantically for the exit. She was very thin and unusually tall, and she hunched her shoulders as if to apologize for her height. She had a habit of hugging books to her chest as if she feared someone might snatch them from her.

At first, Miss Lamont and I got along well enough. She was quite impressed with my proficiency in mathematics, which was considered highly unusual for a girl, even the daughter of Lady Byron, and she praised me for how swiftly and accurately I added up columns of numbers and how perfectly I drew parallel lines. "I know quite a lot about related figures that shall never meet," I told her innocently, and she blinked at me for a long moment, trying to figure out if I meant to be cheeky. I did.

I loved geometry, the way different shapes could be combined or divided to make others in seemingly limitless permutations, and at first Miss Lamont indulged my passion for it, encouraging me to draw shapes and to arrange my wooden blocks into cubes and rectangular prisms. When I went too far and began calling the prisms houses and towers and arranged them into towns and cities, she reprimanded me and took away two tickets. She had evidently been informed about the existing system of rewards and punishments as well as the necessity of suppressing my imagination.

I enjoyed reading on my own and being read to, but when Miss Lamont lectured in geography or French, the minutes seemed to drag by at half the usual rate. As if of their own accord, my hands sought out whatever small items were within reach — pencils, a hair ribbon, pretty acorns I had found on our daily nature walks — and tapped them on the table to make interesting sounds or spun them about to see how long they would revolve.

"Don't fidget," Miss Lamont ordered me over and over, but although I tried, I could not refrain for long. Eventually she began tying muslin bags around my hands to enforce my obedience. When my restlessness then expressed itself in kicking the table leg or drumming my heels on the rung of my chair, Miss Lamont took all of my hard-won tickets away, and when I expressed my outrage by kicking and drumming with redoubled vigor, she resorted to locking me in a small closet beneath the staircase. During a particularly disastrous French lesson, in which I laughed outright at Miss Lamont's hapless inability to force me to do as she commanded, she planted her hands on my shoulders, marched me into the corner, and ordered me to stand there, silent and facing the wall, until she said I might return to my studies. As soon as she released my shoulders and returned to her chair, I snarled and took a bite out of the dado rail above the wainscot.

Miss Lamont spluttered and nearly burst into tears. My mother swept into the room — in recent weeks, my governess's emotional upsets had obliged her to take over my lessons more and more frequently — and ordered me to my room. Miss Lamont was given a two days' holiday while I atoned for my crime, but although I said I was sorry, in truth, I felt strangely exhilarated when I discovered my perfect little teeth marks in the rail. Later, I bubbled up with mirth when I overheard my grandfather chortling about the incident. "We ought to put a gilded frame around those marks to preserve them as a memento of swiftly fleeting youth," he said. "We've all done just as bad in our time."

"Not all of us have," my mother replied levelly, and no one could contradict her — not I, because I had not witnessed a moment of her childhood, and not my grandparents, because apparently my mother had never given in to a single moment of youthful mischief.

On the morning my studies with Miss Lamont were to resume, my mother settled me firmly in a chair, regarded me sternly, and told me that it was disrespectful to waste my governess's time with my antics and sinful to waste my family's money on lessons I did not diligently undertake. "And your behavior upsets Grandmama," she added, when the first two charges did not seem to bother my conscience. "You make her worry about how you will ever grow up to be the sort of accomplished, educated young lady she may be proud of. Is that what you want?"

"No, Mama," said I, mortified. Grandmama had been terribly ill throughout that spring, and although she seemed to be recovering, the thought that I had given her even a moment's concern made me feel ashamed. After that, I did my very best to behave like a good little girl ought, but although there were no more incidents of the wainscot-biting variety, I forfeited tickets, had my hands tied up in muslin bags, and endured lonely hours locked in the closet, though less frequently than before.

My only saving grace was that I excelled in my lessons, especially mathematics and the study of anything mechanical — interests that another, less intellectual, less progressive family would have encouraged in a son but disapproved of in a daughter. I delighted in taking apart clocks and musical snuffboxes, and my grandparents indulged my fascination because I always reassembled the tiny mechanical pieces into perfect working order again. My emerging brilliance pleased my mother and mollified her righteous anger, but her frustration and worry lingered, for she saw something sinister and dreadful in my bursts of passion. "The Byron blood is to blame for her wickedness, I know it," I overheard my mother confiding to my grandfather late one night when I was supposed to be asleep.

"Ada is a good girl at heart," my grandfather said, his voice a soothing rumble. "You worry too much about ordinary childish capers."

"There's nothing ordinary about them. I simply don't understand why she is transforming into *him* when his influence over her is so strictly limited, and when she has my example of virtue, restraint, and piety right before her to emulate." I heard my mother pacing, as she did when she was most anxious. "I'm terribly afraid that we're witnessing the earliest signs of the Byron in her emerging, and no amount of discipline will forestall the inevitable."

Suddenly terrified, I muffled a gasp and scampered back to bed, expecting any moment to transform into a rough, burly man, to feel bristly hairs bursting through my tender skin, to feel thick muscles bloating and distorting my lithe, slender frame. Instinctively I understood that the terrible transformations my mother dreaded were connected to the covered portrait that had disappeared from my grandfather's smoking and billiards room.

She had spoken of my Byron blood as the source of my wickedness. My mother believed in cupping and leeches, and she frequently instructed her physician to bleed her to rid her of unhealthful humors and vapors. When I was safely under the covers once more, I tried to say my prayers, but my thoughts wandered, and I began to think that perhaps the doctor could find a very special leech for me, one carefully trained to drain the bad Byron blood from me and leave the rest. I fell asleep wondering how one would train a leech, because they seemed like little mindless things, not like dogs or cats that would come when you called or do tricks for a tasty reward.

I tried so hard to be good, or rather, not to be bad, but sometimes I was naughty unwittingly. Though I was precocious and bright, I was only five years old, and I was often confused about the composition of my family, and how the father of whom I had no conscious memory fit into it, and why my family did not resemble anyone else's.

I had given these puzzling questions a great deal of thought. One sunny afternoon in July as my mother and I strolled through Kirkby Wood, enjoying the cool shade and admiring the vivid greens of the tree boughs dancing in the breeze overhead, I asked, "Mama, is a grandpapa the same as a papa?"

"No, Ada," my mother replied, moving her skirt out of the way of a fallen branch as we passed it. "A grandfather is the father of one's mother or father. Your grandpapa, Sir Ralph, is *my* father. That is what makes him your grandfather."

"But if Grandpapa isn't my papa, who is my papa? How is it that other little girls have papas and I have none?"

She quickened her pace, and I had to hurry to keep up with her. "You *do* have a father," she said tightly. "Your papa is George Gordon, Lord Byron — my husband. You know that. How could you ask such a stupid question?"

"I —" I trembled, shamed by my ignorance. "I — I'm sorry, Mama —"

"Not another word. We shall discuss this subject when you're older, when I decide the time is right."

Wordlessly I nodded. Tears filled my eyes as my mother seized my hand and strode back to the house with me trotting alongside, struggling to keep up. She left for Seaham early the next morning without telling me about her trip, without saying good-bye or telling me when she would return. It was one of her favorite and most effective forms of punishment.

I still do not know how I could have heard

so much talk about Lord Byron the poet who tormented my mother from abroad with his satire and demands and assertion of parental rights, and how I could have studied the covered portrait above the fireplace before it disappeared, and how I could have heard my mother called Lady Byron, and still have not made the connection that poet and tormenter and father were all the same man. Perhaps I had really meant to ask not why I had no papa, but why my papa was absent. I don't know. It is very curious how children's minds work, the disparate events they believe are connected and the obvious connections they fail to see.

I was too afraid of infuriating my mother to question her again about my absent father, but about a month after I provoked her to anger in Kirkby Wood, she summoned me to her study. Her expression when I entered the room was inscrutable, and I instinctively slowed my pace as I approached her.

She gestured to a chair and invited me to sit. I obeyed, and after a moment she told me to hold out my hand, and when I did, she placed something cool and smooth within it. It was a beautiful gold locket on a golden chain, gleaming in the sunlight that streamed through the open window. There was an inscription around the center engraving, but although I recognized the letters, I did not know the words. They were neither English nor Latin, but seemed to resemble both.

"It is Italian," my mother said, correctly interpreting my silence. "The words say, '*Il sangue non è mai acqua.*' The meaning, as we would express it in English, is 'Blood is thicker than water.' "

I studied the words and murmured them under my breath. Glancing tentatively up at my mother, I asked, "May I open it?"

She waved her hand to say that I could. Releasing the clasp, I discovered a thick, dark brown curl inside — and a thrill of fear and hope and amazement raced through me when I realized whose it must be.

"It is your father's," my mother answered the question I was too afraid to ask. "He has sent it to you, and I do not object to your keeping it. He would like a lock of your hair, if you would agree to send him one."

I did not know what to say. I was happy and excited to have a lock of my father's hair, even happier that he wanted one of mine in exchange, but I worried that if I consented, I would infuriate my mother.

"I think," I said carefully, "that since he's my father, I ought to be obedient and send him what he has asked for. It's my duty as his daughter, isn't it?"

She raised her eyebrows, and I knew even before she spoke that I had not fooled her. "How encouraging it is that you're learning the meaning of duty and obedience at long last."

I flushed and lowered my gaze, closing the locket and slipping it into my pocket. My mother beckoned me closer and produced her shears, and with a quick, careful snip she trimmed a small curl from the nape of my neck, where it would not be missed.

As soon as my mother dismissed me, I scampered off to show my new treasure to my grandmother. Although it was only mid-afternoon, I found her in bed. She had never fully recovered from the illness that had threatened her life earlier that year, and she tired easily. She sat up in bed and smiled when I darted into the room, and as her maid arranged her pillows to support her, she beckoned me to join her in bed.

"Look what my papa sent me," I said, taking the locket from my pocket and holding it out on my open palm.

"Oh, how lovely," my grandmother said, picking it up by the chain and holding it high so it shone in a beam of sunlight peeking through her curtains, which were nearly closed. The windows, too, were shut tight against the mild autumn breezes, for the slightest draft wracked her thin frame as if it were deepest midwinter.

"There's a lock of his hair inside," I said, and when she fumbled with the clasp, I opened it for her.

"Oh, yes," she said, nodding as she examined the curl. "It is exactly as I remember."

"You knew my papa?"

"Of course, child." She closed the locket and returned it to me. "This has come all the way from Italy, from his home to yours. Take very good care of it."

I nodded somberly, slipped the chain over my neck, and touched the precious relic to my heart. "Grandmama, do you think I shall ever meet my papa?"

She hesitated, pondering the question. "I know he wishes to see you," she said carefully, the faint pursing of her mouth suggesting that as for herself, she did not wish to see him. "He has said so in his letters. God willing, you shall meet again when the time is right."

I knew better than to ask when that time would come, for it surely depended upon my mother's goodwill, which must be earned.

"You should run along and let Lady Noel rest now," my grandmother's maid suggested, and when I observed how wearily she sank back against her pillows, I nodded, kissed her soft, papery cheek, and tiptoed away as if she had already fallen asleep.

As that warm, brilliant, vivid autumn slipped into winter, my grandmother more often remained in her bed throughout the day, although in December she roused herself to join the family to celebrate my sixth birthday on the tenth and Christmas a fort-night later.

The effort seemed to drain her remaining strength, and after the New Year, she rarely left her bedchamber. I was only rarely allowed to visit her there out of fear that my youthful exuberance would exhaust her. On days she felt particularly strong she would ask for me, and she liked to lie quietly while I read to her from the newspaper or from Maria Edge-worth's *Early Lessons.*

Such occasions became fewer and farther between as that cold, bleak month stretched on, and in the afternoon of 22 January, my beloved grandmother slipped away, quietly and peacefully, with the same dignity and grace that had distinguished her life for more than seventy years.

CHAPTER SIX:
SHARP IS THE KNIFE,
AND SUDDEN IS THE STROKE

January 1822–March 1825

In the aftermath of my grandmother's death, I was heartbroken, devastated, utterly bereft. Not even the losses of Mrs. Grimes and Miss Thorne and the perpetual absence of my father had adequately prepared me for this, the worst deprivation I had ever known. Yes, my grandfather loved me, and my mother, too, but my grandmother had been a constant, unwavering source of unconditional love, the kind of sustaining love no other person had ever offered me before, or has provided since, in all the years that have followed.

With my grandmother's passing, the Wentworth estate descended to my mother. She — and my father — were legally required to adopt the surname Noel, but Kirkby Mallory and its one hundred sixty acres of oak woodland, hunting grounds, and gardens were my mother's alone. Her annual income increased from five hundred pounds to four thousand five hundred pounds, with another four thousand pounds per annum going to my father. I suppose she could have accepted the title of Lady Noel too, or Baroness Wentworth, but for reasons she never explained to me, she retained the name Lady Byron.

One of her first acts as mistress of Kirkby Mallory Hall was to send to my aunt Augusta game from the estate, with a kind note assuring her that she and her children should expect to grow quite fat on venison in the years to come. The Leigh family had struggled with pecuniary difficulties ever since Colonel Leigh had lost his position as equerry to the Prince of Wales after cheating him in the sale of a horse and using regimental funds to cover his gambling debts, and so I'm sure my mother's gifts were gratefully received.

This was not the first time my mother had shown remarkable, unexpected generosity toward her sister-in-law. Most notably, a few months before I was born, my mother had consented when my father declared his intention to name Augusta and her children the beneficiaries of his will, rather than my mother and me. My grandmother had been appalled that he would leave his son and heir — for I might have been a boy, for all they knew then — only a title and none of his personal wealth, but my mother had known that she could rely on her forthcoming inheritance, while Augusta had nothing, and certainly could expect nothing from Colonel Leigh but more debt and grief. Still, Byron's apparent preference for his sister over herself must have stung, and I can certainly understand my grandmother's point of view.

But now my beloved grandmother was gone, and without her, I became profoundly lonely. My mother traveled often to visit friends and to take the waters at various spas, and my grandfather loved me, but as one might expect, a gentleman of nearly seventy-five years was not an ideal playmate for a six-year-old girl. My only companions were my governess, the servants, and a few of my mother's most loyal friends, mostly spinsters and widows, who came to live with us from time to time.

Though my grandfather usually distanced himself from the womanly business of raising me, I was grateful to him for insisting that I could not be at my books day and night, and that I must be allowed to make friends my own age. Accordingly, a small, select group was assembled, the children of my mother's most distinguished friends and relations. I became very strongly attached to George Byron, the son of my father's cousin and presumptive heir, Captain George Anson Byron. Although I was older than young George by two and a half years, I resolved that he would be my dearest friend and confidant. As I had always wanted a sibling, I decreed him my honorary brother and wrote him many heartfelt letters, confessing my most ardent hopes and feelings and dreams. I can only imagine what his mother thought of my girlish passions, for it was she who responded on George's behalf, at least in the first years of our acquaintance, as he could not yet read or write. Another new friend who could write to me entirely on her own was Fanny Smith, the niece of Colonel Francis Doyle, one of my mother's most trusted advisors. She was clever and unfailingly cheerful, and she sent me the most amusing tales of the mischief she and her cousins got into, usually at their stingy, disagreeable housekeeper's expense. If my mother realized how mischievous Fanny was, I doubt she would have let our correspondence continue.

Although I at last had children I could name as friends, Fanny, George, and the others were rarely with me, and so my loneliness and isolation persisted. I think my unhappiness took its toll on my health, for in the autumn of 1823, when I was not quite eight years old, I fell desperately ill. I experienced sharp, throbbing, debilitating headaches that affected my vision so seriously that my physician ordered my education to cease, which meant, of course, that Miss Lamont was promptly sacked. Two experts were consulted, a Dr. Warner and a Dr. Mayo, and they concluded that I suffered from a fullness of the vessels of the head. My mother prescribed her favorite remedy for her own headaches, the "perpetual leech" — the continuous application of a leech to the scalp, a fresh worm being applied immediately after its predecessor was removed. I found this very unpleasant and not at all effective; a disgusting little worm sucking on my head was a constant distraction and prevented me from achieving the quietude of mind and body that I instinctively knew I required.

Once, recalling that dreadful conversation I had overheard between my mother and grandfather in late spring of the previous year, I asked one of my doctors if a particularly astute leech could be trained to drain only the bad blood from me and leave the rest. The doctor looked at me oddly and said, "Leeches cannot be trained. They can only take blood, breed, and die, in their time. They are good for nothing else."

This discouraged me from any further conversation about leeches.

My mother had mentioned my illness to my aunt Augusta, and she informed my father, who was in Greece at that time, having gone there to fight with the Greeks in their struggle for independence from the Ottoman Empire. It was not until much later that I learned he was quite frantic with worry about my condition — so upset, indeed, that for several months he could not write in his journal, not until he received word from my mother that I was out of danger. My mother did not write to him directly, of course. He submitted his questions to my aunt Augusta, she dutifully transcribed them in a letter to my mother, my mother addressed her replies to Augusta, and Augusta passed along her letters to my father. I imagine this slowed the delivery of news in both directions, which, given the distance between England and Greece, would not have been swift even if they had been on friendly terms, but having Aunt Augusta act as their translator prevented hostile words from turning into bitter arguments.

In October of 1823 — although I did not learn of it until many years later — my father asked Augusta to obtain from my mother an account of my "disposition, habits, studies, moral tendencies, and temper," as well as my personal appearance. He was very curious whether I was "social or solitary, taciturn or talkative, fond of reading or otherwise." He wondered, too, what my own unique "tic," or foible, was, and I thought it generous of him to assume I had only one. Concluding his letter on a note that could have been wry or apprehensive, or perhaps both, he wrote, "I hope the gods have made her anything save *poetical* — it is enough to have one such fool in the family."

My mother enjoyed writing up people's "characters," lengthy, detailed descriptions of their traits, tastes, aptitudes, and weaknesses. In fact, she found composing these meticulous reports such a pleasant pastime that she often created them for people she had only just met and about whom she knew quite little. She knew me as well as anyone could, of course, and she readily took up her pen to tell Augusta — because, of course, she would not acknowledge that my father was the real audience — all there was worth knowing about me.

"Ada's prevailing characteristic is Cheerfulness," my mother wrote, and it was evident even when I was suffering through the worst of my recent illness. Observation was the best developed of my intellectual powers, and the pertinency of my remarks and accuracy of my descriptions were quite advanced for my years. I was not devoid of imagination — here she did not mention her efforts to suppress it — but at present that faculty was devoted to the mechanical, especially the manufacture of little boats and ships of my own design. I particularly enjoyed reading, and now that my vision had been completely restored, I seemed to be making up for the long time I had been deprived of it. I preferred prose to poetry, and I demonstrated some proficiency in music and art. My temper was "open and ingenuous," although my mother noted, "at an earlier age it threatened to be impetuous, but is now sufficiently under control." As for my appearance, my form was "tall and robust," my features "not regular," my countenance "animated." She certainly did not make me sound very pretty, but I suppose I was not.

Four months later, in February, my aunt Augusta wrote my mother to say that my father had been elated with this report, and also with my silhouette, which my mother had kindly enclosed with it. At that time he was in Missolonghi in western Greece, where the rebels had triumphed against a fierce siege by the Turks in 1822. With the Ottoman forces threatening a renewed attack, my father had gone to join the Greek rebels at their stronghold there. My father had proudly shown my silhouette to the men of his garrison and spoke often of his high hopes for me.

"He truly does believe himself to be the hero of one of his own poems," I overheard my mother scoff to her friend Miss Montgomery as she folded the letter and left it on the mantel, but a faint tremor in her voice betrayed her apprehension. Until that moment, I had imagined his travels in Greece to be one great adventure, oblivious to the dangers he could encounter.

I hid my fears and tried to forget them, since I could tell no one. My mother had no idea that I knew half the things I did. She should have included my remarkable skill at eavesdropping in the character she had created about me — but I suppose the omission proves how very skilled I was, since she was unaware of it.

I had fully recovered from my illness by then and had been relieved of the perpetual leech. My doctors decreed that it was safe for me to resume my studies, and I did so with alacrity, under the watchful eye of a new governess, Miss Noble. She was tall, red-haired, and robust, and she was very well traveled and knowledgeable about history. Sometimes she would astonish me with brash, witty asides she thought I either did not hear or would not understand, and occasionally I caught her with a dazed, disconcerted look on her face as if she were quite perplexed as to how she had come to be at Kirkby Mallory as governess to a precocious, lonely little girl. I overheard the housekeeper telling the butler that rumor had it she had been left at the altar when her scoundrel of a fiancé ran off with a foreign heiress. "She is too bold by half and does not know her place," the housekeeper complained, but I rather liked Miss Noble for that.

One April afternoon, I was studying French pronouns in the nursery, impatient to finish so that I might be permitted to go outside and play in the fresh spring breezes and sunshine. Suddenly I heard a carriage approaching the house, and the bustling of the footmen signaled that an unexpected guest had arrived.

"May I go see who it is?" I asked my governess, and without waiting for an answer, I darted from the room. When Miss Noble called sternly after me, I halted at a particular spot where I could observe part of the foyer if I peered between the balusters. "It's Captain Byron," I exclaimed, just as he was escorted out of sight. My heart sank when I realized that he was alone and he had not brought his son George, my honorary brother.

I asked if I might go and welcome him, but Miss Noble steered me back to the nursery. By the time I finished my lessons, the captain had departed, and I was sent out to the garden with strict orders not to disturb my mother in her study. Crestfallen, I went outside to play, alone. Maybe the captain will have brought me a letter from George, I thought, as I swung from a low branch of my favorite oak, and I brightened considerably.

I had not been playing long when a maid brought word that my mother wanted to see me at once. I found her sitting alone in her study, but before I could ask what had become of Captain Byron, she gestured to the chair nearest to hers and said, "Sit down, darling." Her voice was preternaturally calm, but her face was pale, her eyes red rimmed.

I obeyed, my heart pounding. I clasped my hands together in my lap and waited.

"Ada." She paused and cleared her throat. "It is my sad duty to inform you that your father is dead."

"No, he isn't," I replied in a very small voice. "He's in Greece."

"Yes, Ada, he was in Greece, and it is there that he died."

For a moment I couldn't breathe. I stared at her and swallowed hard. "Did a Turk kill him?"

"No. It was a fever, a very sudden and dangerous fever."

It did not seem possible. "Are you sure? Maybe there's been a mistake. Maybe it was another Englishman who died, and the Greeks mistook him for my papa."

My mother's shoulders slumped almost imperceptibly, and as she uttered a wordless sigh, the impassioned light in her eyes declared that no one could ever mistake Lord Byron for any other Englishman. "I am sure," she said steadily. "Captain Byron brought me the news himself."

I began to tremble and then to sob. My mother raised a graceful hand and beckoned, and Miss Noble rushed in to console me so quickly that she must have been waiting just outside the doorway. She led me off to the nursery, but I broke away and ran to my bedroom, where I threw myself upon the coverlet and sobbed.

Despite the estrangement between my parents, when word of my father's death reached us, Kirkby Mallory plunged into mourning, ceremonial yet deeply felt. Lord Byron deserved certain tributes and honors by virtue of his rank, and as his widow, my mother would ensure that every proper service was performed. To those who would sneer that she fulfilled her duties only to make a favorable show for the public — and I know there were many — I assure you, her grief was real.

So was mine, although my mother did not understand it. "Ada shed many tears when I broke the news to her," I overheard her tell a friend, herself a widow, who had come to offer condolences. "I believe she wept more from the sight of my agitation, and from the thought that she might someday lose me too, than from any other cause. She knows almost nothing of her father, and a child like her cannot have any real feelings for someone she has never known. It is a great comfort to me that she does not feel any real grief for him."

But my grief was as real as her own, and I felt it keenly. I mourned the father whom I knew only from glimpses and gleanings, and I mourned what I now realized I could never have — the chance to know him better.

The story of my father's death filled news-

178

paper columns throughout England and around the world, but my mother and grandfather shielded me as best they could from the lurid details. It was not until later that I learned how he had suffered on his deathbed in Missolonghi, how frantic and disbelieving were the doctors who fought desperately to save his life. According to his loyal valet, Fletcher, who visited my mother in early July, in the fevered delirium of his deathbed, my father had spoken of his wife and child.

"He said, 'Oh, my poor child! My dear Ada! My God, could I but have seen her!' " Fletcher reported, hat in his hands, his gaze turned respectfully downward. "And then he said, 'Give her my blessing, and my dear sister, and her children.' "

"Was that all?" my mother cried. "Was there no more?"

"No, my lady. He then said, 'Go to Lady Byron, go to her and say — Tell her everything —' And he went on and on, full near twenty minutes it was, but I couldn't make out his words."

"Oh, do try, try," my mother implored. "What did he want you to tell me?"

"I beg your pardon, my lady. Truly sorry, but I don't know." Fletcher hesitated. "He did say one more thing, at the very end."

"Tell me!"

"He looked at me and said, 'I want to sleep now.' Then he rolled onto his back, closed his

179

eyes, and died."

Soon after his demise, his doctors performed an autopsy, not to determine the cause of death but to discover how a man of such genius differed from other men. They noted that his lungs were extraordinarily capacious and strong, and that his skull was remarkably thick, but they found nothing else unusual that might explain his poetical gifts. They removed his heart, brain, and intestines and placed them in separate containers. Afterward, his remains were placed in a coffin and taken aboard the ship *Florida,* which set sail on 24 May to carry him home to England.

While the *Florida* was en route, a fierce debate raged about where my father should be put to rest. He had fled England overshadowed by dark clouds of scandal and debt, but during his self-imposed exile he had become a hero to the Greek people and had redeemed himself in the eyes of many of his own countrymen. Furthermore, it could not be denied that the gifts of his genius, his poetry, had immeasurably enriched the nation. Should Lord Byron, spurned by English society in life, be forgiven and welcomed back with open arms and grief-stricken hearts in death?

The common people, who loved and admired my father despite his irreverence and iniquities, demanded that he be granted a state funeral and interment at Westminster Abbey. My mother, too, publicly expressed her hopes that at the very least he would be honored with a memorial in Poets' Corner, and when the movement encountered resistance, she composed a poem protesting his exclusion from the ranks of the great men buried there. But her dignified pleas did not move the resolute dean of the abbey, who declared that Lord Byron's sins were so egregious that neither his remains nor a memorial would be countenanced in Poets' Corner or any other sanctified place under his jurisdiction.

In the end, it was decided that my father would be buried in the Byron family vault at the church in Hucknall Torkard, not far from Newstead Abbey.

The *Florida* reached the Thames Estuary on 29 June, and a few days later, my father's closest friend, Sir John Hobhouse, arrived to escort his remains on the final stage of the journey. Many years later, Hobhouse told me that the sight of the ship struck him like a physical blow, his grief rendered all the more painful by the sight of my father's beloved dogs playing on the ship's deck. When he claimed my father's coffin, he requested that the lid be raised so that he might gaze one last time upon his dear friend's face, but thankfully, he spared me the description of what he beheld.

My father's body lay in state in London for several days at the home of Sir George Edward Knatchbull in Great George Street, Westminster, where vast throngs of mourners came to pay their respects. Afterward, the coffin and the two urns holding his brain and heart were placed onto a gleaming black hearse for the journey to his final resting place. The cortege passed Westminster Abbey, where no memorial but the slow tolling of its deep bell was offered him, up Whitehall and Tottenham Court Road and through the city, an astonishing procession of forty-seven carriages following slowly behind. At the tollbooth leading to the Great North Road, the carriages halted and the hearse proceeded northward toward Nottingham alone — but not quite alone, for crowds of the common folk had gathered along both sides of the road to witness its process, and bells tolled in every village it passed, and every night when the hearse paused on its route, great multitudes gathered to mourn and honor him.

On 12 July, thousands of people rose early and lined the streets of Nottingham to meet the hearse when it arrived at five o'clock in the morning. It halted at the Blackamoor's Head Inn, where the coffin and urns were carried inside to a room draped in black fabric, adorned with the Byron coat of arms, and illuminated by six tall pillar candles. From dawn until midafternoon, thousands of mourners were admitted in groups of twenty to file past the coffin, lost in thought, murmuring prayers, many openly weeping. Thousands more, determined to pay their respects, anxious that the body of their hero would be taken away before their turns came, struggled with the constables assigned the task of keeping the crowd in orderly queues.

Later the coffin was returned to the hearse, which carried my father the last eight miles he would ever travel. Clad in mourning black, a great number of people followed on foot, while others stood by the side of the road to watch the funeral cortege go by, the procession swelling as it passed through each village along the way. When it at last reached Hucknall Torkard, the church was already packed with tearful, somber onlookers who had arrived hours before the funeral began at half past three o'clock, to be sure of gaining entrance for the last act of Byron's brief but brilliant life.

Hobhouse was there, and Fletcher, and others my father had called great friends, but my mother and I did not attend. Her health was too fragile to hazard the ordeal, my mother said. Tearfully I begged her to allow Miss Noble to take me instead, but she said it would not be appropriate for me to go without her. "Everyone would stare at you," she warned when I protested.

I quaked at the thought of so many pairs of

mournful eyes fixed upon me searchingly, hungrily, and I immediately acquiesced. And so we marked the sorrowful day at home, in quiet reflection.

In the days that followed, I opened the precious golden locket my father had sent me and touched his dark brown curl so often that it is a wonder I did not damage them both. This precious relic was all that I would ever have of my father that was just for me. His poetry was a greater artifact of his life, but his words belonged to the world. The locket and the curl it protected were mine alone.

Except for the ring that I would receive later, he had left me no other bequest — not a single book, portrait, memento, nothing. All went to my aunt Augusta, as he had decided before I was born. That included his personal wealth of about one hundred thousand pounds, but not Newstead Abbey, as it had been sold, and not his title, for that went to his closest male relative, his cousin Captain George Anson Byron, now the seventh Baron Byron. In another act of selfless generosity, my mother immediately bestowed upon the new Lord Byron her marriage juncture of two thousand pounds per annum, providing him and his family with a living they badly needed.

A cynic would say that my mother, now a wealthy widow, could well afford to make that gift, but she was under no obligation to provide for her husband's successor. I firmly believe that most people would have kept the money for themselves and spent the windfall improving their own estates or buying themselves land, horses, and finery in abundance. I have always been proud of my mother for her generosity, even as I regretted that she had not offered it more frequently to me.

With my father's death, my mother had become financially independent, empowered to live exactly as she wished without deferring to any man, a situation known to very few women of the time. It was little wonder that she never for a moment considered remarrying. She could not enjoy her new freedom, however, thanks to the press, who twisted their lamentations for the great poet into torment for his widow. She was subjected to slander and ridicule, her actions preceding the Separation dragged out and aired before the public once more, her every word parsed, her every decision regarding my upbringing questioned, her absence from his funeral rites condemned. Even her generosity to Captain Byron was misrepresented as parsimonious and grudgingly given.

Nor were her tormentors limited to newspapermen, whose words were damaging but ephemeral. Even before my father was buried, advertisements appeared for a spurious "memoir" allegedly based upon the manuscript my father had sent to his publisher in

1820, which was said to contain "the private correspondence of Lord Byron." That the author was a distant relative of my father's, shamefully exploiting their acquaintance, appalled my mother and outraged my grandfather. Hobhouse, my father's executor, successfully obtained an injunction to halt its publication, but after much legal wrangling in the English courts, the unscrupulous author simply had the book published in France. My father's loyal friend also fought the publication of a biography written by the poet Thomas Medwin, a cousin of Percy Bysshe Shelley, who introduced him to my father in 1821 during their sojourn in Pisa. Hobhouse lost that battle, and in October, six months after my father's death, Medwin's *Journal of the Conversations of Lord Byron, Noted During a Residence with His Lordship at Pisa in the Years 1821 and 1822* cluttered the bookshops. Although the publisher prefaced the volume with a disclaimer, both Hobhouse and my father's publisher, John Murray, threatened to sue. My aunt Augusta begged my mother to join her in a public denunciation of "that Vile Book," but my mother demurred, asserting that it would be wiser to appear as if they had never read it.

Beneath this ongoing assault, it is little wonder that my mother's health suffered. She lost weight, could not sleep, and suffered headaches and ailments of the stomach her physician could not explain. Restlessness overtook her again, as it had years before when the full burden of the Separation had settled heavily upon her shoulders. As before, she traveled from the home of one friend to that of another, from seaside resort to tranquil spa town, as if she could outpace her heartache. I wished she had taken me with her, but she could not regain her strength and vitality with me around to distract her, so I remained at Kirkby Mallory Hall with my grandfather and governess. I wrote my mother many letters, endeavoring to be cheerful, assuring her of my progress in my studies, hoping that she would conclude that I had improved myself enough to be good company, so that she would return to me.

In September, Miss Noble took me to London to see the *Florida,* which had remained in port since carrying my father's remains home from Greece. She was a fine, reassuringly strong ship, with a look that promised swiftness, and it comforted me to think that my father would have had a safe and comfortable passage on his last journey upon the sea. My eyes filled with tears at the sight of it, but I was brave and did not let them fall. I knew somehow that this was the closest I would come to visiting my father's grave until I was a woman grown and, like my mother, could decide for myself.

As the months passed and my loneliness

continued unabated, and as I consumed reams of paper in letters chasing after my mother, I surely had suffered all the losses a little girl could be expected to endure in such a brief span of time. And yet less than a year after my father died, on 15 March 1825, my beloved grandfather also passed away. In his last weeks, when his doctors confirmed that his health was precipitously declining, my mother had rushed home from her travels and had cared for him tenderly until the end.

Now Grandpapa, too, was gone. Only my mother was left to me, and her health was ever fragile, or so she said. A terrible fear seized me then, and never relented, that at any moment Death would come to claim her as well, leaving me utterly alone in the world, unloved and unprotected.

CHAPTER SEVEN:
NEW SHORES DESCRIED
MAKE EVERY BOSOM GAY

March 1826–November 1827

Relentless travel did not quell my mother's wanderlust, and in early 1826 she decided to uproot our entire household from Kirkby Mallory and decamp to Bifrons House near Canterbury in Kent. The estate grounds were quite pretty, with green, gently rolling hills that overlooked picturesque farmlands, but the house was smaller, darker, and draftier than home, and no matter how well the housemaids scrubbed and swept, to me it always smelled faintly of dust, wet boots, and old cheese.

When my mother announced that she had leased Bifrons House for a year with an option to renew, my heart plummeted. Kirkby Mallory was my home, and even though it echoed with the absence of my beloved grandparents, I longed to return. Still, I held out hope that having chosen this particular residence herself, my mother would be willing to settle here with me for a while. To my great disappointment, as soon as she discovered that she was no happier there than anywhere else, she departed for an extended visit with her friend Lady Gosford at Worlingham Hall in Suffolk.

I had scarcely become accustomed to my new surroundings when Miss Noble, too, left me. She left quite suddenly, without giving notice. On her last day with us, she came to my room quite early in the morning and stroked my hair until I woke. "Take care of yourself, sweetheart," she said, smiling wistfully. "Keep to your maths and your science, but let some poetry in now and then too. A little wonder and imagination never hurt anyone." She bent to kiss my cheek, told me good-bye, and left the room. Bemused, I went back to sleep, and it was not until morning that I learned she had gone for good, affronting nearly everyone. Astonishment fueled speculation that she disliked the retiring country life and had found a more amenable situation in London, or that she had run off to America with a handsome doctor she had no intention of marrying. I had become very fond of Miss Noble and I protested whenever I heard such slander, and out of loyalty I did not tell them that she had come to my room before dawn to say good-bye, or that she had encouraged me to use my imagination, which my mother claimed would lead to my utter destruction — a truth I believed less and less with each passing year.

My mother was greatly displeased that Miss Noble's sudden departure required her to return to Bifrons to interview prospective replacements. She was more displeased still to find me unhappy, lonely, clingy, and demanding. "Your *letters* are lively and cheerful," she said, and she made a strange, involuntary gesture as if she were brushing my disgraceful neediness off her sleeves like dust.

Of course my letters were cheerful. I wanted her to come home, and wasn't she more likely to return to a pleasant daughter than a resentful one?

Before long she hired a new governess, a Miss Stamp, whose name I impudently ran together in my mind to signify that she had stamped something badly — misspeak, mistake, mis-stamp. Her business at home complete, my mother was off again, this time to Seaham to check in on the Infant School. I was so annoyed with my mother for leaving so soon to visit with children other than myself that I admit I did not make my new governess's first weeks at Bifrons very pleasant, and it is a wonder that she stayed on. Miss Stamp must have made some complaint or warning about my behavior, however, because when my mother next returned, she called me into her study. "I understand that you have been rather lonely here," she said, a trace of disapproval in her voice.

"Yes, Mama," I cautiously replied, wondering if a punishment was in store.

To my surprise, she smiled. "I believe I have a solution."

My heart soared, and for a moment I thought she was going to either promise to stop traveling so often or offer to bring me along, but instead she turned her head toward the door. "Come in now, John," she called.

In walked one of the footmen carrying a tiny basket, from which came a tiny mewling sound. "Oh!" I cried, bounding out of my chair and rushing over to see. Curled up in the basket was a little bundle of dark gray fur, with a pattern of black fur almost resembling stripes. The kitten's four paws and the tip of her tail were white, and her tiny claws were fine and needle sharp.

"This new friend will keep you company when I'm away," my mother said.

"Thank you, Mama," I exclaimed in a hushed voice so that I would not frighten the kitten. My mother disliked keeping animals in the house, so I understood what a very great gift this was indeed. "May I hold her?"

"You'd better. She's yours to love and care for, your responsibility."

Gently, I lifted the soft bundle of fur from the basket, sat down cross-legged on the floor, and cradled the darling little creature in my lap. She mewled and yawned, making me giggle, and I gently touched my fingertip to each little paw, as soft and snowy white as thistledown.

"I'm going to call you Puff," I declared, and I bent to kiss the top of her head between her ears.

In the months that followed, Puff and I became great friends. Even as I discovered in her a delightful playmate, Miss Stamp found an effective tool for enforcing my good behavior. If I finished a lesson promptly and well, I might have five extra minutes to play with Puff afterward. If I fidgeted through a lecture or spoke impertinently, I could not cuddle Puff during my rest time. I had never been more obedient, and thenceforth when my mother traveled, instead of sending her wistful pleas to come home, I filled my letters with enthusiastic reports of Puff's antics and habits and growth.

In early June, when my mother went to London on a matter of business, she left me in the care of Miss Stamp and Miss Louisa Chaloner, one of her spinster friends. I had finished my lessons for the afternoon, having earned effusive praise for flawlessly reciting my multiplication tables, and I was happily romping with Puff in the drawing room, pretending not to hear Miss Chaloner's requests that I come wash my hands, brush my hair, and go down for my dinner. Suddenly I realized that I was very hungry, and I cried, "I don't need to wash and brush. I want to have dinner now."

"Nonsense, my dear girl," protested Miss Chaloner. "Someone with your looks must always make the extra effort to be tidy."

That brought me up short, as if she had seized me by the scruff of my neck. "What do you mean, someone with my looks?"

"I only mean that you shall never be pretty, but that should never prevent you from being clean and tidy." She drew herself up and regarded me officiously down the length of her long nose. "You might always have a good countenance and be good-looking, but you must know that you shall never be pretty."

I swallowed hard. "I didn't know that I *never* shall be," I said, feigning indifference, pretending that I was well aware of the sorry state of my looks, although in truth, I was hearing it for the first time. "I had hoped I might improve as I grow up."

"Perhaps you shall," she said, nodding indulgently, but I knew she didn't mean it.

After that I did not have much of an appetite, and when Miss Stamp accused me of sulking — she had not witnessed the exchange in the drawing room — I made an effort to nibble a piece of bread. All day long I mulled over Miss Chaloner's words, and later that evening, I took up pen and paper and wrote down my reflections in a letter to my mother, the imperfections of my handwriting betraying my emotion. I repeated what her friend had said about my looks, but not wanting to seem a tattletale, I said that she had spoken "by accident." "I cannot but say that I feel a little regret," I admitted. "On the other hand there are advantages. There are many, many people who are very much liked and loved who are not pretty. Then too there are many people who are very beautiful and very vain — as I should be, I am sure, if I were pretty — and in consequence, they are very much disliked. And after all, of what consequence is it? None. Then why should we care for it?"

I went on at length about the dangers of vanity, and as I sealed the letter, I hoped my mother would be proud of me for my dignified acceptance of my fate never to be pretty. I sent a second letter to my friend Fanny Smith, who promptly replied that she was certain I would be a great beauty when I was grown, and that "the wicked beast Chaloner" would have an apoplexy from jealousy. This cheered me up quite a lot. Although I could not tell my mother, I also found comfort in the fairy tales Miss Thorne had told me. The heroines of her stories triumphed not because they were pretty but because they were kind, clever, and brave. Thus I might still live happily ever after.

When my mother returned from London, I

did not mention the unhappy subject, because my thoughts were immediately taken over by her glorious news. After the Separation, my father had insisted that I never be taken abroad, but with his passing, the prohibition had been lifted. The reason my mother had gone to London was to make travel arrangements for us to tour the Continent.

The wonderful news filled me with elation, followed by a rush of despair when I realized that I would have to leave sweet little Puff behind. Joy swiftly returned, and how could it have not, for I was going to explore wonderful, exotic lands with my good, wise, and brilliant mother. As for Puff, she would be well looked after by the household staff in my absence, and as we packed and prepared, I reassured myself that we would have a happy reunion in a little more than a year.

My elation dimmed when I was informed that Miss Chaloner would be accompanying us, for her unkind though well-intended evaluation of my beauty still stung. Miss Stamp would come along too, to watch over me when my mother was otherwise occupied. A few more of my mother's friends and her cousin Robert Noel would round out the party.

We set sail from Dover in late June, and while Miss Stamp rested below deck with a sour stomach, I held on to the rail and delighted in the rocking of the boat, the wind whipping my hair, the salt spray of the sea upon my face. Our ship docked at Rotterdam, and after spending some time in that city we crossed the Netherlands and entered Germany. I enjoyed our stay in Heidelberg very much, but my mother was eager to visit the spas at Baden-Baden, so we soon moved on.

I marveled at the sublime beauty of the Black Forest as we traveled through it, for it was so unlike the gentler landscapes of Kirkby Mallory that I had once believed the loveliest in the world. How wonderful and inspiring it was to discover how vast and beautiful the wide-open world was, how much of it there was to explore and discover! But despite my admiration for the natural wonders I observed there, for me, our stay in Baden-Baden was marred by an unpleasant experience at our inn. One afternoon while my mother was off taking the waters, I was writing letters in the public drawing room, watched over from a discreet distance by Miss Stamp. I had finished my report on my mother's health and was beginning to inquire about Puff when I noticed a group of tourists congregated by the fireplace who kept giving me quick, curious glances and murmuring among themselves. I smiled politely, but that was a mistake, because it encouraged them to settle into chairs much closer to my table and scrutinize me with no pretense of doing otherwise. They spoke to one another in German, but my German was merely serviceable, and I could not follow their conversation and still concentrate on writing my letter. One word they repeated often stood out clearly: Byron.

Before long, one of the ladies was elected to approach me. "Excuse me, young miss," she said in accented but very good English, "are you not the daughter of Lord Byron, the great poet?"

"I am," I replied.

"I thought so," she said, beaming. "My husband saw your mother's name on the register, and I believed you might be their child." Turning, she spoke to her companions in rapid German, and as one they rose, surrounded my table, and bent close to study my features. At once Miss Stamp rushed over like a frantic hen with wings flapping wildly to chase them off, but not before I heard enough words I recognized — father, face, chin, eyes, hair — to understand that they were searching me for signs of my revered parent.

That evening at supper, a group of Italian men stared at me so boldly that my mother's cousin, Robert Noel, marched over and demanded in fluent Italian that they turn their gaze elsewhere, and the next morning while I played in the garden, a young woman rushed over while Miss Stamp was distracted and thrust a book at me so suddenly that I instinctively took it. *"Küssen Sie bitte das Buch,"* she said, gesturing eagerly, tears in her eyes. I recognized "kiss," "please," and "book," so I hesitantly pressed my lips to the burgundy leather cover. With a cry of joy and a wary glance for my governess, she snatched the book from me, hugged it to her bosom, thanked me half a dozen times more, and darted away, leaving me disconcerted and a trifle angry. I assumed that it was a book of my father's poems, but for all I knew it could have been anything from the Bible to *The Mysteries of Udolpho.*

I disliked being examined like some curious beast captured in the vast woodland wilderness of America, and I was heartily glad when our entourage left Germany. But if I am to confess the whole truth — and I suppose that is what is expected herein — I should add that I think what bothered me most about the tourists' attention was that it had nothing to do with me, and everything to do with my father. I had not earned my small measure of fame for any of my own accomplishments. Mine were borrowed laurels, and they rested uncomfortably upon my brow. I hoped that someday I might earn my own.

We traveled on to Switzerland, where we were not recognized, or if we were, the people exercised enough restraint that we never knew it. Lake Geneva impressed me deeply for other reasons — the astonishing beauty of the Alps rising above the crystal blue lake, the refreshing chill of the water, the graceful gliding of the sailboats, the charm of the villages on its shores, the enchantment of the castles.

One afternoon, I was walking along the shore with Robert Noel, while my mother, Miss Stamp, and Miss Chaloner kept a slower pace some distance behind us. I was happy to have time alone, or close to it, with my mother's tall, handsome cousin, whom I liked very much. He was always impeccably dressed and had studied the law in Edinburgh.

Suddenly I glimpsed something through the trees, and I tugged on his hand to draw his attention to a particularly mysterious castle looming above the far eastern end of the curved lake. "That's the castle of Chillon," he said, a curious note in his voice.

"Is it famous?" I asked.

"It certainly is famous now," he replied, glancing warily over his shoulder, and I understood at once that he did not want my mother to overhear. "The dungeons beneath that castle inspired Lord Byron's poem *The Prisoner of Chillon*. He called the lake by its French name, however — Lac Léman."

A thrill of excitement and affinity passed through me. "My father was here?"

"Yes, Ada. Your father spent a great deal of time in this region." He gestured to the southwest. "You can't see it from here, but at the opposite end of the lake, there's a residence called Villa Diodati. About ten years ago — no, more than that, I think, closer to twelve — your father rented it. He and his guests no doubt had expected to enjoy a balmy summer holiday there, but days of ceaseless rain had kept them indoors. They were amusing themselves by telling ghost stories —"

"I'm not allowed to hear ghost stories," I murmured, not wanting him to stop but thinking I should give him fair warning.

"I know, little cousin. I'm not going to tell you ghost stories; I'm telling you about people telling ghost stories." He grimaced. "Although I suppose this tale wouldn't meet with approval either."

"You've started, so you have to finish."

"Fair enough. As I said, they were staving off boredom by telling one another old ghost stories, reading aloud from a book of German tales. Then your father proposed a competition, challenging each of the company, himself included, to write a horror story of their own. Mary Godwin Shelley was one of his guests, and she wrote the tale that she later turned into the novel *Frankenstein.*"

"Oh, yes," I exclaimed. "I've heard of it — but I'm not allowed to read it."

"That's just as well. You'll appreciate it more when you're older." He gave me an appraising look. "And if I may, you probably shouldn't repeat this story to your mother. It's well-known, but she might not like that I told you."

"I won't say a word," I promised. It was not the first time I had kept a secret from my mother, nor, I was certain, would it be the last.

Knowing that my father had walked along that lakeshore and had bathed in those waters made Lake Geneva even more glorious in my estimation. I spent hours gazing out upon the deep, mysterious lake, admiring the ever-shifting colors and play of light upon its surface. I longed to explore the castle of Chillon and visit the Villa Diodati, and I secretly hoped that curiosity would compel my mother to add excursions to both sites to our tour, but she did not, and I could not ask her to do so without revealing knowledge of my father she would certainly prefer I not possess.

As winter approached we journeyed south, first visiting Milan and then Genoa, where my mother found us lovely rooms at the Hôtel d'Amérique overlooking the sea. The view enthralled me, not only the magnificent sunsets, but also the boats sailing with such effortless grace as they returned from or departed for exotic ports all over the world.

Watching them, I imagined what I would have seen had I stood there in the age of Christopher Columbus, as the great age of exploration was unfolding. How exciting it must have been to watch the explorers' ships embark upon their hazardous journeys when so much of the world was yet unknown and waiting to be discovered!

As we intended to remain in Genoa several weeks, my mother arranged for me to have music and art lessons with local masters in addition to my usual studies with Miss Stamp. I loved my singing lessons more than any other pastime, and I took drawing lessons from a respected artist named Signor Isola. I had some talent but I was no prodigy; but as I happily sketched and painted in the benevolent Italian sunshine, it never occurred to me to wonder why such a renowned master would take on a merely modestly gifted eleven-year-old girl as a pupil.

As spring came, my scientific curiosity compelled me to study the native insect population. The hotel's garden boasted many large anthills, whose busy, indefatigable residents enthralled me for hours on end as I followed their meandering trails and observed their battles and marveled at their feats of strength. At dusk, scattered clumps of moldering leaves fairly crawled with woodlice, and at night, countless clouds of fireflies sparked and danced from the grasses to the high boughs of the cypress and juniper trees lining the paths. My most exciting discovery was a scorpion that I found boldly crawling along the floor of a sitting room; the snakes, locusts, lizards, and black-and-green frogs I found were beautiful and better mannered, for they remained outdoors.

I had settled in quite comfortably in Genoa, so when the day of our departure approached, it was not without regret that I packed my bags and bade my teachers farewell. When I parted from Signor Isola, he gave me a lovely gift, a set of crayons and two paintbrushes. *"Grazie mille, maestro,"* I gasped, delighted with my treasures.

"Use them well," he commanded, smiling. "Ah, little Miss Byron, how I have enjoyed our time together. I see so much of your father in you, the line of your jaw, your close study of a subject, the movement of your hand as you put pencil to paper."

"You knew my father?"

His brow furrowed. "But of course. We spent much time working together when he was last in Milan. You did not know?"

I shook my head, and while I was thrilled to have this new detail of my father's past, I felt wistful, too, thinking of all the people who knew my father better than I ever would. Each fact, each story that was revealed to me, was a precious jewel I threaded on fine golden chain and wore close to my heart.

In early summer we resumed our travels, stopping first in Turin, where I marveled at the beautiful views of the Alps from nearly every street in the city and enjoyed the puppeteers and tumblers parading through the streets. Leaving Turin, we crossed the Alps and returned to Geneva, and after a brief stay there we continued on ninety miles to the southeast to climb Mont Blanc, keeping to the lower elevations. I gazed up at the summit, awestruck, and thought very long and hard about how I might attempt to reach the top — how I would prepare myself with strengthening exercises, what equipment I should carry, whom I would include in my party of brave adventurers. The glaciers we spied from a distance filled me with awe and wonder, and at dinner later that evening, I chattered on about them enthusiastically to an older gentleman who had been introduced to us, an authority on the geology of the Alps, and he kindly and indulgently answered all of my questions.

Our wanderings took us to Vallée de l'Ouche in France for a time, and then back to Germany, where we visited several cities, among which Stuttgart was my favorite. This time my mother had taken the precaution of signing the hotel registers as "Lady Anne Isabella Milbanke," her maiden name, and so we remained incognito — although I suppose it was possible that we were recognized, but the people politely left us alone.

As October waned, we returned to Turin and prepared to set sail for England. I enjoyed my second sea voyage as much as I had the first, and when we reached Dover, I felt as worldly, well traveled, and sophisticated as a young woman of almost twelve years could be. My native England felt both familiar and strange, which is also how I felt to myself. Travel had vastly expanded the boundaries of my carefully circumscribed world, and I felt myself utterly transformed, my curiosity whetted rather than quenched.

Our party dispersed, and the various families and pairs completed their separate journeys home. I longed for Kirkby Mallory, but my mother took us to Bifrons instead. How happy I was to be reunited with Puff, who was no longer a sweet kitten but a proper cat, and even prettier than I remembered.

I was very grateful for her company, for after my exciting adventures on the Continent, Bifrons seemed even more dull and isolated than before. I suspect my mother felt the same, for she soon set out for London to visit friends, who were all very eager to hear about her travels. "Would you take me with you?" I asked her forlornly as I watched her and her maid pack her trunks, which had hardly remained unpacked a fortnight.

"My friends did not extend their invitation to you," my mother said lightly, holding up a silk scarf she had purchased in Turin, considering whether to pack it.

I thought her reply was very bad form and that she ought to at least *pretend* to regret that I had not been invited, but I held back the complaint.

And so she left me, again, and in her absence, I studied with Miss Stamp, played with Puff, and wandered the countryside around Bifrons. I wrote my mother volumes of letters, saying nothing of my sorrow and disappointment that our time together had ended so abruptly. She had seemed to enjoy my company on our tour, although it is true that I was more often with Miss Stamp, and she with Miss Chaloner, than we were alone together. I could not help feeling discarded, as if she could not get away from me soon enough.

But I could not chase after her, and begging her to come home would only provoke her ire. Resigned, I counted the days until her return, and in the meantime, I devoted myself to my studies, for my intellectual accomplishments always pleased her even when my conversation and company did not.

CHAPTER EIGHT: MORE RESTLESS THAN THE SWALLOW IN THE SKIES

December 1827–May 1828

Bifrons was a cold and damp place to spend Christmas, and when my mother returned home to spend the holidays with me, she came down with a terrible affliction of the chest, with wracking coughs, fever, chills, and constant fatigue. At her doctor's urging, she departed early in the New Year to take a rest cure in Devon, leaving me at home with my usual entourage of governess, cat, and servants.

Puff had become quite a naughty little creature, not unlike her mistress at that age. The day after my mother departed, I discovered that my cat had made a secret hiding place in the chimney of my bedroom fireplace. It was a grisly cache, for within it she concealed the poor birds she had caught in the garden, storing them in her makeshift pantry until she wished to eat one.

I spun this event into a lively anecdote in a letter to my mother, but I could not sustain my pretense of good cheer for long. "Yesterday it was exactly a week since you left Bifrons," I wrote seven days later, "and now I have before me two long, dull, tiresome weeks just like the one that has passed only that they will appear rather longer and rather more tiresome."

Bored and lonely, I found myself brooding over the poor birds Puff had slain. I wondered how she had been able to catch them, since they had wings and presumably could have flown away. Puff's stealth and pouncing velocity must exceed the birds' takeoff speed, I concluded, unless she had caught them while they were sleeping.

My contemplation of birds reminded me of our tour of Mont Blanc in Geneva, the summit of which I had glimpsed through the clouds from the foothills. I recalled thinking then that if I had been a bird, I could have soared to the highest peak and enjoyed a spectacular view of the Alps and the valleys below.

Then inspiration struck like a thunderbolt: I could not transform myself into a bird, but perhaps I could create a machine that would carry me into the air like a ship taking passengers upon the sea.

My imagination caught fire and burned brightly. I studied birds in flight and at rest, determined to ascertain how wings — so fragile, yet so powerful and cunningly designed — could lift a bird's body and propel it forward. After sketching several designs, I began building a paper model the exact size and proportion of a bird's wings to its body, working from memory and images of birds that appeared in paintings displayed here and there in Bifrons.

The next morning, when I did not show up for our scheduled French lesson, Miss Stamp found me in the study bent over my model wings, furiously scribbling calculations on paper. "What are you doing?" she asked, a bit taken aback by my intense concentration.

"I'm working out the proportions of a set of wings capable of supporting a human body," I said, my eyes fixed on my work. "A twelve-year-old girl's body, to be precise."

Miss Stamp peered over my shoulder at my sums and figures. "And what have you discovered?"

"That I'm going to need a lot of strong paper and wire." Reluctantly I added, "And that I should probably eat a little less at every meal, if I want to get off the ground."

"I admire your industry, but you cannot sacrifice your other lessons to this project."

"Five more minutes?"

"Now. You're already fifteen minutes late, and that will come out of your playtime with Puff."

Obediently I finished my French lesson, and then music, and then geography, and then my kindhearted governess agreed that working out the proportions for my wings qualified as mathematics, so she allowed me to race back to work.

As the days passed and my plans took shape, I proudly described my progress in a letter to my mother. "I am going to begin my full-scale paper wings tomorrow," I announced on a cold and blustery 3 February, not a good day for flying, but perfect weather for working indoors. "The more I think about it, the more I feel almost convinced that with a year or so's experience and practice, I shall be able to bring the art of flying to very great perfection."

I thought almost constantly about this new art, which I called Flyology, and as I measured and cut and shaped wire, I decided that if my invention worked, I ought to write a book about the art of flying, illustrated with plates, and annotated so that others might duplicate my experiments.

"If I do truly invent a method of flying," I told Miss Stamp one afternoon as we danced a quadrille, for she had dragged me away from my work for my dancing lesson, "think of how useful I'll be to my mother. I'll be able to carry messages to her, or from her to her friends, much swifter than the slow, terrestrial post does now."

"That is very dutiful of you," she replied. "Perhaps you'll no longer neglect your geography studies when you realize how useful they would be for navigation."

I was so captivated by the idea of an aerial post that I devoted most of my next letter to my mother to the subject. "When I fly I shall be able to fly about with all your letters and messages and shall be able to carry them with much more speed than the post or any other terrestrial contrivance," I wrote, my pen barely able to keep up with the flow of my ideas. "To make the thing quite complete, a part of the flying accoutrement shall be a letter bag, a small compass, and a map which the two last articles will enable me to cut across the country by the most direct road without minding either mountains, hills, valleys, rivers, lakes &c, &c, &c, &c." I observed that my book on Flyology should contain a list of the advantages of flying to convince the skeptical. Signing off with a flourish, I declared myself, "Your very affectionate Carrier Pigeon."

In an unused bedroom, which I dubbed the Flying Room, I set up a laboratory for construction, and I devised a system of ropes, pulleys, and a triangular mount upon which I would build and test my wings. The more I worked, the more deficiencies in my knowledge I discovered. I did not know how a bird moved its wings, for example, or what kept it aloft even when its wings were not moving, but rather spread outward in a glide. When I swam, if I stopped stroking and kicking, I sank. What allowed a bird to soar when it did not stroke the air with its wings? Why did it not plummet to the ground? My ignorance did not discourage me, however, or convince me of the impossibility of my scheme, but instead compelled me to work harder, learn more, and vanquish every problem that dared to challenge me.

Miss Stamp found it increasingly difficult to extract me from the Flying Room, but my diligence was rewarded, for by the end of March, I had overcome a very difficult obstacle regarding the motion and extension of the wings, and I had devised a way to attach the wings to the body. And yet many questions remained. "I have now a great favour to ask of you," I wrote to my mother on 3 April, "which is to try and procure me some book which will make me thoroughly understand the anatomy of a bird and if you can get one with plates to illustrate the descriptions I should be very glad as I have no inclination whatever to dissect a bird." Puff's poaching had put me off that particular scientific study.

I fervently wished I could consult with a real scientist, someone who could tell me if my plans were feasible, and since the only men of science I knew were physicians, I asked my mother to write to Dr. Mayo on my behalf, and any other doctors whose opinions I should seek. "Physicians do not build, though," I told Puff as I cuddled her on my lap one evening, for Miss Stamp had firmly declared the Flying Room closed for the evening and only my loyal cat had the patience to suffer through yet another Flyology lecture. "That is a disadvantage. I need to speak with a shipwright, or an engineer of steam engines —"

I gasped as inspiration struck.

I could hardly sleep that night, so excited was I about my newest brainstorm. In the morning, I raced through my toilette, fed Puff, gobbled down my breakfast, and dashed upstairs to the Flying Room to sketch my ideas before I was required to report for my lessons. I had not abandoned my original design of wings that I would wear upon my back, but just as both curricles and barouches drove along the roads, so too could different flying machines traverse the skies.

"Ada," said Miss Stamp sternly from the doorway. "You are ten minutes late for French."

I gasped and jumped up from my chair. Surely I had been working on my new drawings for only a few minutes, but my governess's pursed lips and furrowed brow said otherwise. Meekly I followed her to our schoolroom, where I forcibly pushed aside all thoughts of Flyology and concentrated on conjugations and cartography and every other subject in its turn in hope of winning back her favour. We had become quite close on our European tour, and my recent passion had proven that she was rather more indulgent than I deserved. I could not bear to lose her as I had lost so many other nurses and governesses.

It was not until after tea that I was allowed to turn my thoughts back to Flyology, and then only because it was the subject of my latest letter to my mother. "As soon as I have brought flying to perfection," I declared, after the customary dutiful inquiries about her health, "I have got a scheme about a mode of flying by steam-engine which, if ever I effect it, will be more wonderful than either steam-packets or steam-carriages. I will make a thing in the form of a horse with a steam-engine in the inside so contrived as to move an immense pair of wings, fixed on the outside of the horse, in such a manner as to carry it up into the air while a person sits on its back." I acknowledged that this vehicle probably would present "infinitely more difficulties and obstacles" than my wearable wings would, but how much more magnificent it would be when I succeeded! I added a hasty line about my studies of Louis XIV, lest she think I was neglecting my lessons, I asked her again when she might be returning home, and I again signed myself, "Your very affectionate Carrier Pigeon."

Whenever Miss Stamp permitted, I alternated between constructing my paper wings and planning my equine-avian vehicle, which I began to call the *Icarus* and the *Pegasus*, respectively. I was happy and industrious at work, and frantic and snappish when pulled away from it. I did not leave the Flying Room willingly, except on the afternoon a maid bustled in to announce that Puff was delivering kittens beneath my bed.

For the moment Flyology was forgotten as I ran off to observe this marvel of biology, which was messier than I had expected but no less fascinating. After Puff licked her babies clean, I longed to cuddle them, but the new mother — and who was the father, I wondered? — would not allow anyone but Miss Stamp near them. A few days later Puff carried her babies up into a crevice beneath the roof, where no one, not even the tallest footman perched upon a ladder, could reach them. It was a musty and dirty place, not at all suitable for tiny kittens, but Puff would do as she pleased. She stayed with them throughout the days and came down only for her meals.

"If my wings were finished," I speculated to Miss Stamp, "I could fly up there and have a look." As I imagined myself soaring up to the rooftop to inspect Puff's little nest, I was seized by the urgency to finish the *Icarus* at all speed, and I ran off to my laboratory, refusing to come out for my luncheon and only reluctantly coming down for supper.

The next day, the housekeeper brought me a letter from my mother. Hoping to find news about the bird anatomy book I had requested, or replies to my questions from Dr. Mayo, I eagerly read the letter, only to feel my soaring spirits come tumbling down to earth. "While I admire your diligence and toil," my mother had written, "I am very much concerned that you think too often of these wings when you ought to be thinking of other, more important matters." She went on to tell me that she would be coming home soon, accompanied by her friends Miss Montgomery and Miss Doyle, and Miss Doyle's niece, but even this news did not lift my spirits.

If my mother forbade it, Flyology would be grounded before it fledged.

This realization sent me into a panic. So often had I envisioned myself soaring among the clouds that it was unbearable to think that I might never leave the ground. The thought that all my hard work might be for naught was equally difficult to bear. My father had his poems; my mother had her Infant School; I, too, wanted to create a Great Work for the benefit of the world, and I had determined that Flyology would surely be it.

After collecting my thoughts, I cleared off a section of the table in my Flying Room, sat down properly in my chair, and wrote my mother a careful, sober reply. "I received your letter this morning and I really do not think that I often think of the wings when I ought to think of other things." Quickly I added, "but it was very kind of you to make the remark to me." Indeed it was very kind, although it hurt, because her concerns sprang from love, surely. "You have indeed thought of a great indulgence for me in every respect. In the first place I shall have the satisfaction of seeing you which will be particularly great to me now because you left me in such a state that I really thought at the time that you could not live." When I thought of how terribly her cough had wracked her before she left for Devon, I felt deeply ashamed for giving her even a moment's concern.

I blinked away tears, cleared my throat, and refreshed my pen in the ink.

I continued my letter in a very well-mannered fashion by expressing how much I looked forward to welcoming her and her friends soon — but then a strange impulse overtook me and I became determined to explain, very reasonably and logically, what my project was about, to persuade her that it was not a childish flight of fancy but genuine scientific research. Surely *that* she could understand, and perhaps even admire. "I have now decided upon making much smaller wings then I before intended," I said, as I imagined a man of science might, "and they will be perfectly well proportioned in every respect, exactly on the same plan and of the same shape as a bird's, and though they will not be nearly large enough to try and fly with yet, they will be quite enough so to enable me to explain perfectly to anyone my project for flying, and will serve as a model for my future real wings."

The next day I sent off my letter, and as the day was sunny and warm, I made a great show of ignoring my Flying Room and going outside to play. It was no use: I did not want to let go of Flyology and it evidently did not want to release me. In one of the fields east of the house, I barely avoided treading upon a dead crow lying upside down in the mud, and I confess I could not resist studying its wings. Ignoring my revulsion, I took up a stick and used it to move the wings this way and that and to roll the corpse over so I could examine the wings from above and below.

That evening I wrote to my mother about my anatomical study of the unfortunate bird, and as I sat bent over my letter, Miss Stamp cleared her throat to claim my attention. "I would like you to add a note from me."

I winced. Miss Stamp's postscripts were rarely favorable to me. "Certainly. What would you like me to say?"

"Please tell Lady Byron that I have in some things been very well satisfied with you lately, but that you often have an idle manner which does not please me so well."

"Must I tell her that?" I said, indignant. Miss Stamp might not have approved of how I spent my time, but I had certainly not been idle.

"Yes, indeed you must."

Muffling a sigh, I added the note to my letter and signed off as Carrier Pigeon, a small act of rebellion.

When my mother and her companions finally came to Bifrons a week later, I was so happy to see my mother in such good health that I nearly wept. Her cough had disappeared, her cheeks were soft and rosy, and there was a laughing light in her eyes that I had not glimpsed since we had left Turin. I was as gracious and polite to her friends as I knew how to be, but they glared at me with frank disapproval no matter what I did, even the niece, who was only a little older than myself. I quaked when I wondered what my mother had told them about me to provoke such stern, fusty, censorious glares.

After tea, while the other ladies took a turn around the garden, where they would likely take great pleasure in judging the flowers and deriding the shrubbery, my mother asked me to show her my wings. Delighted, I eagerly led her to my Flying Room, chattering as we went about new discoveries, unresolved problems, and the many practical uses for my invention I anticipated. How proud I was to show her the cables, pulleys, and harness I had arranged; to demonstrate the function of the paper wings; to explain my sketches of *Pegasus,* the steam-engine flying machine I intended to build after the paper wings were perfected.

My mother listened carefully, nodding gravely and asking a few questions, which I promptly and cheerfully answered. When she had seen everything, she took one long, appraising look around the room while I gazed up at her, beaming, anticipating praise and suggestions for improvement.

Instead she sighed heavily. "Oh, Ada," she said, her voice both troubled and tired. "The exuberance you expressed in your letters troubled me, but I dismissed it as youthful enthusiasm. Even when Miss Stamp told me your interest in flight had become a mania, I had hoped she was mistaken. But when I look around and see all this —" She turned in place, gesturing with a graceful hand, her eyebrows drawn together in worry. "I see that we have let you go too far."

"Too far?" I exclaimed. "But I haven't even finished. I haven't taken a single practice flight. I was going to jump from a low height at first, you see, from the top of a barrel or a fence post, and as my wings proved themselves I would progress to ever greater —"

"No, Ada." My mother shook her head. "You have already spent too much time on this folly. Once I believed it was a harmless diversion, but it has consumed far too many hours — days, even weeks — that would have been better spent on study and improvement."

I felt tears rising. "Don't make me stop," I choked out. "Not when I'm so close to flying."

"Ada," she admonished me, and I knew there would be no persuading her.

Miss Stamp helped me dismantle the flight apparatus, gather up my sketches and plans, and fold up the paper wings. Furious, deeply disappointed, I wanted to burn every scrap of paper, every piece of wire, but Miss Stamp objected. I cannot say I was sorry when she collected the remnants of my dream, now sorted into haphazard piles, and carried them off, putting them in safe storage, as she said, in case I wanted them later. Why I would want them when I had been forbidden to fly, or even to complete my models, I did not know, and I was too heartbroken to ask.

My mother's judgment crushed me. I admit that I had not spent as many hours upon my other studies during my investigation of Flyology, but I had mastered my lessons all the same, and I could have learned to distribute my hours more evenly if given the chance. As the days passed, I told myself that my mother had acted out of love, that she feared that my wings would fail and I would be injured or perhaps even killed. I could not say she was wrong. New inventions often failed, sometimes with disastrous results. In breaking my heart, perhaps my mother had saved my life.

I will not allow, however, that I had experienced anything deserving of the epithet "mania." Interest, certainly. Passion, yes. Enthusiasm, perhaps. But mania — never. I deny that now as I denied it then.

In the weeks that followed, I sometimes caught my mother observing me when she thought I was too distracted to notice, and the worry and disappointment in her eyes unsettled me. I resolved to prove that I was not manic, that I was as rational and self-possessed as any child of twelve and a half years who was not tainted with Byron blood.

I devoted myself anew to my lessons with Miss Stamp, and in May, when I began my formal studies of geometry, I embraced theorems and transformations with unfeigned pleasure. By the end of summer, I had taken a great interest in learning to ride, which satisfied my mother very much, for my former wariness around horses had always annoyed her.

And, as I had discovered, if my horse went swiftly enough, riding was nearly as gloriously exciting as I had imagined flying would be — although I did not share that insight with my mother, lest she denounce riding as too provocative of the imagination and forbid it as well.

Chapter Nine:
As a Wild-Born Falcon
with Clipt Wing

November 1828–January 1831

As winter came to Bifrons, I regarded the approach of my thirteenth birthday with dread and resignation, not for any superstitious reasons, but because soon thereafter, Miss Stamp would be leaving me to get married.

The wedding was held at Saint Mary's Church in Patrixbourne, a pretty setting for what was for me a bittersweet occasion. I was happy for Miss Stamp but miserable for myself, although I did my best to show only smiles and a few tears of joy.

As my governess's departure had already thrown the household into disorder, my mother must have concluded that this was as good a time as any to move to another rented residence, a large villa at Hanger Hill in the Ealing district. "I miss home," I complained as I packed my books in the large, sturdy trunk with brass fittings my mother had given me for my birthday. "Can't we move back to Kirkby Mallory instead?"

"Home is wherever we make it, and you'll like the villa," my mother replied, which did not answer my question but would have to suffice since nothing else was forthcoming. The villa was a significant improvement over Bifrons, but it was not home, not to me, and I thought it was inexplicably ridiculous that my mother should continue to rent temporary lodgings for us when she was the mistress of the spacious, comfortable, elegant, and very dear Kirkby Mallory Hall. Since my mother was so often away, wasn't it only fair that I should choose where we lived?

Unfortunately, my opinion was not sought.

As we settled into our new lodgings, I awaited with some trepidation to be introduced to my new governess. To my surprise, my mother informed me that she had decided not to hire one. Instead she had recruited a few of her most intellectual, Nonconformist friends to direct my education. Unlike many of my nurses and governesses, they admired her excessively and could be trusted to do as she bade without question.

The first, Mr. William Frend, was a mathematician and former clergyman of the Church of England who had converted to Unitarianism, which had resulted in his dismissal from Cambridge. Later he was prosecuted for publishing a tract denouncing abuses in the Church of England and condemning much of its liturgy, earning my mother's approval and admiration with his austere doctrine and the courage and dignity he had shown throughout his trials. His daughter, Miss Sophia Frend, one of my mother's closest and most trusted friends, was another of my new educational advisors. She disliked me intensely — I have no idea why — but I was unaware of this at the time, as she craved my mother's friendship so much that she hid her true feelings. Dr. William King, another devout Unitarian, and his wife, Mary, were enlisted to watch over my moral development, while Miss Arabella Lawrence, director of a school in Liverpool, supervised other subjects.

Since they were not all living with us at Hanger Hill — even now the very idea makes me shudder — most of our lessons were conducted by correspondence, meaning that I studied mostly on my own, wrote them long letters about my progress, and awaited their advice and criticism in their replies. There were many aspects of this system I enjoyed — a refreshing sense of independence, for one — but I often thought wistfully of my lessons with Miss Stamp and Miss Thorne, the companionship, the conversations, the more immediate responses to my many questions. I soon grew accustomed to the new arrangements, however, and I worked very hard, not only to please my teachers and my mother, but also to satisfy my own insatiable curiosity.

My education was cruelly interrupted in early 1829 when I contracted a terrible case of measles, which soon worsened dramatically, attacking my limbs and my sight. I suffered vicious convulsions and sudden, stabbing pains so agonizing that they took my breath away. Wretched, feverish, and helpless, I lay in my sickbed utterly powerless to resist as I became paralyzed and almost completely blind.

The fear and grief I felt as my world slowly went dark is greater than I can describe. I could no longer see my mother's face, but her worry and fear were evident in the strain in her voice as she consulted with my physicians and in her forced cheer as she read aloud to me from a chair pulled close to my bedside. I could not forget that she had stayed away when I was afflicted with chicken pox years before, but she had hurried home to nurse and comfort my grandfather on his deathbed. Even in my fevered state, I was more than capable of analyzing this evidence and drawing one bleak, terrifying conclusion.

For weeks I lingered close to death, but gradually the worst of my symptoms eased and my doctors concluded that I was out of immediate danger. Little by little my vision returned — an answer to my most ardent, desperate prayers — and I regained the use of my arms and hands, although the muscles were weak and reluctant to obey my commands. My legs were much slower to recover, rendering me bedridden for months. Autumn came before I could stand unassisted, and even then I could not walk on my own. I had to be carried up and down stairs, so rather than continuously trouble the footmen, for most of those endless days I remained isolated in my room, with Puff as my only companion. By day I gazed longingly out my window at the gardens I had once strolled through without appreciating the privilege. At night I dreamed of my long rambles through Kirkby Wood, of my climb in the foothills of Mont Blanc, and I woke with tears in my eyes.

When it became evident that I would not die, my mother decided that my lengthy convalescence afforded me an excellent opportunity to focus on my studies. I seized upon this plan like a rope thrown to one drowning, and as soon as my vision recovered enough to permit reading, I took up my books with a defiant, determined zeal. My correspondence with Miss Lawrence resumed, and every few weeks she came to Hanger Hill to tutor me in person. As my mother was often away seeking cures for her own ailments at her favorite spas, I welcomed Miss Lawrence's visits with an overabundance of gratitude that must have seemed very pitiable. I certainly pitied myself.

The sluggish pace of my recovery frustrated

me to no end, and when my mother's most esteemed doctors acknowledged that they could contrive no diagnosis to explain the persistence of my illness, I began to despair that I might remain an invalid for the rest of my life. Compounding my distress, on several occasions I overheard the physicians telling my mother that in the absence of an obvious physical cause, they suspected my lingering paralysis had a hysterical origin. This utter nonsense infuriated me. Just before the onset of my affliction, I had been devastated when I was denied the chance to fly. Why would I willingly also relinquish the ability to walk and run and ride?

In early spring of 1830, my mother surmised that a change of scene might do my health some good, so she moved us to another rented residence, Mortlake Terrace, a red-brick Georgian mansion on seven acres in the borough of Richmond upon Thames. "Why can we not return to Kirkby Mallory?" I asked petulantly as I was conveyed out the front door on an air mattress, the only remotely comfortable way I could travel.

"Mortlake Terrace is very pleasant and exceptionally healthful," my mother said, as always offering an unsatisfying, oblique reply to my persistent question. "Your room offers a splendid view of the river, and there are several footpaths on the shore above, ideal for a stroll in fair weather."

"What good are footpaths to me?" I retorted crossly as I was loaded into the coach, mattress and all, and my crutches were passed in after me. "I will not be strolling anywhere anytime soon."

My mother did not dignify my complaint with a reply, but finished supervising our departure while I reclined in the coach, silently fuming.

How impatient I had become in my infirmity, how demanding, how fractious! Not for me was the grateful stoicism of a long-suffering heroine of romance. I wanted to be strong, to run, to dance, not to languish in a sickbed, with lessons my only distraction and Puff's antics my only amusement. I was well aware that other young ladies my age were preparing to enter Society by learning dance, fashion, manners, and the sorts of accomplishments that would emphasize their refinement.

I knew, too, that the point of all this was not self-improvement, my mother's highest ambition, but to prepare them to entice and secure a husband, at the proper time and season. I, too, was expected to marry someday, but in my infirmity, the only feminine accomplishment I could pursue was music. My mother arranged for me to have lessons in singing and in playing the harp, which I took to readily, not only because I had remarkable natural talent, but also because I had little else to do but practice.

I was ambivalent about marriage, as it had certainly not worked out well for either of my parents, and looked upon it as a duty I would be expected to perform sometime in the blessedly distant future. Even so, when my few approved friends — Fanny Smith and the other daughters and nieces of my mother's acquaintances whom in my longing and loneliness I resolutely claimed as friends though we rarely met — wrote about their dance lessons and new dresses, I felt as if they were leaving me behind.

But since the allegedly healthful air of Mortlake and the views of the river Thames, which I grudgingly admitted were splendid, had not yet worked their healing magic upon my uncooperative limbs, I remained bedridden. Since I had nothing else to do, I studied, and my lessons advanced apace. I excelled at geometry and delighted in solving problems, which were to me entertaining little puzzles, and I was fascinated by a subject newly undertaken, astronomy. German and Latin were also added to my curriculum, and I delved into them with great enjoyment.

In time I began to walk about indoors on crutches, but since my doctors admonished me not to overtire myself, most of my exercise was undertaken in secret. Choosing hours when I knew the rest of the household would be preoccupied with other duties, I would hobble from my room as stealthily as I could and set off to explore our new lodgings.

One afternoon when I was feeling particularly rebellious, I invaded the sanctity of the room my mother had claimed as her study. The housemaids had sorted her papers and books efficiently and neatly. I would have been astonished had they not, since her frequent moves had given them many opportunities to practice. Even so, several items lay strewn about the desk in a less orderly fashion, as if my mother had been examining them before her departure and the maids had moved nothing when they cleaned rather than disarrange whatever indiscernible order she might have imposed.

Curious, I hobbled closer to the desk, and after glancing warily at the doorway, I let my gaze fall to the top of the desk. I could not be accused of prying if I happened to see something lying in plain sight.

The object that first drew my attention was a book produced by my father's publisher, John Murray of Albemarle Street, very recently from the pristine look of it. *"Life of Lord Byron, with His Letters and Journals, Volume One,"* I read aloud, and at once I recalled fragments of a conversation I had overheard between my mother and one of her lawyers. She and my father's best friend, Sir John Cam Hobhouse, had long fought against the publication of biographies of my father, for they would assuredly be filled with scandalous anecdotes, half-truths, and utter fabrications. In the absence of an official account of his life, however, spurious works sprang up like mushrooms after a rain. Eventually Hobhouse and Murray agreed to allow Thomas Moore to produce a biography, if only to undermine the success of a competing work they both knew would be outrageously offensive.

Balancing on one crutch, I took the leatherbound volume in hand and examined the title page and frontispiece, an engraving of what presumably was meant to be my father and two companions gazing across a lake at a view of Constantinople. I was tempted to settle into the armchair and read, but I would surely be discovered if I lingered there, and I could not take the book with me without setting off a frantic search. Reluctantly I set it down exactly where I had found it.

To the left of the books were several letters, all with the seals broken, some lying open and easily inspected, enough to tell me that my mother and my aunt Augusta were engaged in some new legal altercation about my father's marriage settlement. Their ongoing disputes bored and exasperated me, so I left the letters alone and spared not even a glance for the documents stacked beneath them.

My gaze fell next upon a small, neat pile of pamphlets in the center of the desk, and the title was enough to make me nearly tumble off my crutches — "Remarks Occasioned by Mr. Moore's Notices of Lord Byron's Life." My mother had written, and had apparently arranged to be privately published, a response to Mr. Moore's biography of my father.

I simply did not have the power to resist reading it, but in my condition I could hardly make a swift escape if someone came upon me unexpectedly. I sized up the height of the pile: How many pamphlets were there? Had my mother counted them and would she remember the number? I quickly decided that there were enough that a single pamphlet would not be missed, and so I snatched one, tucked it into my pocket, and made my awkward way from the room, thoughts racing. What had possessed my mother to respond publicly to Mr. Moore's biography, when for as long as I could remember, she had resolutely followed a policy of dignified, righteous silence, allowing her lawyers to speak for her while she remained above the fray?

In the solitude of my bedchamber, I settled into an armchair near the window, breathless from exertion, but when I retrieved the pamphlet from my pocket and began to read, my pulse only quickened. In response to whatever Mr. Moore had alleged, my mother had composed a detailed account of the events that had led to the Separation. "Domestic details ought not to be intruded on the public attention," she began, sounding very much like the Lady Byron I knew. "If, however, they *are* so intruded, the persons affected by them have a right to refute injurious charges."

She proceeded to do exactly that, describing my father's erratic behavior, her consultations with physicians, the unbearable circumstances that finally compelled her to flee Piccadilly Terrace with her infant daughter. She defended my grandparents against charges that she had parted from her husband "in perfect harmony," and that it was not until they turned her against him that she had sought a formal separation. On the contrary, until she arrived at Kirkby Mallory on the night of 15 January, Lord and Lady Noel had had been "unacquainted with the existence of any causes likely to destroy my prospects of happiness; and when I communicated to them the opinion which had been formed concerning Lord Byron's state of mind, they were most anxious to promote his restoration by every means in their power."

My heart thudded hollowly in my chest. My grandparents had wanted my mother and father to reconcile? My mother had believed he could be cured or redeemed? Never once

had they given me any indication of this —
but, of course, they had rarely spoken of my
father in my presence, not if it could be
avoided.

I read on, learning of my mother's uncertainty regarding whether my father's behavior
sprang from mental derangement or from
moral deficiency, for if the latter were the
cause, "nothing could induce me to return to
him." When Lord Byron rejected her father's
letter requesting an amicable separation,
Lady Noel had consulted the lawyer Dr. Ste-
phen Lushington, who reviewed the facts as
my grandmother presented them and concluded that while a separation would be justi-
fied, the circumstances "were not of that ag-
gravated description as to render such a
measure indispensable." After my mother had
visited him a fortnight later, however, Dr.
Lushington "was, for the first time, informed
by Lady Byron of facts utterly unknown, as I
have no doubt, to Sir Ralph and Lady Noel.
On receiving this additional information, my
opinion was entirely changed: I considered a
reconciliation impossible." Not only that, but
if a reconciliation were attempted, he could
not, "professionally or otherwise, take any
part toward effecting it."

" 'Facts utterly unknown'?" I murmured.
What were these facts? What could my
mother have confided to the lawyer that
would have caused him to entirely reverse his

opinion? What could my father have done to make the idea of reuniting him and my mother so abhorrent?

My thoughts flew to the portrait that had once hung in my grandfather's smoking and billiards room, of the heavy curtain that had concealed my father from my sight, of my mother's fears of the bad Byron and Gordon blood that flowed through my veins just as it had flowed through his. What had he done? I knew he had been unfaithful, but he must have done something infinitely worse, something unimaginable —

I realized that my cheeks were wet with tears, and I could not say when I had begun to weep. Hands trembling, I hastily wiped my face with my fingertips, folded the pamphlet, and hauled myself across the room to hide it in my wardrobe. I wanted to know, and yet I dreaded to know, so it was just as well that I could never confront my mother about these dreadful facts utterly unknown.

I could say nothing about what I had learned, nor could I ask the questions tormenting me, but the turmoil I fought to suppress manifested itself in other ways, in disobedience, impertinence, and argumentation. With my mother I was withdrawn and quick-tempered, either remaining indifferent and stubbornly mute in her presence, or arguing about nearly every word she spoke. Finally, her serenity shattered. "Your prevailing, indeed, your besetting fault at this time is a disposition to conversational litigation," she exclaimed over breakfast one morning when I contested her remark that poached eggs were more delicious than hard-boiled.

"What is 'conversational litigation'?" I asked scornfully, casting my gaze heavenward as if praying for deliverance from such an insufferable parent.

"I can give it no other name," she replied, her eyes snapping with anger and indignation. "You go to law with me more frequently than with anyone else. It is very necessary that this habit should be checked, for it is both disagreeable and inconsistent with the respect owed to me."

"There are certain *facts utterly unknown* that might explain why I disagree with you," I retorted, hardly believing my recklessness even as I spoke. But she missed the allusion, declaring that I disagreed with her only to be disagreeable. I would have been lying if I had denied it.

As the summer passed, I began to regret my impudence. I could not deny that in recent weeks I had sought out argument for argument's sake, but only with my mother. My first inclination was to blame the pamphlet, but when I forced myself to reflect unflinchingly upon my behavior, I realized that whenever I took up any issue, I spoke about it with as much anxiety and vehemence as if the fate of the nation depended upon my words.

For this, I blamed my illness. Throughout my lengthy convalescence, I had lived a quiet and unvaried life for the sake of my health, with so little stimulation and activity that every small matter — and except for the pamphlet they had all been small matters — took on an increased significance, so that the most minor of incidents became to me issues as important as the French Revolution had been to Charles X. I could not expect anyone else to understand why I argued about what were to them the merest trifles but were to me equivalent to the loss of a kingdom.

I resolved to do better, and as summer faded into autumn, I amended my behavior sufficiently so that the tension in the household eased, for until then it had felt like a cord stretched between two horses pulling in opposite directions. I was not perfect, and some days were better than others, but over time I observed that my conduct, my studies, and my health were steadily progressing in the right direction.

By late November, I had regained enough strength and balance that I was able to dispense with the crutches and move about quite well with a cane. A fortnight later, a day before my fifteenth birthday, a specially booked coach delivered a package addressed to me in a hand that seemed familiar, yet not enough so that I could identify the sender. " 'To the Honorable Miss Byron, with every kind and affectionate wish,' " I read aloud. "Oh, there is a smaller note below: 'With Lady Byron's permission.' "

"It is from your aunt Augusta," my mother said, glancing at the package as she seated herself in the chair facing mine. Both were drawn close to the fireplace to ward off the chill of that frosty morning.

"Do I have your permission to open it?" I asked.

"To open it, yes," she replied, leaving unspoken the question of whether I would be allowed to keep it.

Carefully I cut the string and unwrapped the paper. Inside I discovered an exquisite prayer book, beautifully bound, with "Ada" embossed on the cover in Old English letters. "How lovely," I said, moved. I rarely corresponded with my aunt and saw her almost never, which made the gift as rare and meaningful as it was unexpected. "May I keep it?" I remembered to ask.

My mother held out her hand and I placed the book in it. After opening the cover, turning the first few pages, and giving it a quick inspection from front to back, she nodded and returned it to me.

As I paged through the prayer book alone in my bedchamber that evening, I imagined my aunt arranging for it to be bound and embossed. I grew wistful thinking how unfortunate it was that I did not get to see her, my only aunt, more frequently, and that I scarcely knew her children, my only cousins. The eldest, Georgiana, had married shortly before my mother and I had embarked on our tour of the Continent; we had not attended the ceremony, although I believe we had both been invited and my mother had sent a gift. Georgiana and her husband had moved into Bifrons soon after we had moved out, their rent paid by my generous mother, and one of her younger sisters, Medora, had recently joined them there for her sister's confinement, as she was expecting her first child. The sisters were a few years older than I, but it was a shame that we were not friends. Perhaps they had all the friends they wanted, and they had each other and three more siblings as well, but I had almost no one — only my mother, Puff, and an ever-shifting cast of tutors and servants. I longed for siblings, and cousins were certainly close enough to satisfy me, but my mother and my aunt Augusta had become estranged, and I knew my mother would disapprove if I suddenly sought to strengthen our strained ties of kinship.

Christmas should have been the perfect time to invite family to visit, but I dared not suggest it, and Georgiana's delicate condition would have made travel impossible even if my mother had consented. A few of my mother's friends joined us for the holidays instead, but as usual they were a sour, judgmental flock of old hens who evidently defined the word "celebrate" much differently than I did. Thankfully, they departed before Epiphany.

One snowy evening, as I sat alone in the drawing room with Puff curled up in my lap, stroking her soft fur and making mental notes for a letter I owed Miss Lawrence, my mother entered carrying two books. She seated herself gracefully on the sofa nearest me and, as if it were the most ordinary thing in the world, said, "I thought I might study a few of Lord Byron's poems tonight. Would you like me to read them aloud?"

For a moment I was too dumbfounded to do anything but stare at her. "Yes, please," I managed to say. "That would be very nice."

She read first the exquisite verses on Greece from *The Giaour,* which I found lovely, moving, and passionately expressed, and when she prompted me for my opinion, I told her so. Next she read "Fare Thee Well," which afterward I considered an odd choice, for she must have known that my father's lamentations about his doomed love for my mother and his anguish about his separation from me would discomfit me at the very least. I admired her, however, for reading from *Don Juan,* which she called only "the satire," as if wanting to make absolutely sure that I noted the genre and remembered its conventions.

"It's very amusing and cleverly written," I said when she had finished, and then, because I knew she needed to hear it, I added, "but Donna Inez doesn't resemble you in the slightest. Are you sure he didn't mean to portray Miss Sophia Frend instead?"

An involuntary laugh escaped her. "No, Ada, dear. Lord Byron never knew Miss Frend."

"Oh. I suppose not, then." I frowned thoughtfully, then shrugged. "Well, it *is* poetry, after all, not biography."

She smiled, relieved and gratified. "Yes," she said. "That's so."

She set aside the books then, and we chatted about other things with an ease and amiability that rarely graced our conversations in those days. I could not know if we would ever again read my father's poems together, but her willingness to do so that night gave me hope that perhaps she did not despise my father as much as she seemed to. Maybe she loved me and my Byron blood more than I had realized.

CHAPTER TEN:
WHO WOULD BE FREE
THEMSELVES MUST
STRIKE THE BLOW

January–December 1831

How I wish I could say that after that night, my mother and I achieved a new understanding and we became the dearest of friends and best of companions, but that was not so. I was a precocious, lonely, excitable fifteen-year-old girl, and she was the wise and virtuous Lady Annabella Noel Byron. Conflict between us was inevitable.

I willingly accept responsibility for most of our quarrels and the pervasive mood of discord, for I was certainly no model of filial respect and obedience. While the cane was a vast improvement over the crutches, I felt frustrated and constrained by my lingering physical limitations, and instead of enduring them with courage and patience, I waged war against them, and when I lost one battle after another, I became ill-tempered and bitter.

"I would be more comfortable at Kirkby Mallory," I complained one morning when I had woken up to discover my legs unexpectedly aching and stiff, so difficult to move without pain that my mother had come to help the maid dress me. "The corridors are wider and the air more healthful. I'm sure I would be restored to full health much faster if I could convalesce there."

"You will convalesce here," my mother said firmly, and when I continued to grumble under my breath, she sighed dramatically and left the maid to finish the task of dressing me.

"Why do you continue to plague her about returning to Kirkby Mallory?" the maid rebuked me as she took up the comb and began running it through my dark curls, none too gently. "Don't you care about the welfare of your Noel cousins? Not even Robert? You seemed fond of him once."

"I am fond of him still," I said, "but what do the Noel cousins have to do with this?"

"Everything," she said, incredulous. "Your mother has given them the living of the estate."

My heart plummeted. "Why would she do that?"

"Because she is generous and kindhearted, and Kirkby Mallory ought to be theirs anyway." She resumed combing my hair, tugging painfully when the tines caught on a tangle. "The Reverend Thomas Noel is Lord Wentworth's illegitimate son. Your grandmother, Lady Noel, rest her soul, prevented her brother from marrying the mother. If she had not objected, and they had wed, Lord Wentworth's estate would have gone to his son rather than his sister."

"You mean to say," I said, stunned, "that my mother inherited an estate that should have gone to Robert Noel and his brothers?"

"Of course that's not what I mean," she scolded. "The very idea! As a natural son Thomas Noel had no legal claim to the estate. Your grandmother inherited it rightfully, and your benevolent mother has chosen to provide for her Noel cousins. That includes making her cousin Charles Noel her agent for Kirkby Mallory, and buying her cousin Edward that estate in Greece, and paying for her cousins Robert and Thomas to be educated. You know all this, or you should, for you'll have to decide what to do with Kirkby Mallory when it comes to you, pray God that's a long time off."

I understood it in only the vaguest sense, and no wonder, for my mother would not have entrusted to me the secret of a family scandal. I was stunned to learn that Robert's father was a natural child, and I felt foolish for not figuring that out long ago, or at least questioning how the Noel cousins were related to us. I was relieved to know that Robert and his brother would be provided for, and I should have been proud of my mother for looking out for them, but as if I were determined to be contrary, I resented her for giving my childhood home to someone else. *Her* childhood home was Seaham, of course, so she did not cherish Kirby Mallory as I did.

I knew then that I would never again call Kirkby Mallory home.

In my unhappiness and isolation, I developed odd habits, which I now look back upon with embarrassment interwoven with sympathetic amusement for my younger self. I would not sleep in my bed, preferring to wrap myself up in a blanket or rug and curl up on the floor. When visitors called and I was obliged to greet them, I refused to embrace anyone, even when prompted. I would kiss no one but my mother, and even she would receive no more than a grudging peck on the cheek. I developed peculiar routines when it came to meals, eating far too much one day, rejecting anything but water the next.

"You get this from your father," my mother declared one evening at dinner, after I had pushed aside a plate of perfectly roasted duck. "He always vacillated between fat and slim, and he would adopt the most restrictive diets when he wished to lose a few stone."

"I don't get it *only* from my father," I mumbled sullenly, but when she shot me a sharp look, I said no more. Thanks to my many months of inactivity, I had grown quite plump, and I was determined to become slim again and do all I could to thwart Miss Chaloner's dire prediction that I would never be pretty. This, I thought, was an admirable goal, and my mother of all people should not criticize me for it. Perhaps she was unaware that everyone in the household knew about her own peculiar habit of gorging herself on mutton, her favorite food, and then going out onto the lake or the sea in a small boat until the rocking motion sickened her enough so that it all came back up again. Compared to that, my refusal of meals now and then seemed well above reproach.

Eventually my mother became so exasperated with me that she took me to a phrenologist. I was somewhat skeptical of this new science, although I was intrigued by the underlying theory that the brain was composed, like the rest of the body, of different organs, each associated with a particular faculty even as the eyes were for sight and the lungs were for breath. It seemed plausible that just as a laborer would develop broad shoulders and bulging arms by strengthening his muscles, exercising certain aspects of the mind would alter the shape of the skull. Phrenologists claimed they could measure the development of the organs by studying the subject's head, noting the bulges that signified the relatively well-developed organs, and the dips over those that were less developed. Thus it would be possible to discover a person's character by examining his head by touch, noting the locations of bumps and dips, and comparing these to a "phrenological map," a porcelain model of a head with the regions of the brain's organs drawn and labeled on the scalp.

My mother arranged for a consultation with Dr. James De Ville, the most prominent practical phrenologist and maker of phrenological casts in London. I would have agreed to the examination if only for the diversion of an outing, but by the time we set out for Town, I had become quite curious as to what the doctor might find.

I adored London, perhaps because I did not know it as well then as I do now, and because my visits were a rare treat in those days, when I relied upon my mother to take me and I still struggled with my awkward gait and my cane. I did not care if my lingering infirmity attracted curious glances, but my mother's frowns betrayed her embarrassment at my imperfections. That did bother me, but not enough to compel me to stay at home and out of sight.

The city had undergone astonishing growth since I had lived at Piccadilly Terrace as an infant, with new residences and industrial buildings spreading past Greenwich Park, and the gleaming steel rails of the London and Greenwich railway line slicing through the district of Bermondsey. As we approached, I glimpsed the tall masts of a hundred ships rising above the bustling wharfs, the scattering of chimneys in all directions, the church steeples in the City and the East End reaching higher yet, and rising above it all, the magnificent white dome of Saint Paul's Cathedral, the paired columns of the West Front flanking the classical portico. All this I observed through a dense cloud of smoke and coal dust, which seemed particularly thick and choking compared to the fresh country air of Richmond upon Thames.

The streets swarmed with carriages and wagons, oxen and sheep, men on horseback and people on foot, children darting here and there and courting danger with every step, apprentices hurrying off on important business for their masters, aristocrats in the fashionable boroughs and working men and women everywhere else, their attire announcing their professions — a drover here, a washerwoman there. The smell of sewage, manure, and rot was oppressive, but with the aid of a handkerchief pressed to my nose and mouth, I endured it.

Our carriage took us through the busy streets to Dr. De Ville's establishment at 367 Strand in Westminster. A butler received us, but the phrenologist himself joined us almost as soon as we crossed the threshold. He was a square, solid man, with curly light brown hair, a small, neat mustache, and the broad, strong hands of a bricklayer, not that I had known many bricklayers.

"Lady Byron, Miss Byron, welcome," he greeted us, bowing. "Your visit is truly an honor."

He escorted us to a drawing room, where he invited me to sit in a comfortable leather chair with a low back. I seated myself and set my cane within reach upon the floor, suddenly nervous. I grew even more anxious when he put his face close to mine and subjected me to intense scrutiny, as if he were studying an object rather than a girl. He circled the chair, peering at my head from all angles, and when he paused to take notes, a surreptitious glance told me that he was evaluating the overall shape of my head.

"Now, Miss Byron," he addressed me suddenly, the first he had spoken since the examination began, except for the occasional "Hmm" or "Right, then." "At this point, I'm obliged to feel your scalp. You might find it an unfamiliar and unsettling sensation, but your mother will be right here, and if you ever feel too uncomfortable to continue, say the word and I'll stop."

"Very well, Doctor," I said in a small voice. He had an unusual way of speaking, unlike any other doctor I had met. I could not quite place his accent, but he spoke more like a workingman than a gentleman. I rather liked him for that.

"I must also warn you," he continued

gravely, "that I will almost certainly disarrange your hair."

I muffled a laugh. "That's fine. I don't care about my hair."

My mother gave a little sniff, and I knew she was thinking that she wished I cared much more about my hair than I did — my hair, and my attire, and the pleasant feminine ways that I neglected to cultivate, since they would go to waste in my sickroom.

Dr. De Ville rubbed his palms together to warm his hands. "Miss Byron, if I may."

I nodded.

He placed his fingertips upon my scalp, and I sat very still as he explored the geography of my skull. His touch was gentle and pleasant, and not at all intrusive, and I wondered if this was how Puff felt when I stroked her fur. From time to time I stole glances at his face, which was a study in focus and concentration, but nothing I glimpsed there gave me any indication of what he might be learning about my character, qualities that perhaps even I was unaware of.

After a time, he lifted his hands from my head, thanked me with a courteous nod, and returned to his desk, where he wiped his hands on a handkerchief and began writing down his observations. I threw a questioning look over my shoulder to my mother, but her gaze was fixed on the phrenologist. In her pale face and furrowed brow, I saw that whereas I awaited the results with cheerful curiosity, my mother felt only apprehension.

Soon the doctor set his pen aside, straightened, nodded to my mother, and gestured to the chair where I sat. "Lady Byron, if you will?"

I reached for my cane and rose, but as I went to exchange places with my mother, she frowned at me briefly and looked to the phrenologist. "Dr. De Ville, would it be possible for my daughter to wait elsewhere during my examination?"

"Certainly." He bowed, left the room, and returned moments later with a woman I assumed was his housekeeper. "Miss Byron, Mrs. Halsey would be happy to offer you a cup of tea in the dining room, if you'd like."

"Thank you." I could hardly refuse such an obvious dismissal. I nodded to the doctor and my mother and followed the housekeeper from the room.

Mrs. Halsey made me an excellent cup of tea, offered me a biscuit, and kindly kept me company while I waited. We had a very nice chat about cats, and before long the doctor appeared and invited me back to the drawing room to hear the results of my examination.

My mother was seated on the sofa, and when she smiled brightly and beckoned me to sit beside her, I knew that she had already heard her own results and was very pleased with them. My stomach lurched slightly as I braced myself on my cane and sat down, eyeing the doctor warily as he reviewed his notes, the pages spread out before him on the desk near the porcelain phrenological map.

"Lady Byron, Miss Byron," he finally said, "my results confirm something I'm sure you already knew: Miss Byron has a truly remarkable mind."

I felt a wave of relief, and when my mother threw me a proud, exhilarated glance, I smiled nervously back.

"Her intellectual faculties are highly developed," he said, taking a slender wooden baton in hand and indicating a region on the phrenological map. "Also highly developed are her faculties for Imagination, Wonder, Harmony, and Constructiveness. In short, Miss Byron, I'm sure this will surprise exactly no one, but you have the head of a poet."

I felt my mother grow rigid beside me. "What do you mean, Doctor?" she said tightly.

"Only that she has precisely the mental acumen one would expect a poet to possess." He shrugged. "Of course, without sufficient interest and proper guidance, the faculties will manifest themselves in other ways. She could grow up to be an excellent hostess and letter writer, for example, without ever realizing her latent potential."

"I do write a lot of letters," I ventured. "I've had little opportunity to be a hostess, though."

Abruptly my mother rose, startling the phrenologist, who quickly scrambled to his feet. "Thank you for your opinion, Doctor," she said. "You've certainly given me much to consider. Now we must bid you good day. Come, Ada."

She left the room, and I hobbled along after her on my cane. Murmuring an apology, Dr. De Ville hurried past me to catch up with my mother, and I arrived at the front door just in time to hear her bidding him a curt good-bye.

The carriage had taken us halfway home before she finally spoke, as if she were thinking aloud. "I don't understand it. He found my organ of Sensitiveness to be so pronounced that he wanted to call for immediate medical treatment. How could he so accurately read my head and yet be so wrong about —"

When she said nothing more, I said, "Logically, we could conclude that he wasn't wrong about me."

"I don't accept that," she snapped. "He must have missed something. Perhaps he's not accustomed to diagnosing young girls. Your species *is* remarkably difficult to comprehend."

"So I've been told," I replied glumly, but she did not seem to hear me.

In the days that followed, letters flew

between my mother and her usual cohort of friends, and when they visited, I overheard myself discussed in hushed, incredulous voices. I was never supposed to have turned out poetical. Even my genius poet father had not wanted that for me. What had the point of my education been if not to suppress the imagination and enhance the intellect? Had all of my mother's tireless efforts to bring me up in her rational, virtuous image been for nothing?

"Dr. De Ville made a mistake," Miss Montgomery said flatly, sipping her tea. "That's all there is to it. You could not have failed, my dear Lady Byron. It's simply inconceivable."

"Perhaps Ada shifted in her seat during the examination," said Miss Frend.

Naturally she would blame me.

"Perhaps," my mother mused. Unwilling to hear myself further maligned, I crept silently away, as much as one could creep balanced on a cane.

It was with more resignation than surprise that I accepted my mother's announcement a few days later that we would be paying Dr. De Ville a second visit so that he might investigate certain anomalies in my head. "In my head or in his diagnosis?" I queried, somewhat annoyed. "If there's been a mistake, my head didn't make it."

"Of course I meant in the diagnosis. You parse words like the meanest solicitor."

"Evidence of my Intellectual and Constructiveness faculties working together, no doubt."

She brought the conversation to a halt with the oft-declared truth that sometimes she did not know what to do with me, and that she hoped someday I would be blessed with a daughter exactly like myself.

So we returned to London and to the offices at 367 Strand, where an understandably anxious Dr. De Ville examined me more assiduously than before. I sat perfectly motionless in my chair, impersonating as best I could a Greek marble statue, just as Miss Montgomery had admonished me to do in a very sermonic letter.

Afterward my mother and I sat side by side on the sofa again while the doctor studied his notes. "I see where the difficulty arose," he announced after a long, tense quarter of an hour. "I did accurately measure the pattern of bumps and dips in my original examination, but there were other factors I didn't take into account."

"What factors?" my mother prompted.

"Language, for example. While there's no dip above that organ, there's no swelling either, which indicates that this faculty is no more or less prominent than the average. Music and mathematics, however, are strongly indicated by the overall shape of the head, and the diagnosis ought to reflect that."

My mother inhaled deeply, her shoulders squared, her face perfectly calm. "And by this you mean that her organs of Imagination, Wonder, and Harmony do not lend themselves to poetry, but rather to music and mathematics?"

"Indeed. The two are more closely related than most people realize."

My mother smiled. "Of course. It makes perfect sense."

"I do adore music and mathematics," I ventured, "and I had never intended to be a poet."

It was precisely the correct thing to say, apparently, because the doctor heaved a sigh of relief and my mother beamed. I watched them congratulate themselves as he escorted us to the door, hiding my amusement. Why should they not be pleased? They both had gotten exactly what they wanted from repeating the examination. For my part, I had been given another outing to London, so I would not complain.

Privately, though, I scorned them both for interpreting the evidence to conform to the conclusion they wanted, and I remained skeptical of phrenology ever after. My mother, on the other hand, left Dr. De Ville's office wholly convinced of its validity. It had confirmed what she already knew to be true, and therefore it must be a legitimate science. She began to study phrenology in earnest and to attend demonstrations of its practical applications, and she developed the custom of evaluating everyone she met according to the shape of his or her head. She did not go so far as to ask new acquaintances if she might feel their scalps for lumps and dips; that was a privilege reserved for her closest friends.

And what friends they were. I did not care for the women my mother chose as her companions, but how I envied her for having them. I had spent time in the company of my own precious few and maternally sanctioned friends only rarely before my illness struck, and when my vision failed, I had been unable to write to them from my sickbed for many long weeks. Another sad consequence of my affliction was that quite a few of my friends disappeared from my life while I was ill. Others were more faithful, including dear George Byron, whom I still thought of as a younger brother, and my witty, charming friend Fanny Smith.

A few months after my excursion in the world of phrenology, on 10 December 1831, Fanny wrote me an amusing, one might even say cheeky, letter on the occasion of my sixteenth birthday. "My Dear Ada," she began, "I wish you many happy returns of this day, and hope that as it is your birthday, you will begin seriously to think about walking with your *own* legs, instead of borrowing wooden ones, and that your next birthday will not see you still a Cripple . . ."

No one wished for that more fervently than I, and I exercised faithfully throughout the winter so that I might dispense with cane and crutches once and for all — and acquire the graceful slimness required of any young lady who aspired to beauty. But I devoted myself with even greater alacrity to nurturing my active and fertile mind, which thrived, unencumbered, as if to defy the failures of my body.

CHAPTER ELEVEN: BUT SWEETER STILL THAN THIS, THAN THESE, THAN ALL, IS FIRST AND PASSIONATE LOVE

April 1832–March 1833

By April I could walk quite well on my own, and I was obliged to resort to the cane only if I had imprudently overexerted myself the previous day. My mother decided that I was strong enough to endure another move, and before I had time to formulate a well-reasoned argument for returning to Kirkby Mallory without displacing her cousin as the estate agent, she leased Fordhook, an elegant villa on the outskirts of Ealing Common. Fordhook had once been the home of Henry Fielding, author of the immensely popular novel *Tom Jones* and other stories of seventeenth-century manners and debauchery, none of which my mother permitted me to read.

My mother arranged for several tutors to instruct me, each in his or her own particular field of study. I studied French, German, Latin, history, geography, philosophy, natural science, music (which I adored), and mathematics of every sort (which I adored even more). I excelled in geometry, astonishing my tutor and pleasing my mother immeasurably. I have no doubt that her approbation compelled me to work even harder, to progress more swiftly, to master ever more difficult concepts. If she had expressed as much approval for my advancement in geography, perhaps I might have gone on to become a celebrated cartographer or famous explorer instead.

There were days I would have happily given almost anything to escape Fordhook and set off on a journey to the remotest regions of the globe, for my mother had enlisted three of her most trusted, most suspicious longtime friends to watch over me during her frequent absences. Between the three of them, Miss Mary Montgomery, Miss Frances Carr, and Miss Selina Doyle — Fanny's aunt, with none of my friend's kindness and charm — contrived to keep me under constant surveillance. They noted the time I rose from bed, and if I was a minute late, they called me indolent. They studied my plate at mealtimes; if I finished all I had been served, I was gluttonous, and if I left more than a few polite mouthfuls, I was wasteful. If I did not follow instructions the moment they were issued, I was willful. If I did not humbly thank them for their criticism, I was bold and proud and arrogant.

What I resented most about their constant scrutiny was how they robbed me of my contemplative solitude. I have mentioned my pervasive loneliness so often that you might assume I hated being alone, but that was not so. I cherished quiet, uninterrupted hours that I could fill up with my thoughts — often mathematical, occasionally metaphysical, sometimes merely whimsical — but my mother's friends could not bear to see me thus idle, as they perceived it. Perhaps they assumed I was plotting some mischief. If they came upon me lost in reverie, they would order me to take up a prayer book or a pen or needle and thread, work they understood. I gritted my teeth and obeyed, longing for bedtime, when I could lie alone in the darkness and think as much as I liked. They only rarely cracked the door and peered inside to make sure I had not gone astray.

Every day it was the same. If two of the oppressive trio had their eyes upon me, the third was busily writing a report full of recriminations to my mother, and if only one of them was watching me, the other two were surely off somewhere discussing how dreadful, willful, disobedient, and disrespectful I was. They could not fathom how a lady so wise, so good, so pious, and so admirable as Lady Byron could have produced a child as contemptible as myself. The obvious culprit was the influence of my bad Byron blood, for which my mother was blameless.

They were each unmarried, and so, unencumbered by the burden of raising their own children, they had enjoyed an abundance of time in which to contemplate how other women ought to raise theirs. Even now I feel my bitterness rising when I remember how they never gave me a moment's peace, how their accusing, condemning stares followed me everywhere, how they stalked me and crouched and waited to pounce the moment I committed the slightest error. They hated me like poison — why, I cannot say, unless they were jealous of my kinship to my mother, something they could never take from me nor earn for themselves. I have readily admitted that I was far from a perfect child, but they invented and exaggerated stories about me without scruple, as if they sought to drive a wedge between my mother and me. So relentlessly did those odious women hound me that I dubbed them the Three Furies, if only in my own thoughts and in letters to Fanny Smith. I heartily despised them.

I was granted a slight reprieve from their constant scrutiny whenever my mother returned to Fordhook, for the Furies would much rather spend their time admiring her than glaring at me. Unfortunately, her visits invariably meant at least one conference in her study where I was presented with their charges: willfulness, rudeness, idleness, spitefulness, and a whole host of other offenses.

"I've done nothing wrong," I protested, time and again. "They simply hate me and want you to hate me too."

"That is nonsense, Ada," my mother reproached me. "These are good Christian women and they do not lie."

"They exaggerate and embellish, then. Ask them to be specific. Demand exact quotes. I can't defend myself against these generalities!"

But my protests only made her more certain of my guilt. Every conference ended with me exhausted, resigned, and mumbling promises to do better.

My only real escape from the Furies was the occasional trip to London my mother treated me to, sometimes overnight, more often just for the day. I was getting about so well by then that I was usually able to leave my cane at home. Perhaps in my absence, my mother's friends glowered at the cane and wrote scathing reports about its idleness.

In early August, I enjoyed a fortnight's liberation from my jailers when my mother took me to Brighton, one of her favorite seaside resorts in Sussex. We strolled along the beaches, attended concerts, spent leisurely hours reading, and, to my immeasurable joy, went riding. I had not sat a horse for ages, and so at first some of my childhood nervousness reemerged, but my riding master was capable and reassuring, and before long I was comfortable and happy in the saddle. My mounts came in every color — black, gray, chestnut — all equally graceful, beautiful, and strong. Once, after my mother observed me circling round a corner at a canter, she told me, "I believe that was the first time I have ever seen you holding the reins entirely to my satisfaction. Well done, daughter."

"Thank you, Mama," I replied, inordinately pleased by the rare compliment.

While in Brighton, my mother arranged for me to begin guitar lessons, which she said would provide a pleasant accompaniment to my singing. My master was a Spaniard of high rank, Count Urraea, who had been reduced to poverty and expelled from his country along with many other unfortunate refugees. He played with exquisite beauty, and I marveled at his ability to produce the effect of a full band or orchestra, including harp and castanets, from his deceptively simple instrument. I would have declared that his deft, supple hands or at least his guitar had been enchanted by fairies, if I had thought my mother would have been amused rather than annoyed by the fancy.

If only the Queen of Fairies had spirited away my mother's friends before we returned to Fordhook, but alas, they had dug themselves in deep, and there would be no uprooting them, only a temporary pruning. They were present for my seventeenth birthday, but they departed to torment their own families for the Christmas season, and so I celebrated very merrily indeed, playing with Puff, singing and playing Christmas carols on my guitar, breathing freely and sleeping soundly as I had not been able to do since returning from Brighton.

Early in the New Year, my mother decided that I should add chemistry and shorthand to my studies, and she hired two new tutors to instruct me. A retired chemist, gruff but brilliant, instructed me via frequent letters and weekly meetings at Fordhook, where he guided me through instructive and entertaining experiments. The tutor of shorthand, Mr. William Turner, was decades younger but quite accomplished in his own right. He was earnest and patient, even when I became distracted and began sketching Puff or a vase of flowers instead of forming the quick-flowing symbols I was supposed to master.

I don't remember when it was that I first noticed how handsome Mr. Turner was, how his brown eyes shone when he was proud of my accomplishments, how his golden hair fell in a silken wave over his brow when he concentrated, how a charming dimple appeared in his right cheek when he smiled. I endeavored to make him smile as often as I could for the pleasure of watching the dimple appear and vanish and appear again, like a glimpse of the sun through clouds on a stormy day.

We always chatted briefly before our lessons began and for a few moments afterward, but I longed to know more about him. As the weeks passed, I teased out of him that at twenty he was but three years older than myself, that he had studied at London University, that his elder brother had been appointed the first professor of chemistry there, that he was saving his wages to further his education, and that at present he lived with his parents, elder sister, and younger brothers not two miles from Fordhook.

"Do you have a sweetheart?" I inquired innocently.

That elusive dimple appeared and vanished. "No, Miss Byron, I do not have a sweetheart."

"Do you wish to have one?"

He held my gaze for a long moment, smiling faintly, both wary and amused. "If I would happen to meet an amiable young woman who finds me tolerable, I would have no objection."

His words brought a rush of heat to my cheeks, and I found myself compelled to look away. I took a deep breath and addressed myself to my copybook, but after that, whenever our eyes happened to meet, I felt a strange, unfamiliar, tremulous warmth in my chest and in my stomach, so that it was exquisitely unbearable to hold his gaze too long.

Mr. Turner began arriving earlier for our lessons, giving us more time to chat before our formal lesson began, and he often lingered afterward, readily accepting my mother's offer of a cup of tea if she came looking for me in her study and found him still there. "He's a very industrious young man," she told me approvingly one evening at supper. "Far too many young men in his position dash off as soon as the clock strikes the hour. I'm glad he remains until he's certain you've mastered the lesson."

"I am too," I said, taking a quick sip of water to conceal an unexpected stirring of disquiet.

In the days that followed, I could almost laugh aloud at how my least rigorous subject had suddenly become the most important lesson of my day. Even mathematics seemed dull compared to my hours with Mr. Turner, during which I admired his graceful fingers holding the pen, or studied his hands as they made strokes of careless beauty and perfection. Often as I practiced by tracing his marks, I thought I felt his gaze upon me, but if I turned my head, I found his eyes on my pages, his brow furrowed in concentration. Disappointed, I would resume my work, only to feel his gaze light upon me anew.

Once I thought I felt his hand lightly touch my hair where the dark curls tumbled down my back, but that could have been the invention of a wistful imagination. I had enjoyed precious few friendships and little affection in my seventeen years, and I remembered well the painful prediction that I would never be pretty. However much I longed for Mr. Turner to be my friend — and more than a friend — it was impossible to imagine that he might feel the same for me.

As my shorthand improved — for I wanted so much to please Mr. Turner that I made sure to learn despite my distraction — a part of each lesson was given over to dictation. He would read aloud to me from a newspaper or a book, and I would jot down the words and phrases as he spoke. Sometimes he stood by the window, where the light caught the gold in his hair; other times he would walk back and forth in front of me, and it was very difficult not to glance up from my work and admire his form in passing, as my chair put me at a particularly advantageous height.

One frosty February afternoon, he was reading aloud a description of a ball when he interrupted himself to ask why I was shaking my head.

"Was I?" I said, surprised. "I didn't mean to. It's only that I don't remember the quadrille in quite that way."

"How do you remember it?"

"A trifle more spirited, I suppose. Not so staid."

He laughed. "A spirited quadrille. What an intriguing notion."

"It's not so impossible," I protested. "What would you know about it?"

He regarded me with amusement. "Miss Byron, I have danced a quadrille before."

I felt heat rising in my cheeks. "How was I to know? I didn't take you for a dancer."

He smiled, set down the newspaper, and held out his arms. "Allow me to prove it." When I hesitated, he said, "You can't imply that I'm graceless and awkward without giving me the chance to defend myself the best way I can."

I rose and let him take me in his arms, and, humming a brisk, cheerful tune, he led us through a few measures of the dance. I was keenly aware of my hand in his, the touch of his palm on the small of my back. My head grew light and I felt dizzier than the simple turns could account for.

Abruptly he halted, dropped my hands, and stepped back from me. "I hope I've proven my point," he said, his voice seeming to catch in his throat.

Quickly I returned to my seat to disguise how I trembled. "You have, and I hope I have proven mine."

"Yes, you're quite right. A quadrille can be jaunty." He gave me a little bow. "Please accept my apologies."

"Only if you accept mine," I said, attempting lightness. "I was terribly wrong to malign you so viciously, and I beg your forgiveness."

He smiled, and there was that dimple again, and I almost couldn't breathe.

There was no dancing the next day or the one after that, but by the third day we seemed to have returned to level ground. As our lesson drew to a close, we somehow stumbled onto the topic of practical uses for shorthand. "Perhaps someday I'll take dictation from King William and Queen Adelaide," I remarked, smiling at the image this produced in my mind's eye.

His eyebrows rows. "You're nurturing an ambition to become a court scribe?"

"Are there court scribes anymore?" I teased right back. "Has a lady ever been one? No, I only said that because my mother hopes to present me to the king and queen in May. This will be my first London Season."

"Ah, yes. The Season." He nodded, and with an abundance of nonchalance, he added, "They'll be marrying you off to some lucky gentleman soon, I presume."

"Not too soon, I hope," I said, more vehemently than I intended. Composing myself, I forced a smile and said, "The hunt begins in May. Don't tell my mother I said this, but I fervently hope I'll fail to capture a husband for a few seasons."

"Your secret is safe with me." He too tried to smile, but he looked thoroughly unhappy. "Well, Miss Byron, here's to failure in the immediate future and eventual success."

"Hear, hear," I replied, wondering what I should read into his consternation at the prospect of my marriage to some eligible gentleman. Perhaps nothing at all. Perhaps he only regretted the imminent loss of his wages.

Spring came early to Fordhook that year, and whenever the weather was fair, we took our lessons outside to the garden. My mother was away, and even with the Three Furies peeking around hedgerows and glaring over fences at us, I felt an ease and freedom in her absence and a thrill of anticipation in Mr. Turner's company that I had never felt with anyone else.

Sometimes in the middle of our lessons, we drifted from the subject at hand and began to converse like friends instead. He spoke of his family and of his plans to continue his studies at Cambridge and become a professor of literature. "I should like to become a professor of mathematics," I remarked, mostly to make him smile, for there were no lady professors at Cambridge, or Oxford, or anywhere else that I knew of. "Do you think that would be possible?"

When he looked at me, I saw unguarded admiration in his eyes. "Miss Byron, I do believe that you could be the first. The only problem is that —"

"What?" I prompted, dreading that he would say I was not clever enough.

He shrugged, embarrassed. "I was going to say that your beauty would be a most wonderful distraction to your male pupils, but I thought better of saying it, because it sounds like empty flattery, although it isn't. It isn't, and —" He hesitated as if reconsidering whatever it was he had intended to say. "Well, if they can't keep their minds on their studies, that's their problem to resolve, not yours."

I felt all aglow — desired and desirable, bright and lovely and intriguing. No one else but my loyal friend Fanny Smith had ever called me beautiful. "It is a good thing you didn't say it," I teased, basking in the warmth of his gaze, "because you're right; it does ring false. A future professor of literature ought to have a better way with words."

He smiled at me, his eyes shining, until suddenly his glance shifted somewhere behind me. I looked over my shoulder, and there stood Miss Montgomery about three yards away, taking an avid interest in a juniper bush.

By unspoken agreement, Mr. Turner and I resumed our lesson, but I felt Miss Montgomery's glare boring into the back of my skull as if she were trying to carve new dips for the phrenologist to read with the sheer force of her antipathy.

One afternoon, an icy rain kept us indoors. We had just finished our lesson when Miss Carr entered the room carrying my mother's ledger. "Mr. Turner, if you please," she said primly, "may I have a moment to discuss your remittance and your schedule for the rest of the spring? Lady Byron wished me to make arrangements to continue Miss Byron's studies, if we can come to an agreement."

"Certainly," Mr. Turner said, sparing me a rueful grimace, timed perfectly so the Fury did not glimpse it.

As she set the ledger on a table at the other end of the room, Mr. Turner hurried over to assist her into her chair. "Ada," she called to me when she was settled, "this does not concern you. Proceed with your geography."

I plucked my geography book from the pile before me, biting my lips together to hold back the observation that if they were discussing my lessons with my tutor, it most certainly did concern me. I tried to read, but Mr. Turner's smooth tenor enticed my attention away from the page. I wondered if he sang. He seemed to have the voice for it. I watched him, smiling faintly, their conversation fading as I imagined us singing a soaring duet together.

"Ada," Miss Montgomery said sharply over her shoulder. "Your geography."

Immediately I lowered my gaze to the book, but it soon crept upward again. Once Mr.

Turner caught my eye and gave me such a comical look of warning that I nearly burst out laughing, but I managed to conceal it with a cough. Miss Montgomery turned and frowned at me, and something in my face — my bright eyes, perhaps, or my flushed cheeks — made her eyes narrow with suspicion.

I smiled innocently and raised my book to cover my face, but as soon as they resumed talking, I lowered it just enough to permit me to watch Mr. Turner. He had such elegant cheekbones, I thought, and such a perfectly sculpted chin. With such a face he ought to be a prince, or at least a duke. He was certainly more handsome than most noblemen I knew.

Suddenly Miss Montgomery turned in her chair. "Ada Byron," she barked. "If I didn't know better, I'd say that you're more interested in your tutor than your geography."

"How fortunate for us all that you *do* know better," I said brightly.

"Get on with your studies or leave the room."

"I'll study where and when I please," I said, indignant.

Mr. Turner shook his head at me, an urgent, almost imperceptible motion, and I wished I could take the words back.

Miss Montgomery drew in a breath sharply. "That's enough. Ada, leave the room."

"I shall not."

"Ada, go. Now."

Miss Montgomery had worked herself into a near apoplexy, and Mr. Turner looked dismayed, so I rose and left without another word. On my way to my room, I halted in the front hall, fuming. She had no right to dismiss me like a child. Yes, I was more interested in my tutor than in my geography. I would have to be very dull-witted, not to mention severely myopic, not to be.

I hurried to my mother's study and seized paper and pen. "Dear Mr. Turner," I wrote, "I regret that we parted without saying a proper good-bye." I took a deep breath, considered the consequences of what I wanted to write next, and plunged ahead. "If you hate our partings as much as I do, please meet me in the greenhouse at midnight. If I have misunderstood you, then I shall never speak of this again, and you must forget that I did."

When the ink dried, I folded the paper into a rectangle small enough to conceal in the palm of my hand. After composing myself, I strode back into the drawing room. Miss Montgomery had evidently assumed I would be off in some corner weeping with shame, for she gave me a look of such outrage that it could have blistered the paint off the walls.

"I cannot study my geography without my book," I said, crossing the room to collect it and adding my German and Latin texts to the pile in my arms for good measure. Making my way to their table, I inclined my head submissively to the smoldering Fury. "Please accept my apologies for my impertinence." To Mr. Turner, I extended my hand, with the note cupped invisibly in my palm. "Mr. Turner, I'm very sorry for interrupting your meeting."

He nodded, rising, and accepted my hand — and my note passed from my palm to his. When I released him, he put his right hand into his pocket and remained standing. I gave them each one last apologetic nod and hurried from the room.

Never had an afternoon passed more slowly. I retired early, and the Furies were so glad to be relieved of me that no one questioned it. I lay down on the bed, thinking I ought to rest so I would look fresh and pretty for Mr. Turner when he arrived — if he arrived. My heart plummeted. He might not. He was fond of me, that much I knew, but perhaps he did not feel for me what I felt for him.

At half past eleven, I threw back my coverlet, washed my face and brushed my hair, and swiftly dressed in the darkness. I drew on my warmest shawl as I crept downstairs, wincing at every creak of the floorboards, expecting at any moment for the Furies to descend, shrieking and clawing like the harpies they were.

I made my way from the dining room to

the kitchen to the scullery and out a back door. The spring night was cool and misty, with dew clinging in pearlescent globes from the grasses that lined the path to the greenhouse. Though I tried to walk lightly, my slippers crunched the gravel beneath my feet, and the sound seemed to echo off the walls of the house as I swiftly left it behind. I reached the greenhouse with minutes to spare, and as I slipped inside and closed the door behind me, I willed my pulse to stop racing. He would come and we would be together, I thought as I unwrapped myself from the shawl and brushed dewdrops from my curling dark hair. Or he would *not* come, and soon I would slink back to my lonely room humiliated and heartbroken. I would know soon enough, I thought as I folded my shawl and set it on a nearby table where empty clay pots and saucers sat waiting for morning and the gardener.

"Miss Byron?"

I whirled around to face the darkened corner from whence the voice had come, my heart in my throat. "Mr. Turner?" I called softly, just as a familiar form emerged from the shadows.

"Yes. I'm here."

My heart was full as he approached me. He had come. "I'm glad," I murmured, searching his face, suddenly desperate to know his thoughts. He might have come to scold me for my folly, to tell me that he thought of me as his pupil, nothing more.

"I do hate our partings," he said, his voice low, a reluctant confession. "I did not realize you hated them too."

"I despise them," I said. "I loathe them. I wouldn't be able to endure them except for the promise of our next lesson."

He sighed, pained, and I wished I had not reminded him of the vast difference in rank that separated us. "You must know that your mother would never permit me to court you."

But he wanted to, I knew then, and joy and despair warred for possession of me. "You don't know that for certain."

"I do. We both do."

"My mother chooses her friends from all stations in life."

"But she will not choose her daughter's husband from one beneath her." He bowed his head and took my hands in his, interlacing our fingers. "I am a tutor. You are an heiress, and young. Your mother — and everyone else — will assume I'm after your fortune —"

"I don't care what other people think. I know it isn't true."

"Of course it isn't true. My God, how much easier this would be if you were a shopkeeper's daughter, or a governess. If you were, I could kiss you now and —"

"You *can* kiss me now," I said, tears in my

280

eyes, as I lifted my face to meet his. A moment later, his lips were on mine, soft and warm, insistent and tender. He took me in his arms and pulled me against him, and I pressed myself closer yet, and on and on we kissed, until we were breathless, until we were gasping, until a powerful undertow seized me and pulled me into depths I was only too eager to drown in.

Then his hands were on me, and mine on him, touching, exploring, caressing. He tangled his hands in my hair, which had come loose from its chignon and tumbled down around my shoulders. We kissed again and again, deeply and breathlessly, his tongue in my mouth and mine in his. I felt him fumbling with the buttons of my dress and I was seized with the urgency to help him, because I wanted nothing between us.

He snatched up a blanket draped over a table of new cuttings and spread it upon the floor, his other hand on the back of my neck, holding me close to him. He eased me to the ground, kissing me, caressing me, and then he was on top of me, and my hands were unfastening his trousers, and he was kicking them off, and kissing my neck, and murmuring my name, "Ada, Ada, Ada." I felt him erect and strong pushing against the tender flesh of my inner thigh, and at the same moment the thought flashed through my mind that I could not believe what was happening, he clenched his jaw, his urgency slowed, and after breathing heavily against my neck while I kissed him again and again and ran my hands over his smooth, muscular back, he suddenly groaned and heaved himself off of me.

"Mr. Turner?"

He laughed, but his frustration was evident. "I think you can call me Wills, Ada."

"Wills." His name was delicious in my mouth. "What's wrong?"

He rolled onto his side, brushed my hair away from my face, and kissed me on the cheek, his mouth lingering there, close to mine. "Nothing. Everything."

"Why —" The racing of my heart was slowing. "Why did you stop? Did I —" I took a deep, shaky breath. "This was my first — Do I not please you?"

"My God, Ada, yes, you please me. You please me so much it's almost killing me."

"Why, then?"

He kissed me, but my lips were trembling, and then my chin joined in, and I squeezed my eyes shut against tears. I could not bear it if I compounded my humiliation by breaking down in front of him.

"Why?" he echoed. "Because I love you, Ada, and I will not be the cause of your ruin."

He loved me. I thought I might die of happiness and misery. "What nonsense this is to talk about ruining a woman by making love to her," I said, my voice shaking. "No one speaks of ruining a man in this way."

"It's different for men. You know that. It's not our doing, but that's how it is."

"But are we not both made for this very thing? If you pluck an apple from a tree, is the tree ruined? If you use a new pen, is it ruined, or is it finally fulfilling the purpose for which it was created?"

His breathing was labored, as if it required every ounce of his strength not to press his mouth to mine, to my lips, to my neck, to my breasts. "You are not a pen, Ada."

"Nor am I a child," I cried. "If to love is to ruin, then shatter me beyond mending!"

Wills tangled his hands in my hair again, a moan like a low growl escaping his throat. "You have no idea how much I want to."

"I think I have some idea! You're aren't alone in this — this thwarted desire." I kissed him, hard. "Wills —"

"We can't, Ada." He stroked my cheek. "What if I got you with child?"

Only if my mother had suddenly walked into the greenhouse would my desire have been more swiftly quenched. "That would be . . . very difficult to explain."

"The explanation would be the easy part. Everything that followed —"

He did not need to say more.

He helped me back into my dress and pulled his own clothes on as I tried in vain to arrange my hair. I gave up when I realized that it hardly mattered; if the Furies discovered me sneaking back into the house in the middle of the night, unkempt hair would not be what condemned me.

Before we left the greenhouse, Wills cupped my face in his hands and kissed me. "Ada, my love, this can't happen again."

A tide of regret and grief washed over me, although I had expected this. "I know," I choked out, blinking away tears. I put my arms around his neck and pulled him close for one last kiss, soft and lingering. How I loved the scent of him, paper and graphite and something indefinably male. How I ached to be his, and for him to be mine.

That was meant to be our last kiss, and as he escorted me back to the scullery door, my hand tucked into the crook of his elbow, I wondered how I could return to what we had been before. How could I trace the strokes of his pen with mine, how could I sit and transcribe what he read to me, without remembering his taste, the feel of his lips on mine, the strong, supple muscles of his naked back beneath my hands?

In the days that followed, during our lessons we upheld the strictest propriety, which was necessary for another reason, as my outburst and impudence to Miss Montgomery had prompted the Three Furies to watch me more closely than ever. Then, when we found ourselves alone on the second day after our encounter in the greenhouse, he suddenly pulled me behind the drawing room door and kissed me, long and deep, until I thought I might melt into bliss. I had never felt so thoroughly loved, so wanted, so . . . so entirely accepted for who and what I was. Of all the people I cared about, of all the people surrounding me, only Wills looked at me that way.

More stolen kisses followed, and twice more we met in the greenhouse under the cover of night. Wills's touch awakened dormant passions that I never could have imagined dwelt within me, but although we brought each other to ecstasy, he did not enter me. "Someday, perhaps," he murmured, kissing my face while I clung to him. I knew he meant if we were ever married, but that seemed an utter impossibility. My heart ached to think that the most we could ever have would be our lessons and our clandestine passion.

As our intimacy grew, it became more difficult to conceal our affections from the Furies. Smiles, glances, banter, little jokes spilled over into our lessons and our conversations before and after. We became careless — or rather, I did. We were practicing dictation in a secluded spot in the garden when Wills compared me to the lady in the story he was reading aloud, a generous and flattering comparison that warmed my heart and made me laugh aloud for joy. And so it happened that I was sitting on his lap, one arm around his shoulders, the other tickling his chin with a daisy I had plucked, when Miss Doyle came upon us.

"Ada," she exclaimed, striding toward us as we scrambled to our feet. "Mr. Turner, I am shocked. I would expect such impropriety from this willful child, but you —"

"He didn't do anything," I protested as she seized me by the upper arm and pulled me away from him. "He was just sitting there reading and I decided to play a trick on him."

"A fine trick it is too." Miss Doyle glared at Wills. "Mr. Turner. You are her tutor, and a gentleman, or so we believed. How dare you take advantage of a foolish, impetuous girl? How dare you betray the trust Lady Byron placed in you?"

He held up his hands, a futile attempt to calm her. "Miss Doyle, please —"

"Don't say another word. Gather your things and leave Fordhook at once." She propelled me toward the house, and in my distress, I did not struggle. "You will hear from Lady Byron soon enough."

"Wills," I cried out, but Miss Doyle spun me around and drove me ahead of her down the gravel path and into the house.

I was ordered to my room, and there I suffered, pacing anxiously, worrying about Wills, pounding my pillow in rage. My mother was summoned from Brighton, and she reached Fordhook by twilight. I expected to be called to her study, but she punished me by obliging me to wait, anguished and alone, until I finally dropped off to sleep, utterly dispirited.

The next day I rose early and began to wash and dress, but I had not quite finished when Miss Doyle knocked on my door and announced that my mother awaited me in her study. "I will escort you," she said primly. On any other occasion, I would have laughed and assured her that I would not get lost along the way, but I was too upset and apprehensive to refuse.

My many hours of solitude had given me time to compose and rehearse my defense, but when I finally stood before my mother, seated behind her desk with all the solemn dignity of a judge, she refused to hear it. "Mr. Turner will be discharged at once," she told me, her expression that of someone whose expectations of disappointment have been fulfilled. "Given the circumstances, I could not possibly offer him a character."

"That's not fair," I protested. "He's an excellent teacher. How will he find another situation without a reference?"

"An excellent teacher does not become overly familiar with a pupil."

If only she knew. My knees nearly buckled when I imagined what punishment she would have arranged for Wills if the Furies had discovered us in the greenhouse. "Please don't make him suffer for my wrongdoing. As I told Miss Doyle, Mr. Turner was sitting and reading aloud when I dropped myself onto his lap. It was only meant to be a joke, but he was so startled that he did not push me away, and that's when she discovered us."

"Miss Doyle has already told me your excuse." Sighing, she interlaced her fingers and rested her hands on the desktop. "However, Miss Carr informed me that she had previously observed you flirting with him, and he did nothing to discourage you."

"There was nothing to discourage! Whatever Miss Carr thinks she saw —"

"Ada, enough," my mother interrupted wearily. "I've made my decision. After you've had time to reflect, you'll be thankful, as I am, that this flirtation was nipped in the bud. Whatever tendency for reckless passion you might have inherited from —" She broke off, inhaled deeply, and continued. "Whatever your natural inclinations might be, you can and must control them."

She dismissed me, sending me off with suggestions for books and tracts to help me understand fully the ruinous consequences I had narrowly avoided. I could not promise to read them, so I clenched my jaw and offered a sharp nod that might have been interpreted as submission.

My presence was required at breakfast, but

my stomach was in knots and I could not bring myself to swallow more than a few mouthfuls. My poor, darling Wills. How would he explain to potential employers why he had been peremptorily dismissed from Lady Byron's service? What would become of his dream to continue his studies? I seethed with anger as I watched my mother serenely sip her tea at the head of the table, untroubled by the slightest pang of conscience for having arranged to destroy a man's future.

After breakfast I was ordered back to my bedroom to contemplate my transgressions, but instead I burned with resentment even as my heart twisted in anguish. How could I carry on as before, cowed into obedience, when the man I loved stood to lose everything?

By the time I was commanded to join my mother and the Furies for supper, I had decided.

That evening I packed a few necessities into a small satchel — two dresses, undergarments, the locket and ring my father had given me, my favorite geometry text — and concealed it beneath my bed. Then I waited. The hours passed, darkness descended upon Fordhook, and as soon as I was certain the household slumbered, I took my satchel in hand and stole from my room and out the scullery door into the night.

I knew his parents' home was about two

miles away, and I knew which road to take to get there, and I fervently hoped that when I reached the village, I would recognize the Turner house from Wills's descriptions. I walked with great haste in the light of a quarter moon, stumbling now and then when the shadows concealed the edge of the road. My satchel was not unduly heavy, but I was not accustomed to the exercise and my arms and shoulders began to ache, even though I shifted my burden from hand to hand when one grew weary. A cramp pinched my side, and my right shoe began to rub a blister on my heel, but it never occurred to me to turn back.

At last I came to the village, and I wandered about, searching the houses for the details my beloved Wills had mentioned — a two-story stone farmhouse with red shutters, lush blackberry bushes in the side garden, an abandoned rope swing dangling from an ancient oak out front. When I finally found it, I grew faint with relief — but then my heart began to pound with trepidation. I had not planned my arrival, only my escape.

I stood there for several minutes, uncertain, but then I began to shiver from the chill and the mist despite my warm shawl. I could not stand there until morning hoping Wills would appear, and I refused to go home, so I summoned up my courage and knocked on the front door.

A young woman with hair the same golden hue as Wills's answered, and I knew at once she was his sister, Marjorie. "Yes, miss?" she greeted me, her eyebrows drawn together in concern.

"I beg your pardon for disturbing you at such a late hour," I said, breathless. "May I please speak with Mr. William Turner?"

"Of course." She opened the door wider. "Please come in out of the damp. Did your carriage break down?"

"No — no carriage," I said, looking about the cozy sitting room for a place to rest. Without another question but with a thorough, appraising look, she offered me a chair, excused herself, and disappeared down the hall. It seemed an age until Wills appeared, his sister trailing after him.

"Ada," he greeted me, astonished. Remembering his sister, he quickly amended, "Miss Byron. What's the matter?"

"What's the matter?" I echoed. "Haven't you been told?"

"Yes, of course I have." He knelt beside my chair and took my hands, and to his sister he said, "Marjorie, would you excuse us, please?"

"I think that's the last thing I should do," Marjorie said, eyeing us, "but I'll put the kettle on and be back soon with tea."

She shot her brother a look of warning as she left, but Wills's gaze was on me and he missed it. "You're cold," he said, rubbing my hands, transferring warmth to them from his own.

"Wills, what are we to do?"

"I don't know that there's anything we can do," he said, avoiding my gaze. "I'm finished as your tutor. As anyone's tutor, I suppose."

"Wills, I'm sorry, so very sorry —"

"It's all right." He cupped my cheek with his hand, and I closed my eyes and pressed my face against it. "It's not your fault. I should have — resisted."

"I'm heartily glad you didn't," I exclaimed. "Wills, I love you. Don't you love me?"

"Of course I do." To prove it, he kissed me, and I believed. "I want to marry you."

"Done! I accept," I said, my laugh a little frantic.

He smiled, and I quickly kissed his cheek before the dimple vanished. "I could ask your mother for your hand," he said. "I have nothing to lose at this point. She could say no, or she could take pity on us and say yes."

"She shall refuse," I said bitterly. "There is nothing to compel her to consent."

He took both of my hands in his and raised them to his lips. "Perhaps —" He hesitated. "Perhaps we could provide the impetus. If we eloped —"

"Yes," I said, a thrill of hope racing through me. "She would have to let us marry. But —" I could not mislead him. "My mother controls my fortune. She could disinherit me. She cares so little for me, she probably will."

He kissed me so long and tenderly that my head spun. "I don't love your fortune. I love you. I can provide for us, if you can reconcile yourself to a more modest way of life."

"Happily," I said. "I can help too. I can tutor young girls — mathematics, science —"

"Ada," he said, suddenly serious, "are you sure this is what you want? I wouldn't want to coerce you down a path you'll later regret taking."

"Look where I am," I said, lifting my hands and letting them fall to my lap. "I've run away. I've half eloped already."

We laughed together, and we kissed. Just as Marjorie returned with the tea, Wills seized my hand and led me off to a small bedchamber on the upper story, where he took a traveling bag from the wardrobe, set it open on the bed, and began filling it with clothing.

"We'll go to Edinburgh," he said, striding back and forth between wardrobe, bureau, and bag. "I have an uncle there, my mother's younger brother. We'll tell him we married here, and he'll take us in. By the time anyone thinks to look for us there, too much time will have passed, and our parents will realize that allowing us to marry is the only option."

"Oh, yes, Wills, yes," I said, overcome by happiness.

He grinned at me and looked as if he were

about to speak, but then he froze, his smile fading. He hurried to the window, and as he did I heard it too — a carriage halting before the house. "Stay here," he urged, his expression darkening as he strode from the room.

"Wills —" I darted to the window and peered outside, where I discovered my mother's carriage parked at the front door. Reeling away, I stumbled to the bed and sank down upon it. Our elopement had been thwarted before it had properly begun.

Later I learned that someone within the Turner household had overheard us planning and had sent word to Fordhook. My mother had not come herself, of course, but had dispatched Miss Doyle and Miss Montgomery to collect me. After an ugly, angry scene in which Wills stormed and I wept and his parents and sister stood resolutely against us and the two Furies glared with cold malevolence and made veiled threats, my hand was torn from Wills's and I was forced from the house and into the carriage. The Furies scolded me the entire way home, but I scarcely heard them. Our plans lay in ruins, my hopes shattered beyond repair.

As soon as I crossed the threshold, the waiting for my mother's judgment commenced. It would not come that night, for the Furies would have their way with me first, whisking me upstairs, undressing me, subjecting me to horrid questions and humiliating examinations, all to determine how much damage had been done.

Once the ordeal was concluded, they saw me to bed, and after they left and shut the door, I heard a chair scrape the floor in the hall outside my room. I knew one of the Furies would be stationed at that post throughout the night.

The next day my breakfast was brought up to me on a tray, and my luncheon. I could not touch them. I spent the hours pacing, writing desperate, passionate letters to Wills, brooding over our plan to elope, despairing of bringing it to fruition. Then, when I had exhausted myself with anger and worry, the summons finally came.

My mother sat behind her desk, looking every inch the adjudicator. She gestured to a seat, I declared that I preferred to stand, she waited with infinite patience, and eventually I gave up and sat down, scowling.

"You will be pleased to know, I'm sure," she began, "that I have decided not to press charges against Mr. Turner."

I stared at her, aghast. That possibility had never occurred to me.

"Not because he did not break the law," she continued, "but because if this incident is brought before the courts, the press will seize upon it, and we will lose whatever small chance we might yet have to keep this matter quiet."

"He has done nothing wrong," I said levelly. "I'm seventeen, a woman grown. I consented to everything."

"You don't have enough understanding to consent to anything."

I shook my head, disbelieving. "How can you believe that when you're planning to have me married off within the year?"

"Yes, about that," she said brittlely. "You do realize that you've cast aside any chance you had of making a good match, do you not? You are *ruined*. Do you understand me?"

"I understand what you're implying, but I vehemently disagree. There was no —" I flushed with anger and embarrassment, but I forced myself to say it. "I am still a virgin."

She shook her head, rendered incredulous by my immeasurable ignorance. "There is virginity, and there is purity. Do you think Society cares whether you actually consummated your foolish little affair? You fled to his house in the middle of the night. He took you in. When you were discovered, you were preparing to elope. That's all anyone would need to know. How things *look* matters as much as how things *are,* perhaps more so."

I could not believe what I was hearing. "You shouldn't have come after me. I've always disappointed you, and this was your chance to be rid of me."

"I don't want to be rid of you. I want you to stop acting like a foolish child and live up to my expectations, to do your duty."

"What about my duty to myself? I love him."

" 'Love him'?" she echoed. "Do you think your Mr. Turner loves *you*? He has ruined you. He has destroyed all hope of your future happiness, just for a few ephemeral moments of pleasure. Would love do that?"

"If I am ruined," I retorted, my voice shaking, "then let me marry Wills."

"I shall not. It is out of the question. Ruined or not, no daughter of mine will marry a tutor." She uttered the last word as if it were an epithet.

"Then —" My thoughts raced. "If I cannot marry Wills, and I am unfit to marry anyone else, what will become of me?"

"We must keep this sordid business quiet and hope the secret never comes out."

The edge to her voice and the set to her jaw told me she had already taken measures to make this so. That must have been how she had spent her morning, while I had paced overhead and clung to vain hopes that I might yet be reunited with Wills.

One last chance remained, and I seized it. "And if the secret does come out?"

For a moment I dared hope that I had her, that she would admit that in that case, she would have no choice but to let me marry Wills.

But she brushed aside my challenge with a

graceful wave of her hand. "Why, then, you would not marry. You would still have your fortune, although I would mourn the loss of your heirs that will never be. As for how you would live, you would follow the excellent example provided for you by my friends."

I recoiled as if I had been struck. She meant the Furies. She expected me to accept their fate as my own and to become as miserable, condemning, and bitter as they were, begrudging other people their happiness because they had not found any for themselves.

"I will never be like your friends," I said, my voice shaking. "I would rather die."

She regarded me coolly. "Then you had better pray we find someone willing to overlook your shortcomings and marry you."

Chapter Twelve:
Thus the Heart Will Break, Yet Brokenly Live On

March–May 1833

Later I learned that my mother had paid Wills his salary for the rest of the spring and had written him an acceptable reference, which he used to secure a new situation with a family in Suffolk. It was understood that this generosity would purchase his silence, and he must never ask for more.

While I was confined to my bedroom, Wills's sister came to collect the papers and payment, for Wills had been warned that he must not attempt to communicate with me. If he ever set foot on the Fordhook grounds, or on any property belonging to my mother, he would be arrested, and she would do everything in her considerable power to ensure that he was imprisoned for life or transported to Australia.

Though I understood well the severity of the consequences Wills would face, at first I dared hope that he would come for me regardless. We could elope to the Continent and marry; we could find work as tutors with sophisticated French or Swiss families who did not fear my mother's wrath; we would be poor but happy and in love. When I was allowed to leave my room for exercise escorted by a Fury, I invented reasons to visit the greenhouse to see if he had left a message for me, a token of his affection, a letter explaining where and when to meet him so we could run off together. In vain I looked and returned another day and looked again, but there was never anything to be found.

Reluctantly I concluded that Wills could not come to Fordhook, yet I still held out hope that he would send word to me. I did not expect him to send me a letter through the post, because, of course, my mother would intercept it. Nor did I think he would bribe a servant, because everyone in the household was fiercely loyal to their mistress. I did think that he might persuade a sympathetic deliveryman to smuggle me a message, or enlist the help of a daring child from the village with the promise of a coin, but still he sent no word.

I could not blame him for his reluctance to defy my mother, and yet I wished he would. Every day he failed to do so proved that his fear of my mother exceeded his love for me. Though I was deeply saddened and disappointed, I forgave him, and I even convinced myself that he had made the right decision. If

I truly loved him, I could not ask him to throw away his prospects and his dream of becoming a professor of literature just for me, especially if it would bring scandal crashing down upon his head and doom him to exile. What else could I do? In my heart, I bade him a sorrowful good-bye and wished him well.

I never saw him again. I did not know that then, of course, and for years thereafter, whenever I traveled through Suffolk, I looked for him. My heartbeat quickened at the glimpse of hair in a particular shade of gold, of a familiar stride, of a certain curving line between steady shoulders and tapered waist. These vain hopes faded as the years passed, although I confess they never left me entirely.

I hope that wherever Wills is now, he is well and content.

In the aftermath of my thwarted elopement, my relationship with my mother changed irrevocably. All my life my mother had worked tirelessly to rid me of the influence of my Byron blood, but in loving Wills, I had confirmed her worst fears — I lacked self-control, craved independence, was contemptuous of authority, and heedlessly indulged my passions. But if her understanding of me had altered, so, too, had my feelings for her. I knew I ought to love, revere, and respect my mother, but what I felt for her then was more akin to awe and admiration than love and affection.

I sank into melancholy as deep and as painful as if I were mourning a death. Listless and quiet, I could find no comfort in my books or studies or horses. My appetite fled, and I lost more than a stone, which at first pleased my mother, who thought I was too plump, but she grew alarmed as my weight continued to drop. She summoned her most trusted doctors, who examined me and agreed that leeches and cuppings were required, but after their treatments, I felt more fragile and lethargic than before.

You might blame my mother for causing my misery — I certainly did — but to her credit, she did more than anyone else to draw me out of it. She ordered the cook to make my favorite dishes and she cajoled me to eat. She took me to a spa in Brighton to give me a change of scenery and to put color in my cheeks. When we returned home, she reminded me that our poor horses suffered from my neglect, and so out of guilt more than any expectation of pleasure, I resumed riding.

As for my spiritual needs, my mother enlisted the services of Dr. William King, the devout Unitarian who, along with his wife, had guided my moral education while we were at Hanger Hill. Dr. King escorted me on long walks around the Fordhook estate, during which he urged me to rigorously scrutinize my recent behavior, examining what I had done in the cold, clear light of reason rather than through the rosy glow of infatuation. "The imagination is a dangerous asset," he asserted, his brow furrowed in earnest concern. "It is essential that you learn to control it and not allow treacherous thoughts to wander about your mind unrestrained. You must rule your emotions, not allow them to rule you."

Though our talks unfolded beneath azure skies amid the fragrant spring blossoms of the Fordhook gardens, as we followed the circuitous paths again and again and wore away at the gravel beneath our feet, so too were my pride and certainty ground into dust beneath our constant, unflinching scrutiny. Gradually he helped me to realize how reckless I had been and how close I had come to bringing catastrophic ignominy upon myself. Another young woman, even one nobly born, might have been able to elope and live out her days in anonymous, genteel poverty in some foreign land with the man she loved, but not so the daughter of Lord Byron, who would be relentlessly pursued and gleefully harassed by the same newspapermen and gossipmongers who had persecuted him. The public, greedy for scandal, envious of unearned fame, would never have allowed Wills and me to live in peace. If we had eloped, I would have destroyed us both.

This new understanding dealt me a staggering blow. I had always prided myself — undeservedly, the Furies would say — on my intellect and perception, and yet I had entirely failed to foresee the inevitable outcome of the reckless course I had charted. For the first time in my life, I began to fear that something was very wrong with me, some inherent perversity that no amount of prayer or deep reflection could expunge. I brooded over my bad Byron blood, and the mysterious covered portrait, and the unspeakable "facts utterly unknown" that had forced my mother to separate from my father. Now I had a terrible secret of my own to conceal, the secret of my near ruin, which, if discovered, would condemn me to shame and loneliness.

More leeches and cuppings, my mother's panacea, afforded me no relief. I became anxious and timid, jumping at sudden noises and cowering in my room during thunderstorms. "Her sense of guilt rivals a Papist's," I overheard my mother tell the Furies one evening as they observed me through the open doorway to my bedroom while I feigned sleep to avoid another sermon.

"A little shame will do her good," said Miss Montgomery.

"A little, perhaps," my mother conceded, "but this is excessive, and the Season will begin soon. I cannot take her to London in this condition, and if I leave her behind, people will grow suspicious and begin asking dangerous questions."

And thus I had a new worry. I must get better, and I must be quick about it.

I went riding nearly every day, because the vigorous exercise and the excitement of daring velocities brought me as close to happiness as I ever expected to be again. With Dr. King's encouragement, I resumed my studies, and when they seemed to bring me solace and distraction, I threw myself into them with a vengeance. Eventually my pervasive sense of dread receded, but a trace of nervousness remained, and I experienced a slight recurrence of my old symptoms of weakness and paralysis, so that on particularly bad days I was obliged to lean upon my cane.

I knew that a spark of my old spirit had returned when, after Miss Doyle berated me for using my "gentleman-like stick" instead of a more feminine parasol, I replied, "I appreciate the suggestion, but if I wanted fashion advice from a dowdy old hen, I would have consulted Miss Carr." That remark earned me a rebuke from my mother, but I felt immensely better for having made it.

This improvement came just in time, too, for my mother and I were preparing to move to London for the start of the Season within the week. In an act of true mercy for which I silently and irreverently thanked all the gods that ever were, she did not invite the Furies to accompany us.

My mother had arranged comfortable and gracious lodgings for us in a fashionable neighborhood, and the moment we crossed the threshold she launched us into a frenzy of last-minute preparations for my presentation at court. An excellent dressmaker had been toiling over my gown for weeks, but I had grown very slim in my melancholy, and after I was measured the bodice had to be refitted, nearly every seam plucked out and sewn again. The gown was a lovely confection of white tulle with a broad white satin sash and a low, curving neckline, the design entirely my mother's and the dressmaker's since I had no sense for fashion. The appropriate slippers, jewels, and fan were selected, as was the requisite headdress, an elaborate creation with a profusion of white ostrich feathers and an ethereal veil long enough to cascade to the train of my gown. It was the most beautiful dress I had ever worn, and I was torn between delight for its beauty and regret that Wills would never see me wear it. He would not have recognized me.

In the drawing room and the longest hall of our London residence, my mother made me practice walking in this ensemble, forward and backward in a perfect, smooth, graceful glide. I also rehearsed my curtsey, no ordinary dip but a full court curtsey in which one had to bend the knee until it nearly touched the floor and rise again without toppling over, tripping over one's gown or train, or allowing one's headdress to tumble off one's coiffure. All this was to be completed with elegance and grace, evidence of one's good breeding and proper upbringing.

If I had been obliged to use my cane, I cannot imagine how I would have accomplished it, but I was anxious not to make a mistake, so I obediently practiced walking, curtseying, and backing out of a room as my mother commanded. Only once, when we had rehearsed so long that my knees and neck and shoulders ached, did a complaint escape my lips.

"You have no idea how easy young ladies have it today," my mother admonished me. "When I was presented to the court of King George and Queen Charlotte, the queen insisted upon the court dress of the previous century and required the young ladies to wear cumbersome, wide hoops. Climbing in and out of a carriage was an ordeal one could not accomplish unassisted, and simply navigating a room taxed one's endurance and agility almost to the limit. In comparison, you have nothing to complain about."

I had *less* to complain about, but still a rather long list of grievances, I thought, though I did not say so aloud. My mother was my only ally in this mission, and I was grateful for her help. I suspected I required it far more than most girls my age, who had not squandered precious preparatory years confined to a sickbed.

I was to be presented at Saint James's Palace at the fourth Drawing Room of the Season, and as the occasion approached, I practiced diligently, my excitement and trepidation rising as my mother received word of the illustrious guests who were expected to attend — various dukes, a host of other nobles, and many visiting foreign dignitaries. Although my mother never explicitly said so, perhaps because she did not wish to terrify me, I understood that even among this august gathering and as only one of dozens of young ladies making their debuts, as Lord Byron's daughter, I should expect to attract a great deal of notice. "This might inspire some jealousy among the other girls," my mother warned me.

"I want them to like me," I protested. "I want friends. I don't want attention simply because of my father."

"You'll have it whether you want it or not," she said, "so take care to acquit yourself well."

She turned away to fuss with the lace on the sleeves of her gown, and as I studied her, I realized that she was almost as anxious as I. If I failed in any manner of my deportment or appearance, I would ruin not only my own reputation and prospects, but my mother's as well.

I imagined other young ladies looked forward to their presentations with excitement and anticipation, but I could not wait to have it over and done. Although Dr. King would not have approved, in my nervousness I found some illicit comfort in my memory of Wills's affection. He had found me lovely and charming, so perhaps others would too.

The momentous occasion arrived at long last on 10 May 1833. Although the actual ceremony would not begin until two o'clock, we were up early to eat — it would be a long day, and my mother had a terror of me fainting from hunger into a pile of tulle and silk at the king's feet — and to attend to my toilette and to dress. A maid helped me with my gown as my mother escorted me into the carriage, which carried us swiftly through the city toward Pall Mall until we turned onto Piccadilly Street and joined the long procession of carriages bringing other young ladies to the palace.

I was fairly confident that I had studied and prepared well, and my mother was in good spirits, so I was feeling quite hopeful and happy as we passed through the main entrance of the redbrick Tudor palace. Guided by palace attendants, we merged into the parade of young ladies in white gowns and proud, watchful sponsors who were shown into a salon to await the announcement of our names.

"I will try to find you a chair so you may rest," my mother said, glancing about. The room was elegantly appointed, the walls covered in gold damask that seemed to glow in the light of the chandeliers, but it seemed that most chairs had been removed to make room for more ladies and sponsors to stand. "Don't move from this spot."

I nodded, my mouth suddenly dry. While I waited for her to return, I smiled and nodded politely to any young lady who glanced my way, silently willing my mother to hurry. I exchanged a few pleasantries with the friendlier girls who deigned to speak to me, but I recognized no one and felt quite alone. From the conversations I overheard, I gathered that I had little in common with most of them. In a discussion of the sublime beauty of the Pythagorean theorem I would have outshone them all, but since old Pythagoras was not an unmarried lord with four thousand a year, I suspected that these young ladies neither knew him nor cared to.

My mother had not yet returned by the time we were instructed to line up and await the announcement of our names, and my heart sank with dismay when I realized the escorts had themselves been escorted into the drawing room to await us there. I had hoped for some parting word of encouragement from my mother before the moment came, but it seemed I would not get it.

I was silently assuring myself that all would be well, and mostly believing it, when the young lady in front of me turned around, gave me an appraising look, and smiled in recognition, although I was certain we had never met. "My goodness, isn't this terrifying?" she said cheerfully, although she seemed not a bit afraid. Her silken blond hair seemed to have been spun from gold, her eyes were the blue of an early summer sky, and her gown was of white silk exquisitely embellished with lace and pearls. Her face looked as if it had been created to inspire love and poetry, and her figure was so graceful and elegant that she could have been a model for an artist's rendering of Aphrodite or Helen of Troy.

"Exciting, yes, but not terrifying," I said, smiling tentatively at this extraordinary creature, who was surely the most beautiful young lady in the room. "Thousands of other girls have been presented before this, and they have all survived."

"Not all of them," she said darkly, and my eyes must have widened, because she quickly amended, "Oh, they all lived, as far as I know, but some departed with their reputations in tatters." Drawing closer, she murmured, "Every year there is always one girl who collapses, or flees from the salon to be sick

311

before her name is called, or babbles non-sense when the queen questions her. No one ever forgets her. Whatever else we do today, we must take care not to be *that girl*."

"No," I said faintly. "I certainly wouldn't want to be."

"Nor I." She fixed me with a look of imperative warning. "Whatever you do, you must not think of being sick. Don't think of all those strangers staring at you. And especially, don't *ever* think about how humiliated your family will be if you fail. Think of something pleasant instead, such as . . ." She put her head to one side, considering. "Kittens. Do you like kittens?"

I nodded and swallowed to clear my constricted throat. "Very much. I have a cat I'm very fond of."

"Perfect. Think of your cat and I'm sure you'll do just fine." Smiling brilliantly, she turned around to face front and was soon engaged in a conversation with two other young ladies, who greeted her like a dear friend.

Inhaling deeply, I squeezed my eyes shut and imagined playing with Puff, teasing her with a ball of yarn in my old bedroom at Kirkby Mallory, but the more I concentrated on not being sick or fainting or toppling over in my curtsey or getting tongue-tied in front of the king and queen, the more my imagination filled with precisely those heart-quaking scenes. "Puff," I murmured, thinking of soft fur and gentle purrs.

I swallowed hard and wished frantically for a glass of water. To steady my nerves, I opened my eyes, fixed my gaze on a point straight ahead of me, and began calculating cube roots of random numbers. A sudden motion drew my attention, and I shifted my gaze in time to observe the golden-haired goddess observing me, a sly smile playing on her lips as she whispered to her two companions. She looked away when she caught me watching her, but it was too late — I had figured out her scheme. I might not have enjoyed the company of other girls often in my childhood, but I had read a great deal about them. That wicked creature wanted me to embarrass myself, but I was determined not to give her the satisfaction of knowing that she had rattled my nerves.

When she reached the top of the queue and was announced, I learned that she was called Miss Mariah Bettencourt, but the name was not familiar to me. Three other young ladies followed her, and then it was my turn. "Miss Augusta Ada Byron," the yeoman called out in a voice that carried across the drawing room, and from the entrance I beheld a large, splendid chamber with floor-to-ceiling windows with curtains of crimson velvet on one long wall, enormous portraits of royals past and present displayed in gilded frames on the three others, a vast fireplace opposite the windows adorned with crests of arms, and a pair of grand gilded chandeliers and elaborate cornices high above it all. There were no chairs, for here no one sat in the presence of the king and queen, but the room was full of girls in white dresses who had preceded me and, in several times their number, ladies and gentlemen dressed in their finest silks and suits and costumes of foreign lands, glittering with jewels, fragrant with perfume and pomade.

It was rather dizzying, and I took a quick breath to steady myself, but I did not pause after I heard my name but entered the drawing room, where I was greeted by a murmur of interest and more curious, intrigued glances than I could count. Unsettled, I nonetheless smiled serenely, glided across the floor to where His Majesty and Her Majesty were seated, and performed my curtsey without the slightest wobble. When I rose, Queen Adelaide said, "Welcome to court, Miss Byron. We are very fond of your father's poetry."

"Thank you, Your Majesty."

"We believe 'She Walks in Beauty' is the most lyrical and beautiful of his poems."

"Thank you, ma'am. It is my favorite of his works." In truth, I preferred *Don Juan,* but my mother had told me to agree with everything the king and queen said, even if they misspoke my own name.

They dismissed me pleasantly, and I backed away demurely without tangling my feet in my gown and falling on my backside. I felt hundreds of pairs of eyes upon me, but a sidelong glance told me that none of them were Miss Mariah Bettencourt's, for she was looking deliberately away, as if I were so dull that she had already forgotten me.

My mother quickly made her way to my side. "You acquitted yourself tolerably well," she murmured, so no one would overhear.

Coming from her, this was high praise indeed, and I flushed with pride. "Thank you, Mama."

"Your expression was pleasant and digni-fied, and your curtsey was as graceful as we could have hoped."

"Our practice was rewarded."

"Indeed it was."

"Mama," I said, inclining my head dis-creetly at Miss Bettencourt, "do you see that young lady across the way, the tall blonde next to the woman in the yellow gown?"

"Yes, that's Lord and Lady Bettencourt's eldest daughter, Mariah. They have Mortimer Hall in Somerset. It's said to be lovely, and Miss Bettencourt is reputed to be quite ac-complished."

"Accomplished, perhaps, but not very nice." I quickly related how she had tried to unsettle me just before I was announced.

My mother's self-possession was legendary, and only a slight pursing of her lips betrayed her vexation. "I'm pleased you did not lose your composure," she said. "I warned you that you might be the envy of young ladies who resent that your fame eclipses their own."

"You mean my father's fame," I said. "I have won no accolades for myself. My only accomplishment thus far has been to cleverly arrange to be sired by the greatest poet of the age."

"And you managed that with aplomb," she replied. "Forget Miss Bettencourt. Spite and beauty are all she has. It is rumored that her father is thousands of pounds in debt, and it is certain that Mortimer Hall is entailed and will pass to her father's cousin upon his death. Her only hope is to enthrall a very wealthy man with her pretty face so he will forgive her lack of fortune and marry her. You have nothing to fear from her."

Were there people I did have something to fear from? "Mama —"

"Come," she interrupted, taking my arm. "There are people here far better than the Bettencourts whom you ought to know."

My mother introduced me to the Duke of Wellington, the Hero of Waterloo, whom I liked for his straightforward manner, and the Duke of Orléans, whom I found very gracious and sympathetic. I also met Talleyrand, the French elder statesman, but he seemed a bit distractible and rather reminded me of an old monkey. The many other dignitaries and foreign ministers I met that afternoon were all very proud and fine, and I believe that most of the ladies and gentlemen found me to be a pleasant, amiable young woman. At least, I hope they did. This I knew to be true: Of all the young ladies who had been presented that day, none had attracted more attention than myself, even though there were many others more beautiful, more graceful, and more deserving.

Afterward, as we rode home, my mother told me that I had conducted myself like "a young lioness" and that she expected similar success at the Court Ball the following week. The ball was to be the highlight of the Season, and I was thrilled that she had decided I should attend. My mother did not enjoy Society as much as other ladies of her rank did, although she once had. At my age she had reveled in the pleasure of parties, balls, and the whole whirl of gaiety, but now she preferred the company of her intellectual friends, who like herself were devoted to good works and moral improvement. "I have no intention of spending the entire Season in London," she had cautioned me before we had left Fordhook. "We will come and go as the occasion requires."

Knowing that she considered our appearances in Society to be an obligation of her rank and title as well as an undertaking essential to finding me a husband, I was glad that she had added the Court Ball to her list of necessary engagements. Remembering Miss Bettencourt's malice, however, I felt the luster of my excitement dimming. It unsettled me to think that I might again be the center of attention at another glittering event where there were so many others more worthy, as well as more desirous, of meriting observation.

"I don't want you to occupy yourself with frivolities," my mother told me the day after my presentation at court, "so I will choose your gown." Relieved, I thanked her, but I resolved to learn more about fashion so that the next time, I could at least offer a few suggestions regarding the style and fabric of my attire. My mother chose an ashes-of-rose silk ball gown cut in a simple but elegant silhouette, embellished with pearlescent satin ribbons and a touch of lace trim at the wrists and neck. It fit me perfectly, emphasizing my slender waist and my long neck. For jewelry, she selected a lustrous, sparkling pearl-and-ruby necklace with matching earrings to draw attention to my bosom and away from my strong chin, which reminded my father's admirers fondly of him but did nothing to enhance my beauty. As it happened, my mother's friend Miss Louisa Chaloner had been very wrong indeed when she had predicted that I would never be pretty. I was no Miss Bettencourt, but Wills had shown me that I was far from plain and had more than my fortune to recommend me.

"When I was your age, balls at Saint James's were astonishingly dull," my mother remarked as she and her maid dressed me on the evening of 17 May. "The protocol for dancing was so restrictive it's a wonder anyone danced at all. If one wished to dance a minuet, one was obliged to submit one's name to the king's chamberlain a day ahead of time, and at the ball he would summon the ladies and gentlemen forward to dance according to rank. Only one couple danced at a time, and since there were invariably more ladies than gentlemen, each lady danced one minuet, each gentleman two." She stood lost in reflection for a moment before resuming her story and the task of getting me into my gown. "The dance floor was separated from the rest of the chamber by a wooden railing. Only the royal family, their particular companions, and the dancers were permitted there. Everyone else, including the band, was obliged to look on from a crowded gallery."

"It doesn't sound very enjoyable," I said.

"I don't believe enjoyment was the point. Oh, the country-dances that followed the minuets were more pleasurable, and not all balls were as formal as those at Saint James's. Queen Charlotte gave a wonderful ball at

Windsor one year, with country-dances set to sprightly Scottish reels. The supper was excellent as well." As her maid fastened my last button, my mother looked me up and down and nodded approvingly. "Those days are gone. England has been changing so rapidly and London most of all. The young today expect pleasure in every occasion far more than my generation ever did, and those expectations are usually gratified." She sighed. "I'm sure you'll have a lovely time."

She made it sound as if she would consider it an ethical lapse if I did. I resolved that I would enjoy the ball, if only for the sake of the music, which I had been looking forward to with great anticipation. Afterward, my mother would not have to know that I had felt anything more than satisfaction at fulfilling my duty.

And for the most part, I did have a wonderful time at the ball. The music was excellent, fulfilling all my youthful expectations of pleasure, as was the dancing, whether I was participant or observer. While it was true that I was uncomfortably conscious of the curious glances and the voices that murmured, "Byron's daughter, Byron's daughter," wherever I turned, I did not flee the ballroom in a panic or cower in the corner, head bowed, staring at the hem of my gown and praying no one would address me.

Such prayers would have been futile, as I

found myself besieged by a throng of handsome young gentlemen. They paid me the usual compliments, and I confess that after I deliberately forced thoughts of Wills and his dimple and his caresses from my mind, I enjoyed basking in their admiration and flirting back and forth. Oh, I realize that the enormous Wentworth estate I was expected to inherit from my mother, worth eight thousand pounds per annum, might have made me more attractive than if I had been poor, but the gentlemen would not have lingered so long to converse with me after we danced if my charms were limited to my fortune.

The more attention the gentlemen paid me, the more alluring I felt, and I thought my delight had surely reached its summit when I spotted Miss Bettencourt among the dancers. She was offering a winsome smile to her partner, an older gentleman — not elderly, I don't mean that, but closer to my mother's age than to my own. He was quite distinguished, if not as richly dressed as many others present, although he was still attired according to protocol. It occurred to me that he was one of the few men who had not tried to arrange an introduction with me. Though it makes me look petty and jealous, I freely confess that I found myself very displeased that anyone could be blind to me because he was dazzled by the brilliance of Miss Betten-court.

Soon thereafter, I observed that Miss Bettencourt had left his side and her place had been usurped by Mrs. Dallas — the wife of the uncle of the seventh Baron Byron, Captain George Anson Byron. Although ours was not a particularly close family connec-tion, I had met her on several occasions, and she and my mother exchanged occasional let-ters. Possessed by some mischief, as soon as Mrs. Dallas left the gentleman, I made my way through the crowd to her side.

"Why, Miss Byron," she greeted me, pleased. "How lovely it is to see you looking so well. How is your most excellent mother?"

"She is very well, thank you," I replied. "Dare I hope that your great-nephew George accompanied you here this evening?"

"I'm sorry, dear, he did not." The ostrich plumes in her headdress bobbed when she shook her head. "He will be very sad to hear that he missed seeing you."

"Not half as sad as I am." I was sincere, but after catching up on all the family news, I quickly changed the subject to inquire about the gentleman with whom I had seen her speaking.

"What gentleman?" She glanced back over her shoulder as if he might have remained there to refresh her memory. "You must mean Mr. Knight, Mr. Charles Murray Knight."

"Indeed?" I was surprised by the lack of title, as a young lady in Miss Bettencourt's pecuniary circumstances surely needed to ensnare a lord or an admiral, at least. Perhaps he had earned his own fortune through diligence and cleverness; it had been known to happen. "I thought I recognized him as the father of one of my friends, but I was mistaken. Perhaps I should meet him anyway, if he is a friend of yours."

"Meet Mr. Knight? I don't think that's necessary, dear. He's not really a friend of mine, more of an acquaintance of Lord Byron."

But I persisted, gently, and soon she dubiously acquiesced. After we exchanged the perfunctory greetings, he was courteous and charming, and he complimented my father's poetry without being obsequious. Thus satisfied that I would come to no harm, Mrs. Dallas left us to converse.

I soon learned that Mr. Knight was a railroad investor who also held various impressive posts within the government. "I have always had to make up for what I lack in titles and rank with my wits and hard work," he said modestly, which I found refreshing.

He knew London and its history very well, and when I mentioned my interest in science and mathematics, he told me of several places that I ought to visit. He described the red Time Ball recently installed on the roof of the Royal Observatory in Greenwich so earnestly that I thought he was about to invite me to accompany him on a trip to see it. Just as I was wondering how I would respond if he did, my gaze fell upon Miss Bettencourt, who was observing us from a rather close distance, her face expressionless.

Immediately I brightened my smile and gazed more warmly at Mr. Knight, and when he made a humorous remark, I laughed as if I had never heard anything more clever or amusing. That pleased him, and as our conversation continued with even greater animation, Miss Bettencourt's lovely face suddenly became crestfallen and weary, and she turned and disappeared into the throng.

At once I felt a stinging jolt of shame. Although I did like Mr. Knight, I had sought his acquaintance only to see whether I could lure him away from Miss Bettencourt. I was successful, and the attention he paid me clearly wounded her.

I thought of Wills and felt dizzy with self-loathing.

I had never really wanted Mr. Knight, and although it was pleasant to chat with someone who shared my interest in science, I knew my mother would never allow me to marry him. Only the worst sort of conniving coquette would wedge herself between a rival and the man she admired out of pure spite, and I could never be that.

Smiling and thanking him for the news about the Royal Observatory, I made my excuses and hurried off to find Mrs. Dallas again. I felt sick from the intoxicating draft of admiration and attention I had taken in too quickly, and I knew I needed a good dose of maternal common sense and kindness to sober me up.

I did not see Miss Bettencourt or Mr. Knight again that night, but the following day, when my mother and I attended a party at the home of her longtime friend Mary Acheson, Countess of Gosford, I saw Mr. Knight approaching me, but before I could hurry away pretending I had not seen him, he was at my side, smiling.

"Miss Byron." He bowed, and I curtseyed in turn. "What a pleasure it is to see you again. Do you know, I enjoyed our conversation about the Royal Observatory so much that as we parted, I thought of several other mathematical and scientific subjects I wanted to seek your opinion about."

"You wanted my opinion?" I echoed. I was seventeen, and he looked to be nearly forty. In my experience, people of his generation were more inclined to give me sermons than seek my opinion.

"Certainly. First, have you read Mrs. Somerville's book, *Mechanism of the Heavens?*"

"Have I read it? Only so often that I have

nearly worn off the cover." Mrs. Mary Somerville was a renowned mathematician and astronomer, and I had long worshipped her from afar. Her mathematical papers revealed true genius, a marvelous insight and depth of understanding that rendered me awestruck. I absolutely revered her as the model of the sort of mathematician and scientist I hoped to become. "Her translation of Laplace's *Mécanique Céleste* far surpasses the original."

"That was no mere translation," said Mr. Knight. "She illuminated Laplace's complex subject and made it comprehensible for the ordinary reader. I hear she's working on a new book on the physical sciences."

"Is she?"

"Rumor has it that it will be published next year."

"No sooner than that?" I lamented. "I cannot wait to read it."

"You should ask her about it. Likely she'd be willing to divulge a few secrets to a sister mathematician."

"Sadly, I've never had the pleasure of meeting Mrs. Somerville."

"Haven't you? Well, we shall have to see what we can do to remedy that."

"You know Mrs. Somerville?" I exclaimed with such reverence that he might have told me he had met Sir Isaac Newton or John the Baptist.

"I'm acquainted with her son," he replied.

"I'm sure I could persuade him to introduce us."

The "us" rang with promise, and suddenly I remembered Miss Bettencourt's unhappiness, and my own misery when Wills was lost to me. "Mr. Knight," I began, but then I sensed rather than heard someone approach me from behind, and I turned to discover my mother. I greeted her with a smile and quickly made introductions. Her face remained serene throughout, which told me she was likely agitated about something. I was not surprised when she offered Mr. Knight a polite excuse and led me away.

"I don't like him," she told me when we were out of earshot. "He seems too eager to ingratiate himself with his superiors."

"Every day you're surrounded by people who seek to ingratiate themselves with you," I said, a trifle exasperated by the tightness of her grip on my arm. "What's one more?"

"There's something different about him. Something oily." She halted, bringing me to a stop as well, and fixed me with a look that would suffer no disagreement. "I don't want you to speak to him again."

"You can't ask me to cut him," I protested.

"Of course not. He hasn't given you just cause, and —" She glanced about, frowning. "I suspect he has numerous friends here."

"Perhaps he won their friendship by being a good and decent gentleman."

"Or by learning their secrets and placing them in his debt."

"Mama, you must let me keep this acquaintance," I pleaded. "He offered to introduce me to Mrs. Mary Somerville."

"Nonsense. He is no more acquainted with Mrs. Somerville than he is with Napoléon. I shall find a mutual friend to introduce you." She linked her arm through mine, but her touch was less possessive than before. "Let us go find more suitable company."

I acquiesced, not only because I was reluctant to make a scene, but also because her promise of an introduction had mollified me. In truth, I preferred not to encourage Mr. Knight. I knew how it hurt to be disappointed in love, and I did not want to bring Miss Bettencourt further grief — and yet, I could not forget that she had not shown me any such kindness on the afternoon we were presented at court.

The following evening, although my mother complained that she had tired of revelry and wished the whole Season were over, we attended a ball at the residence of the Contessa di Passarelle, who was visiting from Milan. Miss Bettencourt was present; I greeted her with a polite nod, which she returned gracefully, and we proceeded to deliberately ignore each other. It was not until much later that I spotted her dancing with Mr. Knight, and although I irrationally regretted ceding victory to my rival, I felt no sorrow over losing the gentleman himself. How could I, when if Wills had walked into the room and beckoned to me, I would have thrown myself into his arms and wept for joy?

Soon thereafter, I was strolling through the gallery admiring the paintings when I heard footfalls behind me and turned to see Mr. Knight striding my way. "Good evening, Miss Byron," he said when he reached me, bowing. "Are you not dancing this evening?"

"I'm a little fatigued," I said, smiling ruefully, hoping he would take the hint and not ask for a dance.

"Are you too tired to meet someone extraordinary?"

I gasped. "You don't mean —"

He smiled and offered me his arm. "Why don't you come and see?"

Eagerly I took it, my thoughts racing as I tried to plan what I would say to my idol. "I'm as nervous now as when I was presented to the king and queen," I confessed, laughing tremulously. "More so, I think."

"A little nervousness is to be expected."

He had led me away from the rest of the party, and as the sound of music faded behind us, I hesitated. "Why is Mrs. Somerville not with the other guests?"

"Come along," he urged, leading me toward the staircase. "Don't be shy."

I did not want to keep her waiting, so I nodded and we started climbing the stairs. Perhaps Mrs. Somerville had taken ill, I thought, and had gone upstairs to rest. But if that were so, I would not wish to disturb her. "Perhaps not," I said, halting on the staircase and releasing Mr. Knight's arm.

He caught hold of my hand before it could slip free from the crook of his elbow. "Why not? We might not have another opportunity."

"I'm sure we will. I'd prefer to wait until she's feeling better. Bursting in on her when she's indisposed will hardly make a good impression."

"Miss Byron?" a woman called to me from below.

I glanced over my shoulder and saw my mother's friend Lady Gosford peering up at me curiously from the foot of the stairs. "Yes, Lady Gosford?"

"Your mother was asking for you." Her gaze darted between me and Mr. Knight and settled firmly upon him. "I don't think she's feeling well."

"Something must be going around," I said, shaking my head as I made my way down the stairs. "Mrs. Somerville has taken ill too. I was just going to see her."

"Who?"

"Mrs. Somerville, the mathematician."

"Yes, Miss Byron. Of course." Lady Gosford extended her hand as I approached and drew me to her. "Mr. Knight," she said

330

imperiously, "I believe you should either rejoin the party or go home."

Wordlessly he bowed to her, but Lady Gosford steered me back to the ballroom so quickly that I did not see which of the two astonishing suggestions he chose. She did not release my shoulders until she had delivered me to my mother, who stood in a quiet corner of the salon adjacent to the ballroom. My mother was ashen faced, and her eyes and mouth were lined with tension, and I knew at once that I was the cause.

We did not leave the party immediately because my mother did not wish to draw attention to our departure. Soon, however, we were in the carriage speeding toward our London home, my ears ringing from my mother's scolding. "How could you have been such a fool?" she berated me. "You're supposed to be so clever. Haven't you courted disaster enough already? Do you *want* to be ruined with all of London watching?"

"Of course not."

"What, then? What were you thinking?"

"He offered to introduce me to Mrs. Somerville."

"There and then? At the party?"

"He was taking me to her."

"He said so?"

"Yes, he —" I hesitated, thinking. He had asked if I were too tired to meet someone. I had filled in the rest myself.

I felt faintly ill.

"Let me be very clear," my mother said sharply. "If, at a social gathering, a man you scarcely know attempts to lead you to a secluded place some distance away from the other guests, the correct answer is always no!"

My heart was pounding. "I don't think — Mama, you must believe me. I wouldn't have consented —"

"He might not have cared whether you consented."

"I — I don't think he would have forced me."

"You don't know that, and perhaps that was not his intention. All he needed was to get you alone in a compromising situation. If anyone had discovered you — and I've no doubt he had a friend lurking nearby to ensure that you were — your reputation would have been ruined. Our only choice would have been for you to accept disgrace or marry him."

I squeezed my hands together in my lap, closed my eyes, and let my head fall back against the seat. She was right. Clever though I was with books and lessons, in every other respect, I was a fool.

We rode on for a moment in silence, but it was not to last. "I am constituted by God to be your guardian forever —"

"Not forever," I exclaimed. "Not when I am a woman grown!"

"Indeed, forever and always, and you must let me guide you," my mother said, glaring at the interruption. "You must learn obedience if you cannot learn caution."

"I choose caution, then," I said wearily, a trace of anger in my voice. Silence again descended upon the carriage, and when we finally reached home, we parted in the foyer without a word.

In the morning, I woke to find my mother gone. The housekeeper informed me that she had returned to Fordhook, and that in her absence I was to stay with Lady Elizabeth Byron, the seventh Lord Byron's wife and George's mother.

After breakfast, as instructed, I packed a satchel with enough clothing for a few days. Although I recognized my mother's tried and true punishment, I felt abandoned nonetheless, and angry with myself for feeling that way, and resentful of my mother for deliberately causing me distress. I knew I had made a mistake, but I had not intended any wrongdoing, and punishment would not help me learn from it any better.

Fuming, I closed my satchel and set it by the door for the footman to load into the cab, but before I departed, I went to my mother's study, seated myself at her desk, snatched up pen and paper, and poured out my anger and frustration onto the page, without the civility of a salutation.

The principle point on which I differ from you is "your being constituted my guardian by God *forever.*" "Honour thy father & thy mother," is an injunction I never have considered to apply to an age beyond childhood or the first years of youth, in the sense at least of *obeying* them. Every year of a child's life, I consider that the claim of the parent to that child's *obedience,* diminishes. After a child grows up, I conceive the parent who has brought up that child to the best of their ability, to have a claim to his or her gratitude. The child should serve the parent & next himself to make him or her comfortable, the same as a friend to whom he was under an obligation. But I cannot consider that the parent has any right to direct the child or to expect obedience in such things as concern *the child only.*

I will give a practical illustration of my meaning. If you said to me, "Do not open the window in my room," I am bound to obey you whether I be 5 or 50. But if you said to me, "Don't open your room's window. I don't choose that you should have your window open," I consider your only claim to my obedience to be that given *by law,* and that you have no *natural* right to expect it after childhood. The one case concerns *you & your* comfort, the other concerns *me only* and cannot affect or signify to you.

Do you see the line of distinction that I draw? I have given the most familiar possible illustration, because I wish to be as clear as possible. Till 21, the law gives you a power of obedience on *all points;* but at that time I consider your power and your claim to cease on all such points as concern me alone.

I signed the letter, sealed it, and gave it to the housekeeper to put in the post. Never before had I spoken so bluntly and defiantly to my mother, but I meant every word, and my declaration was long overdue. She could command my obedience only until the age of twenty-one, at which point the law could not compel me to follow her commands. The intervening years would be scarcely tolerable if she made them so, but knowing they would eventually come to an end would help me endure them.

As I climbed aboard the carriage, I realized that the only way I could escape her control any sooner would be to marry.

CHAPTER THIRTEEN:
ONCE KINDLED,
QUENCHLESS EVERMORE

May–June 1833

I learned that my mother had informed Lady Elizabeth Byron about my most recent brush with infamy when, mere moments after I had crossed her threshold, she sat me down with a cup of tea and told me that Mr. Knight was a notorious fortune hunter.

"He can't be a very good hunter," I said with feigned nonchalance, "or he would have caught himself a wife by now. Regardless of what you might have heard, I was never in any danger of being ensnared."

"Of course you weren't," she said sympathetically, passing me a plate of scones.

I had a fleeting thought that perhaps I ought to warn Miss Bettencourt to avoid Mr. Knight, but I concluded that she probably would dismiss my warning as a rival's deceptive stratagem. Furthermore, since she had no fortune to tempt him, he might admire her, but he would surely not attempt to seduce her. A fortune hunter did not scheme to compel into marriage a young woman without a penny to her name. But while Miss Bettencourt was safe from him, other young ladies would not be. I resolved to keep a watchful eye on that villain, and if I ever discovered him leading another innocent young woman into peril, I would fly to her rescue.

I spent several pleasant days with my Byron kin, and I was delighted by an unexpected visit from the cousin I claimed as an honorary brother, George. Before long it occurred to me that I loathed my mother's favorite punishment much less than I once had. I could not share this insight with her, however, or she would contrive some new and more injurious punishment next time. Not that I intended there to be a next time, but it seemed inevitable.

Our separation had the additional benefit of giving us time for our tempers to cool. When my mother returned to London in early June, I joined her in our rented lodgings, she greeted me with a kiss, and nothing more was said about my blithe stupidity. Soon thereafter, either to show me that all was forgiven or to reduce the likelihood that the odious Mr. Knight would succeed in a second attempt to deceive me, my mother accepted an invitation for us to attend a party at the home of Sir Richard Copley, a member of the Royal Society and one of the presti-

gious science society's most important bene-
factors. Many scientists and philosophers
were on the guest list, and she believed that
Mrs. Somerville might be among them.

Thrilled, I thanked my mother profusely
and immediately began planning what I
should wear to make a good impression, and
more important, what I would say. With my
mother's help, I settled on a lemon-yellow
day dress with a low waist and gigot sleeves,
and a white lace pelerine to drape over my
shoulders. I had memorized how I would
greet my idol, rehearsing the phrases while
studying myself in the mirror, but what I
would say after that, I still did not know even
as my mother and I climbed into the cab on
the evening of 6 June.

"Be natural and at your ease," my mother
advised me as we rode toward Whitehall.
"Sometimes you appear overconfident. If you
do meet Mrs. Somerville, do not try to
impress her with your mathematical knowledge, because hers surpasses yours, and you
will look like a foolish child."

I nodded, not wishing to spoil the evening
with an argument. If I sometimes seemed
overconfident, it was only because I was trying to conceal my uncertainty.

Lady Copley's London residence boasted a
flourishing garden in front and ornate white
pillars flanking the entrance. When we entered, the music of a harp drifted to us above

the murmur of conversation, and I eagerly turned toward it. I adored the harp, and I esteemed Mrs. Somerville so much that I was certain she must adore it too. Surely I would find her near the source of that music.

"Ada, wait," my mother said, placing her hand on my arm. "Before you hurry off, we must greet our hostess."

We soon found Lady Copley in a sitting room just off the foyer, and we went to pay our respects. Young, auburn-haired, and graceful, Lady Copley looked splendid in a cream silk dress with an embroidered bodice and a sash of pale green, and her glowing complexion intimated that the rumors of her delicate condition could be true. Lord Copley had been a widower twenty years her senior when she had married him two years before. She had a stepdaughter only four years younger than herself, and by all accounts they had become the best of friends. I confess I envied Miss Copley for that.

Lady Copley welcomed us warmly, and as soon as we got through the usual pleasantries, I blurted, "Did Mrs. Somerville come? I do so want to meet her."

"I'm very sorry, Miss Byron," she replied, shaking her head, "but Mrs. Somerville has been traveling abroad for the past year or so. I believe she's now in Paris, working on her new book."

"Oh, dear," I lamented. "What a pity!"

"Never mind," my mother said briskly, smiling to compensate for my poor manners. "We'll make her acquaintance another day. In the meantime, we have many friends here we look forward to seeing, and other ladies and gentlemen we cannot wait to meet. Thank you, Lady Copley."

We exchanged curtseys and my mother took me by the arm and guided me away. "I so wanted to meet Mrs. Somerville," I fretted in an undertone.

"I know you did," she murmured back, nodding to an acquaintance in passing, "but that's no reason to make Lady Copley feel as if she's failed you by not conjuring the lady upon demand."

While my mother followed after me at a more leisurely pace, pausing to greet friends along the way, I traced the harp's melody to a drawing room. Nearly two dozen ladies and gentlemen mingled in the sunny room, gathered in small groups or pairs near the window or in comfortable seats arranged here and there. The harpist, seated in the far corner, was a silver-haired woman attired in a modest dress of midnight blue, so engrossed in her music — an adaptation of a Haydn piano sonata in F major, if I was not mistaken — that she seemed unaware of anything but her instrument and the enchanting melody she spun from it.

As I drew closer, nodding politely to other

guests who glanced my way, I overheard bits of fascinating conversations — one of which I was sure was led by Mr. Charles Lyell, the preeminent geologist, for he strongly resembled the portrait on the frontispiece of the book *Principles of Geology*. "Aquatic creatures lived in ancient seas," he was telling his enthralled audience. "When they perished, their bodies sank to the bottom, where their soft parts decayed and their sturdier shells remained, creating a layer blanketing the seabed. Over the centuries, subsequent layers built up, one upon the other, and they were compressed to form stratified rock. Eons later, the seas dried up, great subterranean geological forces thrust these layers upward to great heights, and they were carved by rivers into the mountains we see today."

How delightful it was to be present at a party where such fascinating subjects were discussed! Just as I was about to work my way into the circle of attentive listeners, a burst of laughter caught my attention. Turning toward the sound, I spied a gentleman who looked to be not much older than my mother speaking earnestly to a group of four gentlemen and three ladies who seemed both amused and intrigued. The gentleman stood while his companions sat in a half circle around him, as if he were a teacher addressing a class. He was slightly taller than average height, and animated, with broad shoulders and a barrel chest. His square face bore an expression that suggested rationality and a jaw that implied stubbornness. My mother and her phrenologist friends would have frowned at his brow, which suggested intelligence without reverence, and at his mouth, which warned of an impatient nature. Fortunately, I was no phrenologist.

Glancing back the way I had come, I searched the crowd for my mother, only to find that so many acquaintances had stopped her for a chat that she had not proceeded very far beyond the entrance. She seemed perfectly content without me, so rather than wait for her to make introductions, I approached the lively gentleman and his enthralled audience alone.

"And so after years of dangerous, difficult surveying, the meridian was measured from the North Pole to the equator, passing through Paris, naturally, and from thence we derived the meter," the gentleman was saying as I drew closer. "For almost thirty-five years we have benefited from having a standard distance of measurement, as Delambre himself said, 'for all people, for all time.' But what of all of the old tables, which until then had been used to make complex scientific calculations?"

"They would be no good anymore, I suppose," said one of the ladies. "They don't conform to the meter."

"Exactly right, Mrs. Crawford," the gentleman replied. "So our intrepid Frenchmen were faced with a daunting conundrum: How on earth could they draw up new tables when the number of calculations required to create them vastly exceeded the total number of calculations that could be completed by all the mathematicians in France?"

"The simple answer is that they could not," remarked the eldest gentleman in the circle.

"Yes, Lord Mitchell, quite so. It was a physical impossibility. Or so it was until the French mathematician Gaspard Riche de Prony was inspired by the economist Adam Smith's study of the division of labor."

The Wealth of Nations," I heard myself say. His companions suddenly shifted their gazes to me, and I felt myself blush beneath their scrutiny.

"Yes, indeed, miss," said the gentleman, smiling approvingly. Emboldened, I seated myself in an empty chair on the edge of the circle, and when one of the gentlemen moved to make room and Mrs. Crawford smiled and beckoned, I drew my chair closer. "De Prony was fascinated by Smith's description of the manufacture of pins. One man drew out the wire, a second straightened it, the third cut it, the fourth sharpened it to a point, and so on and so forth so efficiently that twenty pounds of pins could be produced in a day."

"And de Prony thought this process could

be applied to creating the new mathematical tables?" queried another woman.

"Yes, Lady Addicott, he did. Why should he not manufacture logarithms as one manufactures pins?" Smiling, he spread his hands and shrugged as if the idea were so obvious, someone should have thought of it years before. "With Delambre's help, he contrived a sort of mathematics factory. The first room was assigned to the smallest group of workers, the most highly skilled, and therefore, the most expensive: the professional mathematicians."

"You would include yourself in this most exclusive group, I presume?" teased Mrs. Crawford.

"I think not," said Lord Mitchell. "Mr. Babbage is meant to be Monsieur de Prony in this scenario, the master in charge of all."

As laughter went up from the circle, Mr. Babbage grinned and waggled a finger at the gentleman. "You know me too well, all of you."

"What was the function of these mathematicians?" I inquired.

"The most important one, Miss . . ."

"Byron," I supplied, pretending not to notice the raised eyebrows and significant glances that greeted the revelation.

"Ah, yes. Miss Byron. Their role was to determine the formulae that were required to solve a particular calculation, and then to

reduce each formula to its smallest compo-
nents, to forms of mathematical operations
simple enough to be used by non-
mathematicians."

"Who were seated in the next room?"
ventured Lady Addicott.

Mr. Babbage nodded. "Exactly so. The
second room, larger than the first, accom-
modated the calculators. They were not as
skilled as the mathematicians, but still were
quite accomplished, and there were more of
them. Their role was to determine the range
of values for the calculation in question, as
well as the layout of the table."

As he spoke, I imagined a bustling workshop, much like the engraving of a mill I had
once seen, but instead of workers laboring
over their looms, clerks were seated at rows
of tables, diligently toiling with pencil and
paper. I wondered if de Prony allowed women
to work as calculators. Women worked in the
mills, enduring arduous labor in dusty, loud,
and potentially dangerous conditions; why
couldn't a sufficiently bright young lady work
in a mathematics factory too?

I wasn't thinking of myself, of course. Peer-
esses did not work in factories, and I wanted
to be the next Mrs. Mary Somerville, not a
mere calculator.

"The third room was necessarily the larg-
est," Mr. Babbage continued. "Therein
worked roughly sixty to eighty computers,

the least qualified — and least expensive — employees. Their task was to compute the results of the calculation in question using the formulae and values provided to them."

"You say they were the least qualified," said Lord Mitchell, brow furrowed, "but I must assume they had some knowledge of arithmetic."

"Certainly. The same basic skills any shopkeeper, weaver, or laborer must possess in order to conduct business — simple addition, subtraction, multiplication, and division." Mr. Babbage's smile turned wry. "De Prony had an ample supply of suitably qualified and recently unemployed workers eager for these new jobs, and you'll never guess what their previous occupation had been."

After a moment, one of the gentlemen said, "Clerks of some sort, I gather?"

"Hairdressers," said Mr. Babbage, a dark undercurrent in his voice. "After the Revolution, so many aristocratic heads had been parted from their unfortunate owners that the demand for workers proficient in wig powdering and pompadour constructing no longer existed. Thus many former hairdressers became computers instead."

For a moment a chilling shadow seemed to fall over the circle, and I shared the sudden apprehension. What had happened in France would never happen in England, I reminded myself firmly. My mother, Dr. King, and many other intelligent people whose opinions I trusted said it was so. And wasn't my mother, through her tireless efforts to educate the children of the working poor, doing all she could to help the lower classes improve their lot without the violent chaos of revolution?

"But as I have said —" Mr. Babbage sighed comically, and the shadow lifted. "The computers and the calculators were not skilled mathematicians, and errors could be introduced at any stage of the process, and those errors would be compounded as the process moved along. When I visited Paris — oh, what was it, about ten years ago — and I observed de Prony's mathematical factory, I was intrigued, but I thought to myself: How much more wonderful it would be if those computations had been accomplished by machine!"

Mrs. Crawford and Lady Addicott smiled indulgently, and one of the gentlemen chuckled, but I perched on the edge of my chair, enthralled.

Mr. Babbage's eyes were bright with excitement. "I knew that a machine could do everything the computers did —"

"Except arrange hair," one of the gentlemen broke in.

Everyone laughed, including Mr. Babbage. "Fair enough, but that skill is not required in mathematics. What is needed is the ability to calculate finite differences. Using this method, one can create a multitude of different numerical tables using simple addition and subtraction." He rubbed his hands together and beamed, brimming over with enthusiasm. "A machine performing the series of steps that comprise the technique of finite differences could carry out mathematical operations indefinitely and flawlessly."

"De Prony's calculators and computers could not do this sufficiently well?" queried Lord Mitchell.

My thoughts flew to the obvious answer, but before I could offer it, Mr. Babbage shook his head. "Even the best men require rest and make occasional mistakes. One of the great advantages that we may derive from machinery is the check that it affords against the inattention, the idleness, or the dishonesty of human agents."

Lord Mitchell frowned. "Perhaps, but if you were to replace the calculators and computers with machines, then you've reintroduced the problem of mass unemployment."

Several of Mr. Babbage's listeners nodded, but before he could address that concern, Mrs. Crawford spoke. "Forgive me, Mr. Babbage, but if de Prony's mathematics factory has already produced these tables, why would a calculating machine be necessary?"

"Ah, yes." He held up a finger, smiling, clearing enjoying the debate. "But de Prony's factory hasn't created all the tables the world shall ever need, nor could it. His system is limited to six digits, whereas my machine would go up to thirty." His smile broadened as his listeners exchanged glances, clearly impressed. "Also, de Prony has never been able to publish his tables. The cost would be prohibitive, and the problem of the likelihood of introducing error is insurmountable. His tables remain in manuscript form, and only those few individuals with access to the volumes held at the French Ordnance Survey can make use of them. My machine would have a printing mechanism built into it, so that any result could be immediately produced on paper, quickly and efficiently, with no risk of transcription or typesetting errors."

"Mr. Babbage," I said, "you speak with such certainty. Do you mean to say that you already know how to build such a machine?"

Everyone else smiled. "My dear Miss Byron," said Lady Addicott, amused, "you must be the only person in London who has not heard of Mr. Babbage's famous Difference Engine."

Difference Engine. The phrase had an aura of magic about it.

"Not everyone has heard of it," Mr. Babbage demurred, eyes twinkling. "Not yet, anyway. Give me time."

"Then you *have* built it," I exclaimed. "How marvelous!"

"I've built a demonstration model only," he replied. "The full-scale version of my Difference Engine is, shall we say, a work in progress."

"It shall be completed, Babbage," the youngest gentleman said stoutly, and all except Mr. Babbage, Lord Mitchell, and I myself nodded. I did not because I had only just heard of the Difference Engine and its aspiring creator, and I could not possibly judge. I don't know why Lord Mitchell declined to offer Mr. Babbage reassurances, unless he sympathized with the hairdressers who would be sacked if Mr. Babbage succeeded.

"It shall be completed," Mr. Babbage agreed, sighing. "One day the stars shall align, and the tightfisted government will release the funds they have promised me, and my recalcitrant engineer will resume the manufacture of the parts I need, and then we shall see what we shall see."

I longed to be there to see it.

The circle broke up and its members dispersed, as will happen at a party, but I lingered, eager to hear more about Mr. Babbage's wondrous Difference Engine. My mind raced with the variety and number of practical benefits that would result from such a machine. The tables it could produce for sailors navigating on the open sea, the tedious mental labors that could be delegated to a device that suffered neither boredom nor fatigue — the possibilities were themselves incalculable.

I approached Mr. Babbage, and we had scarcely exchanged greetings when my mother joined us and I promptly introduced them. "I observed from across the room that you had my daughter quite enthralled, Mr. Babbage," my mother said, smiling. "I must assume that you were discussing mathematics, music, or horses to have captivated her so."

"Mr. Babbage has invented the most wonderful machine," I told my mother, my words tumbling over one another in my excitement. "He calls it the Difference Engine, and it uses the technique of finite differences to tabulate polynomial functions."

"How delightfully well you describe it, Miss Byron," said Mr. Babbage, a trifle surprised. "I had no idea I was addressing a fellow mathematician."

His compliment pleased me immensely, but I knew my mother would not want me to seem proud. "I am a student only, with a great deal yet to learn," I said modestly, "but I find your Difference Engine absolutely fascinating."

"You must come and see it, then," he said, nodding to us both. "I give weekly soirées — which I confess I exploit to introduce people to my work — and I would be honored if you would attend."

I wanted to blurt out that we would not miss it for the world, but I wisely held my tongue to give my mother a moment to consider. "Thank you, Mr. Babbage. We would be delighted," she said, and if I had been only a few years younger, I might have jumped up and down for joy.

He assured us that we should expect his invitation without delay, and we parted with great satisfaction on all sides. Thus even though I had yet to meet Mrs. Somerville, I could no longer consider the party in any way a disappointment.

The following evening, in order to provide a contrast to the intelligent, edified conversation we had enjoyed at Lord and Lady Copley's the day before, my mother allowed me to attend the opera with Lady Elizabeth Byron. My mother did not join us; she disliked opera but said that since I loved music so dearly, I might go and judge for myself.

I cannot recall precisely what I had expected, but I was surprised by what I saw. The celebrated Italian soprano Giuditta Angiola Maria Costanza Pasta starred in *Anna Bolena,* in a role Donizetti had written specifically for her voice. She was quite wonderful, both as a singer and as an actress, and was especially gifted in expressing intense passions, but I confess the unfamiliar conventions of opera, which the other members of the audience took for granted, were quite lost on me.

But that was not the fault of the singer or the music. I did not understand what I beheld, and my thoughts were elsewhere — on Mr. Babbage, his Difference Engine, and the invitation I fervently hoped he would not forget to send.

CHAPTER FOURTEEN: WHAT WONDROUS NEW MACHINES HAVE LATE BEEN SPINNING!

June 1833

How I rejoiced when Mr. Babbage's invitation duly came and my mother agreed that we should accept. In the days following Lord and Lady Copley's party, we had discovered that Mr. Babbage's soirées were all the fashion in London among scientists, philosophers, and authors, as well as the aristocrats interested in knowing them. In Mr. Babbage's drawing room and salons, duchesses mingled with doctors, engineers with earls. We had heard, too, that Mr. Babbage and Mrs. Somerville were good friends, so I held out hope that he would introduce me to her after she returned from abroad.

My mother had, of course, made discreet inquires about Mr. Babbage before accepting his invitation. She learned that he had studied mathematics at Trinity College and Peterhouse at Cambridge, where he had been regarded as the top mathematician. After graduation, he had sought several academic posts and had been chosen for none, and so he had worked as an independent scholar in mathematics, astronomy, and electrodynamics and had dabbled in actuarial and insurance businesses. He had been elected a fellow of the Royal Society in 1816, and upon the death of his father, a prosperous banker, he had inherited a substantial estate worth one hundred thousand pounds. Such a fortune impressed even my mother.

On Monday evening, 17 June, my mother and I rode to Mr. Babbage's residence at 1 Dorset Street in Marylebone, a relatively quiet, remote neighborhood near Regent's Park. He had moved there in 1828 after the deaths the previous year of his father; his beloved wife, Georgiana; and two of their eight children, of whom two others had perished earlier in childhood. His eldest son was away studying engineering and architecture, and his daughter and two younger sons lived with his mother elsewhere in London.

Mr. Babbage's Georgian home, aesthetically pleasing in its symmetry and proportions, was white stone and redbrick outside, all polished wood, bright windows, and gleaming brass within. Although it missed the feminine touches his late wife might have brought to each room, it was gracious, comfortable, and tastefully decorated, indicative of a master who preferred clean lines and admired beauty from function.

The soirée was already merrily in progress when my mother and I arrived. We found Mr. Babbage mere moments after we entered, bustling about in the role of genial host, encouraging his guests to partake of food, drink, and fascinating conversation. His face lit up when he spotted us, and he quickly worked his way to our side. "Welcome, Lady Byron, Miss Byron," he said. "What a great honor and a pleasure it is to have you join us."

"I don't suppose Mrs. Somerville has come?" I said, ignoring the exasperated look this evoked from my mother. "I would so like to meet her."

"I'm sorry, Miss Byron," said Mr. Babbage as he led us into a spacious sitting room with tall windows overlooking the front garden. "As far as I know, Mrs. Somerville is in Paris."

"I had hoped she had returned."

"Not yet, I'm afraid. I'm happy to count Mrs. Somerville as a good friend and a frequent guest, however, so perhaps another time you visit, I shall be able to introduce you."

It was all I could do to restrain myself from skipping with glee. Mr. Babbage had already decided there would be another visit.

"I do have another lady I would like you both to meet," he said, his smile turning mischievous. "You've come just in time. I was just about to show her off."

Mystified, my mother and I exchanged a look — my mother raised her eyebrows; I shrugged — and we followed Mr. Babbage into an adjacent drawing room, where already at least three dozen other guests had gathered. I recognized a few of them from Lord and Lady Copley's party, and still others from the Court Ball, including Arthur Wellesley, first Duke of Wellington, former prime minister and great military hero who had defeated Napoléon at Waterloo. When Mr. Babbage entered, conversations trailed off and everyone turned to face him, expectant and curious. When the people shifted, I glimpsed a gleam of silver behind them, and I realized they had gathered around an object standing upon a table in the center of the room.

"Come closer, everyone," Mr. Babbage beckoned as he headed toward the table where the mysterious object was displayed. His guests parted for him, but I was obliged to wend my way through the crowd to a better vantage point, quickly, so that I did not miss a moment of whatever exhibition was about to begin.

What I saw made me gasp in wonder: an exquisite silver automaton, a perfectly and delicately fashioned female figure about a foot tall, every feature rendered in astonishingly lifelike detail. Clad in the pink-and-green Chinese crêpe costume of a ballerina, she was posed in a graceful arabesque, and upon her right forefinger perched a tiny silver bird.

A hush fell over the room as Mr. Babbage pressed the dancer's back, activating a mechanism concealed by her costume. With scarcely a sound, she gracefully glided forward, raised her hand, and tilted her head as if to observe the tiny bird on her finger as it flapped its tail, spread its wings, and opened its beak. The bird held still once more, the dancer pirouetted and glided back to her starting position, and after a moment, the mechanical dance began anew.

A murmur rose, and a smattering of applause broke out. Enchanted, I gazed at the graceful silver figure as it smoothly danced forward and back, compelled by some sort of clockwork mechanism concealed within the slender silver form. "How marvelous," I breathed, drawing closer, longing to trace the lines of the dancer's face with my fingertip. Even her eyes seemed alive, full of mischief and imagination. "Did you create her, Mr. Babbage?"

"I did not design her, but I did assemble her," Mr. Babbage clarified, addressing his reply to the room. "I first observed my Silver Lady as a boy, when my mother took me to visit Merlin's Mechanical Museum in Hanover Square." A few chuckles of recognition and remembrance went up from the older members of his audience, but I had never heard of it. "Clockworks and automata fascinated me, as did nearly anything mechanical, and as I gaped at the musical clocks, and the steel tarantula that crawled out of its box and scurried about, and the umbrellas that opened and closed without the touch of a human hand, Mr. John Joseph Merlin himself took note of my precocious understanding of mechanics. He invited me to tour his attic workshop, where he was constructing newer, more extraordinary mechanized wonders." He gazed at the dancer with fond admiration. "This lovely creature was among them."

"She is rather scantily clad," said one gray-haired lady, raising a lorgnette to her eyes and studying the Silver Lady reprovingly. "She is in need of a petticoat."

"My dear Lady Morgan, I am very much indebted to you for your helpful suggestion," said Mr. Babbage, so dryly that I suspected he had already dismissed it. "As I was saying, Mr. Merlin had many astonishing works in progress in his workshop, but many of them were yet incomplete when he died thirty years ago. His museum closed in 1803, and his collection, including the contents of his workshop, was acquired by Mr. Thomas Weeks, a jeweler, who opened his own mechanical museum on Tichborne Street in Haymarket. Perhaps some of you remember it."

I glimpsed a few nods here and there, but I did not offer one, nor did my mother, who had joined me in the innermost circle around the Silver Lady. She frowned slightly to rebuke me for darting off, but I kept my gaze fixed on the dancer and pretended not to notice.

"It was a rather impressive museum, one of the better of its kind, with a main gallery more than one hundred feet long, lined with blue satin." For a moment, Mr. Babbage's eyes took on a faraway look. "But as we all know, fashions change. The mania for intricate automata faded, and eventually, Weeks's Mechanical Museum closed too. His collection went up for auction —"

"And you were first in line to purchase the lot?" a man interrupted, to the amusement of the other ladies and gentlemen.

Mr. Babbage shook his head, smiling, and waited for the laughter to fade. "Not the entire collection, certainly not. Only this exquisite creature, which I discovered in pieces in an attic, utterly and disgracefully neglected. For a bid of twenty-three pounds, I acquired the dancer and a box of her spare parts, which I brought home, carefully restored, and meticulously assembled into the Silver Lady you see before you."

"Money well spent," remarked another gentleman.

"You have certainly been a skilled and faithful Pygmalion to your lovely Galatea, Mr. Babbage," said a lady.

He gave her a little bow. "Thank you, Lady Bennett." He pressed the dancer's back a second time, and she halted, frozen in a graceful arabesque once more. "Now, my friends, if you would follow me into the next room, I shall show you an even more astonishing mechanical marvel."

My pulse quickened as Mr. Babbage opened a different door than the one we had entered through, and I joined the throng filing into the adjacent chamber. I was at the trailing end, and I paused just inside the doorway to allow the crowd to disperse throughout the room, the better to take in the miraculous invention from a distance before drawing closer to inspect the details.

And there it was — Mr. Babbage's Difference Engine. Like the Silver Lady, the model stood upon a table in the center of the room, an intriguing apparatus of gleaming brass and steel about the size of a steamer trunk placed on one end. Sturdy brass columns supported two heavy brass plates between which were an assemblage of interlocking gears and levers, as well as many wheels with numerals engraved upon their edges, horizontally aligned and arranged in vertical columns along axes. A crank handle was fastened to the top of the machine, the handle facing downward. There was neither ornamentation nor embellishment, and whereas a watchmaker usually concealed the workings of his timepieces behind a decorative clockface, the functioning mechanisms of Mr. Babbage's demonstration model were visible to the observer from every angle.

"Your Grace, ladies, and gentlemen," Mr. Babbage intoned from the top of the room, "you are about to behold a calculating machine like none ever created before, or even dreamed of. At one-seventh the finished size, I give to you . . . the demonstration model of the Difference Engine."

His audience applauded, myself perhaps loudest of all, and our eyes followed the inventor as he strode toward the large central table supporting the machine. He circled it once, inspecting it thoroughly, and then, tucking one hand behind his back and grasping his lapel with the other, he said, "Earlier today, I set up the Difference Engine to execute a simple mathematical operation, the increase of a number in increments of two. We will begin at zero." He smiled. "We are all so familiar with this particular calculation that each of us will know immediately if an error occurs."

A few chuckles went up from the crowd, and I observed many nods and murmurs of anticipation too.

Mr. Babbage placed his hand on the crank at the top of his machine. "And now, my friends, you're going to witness something truly extraordinary."

I felt a thrill of excitement, even as my mother gave a skeptical sniff. Mr. Babbage cranked the handle vigorously, and with a whir of cogs and wheels, the entire array was set in motion. He stepped back, his gaze fixed on the engine, and even as he did the figure wheels began displaying the anticipated sequence, 0, 2, 4, 6, 8, 10 . . . and on and on. It was most impressive in its accuracy and regularity, but after a time I sensed the people around me losing interest in its perfection. Just as I, too, was beginning to wonder if Mr. Babbage intended to show us anything else, he suddenly gave the handle another vigorous crank. Suddenly, without any intervention on his part, the number displayed leapt ahead a few dozen to 121, which became 123, then 125, 127, and on and on in the sequence he had originally promised.

There were a few gasps and murmurs of surprise. "How did it do that?" I asked, incredulous. "How did you make it change to a new value out of sequence and then continue on as before?" Machines simply did not behave that way. They were never so . . . erratic. Not like people.

"Something must have gone wrong," a gentleman declared, gesturing imperiously at the machine. "A fly, or perhaps a large spider, got caught in a cogwheel and threw it off kilter."

"I assure you, my good fellow, nothing has gone wrong." With a touch upon a lever or two, Mr. Babbage stopped the whirring and spinning of the engine. "We shall try again, and prove it. This time you may give me the values." He turned to his right, and his gaze alighted upon the Duke of Wellington. "Unless the honor should go to His Grace the duke?"

"By all means, His Grace should decide," said the other gentleman diffidently.

The duke thought for a moment and said, "Let us make the interval of increase be five, and let the value leap ahead fifteen when it reaches thirty."

"Very good, sir." Mr. Babbage nodded approvingly and commenced working behind the machine. I heard the faint click of levers, and I quickly made my way around the edge of the table so that I could better observe what he was doing, but the calculation was apparently so easily arranged that he was almost finished by the time I drew close enough to see. I did glimpse something that had been hidden from my view before: several pieces of sheet music apparently left upon the table and forgotten.

"Remember His Grace's formula," Mr. Babbage instructed us, and again he turned the crank, releasing it with a flourish. I quickly returned to the front so I could see the display wheels — and there the sequence was, exactly as it should have been: 0, 5, 10, 15, 20, 25, 30, 45, 50, and onward.

An exclamation of surprise rose from the onlookers, and this time the applause was not merely polite. But Mr. Babbage was not finished. Adjusting the levers, he had his Difference Engine raise numbers to their second and third powers, quickly and perfectly every time. Next, he extracted the roots of a quadratic equation, and although we did not have sufficient time for him to show us, he declared his machine was capable of a great many other astonishing mathematical feats, including the generation of a table of all the prime numbers between zero and ten million.

"This machine is sublime," I heard my mother say in an undertone, and I tore my eyes away from the machine to stare at her, astounded. I could not believe that she had been converted from a skeptic to a believer in the space of a quarter hour.

"Pray, Mr. Babbage," ventured a lady, "if you put wrong figures into the machine, will the right answers still come out?"

To me the answer was so obvious that I could not believe anyone would ask the question, but Mr. Babbage smiled affably and said, "No, my dear lady. The Difference Engine is not capable of guessing what I *intended.* It knows only what I instruct it to do."

"Your machine is most impressive, Mr. Babbage," said the Duke of Wellington, nodding thoughtfully. "Aside from not reading our thoughts, which I'm rather glad is beyond its abilities, is there nothing mathematical your Difference Engine cannot do?"

"Nothing," Mr. Babbage replied firmly, but then his gaze fell upon the sheet music lying on the table. Snatching up the pages, he quipped, "It can do everything except compose country-dances."

A ripple of laughter went up from the room, but my own amusement dimmed when I realized that my mother had not joined in.

"I can see how your Difference Engine would be very useful to a general conducting a military campaign," the duke said, "with so many numbers and factors to consider."

"Indeed, but I think its greatest benefits will be seen in commerce and industry." Mr. Babbage paused significantly before adding, "However, we will not fully realize the extent of its capabilities and the vast reach of its benefits until the full-scale Difference Engine is constructed."

He regarded the Duke of Wellington with eager anticipation, but if he had expected a grand pronouncement, he was disappointed, for the duke merely nodded, thanked him for the demonstration, and departed the room accompanied by a few companions. This signaled to the rest of us that the exhibition was over, and while some guests lingered to admire the Difference Engine, still more returned to the drawing room to admire the Silver Lady again, and almost everyone else followed the duke's example and rejoined the rest of the party.

I was among those who remained with the Difference Engine, my heart pounding with excitement as I circled the table, admiring the beautiful instrument from all sides. It was ingeniously crafted, not as enchanting to the general observer as the Silver Lady, perhaps, but more complex and impressive. A closer look revealed to me that the numbers were arranged on consecutive carriages comprised of toothed wheels, each of which was marked on the edge with ten digits. When in the course of performing addition a wheel passed from nine to zero, the projecting tooth moved a lever to activate values in other places — tens, hundreds, thousands, and on.

How enraptured I was as I beheld the Difference Engine in all its mechanical wonder! Tears sprang to my eyes as if I gazed upon Michelangelo's *David* — for to me, it was no less a profoundly magnificent work of art.

"I confess I have but faint glimpses of the principles by which it works," my mother said in an undertone when I passed her a second time. I almost laughed, certain that she was joking, for she had studied Euclid in the original Greek when she was quite young, and her understanding of various intellectual concepts had always surpassed mine, except for subjects that she deliberately avoided due to profound lack of interest, such as Flyology and animals. It was disconcerting to think that I might grasp the intricacies of Mr. Babbage's invention better than my mother.

Yet the Difference Engine was as mechanical as it was mathematical, and unlike myself, my mother had not spent a good amount of her childhood dismantling clocks and windup toys to see how they worked. That surely explained how something that was obvious to me mystified her — although why I was so anxious to prove my mother's intellectual superiority, I could not say.

Mr. Babbage approached us then. "Lady Byron, your reputation as a lady of singular understanding precedes you," he said. "I'm very curious to know what you think of my engine."

Her expression was serene as she studied it critically. "I believe your thinking machine has utterly captivated my daughter's imagination."

That last word always carried a note of warning whenever my mother spoke it, but Mr. Babbage would not know that. "It isn't a *thinking* machine, Mama. It cannot think," I said in a rush.

"It has captivated Miss Byron, you say," Mr. Babbage mused, regarding my mother appraisingly. "What about you?"

"I marvel at it," she admitted. "To think that your apparatus could carry out these finite differences swiftly and with unvaried perfection indefinitely, to make more calculations than the world has known of days and nights — I find myself astonished and humbled."

"Thank you, Lady Byron."

"There is a sublimity in what you have shown us, perhaps unwittingly, of the ultimate results of intellectual power." She regarded him frankly. "One question remains."

"Only one?" Too late, I pressed my lips together. I truly did not mean to be impertinent.

My mother gave me a slight frown. "One for now." Turning back to Mr. Babbage, she said, "Your demonstration of the Difference Engine was well done, despite the occasional touch of a showman's hyperbole." Mr. Babbage seemed to strangle back a laugh, but my mother ignored it. "Why did you have to diminish the good impression you had made with that reference to country-dances — and in the presence of the Duke of Wellington, of all people?"

"Ah. You think I blundered." He shook his head. "My good lady, don't assume for a moment that the sheet music had been left on the table by accident. I need the Duke of Wellington. I need him to be impressed by my engine, and I need him to remember how he felt upon seeing it work its marvelous calculations, and not to allow those impressions to be buried beneath the flood of other concerns that I've no doubt inundates him every day." He threw me a comically helpless look, and I nodded encouragement. "The duke frequently attends balls, and country-dances are in fashion. I hoped my little jest would linger in his memory so that every time he encounters a country-dance, whether as dancer or observer, he shall be reminded of my Difference Engine."

"You desire his patronage?"

"Miss Byron, if I am ever to complete the full-scale Difference Engine, I fear that I desperately *need* his patronage." Suddenly he smiled, and his serious mood seemed to lift as his genial gaze took in each of his listeners in turn. "I believe that there is no aspect of our lives which cannot be improved by the uplifting benefits of technology. The challenge is to convince the gentlemen who control the national purse to give me enough funding to prove it."

His remark evoked somber nods and sympathetic smiles from the others, which made me suspect that a tale of financial woes and torturous politics had inspired it. Before I could inquire, Mr. Babbage gestured to the door and urged us all to rejoin the other guests before they polished off all the delicious food and drink he had prepared for us.

My mother took my arm, as if she sensed my mind working frantically on a scheme to remain behind to study the marvelous machine in solitude. Reluctantly, I followed Mr. Babbage from the room along with everyone else, but I gave the Difference Engine one last, long, yearning glance over my shoulder before our host closed the door behind us.

In the days that followed, my conversation and letters overflowed with descriptions of the party — of the splendid assemblage of intellectuals, the clever and delightful Mr. Babbage, and most of all, his marvelous Difference Engine. "I cannot wait until he invites us to another soirée," I declared unfailingly every day as the hour we expected the post approached.

My mother grew so weary of my rhapsodizing — and of my panicky lamentations when no invitation immediately appeared — that she declared she almost regretted taking me to Mr. Babbage's that night. That "almost," I knew, reflected her appreciation of the elite company and the marvelous Difference Engine, but not for our host. To my dismay — because it surely meant that she would limit our time in his company — although I had liked Mr. Babbage from the first, my mother did not care for him.

First, of course, was the matter of his jest about country-dances. I accepted his explanation, and indeed thought it clever of him to encourage the Duke of Wellington to remember the Difference Engine whenever he attended a ball, but my mother thought the joke rather flat and beneath the dignity of both the machine and its inventor. Furthermore, she was wary of certain defects of character revealed by his physiognomy, and she judged him "too finical" in his choice of attire and furniture. "He impresses me when he discusses mathematics and engineering," she acknowledged, "but he applies worldly means to the attainment of his ends, and he pays too much attention to trifles."

"What sort of trifles?" I asked, genuinely bewildered.

"Money, for one," she replied. "His desperation to acquire the patronage of the Duke of Wellington is most off-putting."

"The duke did not seem offended," I said, a bit defensively, "and only those who enjoy great prosperity ever consider money a trifle."

"*You* do not need to educate *me* on the struggles of the poor," my mother rebuked me, "and Mr. Babbage has done quite well for himself. If you cannot curtail this impertinence, Ada, I'll decline his invitations out of concern that he has already been a bad influence on you."

I immediately apologized and promised to

amend my behavior, though I doubted my mother would follow through with her threat. She had seen for herself that Mr. Babbage's soirées were where fashionable and intellectual society mingled, and a lady of her rank and accomplishments belonged in that illustrious company if anyone did.

An invitation from Mr. Babbage finally did arrive, and then several times more throughout the Season, and while my mother did not accept every invitation, she did so more often than she refused. Although at forty-one Mr. Babbage was nearly twice my age, we shared a love for all things mathematical and mechanical, and we soon became quite good friends. My admiration of the Difference Engine pleased him, and when he discovered that I could be a sympathetic listener, he confided that he had reached an impasse in his struggles to complete the full-scale version. "It's a fraught and frustrating tale," he warned, but I longed to know every detail, so I urged him to confide in me.

As I had overheard him explain at Lord and Lady Copley's party, he had been inspired to create a mechanical version of de Prony's mathematical factory after touring it in Paris in the early 1820s. Within two years of planning and tinkering, he had the design worked out and the demonstration model completed, and he announced his invention in an open letter to Sir Humphry Davy, the president of the Royal Society. "A copy of the letter was sent to Sir Robert Peel, who was the home secretary at the time," said Mr. Babbage as we sat together in his library, the conversation and laughter of the soirée a distant, pleasant hum in the background. "He had no time for it, or for me. I have it on very good authority that he dismissed my invention with the phrase, 'It is an engine designed against our walls or some other mischief hides in it.' "

I recognized the quote from the *Aeneid.* "He accused you of creating a Trojan horse to — I can't imagine what. To bring down the British Empire?"

Mr. Babbage shrugged. "Apparently so. Nevertheless, despite Peel's ignorant and shortsighted rejection of my engine, the Royal Society gave me their wholehearted support, and with that, I was able to interest the Treasury. The chancellor of the exchequer himself invited me to meet. I put the demonstration model through its paces and answered all his questions, and he was sufficiently impressed to offer me a grant of one thousand pounds from the Civil Contingencies Fund then and there."

"Excellent," I said. "The funding is significant, of course, but so is the recognition of your work by the government."

"The funding is *essential,*" Mr. Babbage said emphatically. "Without it, there is no Difference Engine, just ideas on paper and an exasperated philosopher tinkering in his workshop to no practical end. It is quite unusual for the government to fund research such as mine, you understand, but they thought my invention would have certain applications for the Royal Navy, generating accurate tables used in navigation foremost among them."

"Yes, I thought of that too, when I first heard you describe your engine."

"So, I had money in hand, or rather some of it, and more forthcoming." Mr. Babbage smiled, remembering. "My good friend John Herschel and I celebrated with an excursion to see a telescope, and then I set myself to work. I built a workshop in the stables behind the house — I shall show it to you later, if you're interested — and I converted an empty room into a forge. I also hired Mr. Joseph Clement, a brilliant engineer renowned for his precision work. Having seen the model in operation, you can imagine the vast number of wheel, dials, cogs, axles, and other parts I required him and his subordinates to make, all to exact specifications."

"With all of those resources at your command," I said, as delicately as I could, "one might wonder why, eleven years later, the project is not yet complete."

"One might indeed wonder," said Mr. Babbage mournfully. "My dear Miss Byron, I pray you will be spared the frustration and indignity of ever going hat in hand to collect funds that have been promised to you but are very reluctantly handed over. The money has come only in dribs and drabs, and on many occasions I have been obliged to draw upon my own accounts to keep the project from grinding to a screeching halt." He sighed and managed a rueful smile. "Ironically, some critics and professional curmudgeons imply that I've squandered taxpayers' money on myself, when the exact opposite is true. I've spent a substantial portion of my inheritance on my Difference Engine. I don't regret it, but I cannot continue to do so."

"That's why you're courting the Duke of Wellington."

"Yes, 'courting' is an apt word for it. The ritual does indeed feel as capricious and calculated." He sighed. "I'm confident that a gentleman with his prestige and influence could open the floodgate with a single letter, and he would be perfectly right to do so, for enough of the Difference Engine has been completed to justify every promise I've made about its capabilities, every expectation I've raised of its ultimate success."

I shook my head, sympathetic. "If so much has already been built, can you not continue to work with the expectation that the money you've been promised will eventually be disbursed?"

"I did indeed do so for quite a while, but

that arrangement has proved to be untenable. Early on, my engineer, Mr. Clement, who has nerve to match his prodigious talent, informed me that he could not pay his workmen unless I advanced him the funds. To prevent delays, I would pay him out of my own purse, sometimes five hundred or one thousand pounds at a time, and reimburse myself when the Treasury warrants were issued. This, eventually, became something I could no longer afford to do."

"Perfectly understandable," I murmured, abashed, for I knew very little about how workers were paid. My mother always took care of such matters — my mother, who had political connections that were every bit as highly placed as the duke. Perhaps I could persuade her to use them to help Mr. Babbage, although I would say nothing to him yet, rather than give him false hope.

"So I advised Mr. Clement that in the future I should no longer pay him until I had received the money from the Treasury," Mr. Babbage continued. "My engineer immediately ceased construction of the engine and sacked his workers."

"How disgracefully disloyal!" I exclaimed. "Did the privilege of working on this magnificent machine mean nothing to him?"

"Apparently less than it would to you or me, but in his defense, he does have to eat and keep a roof over his head."

"You would have paid him, just not as soon as he liked," said I. "I trust you fired him and hired a new engineer, one more dedicated and faithful."

"Even if I could find Mr. Clement's equal, I cannot fire him. When he left, he and his men took all of my drawings and tools with them."

"That cannot possibly be legal."

Mr. Babbage spread his hands, helpless. "These were new tools, ones they built especially for this work. It is common practice that even if the costs of construction are borne by their employers, engineers and mechanics have the right to keep all the tools they themselves made." His voice took on a slight edge. "The fact that I invented many of these tools, and that the workers made them from my instructions, apparently does not matter. Alas, the only way my tools and the men to wield them will be restored to me is if I pay Mr. Clement in advance for their labor."

"And you cannot do that until the Treasury pays you."

"Exactly."

I sighed and sat back in my chair, greatly vexed. "How outrageous that a bureaucratic snarl and one engineer devoid of a greater sense of purpose could prevent the completion of an ingenious machine that would transform the world."

Mr. Babbage managed a wan smile. "You praise me and my Difference Engine too generously, Miss Byron, and I am ordinarily the last person to object to that."

"But it is true," I said, puzzled. "Let us have no false modesty, Mr. Babbage."

"I do not doubt that my engine could transform industry, and commerce, and perhaps the navy," he conceded, "but not the world, although I thank you very much for believing it possible, and for believing in me."

I did not quite know what to say, so I inclined my head gracefully in imitation of my mother in a gracious moment. "I would be delighted to accept your invitation for a tour of your workshop at your earliest possible convenience," I said instead. "For now, I would be satisfied with another look at the demonstration model."

"Of course, Miss Byron," he agreed, rising and offering me his arm.

I took it, and off we went, while the soirée continued all around us.

Mr. Babbage remained with me for a while, but he could not neglect his other guests, so he soon excused himself and left me to admire the Difference Engine alone. But not entirely alone. Other ladies and gentlemen wandered in and out of the room while I stood nearly motionless, studying the amazing machine, but before long I became aware of the presence of another similarly still and studious figure on my left. A discreet glance revealed a gentleman perhaps two or three years older than myself, rather handsome, with soulful eyes, full cheeks, and a sensuous mouth. His thick light brown hair was parted on the right to reveal a high forehead that my mother would have approvingly noted signified well-developed faculties for Intellect and Conscientiousness.

"It is quite extraordinary, is it not?" I ventured, glad to make the acquaintance of someone who seemed to admire Mr. Babbage's creation as much as I did.

"Indeed it is," he said, but there was a wary note in his approval. "Ordinarily I am ambivalent about machinery, especially when men proclaim that it will improve our lives beyond imagining, but in this case, I believe Mr. Babbage is correct."

"I'm confident he is," I said, lifting my chin. "And when his funding comes through, he will prove it."

"*If* his funding comes through," said the young gentleman wryly. "The moment a gentleman perfects an invention and petitions the government for aid, he ceases to be an innocent citizen and becomes a culprit, a man to be shirked, browbeaten, and sneered at. I have never heard of any mechanician, inventor, or natural scientist who failed to find the government all but inaccessible, and whom the government did not discourage and treat badly."

"I hope you exaggerate," I said, dismayed.

"I wish I did. Of course, I speak only of the English government. When Englishmen take their inventions into other countries, it is quite a different matter, which is why so many of them eventually go abroad."

My heart sank lower. I could not bear to imagine Mr. Babbage packing up his demonstration model, notes, and drawings and carrying them off to some foreign land where I would likely never see them again. "Are you an inventor yourself?" I asked, hoping to learn that his dim view of an inventor's prospects sprang from his own disappointment, or from total ignorance, in which case I could ignore it.

"No, miss, not I." He bowed courteously. "I am Charles Dickens, aspiring author, currently employed as a reporter for *The Mirror of Parliament.*"

"So you do understand the workings of government."

He shrugged and offered a self-deprecating smile. "As well as any man can understand that inscrutable and indifferent beast."

I smiled, charmed despite his unfavorable assessment of Mr. Babbage's prospects. "I hope that you're a better writer than you are a prognosticator, Mr. Dickens, because I choose to be confident that our mutual friend will meet with success."

I did not know it then, but in the years to come, Mr. Dickens would become an enormously popular and successful author, and we would become great friends. As for his foresight —

"Ada?"

I glanced over my shoulder and discovered my mother standing in the doorway. It was time for us to depart, but it was with great reluctance that I bade my new acquaintance good-bye and cast one last longing look toward the machine that fascinated us both.

I could not wait to see the Difference Engine again, to delve more deeply into its mechanical genius, to explore and understand all its mysteries. I cannot explain it, but even then I suspected that Mr. Babbage did not truly know how revolutionary his invention was and could be, and that he did not fathom, as I was beginning to, that it was capable of vastly more than he could yet imagine.

CHAPTER FIFTEEN:
THE COMMENCEMENT OF ATONEMENT IS THE SENSE OF ITS NECESSITY

June 1833–March 1834

As soon as my mother and I were settled in the carriage, I shared with her Mr. Babbage's unhappy tale of bureaucratic stalemate. "That is why he seeks the Duke of Wellington's patronage so avidly," I said, "but I was thinking that the home secretary would have even more influence, and greater power to release the funds Mr. Babbage has been promised, don't you agree, Mama?"

She sighed. "No, Ada."

I knew she was not disagreeing with my point, but with the request she knew was forthcoming. "But why shouldn't you speak to him? He's your first cousin."

"I haven't seen Lord Melbourne in years," she said, frowning as she drew her fine wool shawl around her shoulders. "I've always thought very highly of him, but there is some . . . estrangement. His mother betrayed my confidence in a very hurtful manner when I was younger and relied upon her counsel, and as for his wife, Caroline —" She shook her head. "I'll say no more of her."

"But you haven't argued with your cousin," I persisted. "And forgive me, but aren't his wife and mother both deceased? Perhaps the time has come to mend fences."

"It's true that my cousin never wronged me, and he couldn't have prevented my aunt and his wife from doing so. The fault was never his." She fell silent for a moment, then sighed. "I should resume my correspondence with him. We are family, after all, and it is not right to neglect those ties. I shall not, however, ask any favors of him on Mr. Babbage's behalf. Has he put you up to this?"

"Of course not," I exclaimed. "I don't even think he knows we're related to Lord Melbourne."

"Likely not, or he would be courting me as relentlessly as he pursues the Duke of Wellington." She fixed me with a look that would suffer no disagreement. "I cannot beg favors of Lord Melbourne indiscriminately. If I ever do seek his help, it must be for something absolutely essential that I could not obtain without his help, and it must be directly to my benefit or yours."

"But helping Mr. Babbage build his Difference Engine *will* benefit me directly."

"How so?"

I could not answer that, because I was not entirely sure myself. I was drawn to the amazing machine, fascinated by it, and I longed to see it completed, to have a hand in its completion. Not since my studies of Flyology had my imagination been so fully enraptured by a technological marvel. But that would sound like dangerously enthusiastic nonsense to my mother, so I murmured something about scientific advancement benefiting us all, and my mother sighed, and the subject was closed.

Although I had become thoroughly enamored with Mr. Babbage's marvelous Difference Engine and happily would have spent all day studying and discussing it, I was not permitted to ignore my studies, either of the intellectual or of the moral kind. I read and wrote and calculated and analyzed as always, communicating with my tutors through the post, and my mother and I frequently attended edifying lectures on various scientific, philosophical, and historical subjects. Dr. William King, too, continued to advise me on spiritual and ethical matters in lengthy letters, which I did not mind, since he truly was a good, kind man deeply concerned for my welfare. I sincerely wanted to be good, and with Dr. King as with no one else I could ruthlessly examine my conscience without fearing that he would condemn me for what I found.

Nor was the business of finding me a husband neglected. My mother and I attended balls, parties, dinners, luncheons, dances, concerts, and soirées. We went riding in Hyde Park and browsing in the shops on Bond and Regent Streets. We paid calls on my mother's friends and received callers at our residence in Mayfair. Most of the time we got along quite well, and though we were not quite confidantes, we had grown closer than ever before. I was grateful for my mother's guidance, and I had resolved to put aside my youthful rebellion for the sake of my future. More often than not, I succeeded.

Basking in my mother's full attention, which I had so long desired, I blossomed. I attracted more than my fair portion of attention from the eligible young gentlemen making the rounds, but I was mindful that in all probability most of them were more interested in my fortune than in my mind, and I did not lose my heart to anyone, no matter how handsome or clever. Some of the young men were amusing and intelligent, others as dull as a lead whetstone. I never failed to introduce mathematics or science into our conversations, and if a fellow returned a blank-eyed stare, I crossed him off my mental list regardless of his handsome face or impressive title or substantial fortune. One had to narrow down the field somehow.

I flirted; I will not deny it. Most of the young gentlemen flirted right back. It was light and fun and meant nothing, and everyone knew it. I'm sure three-quarters of our clever banter was forgotten within the hour, but it was diverting for the moment, and it did no harm. But despite the distraction of frivolities and flirtations, my thoughts were never far from matters mathematical and scientific, especially Mr. Babbage's Difference Engine.

By mid-August the Season was winding down, and my mother was more than ready to retire to the country. As for me, I departed London with mixed feelings. I had not seen Mr. Babbage and his Difference Engine as often as I would have liked, and to my regret, I had not been introduced to Mrs. Somerville, who was still abroad. I had done my duty to my mother by meeting prospective suitors, and I had served myself by failing to get engaged to any one of them. I had passed the test of my presentation to the king and queen at the royal court; I had made only one enemy in Miss Bettencourt, and that was entirely her design; and I had done nothing more scandalous than climb halfway up a staircase with the fortune-hunting and incongruously named Mr. Knight. In sum, I calculated that my first Season was a success.

I enjoyed the liveliness of London and would miss it, but that was not why I dreaded returning to Fordhook. While I longed to see my horses and Puff, who had grown curmudgeonly in her middle age but remained fond of me, the Three Furies were also awaiting our return. Distance had afforded me some relief from their constant scrutiny, but our weeks apart had not weakened their resolve to improve me. In all the time I had been in London, they had continued to harangue me through the post as vigorously as they had stalked me around Fordhook.

One might assume that the learned Dr. King's guidance on ethical matters would have sufficed for one seventeen-year-old girl, but his were not the only sermons I was obliged to endure. My mother's friends — the Three Furies most of all but also several others — wrote to me often, accusing me of vague crimes they had not observed but were certain I had committed, because defiance was my nature.

Time and again they reproved me for not appreciating my exemplary mother as I ought. "You have a parent to whom you have at times behaved in a manner unbecoming the child of so invaluable a mother," admonished Miss Briggs, a former governess who apparently believed I was still in her charge. "The time will come when you will no longer have it in your power to make amends for the omission of any filial duty, and when you probably will wish in vain for the opportunity of doing so." Miss Doyle, who until the end of her days would probably picture me sitting on Wills's lap in the garden whenever she heard my name, wrote, "In your dear and excellent mother you have all that can be offered as an example short of the character of our Saviour, and she is still with you. Cherish this advantage, my dear Ada, while it is yours and do not let it be the subject of regret hereafter that you have not made proper use of it or valued it as it deserved to be valued."

Was it not perfectly natural that their letters upset me? It eroded my happiness and confidence to be told so often, day after day, that I was a wicked, incorrigible girl, that I was the ungrateful daughter of a perfect mother, and that I would regret taking her for granted after she was dead. Their condemnation exhausted me. Their predictions of my mother's imminent death worried me. The impossibility of satisfying them frustrated me beyond measure.

There was no point trying to defend myself, not only because that would add denial and defensiveness to the list of my infractions, but also because their complaints were vague and therefore all-encompassing. They berated me for a general *wrongness* intrinsic to my character. Humbly thanking the Furies for their concern and for the affection they showed by correcting me did absolutely no good, for even my repentance aroused their suspicions. "The sense you expressed of your faults and imperfections I believe to have been perfectly sincere," Miss Briggs wrote in reply to a particularly contrite letter, "but let me warn you against the error of supposing that a merely professed intention of amendment is sufficient to satisfy either myself or your mother, or your own conscience. You will have to search yourself continually — to form fresh determinations daily."

I tried. When some contrary part of my nature — my bad Byron blood, perhaps — boiled up within me and spilled over, compelling me to snap at my mother impatiently or tell a lie because I did not want to have to explain why I was engrossed in an activity that she would dismiss as a ridiculous waste of time, or when I found fault with everything she did and just wanted to go to my room and be *away* from her for a while — then I felt deep shame, followed by guilt, and joined soon thereafter by horror, because my wickedness was no doubt pushing her toward an early grave.

I know I've described how often throughout my childhood my mother was obliged to leave me to take various rest cures at spas, and how frequently her physicians prescribed leeches and cuppings to ease her symptoms. However, I neglected to add that I was considered the cause.

Real or imagined, all of my mother's complaints about her poor health were blamed upon a disorder of the womb that, it was said, had originated on the day of my birth. While the pregnancy and delivery were in every way normal, my mother's physicians and phrenologists agreed that as a consequence of bringing me into the world, the blood vessels in the region of her womb had become chronically overloaded and thenceforward required continual depletion.

My mother did not blame me, or so she assured me on many occasions, because of course I had not done it on purpose, but the simple fact I was reminded of time and again was that my mother had sacrificed her good health and vitality for me. It is little wonder that I suffered great remorse for the slightest wrongdoing, and that I so intensely resented the Three Furies' constant remonstrances that I was an undeserving daughter. Simply this: I believed they were right, but I was powerless to repair the damage I had allegedly done.

It did not occur to me then that my mother's various, vague ailments never prevented her from doing anything she wanted to do but gave her a ready excuse to decline invitations she did not wish to accept and to avoid people, including myself, whom she did not want to see. The guilt and fear that her fragile health evoked in my heart gave her tremendous power over me as well.

My mother did not need to remind me of how birthing me had injured her, for her loyal friends readily took on that task. When we left London for Fordhook, within days the Three Furies flew in from whatever gloomy roosts they had perched upon in our absence. At first they were too thrilled to be reunited with my mother to pay much attention to me, but the moment she departed for a favorite spa, with grim resolve they settled in to the task of supervising me, determined that I should not sin on their watch. Forgive me if I choose not to relive those unpleasant, endlessly frustrating days in these pages. Suffice it to say that I cannot imagine how I would have endured them if not for my books and my horses. They offered me the escape I desperately needed, for Dr. King himself had recommended diligent study to give order to my unruly mind, so the Furies did not interrupt if they came upon me bent over a book. The Furies could not keep up with me on horseback, nor did they dare try, so riding offered me a few hours of glorious freedom that did much to relieve the burdening sense of oppression that weighed me down so heavily that autumn.

In early November my mother granted me a most welcome holiday from my jailers when she accepted Queen Adelaide's invitation for us to attend a royal Drawing Room at the sumptuous Brighton Pavilion in that seaside resort town. Unlike my first appearance before the king and queen, this court was to be semiformal, although the setting would still be quite lavish, for the pavilion, designed by King William's more decadent predecessor, George IV, had been newly refurbished as a royal palace.

I wore a peacock-blue satin gown embellished with elaborate floral embroidery around the skirt at the height of my knee. Ribbons adorned the full gigot sleeves and a belt emphasized my slender waist. My mother looked very youthful and pretty in a gown of figured satin in a rich maroon hue. The neckline was fashionably low and curved, but it rose to a peak in front, a style that complemented her figure particularly well. White and blond satin covered her neck to the throat, so no one would realize that she wore her flannels underneath, as well as a plaster on her chest, for the sake of her health. Her hat, too, was crafted from white and blond satin and was adorned with white ostrich feathers.

No one was more pleased with my mother's splendid appearance than the dressmaker herself, who went into ecstasies when she beheld the perfection of her own handiwork. *"C'est divine,"* she exulted when my mother tried on the finished gown for the first time. *"Vous êtes un ange! Mais regardez donc, madame! Oh, elle est céleste! Elle va si bien!"*

On and on she rhapsodized with such ardor and enthusiasm that we would have been alarmed if the scene had not been so comical. After a while my mother and I could hardly maintain our composure, and we exchanged amused glances, stifling laughter, until we could no longer meet each other's eyes for fear that we would burst out laughing. Such moments of shared levity between us were rare, and I knew this one would swiftly pass, so I cherished it.

Our conviviality lingered long enough, however, to infuse our appearance at court with anticipation and delight. It was a triumphant evening for my mother, and I fairly burst with pride when the queen honored her with a request to join her private circle — and to my delight, as her daughter, I was allowed to accompany her.

The pavilion was divided into numerous salons, the most splendid of which was reserved for the royals and their most favored guests. I tried to imitate my mother's expression of implacable serenity as we were escorted into their illustrious company, but inside I trembled and quaked, wishing that I had practiced my graceful glide and silently praying that I did not stumble as we approached the place where Queen Adelaide and her companions were seated. My mother was shown to a gilded and embroidered chair a mere few feet from the queen, and I was taken to a large ottoman a little farther away, where a few young ladies already seated upon it smiled and made room for me.

The queen spoke graciously with all of the ladies honored with places in the semicircle around her, but since a vast number of topics were, for reasons of decorum and politics, excluded from royal conversation, much of our talk was rather bland, or as my mother sighed the next morning, "comparatively insipid." "It is a pity," she lamented, "that apparently it is proper etiquette to stultify oneself." I cannot say that I agreed. From where I sat, it seemed that Queen Adelaide valiantly enlivened the exchange as much as anyone could have done, and I was too pleased and honored by the favor Her Majesty showed us to critique the conversation as if I were reviewing a play for the London *Times.* King William also distinguished my mother by pausing by her chair as he made his rounds of the room and engaging her in a lengthy conversation.

From my place on the ottoman with the other younger ladies, I could not help observing that the royal salon seemed to be regarded as a sort of sanctum sanctorum to those guests who had not specifically been invited to enter. Very few people possessed the courage to cross the threshold, and I was at first surprised, and soon amused, to watch one finely dressed, dignified guest after another approach the doorway, peep inside the salon, and timidly retreat. One young lady — tall, slender, blond, attired in an elegant gown of emerald silk — lingered longer than the others, her gaze taking in the scene without a hint of bashfulness. When her gaze settled on me I recognized her as none other than Miss Bettencourt. I started in surprise, she inclined her head, I nodded politely back, and after a moment more, she glided from the doorway so gracefully she would make a dancer envious. I watched for her throughout the evening, but she did not return.

My mother and I stayed at court until almost midnight. We could not have left earlier even if we had wanted to, as it would have been the height of rudeness to retire before Their Majesties did. We were both quite fatigued by the time we boarded the carriage, but we enjoyed a pleasant ride back to our lodgings even so, for I was proud of my mother and she was pleased with me.

It was only later, as I reminisced about the evening while preparing for bed, that I remembered Miss Bettencourt. It occurred to me that I could have made a show of going to speak with her, and perhaps the gracious queen would have invited her to join our prestigious circle, and Miss Bettencourt might have been grateful, and we could have become fast friends evermore. But I thought of it too late. Never mind, I told myself as I sank into sleep. The idea that Miss Bettencourt would ever like me was surely wishful thinking.

I still longed for more friends my own age, and though my first London Season had been a whirlwind of social activity and I had made many new acquaintances, I had not really found much opportunity to develop strong friendships with other young ladies. I suppose the atmosphere was not conducive to friendship, as we were under such pressure to look our best and impress with our conversation and delight with our accomplishments, all while competing for the elusive prize of a good match. There were only so many eligible young gentlemen to go around who were handsome, wealthy, titled, intelligent, and agreeable, and I am sure we were all mindful of the disgrace that would follow if we did not acquire one. It was little wonder we regarded one another as rivals.

My mother and I returned from our holiday in Brighton in good spirits and more satisfied with each other than we had been in a long time. Naturally, this disruption to the natural order alarmed the Three Furies, who promptly set themselves to the task of reminding my mother that I could not be trusted and that if I seemed obedient and repentant, it surely meant that I had learned to better deceive her.

The situation became increasingly frustrating to me as the autumn days grew shorter and winter sent in. As I began to despair of ever becoming perfectly good, I grew resentful, and my old habit of "conversational litigation" reemerged. If I could not be good enough to please my mother and her friends no matter how hard I tried, why bother trying? Why not indulge myself and say what I really thought?

"I am not who I was a year ago," I told my mother on the eve of my eighteenth birthday as we sat alone in her study. "The more I see and the more I think and reflect, the more convinced I am that no person can ever be happy who does not possess deep moral feeling and who does not let that feeling be one's guide in all circumstances throughout life. What more can I do to prove to you that I am an altered person?"

"I do think you have lost your sense of infallibility," my mother acknowledged, studying me. "However, you have not yet substituted that with reliance upon the Infallible Guide."

"I do place my trust in God," I protested. "Of course I do."

My mother sighed, interlaced her fingers, and rested her hands on her desk. "Ada, I know you better than anyone, and you cannot fool me. What disturbs me most is that, despite all of our best efforts to instruct you, you seem to lack any sort of a moral sense."

I felt a chill of apprehension. What she described was a form of madness. People were sent to asylums for that. "Mama, I assure you, that is not so. What have I done to make you think so little of me?"

"When you do adhere to principles of truth and virtue, you do so only because we expect it of you, not because you have any understanding of, or esteem for, their inherent goodness."

For a moment I was going to retort that as long as my behavior was exemplary, what difference did it make, but I held my tongue, because I knew it made all the difference in the world to my mother. I felt trapped, judged, powerless. How could I prove how I felt if my actions would not be accepted as evidence of my feelings?

I was struck by a curious, fleeting thought: If I had a Difference Engine inside me instead of a brain and a heart, how much easier my life would be. No one could doubt me then. The Difference Engine's "thoughts," or rather, the calculations it provided, were always correct and always readily visible. No one could argue with it or accuse it of deception or manipulation.

Imagining myself as a young woman on the outside but with gleaming brass mechanical innards, and oil instead of blood, I felt a frenzied mirth bubbling up in my chest, threatening to spill out in a cascade of manic laughter. I pressed my lips together and bowed my head, but it required every ounce of my strength not to laugh and cry all at once.

My mother must have interpreted my struggle as the first true sign of my contrition, for she sighed, relenting. "I think I know something that may help you."

I lifted my head warily and watched as she retrieved a book from a drawer and passed it across the desk to me. Dubious, I took it up, frowned at the blank spine where the title should have appeared, and opened the cover to find that all the pages were blank. "A journal?"

My mother nodded. "One with a very specific purpose. Dr. King has been an excellent spiritual advisor, and he has shared with you many important moral precepts. I believe it would help to reinforce those principles in your mind if you wrote them down in a book. The act of transcribing his words will cause you to ponder them more deeply, and in the end you will have collected them in a reference you can refer to in moments of weakness or doubt."

It seemed too easy; I had expected a harsher punishment, or at least a more demanding exercise. "I think that's a very good idea," I said carefully, closing the book and holding it on my lap.

When my mother advised Dr. King of her plan, he readily agreed that it was sound, and he promised to write to me even more frequently and to come to Fordhook to resume our old walks and chats when his schedule and the weather permitted. He also advised me to focus my studies on mathematics and science to keep my imagination in check and to fill up the void in my mind created in the absence of the stimulation of London. In particular, he recommended the "close and careful" study of Euclid's geometry, which to me sounded like a delightful holiday.

Never before had I been happier to accept corrective measures, and all winter I studied vigorously. Early in the New Year, I wrote to Dr. King to express how happy I was to follow his recommendation, that I felt its benefits already in helping me to discipline my disordered thoughts, and that I wanted to add a course of arithmetic and algebra to the program, as well as astronomy and optics as soon as I had mastered the requisite mathematics to comprehend them.

How wonderful that the study of mathematics figured so prominently in Dr. King's prescription for the mastery of my passions and imagination! Ardently I embraced Euclid's geometry and algebra and all the rest, and it seemed that the more I learned, the more I discovered I had yet to learn. I feasted gloriously on knowledge, on formulae and proofs, and I thought how wonderful it was to live in an age when so many new scientific and mathematical concepts were being discovered every day.

It must be Providence, I decided, that I had entered the world at precisely the right time. Or perhaps instead, this glorious wellspring of knowledge had waited for me to arrive before it began to surge and flow.

"Ada, remember moderation," Dr. King cautioned me. "Mathematics, self-improvement — even these can be practiced to excess. You must not allow a new mania to replace the old."

Mania, again. Always that word was banded about whenever I pursued my passions. Whatever my mother and her host of advisors did not understand or approve, they labeled an illness. I longed to return to London, to Mr. Babbage, Mr. Dickens, and the elusive Mrs. Somerville, where genius was celebrated and imagination encouraged, not regarded fearfully like a house fire that must be extinguished before it destroys the entire village.

Chapter Sixteen:
A Mind to
Comprehend the Universe

March–May 1834

I had not yet achieved perfection by the time my second London Season began, and in hindsight I am heartily glad for it, for I would have become a very dull young woman indeed had I succeeded. The perfection I admired in Mr. Babbage's Difference Engine was not only impossible for a human being to achieve, but also undesirable. I understood that at eight years of age, but I had forgotten it by eighteen. Fortunately, that crucial piece of wisdom I lost between childhood and womanhood was restored to me while I was still young and optimistic enough to make use of it.

But that was yet ahead of me. When my second London Season began, I was still determined to become the sort of exemplary young woman my mother had been at my age. But even then, I could not dread my imagination as much as she and Dr. King thought I should. I understood its dangers, its seductive powers, and yet I hated to hear it maligned. When they exhorted me to quash it, to contain it, I felt myself taking my poor, disparaged imagination in my arms and bending over it protectively to shield it from the slings and arrows of outraged parents and those *in loco parentis,* as if it were a helpless newborn kitten.

I suppose the very fact that I did imagine this proves how badly I failed to subdue my imagination.

Although I strove for honesty and obedience, as my mother and I settled into new lodgings in Mayfair, I resisted confessing that my imagination thrived, more curious and exuberant than ever. I was secretly pleased that it had turned out to be the rare sort of wild creature that survived fairly well in captivity.

Not long after we returned to Town, we attended another royal Drawing Room at Saint James's Palace. This time I stood by my mother's side attired in a beribboned silk gown of pale green while other young ladies in white satins and silks were presented to the king and queen. A few of the girls looked utterly terrified, some were a trifle unsteady in their full court curtseys, but not one committed any of the errors that would condemn her to the sort of eternal ignominy that Miss Bettencourt had warned me of, or rather, had wished upon me.

Miss Bettencourt. I had not seen her or thought of her in months. I glanced around the drawing room, but I did not see her, and I wondered why she was absent. Perhaps, I thought, more curious than spiteful, she had not been invited.

As I searched the room, my gaze fell upon a gentleman I recognized — Colonel Francis Doyle, my friend Fanny's uncle, brother of the Fury Miss Selina Doyle, and one of my mother's most trusted attorneys. He was chatting with a gentleman who looked to be a few years older than my mother, and as I studied him, I felt a strange sense of recognition. He had thin brown hair and features that, while not unpleasant, were not regular enough to be called handsome — full cheeks, an aquiline nose, and a small pursed mouth. As he felt my gaze upon him, he looked my way and froze, his face draining of color. Colonel Doyle, realizing he had lost his friend's attention, looked along his line of sight to see what had distracted him, and found me. The two conversed briefly in quick, terse sentences; the strange gentleman nodded; and Colonel Doyle led him through the crowd toward me.

Suddenly wary, I glanced around for Fanny, and when I did not see her I looked for my mother. Unfortunately, she was engrossed in a conversation with Sir Robert Peel and I knew she would not thank me for interrupting.

"Miss Byron?" said Colonel Doyle, halting before me. His companion fixed me with a stare so intense that I could not hold his gaze.

Ignoring the stranger, I offered the colonel a polite smile. "Yes, Colonel Doyle?"

"My companion was a dear friend of your father's since their school days, and he would very much like to meet you. Miss Byron, please allow me to introduce Sir John Cam Hobhouse. Sir John, this is Miss Augusta Ada Byron."

Hobhouse. I felt a jolt of recognition at the name, and I struggled to hide my sudden distress as we exchanged the usual pleasantries. The man who stood before me had been my father's best friend, and I knew my mother despised him. She considered him the worst of the "Piccadilly crew," as she called my father's loyal friends and drinking companions who had led him into insobriety and degradation, undermining his marriage, contributing in no small way to the Separation.

"What a true pleasure it is to see you again, Miss Byron," said Hobhouse, smiling. "You will not remember me, of course. The last time I saw you, you were but six weeks old."

I felt my throat constrict and I swallowed hard. This man, who my mother had raised me to believe was the most vile and conniving of men, had known my father better than anyone. "I do not remember you," I managed to say, "but I have heard of you."

He nodded sadly. "I suppose most of those stories have not been kind."

A flood of memories — not mine, but stories I had overheard, exchanged between my mother and her friends — crashed over me. "I trust you do not mean to suggest that my mother has spoken untruthfully about you," I said. My voice trembled and trailed off as if a hand had closed around my throat.

"No, certainly not —"

"Because that's precisely how it sounded to me." I nodded sharply to him and then to Colonel Doyle. "If you will excuse me, gentlemen, I believe my mother wants me."

I turned and strode away, losing myself in the crowd, gulping air, fighting back tears. It was inevitable that I should meet some of my father's old friends once I entered Society, I told myself, fighting to regain my composure. I had grown accustomed to encounters with his loyal readers because they were legion, but someone who had known him intimately — that was completely different, somehow, although I would never have imagined it would have affected me so intensely —

"Miss Byron?" I felt the touch of a woman's hand on my arm. "Are you quite all right?"

I halted, but in my distress I needed another moment before I could speak. "Good evening, Lady Byron." Not my mother, but her successor, the wife of the seventh Baron Byron, Captain George Anson Byron. "How do you do?"

"Quite well, my dear, but forgive me, your expression tells me you cannot say the same." She put an arm around me and led me to a less crowded part of the drawing room, where we could speak with some measure of privacy. "What's wrong? Do you want me to find your mother?"

"Not just yet, please." I inhaled deeply and forced my heart to stop racing. "I had . . . an unpleasant introduction to a dreadful man, an old acquaintance of my father, Sir John Cam Hobhouse."

"Sir John, a dreadful man?" Lady Byron shook her head, puzzled. "I've never heard him called that before. I can't imagine what he might have done to deserve it, especially if you have only just met him."

"Well —" I hesitated, flustered. "He didn't really do or say anything offensive, I suppose, but — well, his reputation precedes him."

"Oh. I see." Lady Byron nodded knowingly. "My dear girl, I would not wish to contradict or criticize anyone to whom you owe your first and strongest loyalty, but let me say this." She paused, choosing her words with care. "I have always known Sir John Hobhouse to be a perfectly respectable and honorable gentleman, and while it is wise to consider the

408

opinions of our elders, we must be careful not to absorb their prejudices along with their wisdom."

"Prejudices?"

"There comes a time in every young woman's life when she must learn to trust the evidence of her own senses, of her own experiences, if it does not confirm what she has heard from others." She smiled and lowered her voice conspiratorially. "I trust you will not get me in trouble with *your* elders for telling you that."

"No, certainly not."

"Good." She glanced past my shoulder. "I think I see your mother over there, if you need her."

We parted, and I made my way through the crowd to my mother's side, my thoughts churning. I had left Hobhouse so abruptly that I had scarcely had a chance to gather any evidence of my own senses and experiences. If my mother's own lawyer considered him a friend, if Lady Byron called him honorable — could it be that my mother was mistaken? I could not believe that she would deliberately deceive me, but perhaps she knew only his worst elements and none of the good.

My heart sank when I realized how rude I had been to him, and to Colonel Doyle. I could only hope that they would excuse my behavior on the grounds of my youth, although I could not rely upon that excuse much longer. If only I had kept my composure and had reserved judgment, what fascinating stories about my father might I have learned from his dearest friend?

Suddenly my imagination returned me to the shores of Lac Léman and to the stories my mother's cousin Robert Noel had shared with me about my father, the castle of Chillon, and the Villa Diodati; to Genoa and the studio of the master painter Signor Isola, who had glimpsed signs of my father in me — the line of my jaw, the way I studied my subject, the motion of my hand as I sketched. These were precious glimpses into the past that my mother could not, or would not, have ever shared with me.

What new stories might have been captivating my imagination at that very moment, if not for my presumptions? Silently I berated myself for squandering an opportunity that was unlikely to come again. All I could do was learn from it. I was no longer a child, and I needed to think for myself.

I realized that these were dangerous, transgressive thoughts, but rather than drive them away, I resolved to hold on to them for a while and see where they led me.

Soon thereafter, I had the very different experience of meeting someone whom I was predisposed to like exceedingly well. The momentous occasion was at a dinner party I attended with Lord and Lady Byron and their son George, my honorary brother. My mother did not come, being indisposed, but soon after our arrival I discovered that my father's publisher, Mr. John Murray, was also present.

Although we had been introduced before, I did not know Mr. Murray well. He and my mother occasionally corresponded about my father's work, but while they had a civil relationship, they were not friends. Through the years I had heard my mother make certain scathing remarks about him — most recently, a few years ago regarding a dispute about the publication of my father's memoirs and the subsequent burning of the manuscript. A fortnight earlier, I might have shunned Mr. Murray as I had Hobhouse, but I had learned my lesson, and I resolved to be cordial.

He greeted me warmly when I approached him, and he politely inquired after my mother. He courteously said nothing of my father's memoir or any other potentially distressing subjects but instead offered several thoughtful, amusing reminiscences of working with my father.

"There was another occasion, I recall, shortly before Christmas of 1822," said Mr. Murray, his gaze faraway. "Lord Byron was in Genoa at the time, and he wrote me a letter of at least six pages berating me for a decision that I now regret."

"What decision, if I may ask?"

"Of course you may ask. You may always ask." Mr. Murray ran a hand over his jaw, his expression sheepish. "I confess I had found Lord Byron's most recent cantos of *Don Juan* too shocking, and I had refused to publish any more of his work. In one letter, he urged me to continue to publish his poetry, claiming that he trusted no one else to do it properly — which, I admit, flattered me. He also assured me that he would compensate me for any financial losses I might suffer if the new volumes did not sell." He smiled wryly. "The very next day, he wrote again to complain about my poor editing and to criticize me for cutting a dedication to Goethe from one of his poems."

"I imagine poets can be difficult to please," I replied, amused.

"Some more than others," he acknowledged, and instinctively I knew that he would never say anything more critical than this about my father in my presence, and that endeared him to me. "Other authors are more congenial, as long as I print their books correctly and don't omit essential facts or, heaven forfend, entire pages of the manuscript."

I smiled. "I think they would have a right to complain in such circumstances."

"I quite agree with you, which is one reason I endeavor to make no mistakes." He frowned thoughtfully, tapping his chin with a forefinger. "I understand that you have an interest in mathematics and science, much like your mother. Is that so?"

"Very much so, a keen interest."

"I think you'd enjoy a new book I'm publishing later this month. I'll be sure to get you a copy. It's about how the various branches of the sciences are actually closely connected. It's called *On the Connexion of the Physical Sciences,* by Mrs. Mary Somerville. Are you familiar with her work?"

"I surely am," I exclaimed. "I've been looking forward to reading her new book ever since I heard a rumor about it almost a year ago. I'm delighted to hear that the wait is almost over."

"I'm sure Mrs. Somerville would be pleased to know that. Would you like to meet her?"

"Indeed, with all my heart," I said, wistful. "I've long hoped that our paths will cross one of these days and some kind person will introduce me."

"Your paths could cross in about five minutes, if you like," said Mr. Murray, smiling. "Mrs. Somerville is in the library, and I'd be very pleased to introduce you."

If I were the sort of young lady who swooned, I probably would have done so at that moment and would have missed the opportunity to meet my idol at long last. Fortunately, I was more levelheaded than that, despite all other evidence to the contrary, and I eagerly accepted Mr. Murray's offer.

He escorted me into the adjacent chamber, where I immediately felt at home, thanks to the walls lined with bookshelves and the pleasant, familiar smell of beeswax and old paper and leather bindings common to libraries everywhere. Several guests mingled here and there in the room, which was about twice as long as it was wide, but Mr. Murray led me past them all to a wide bay window on the far end, where two armchairs and a sofa were arranged to create a cozy reading nook. A woman in her midfifties was seated in one of the chairs. A gentleman and a lady a few years older sat together on the sofa across from her, and a younger man, perhaps about ten years older than myself, stood at the first woman's side, one arm folded behind his back, the other resting upon the high top of her chair. He looked familiar, as if we might have been introduced at a ball or a party once but had not cultivated the acquaintance.

The four guests were chatting when Mr. Murray and I entered the room, but as we approached, the couple rose, made their farewells, and strolled off, leaving the way clear for us. My heart pounded and my mouth went dry, but it was too late for second thoughts, because suddenly there I was, standing before the woman I had so yearned to meet.

Mrs. Somerville had strong, pleasing features in an oval face, her eyes a clear hazel, her lips full with a hint of a smile. She wore her chestnut brown hair in an intricately braided knot on the back of her head, with graceful curls arranged on the sides. Though her gaze was piercing, her expression was calm, kind, and intelligent, and yet I was terrified.

I managed to stammer out a coherent reply when Mr. Murray introduced us and Mrs. Somerville addressed me, and I'm sure I said something polite when I was introduced to the gentleman standing by her side, who turned out to be Woronzow Greig, the eldest son of her first marriage. For a fleeting moment I considered asking him if he knew Mr. Charles Murray Knight, but I realized just in time that Mr. Knight had probably lied about their acquaintance as he had lied about everything else, and I did not want to admit to knowing such an awful person.

Mrs. Somerville invited us to sit, and her manner was so natural and gracious that I soon felt at ease. I inquired about her forthcoming book, and she seemed charmed by my eagerness to read it. "I've worked on the manuscript so long — focusing the subjects, honing the prose so that the writing is as clear and yet as informative as possible — that I confess there were times I wondered whether I would ever be sufficiently satisfied with the book to publish it," she said, her voice a compelling alto. "Now here I am, preparing to send it out into the world for its judgment — with Mr. Murray's help, of course."

He bowed and seated himself in the other armchair. "Miss Byron shares your passion for mathematics and science."

"Indeed?" Mrs. Somerville's eyebrows rose. "Do you regard them as a pleasant pastime, Miss Byron, or do you hope to make a career of them?"

"The latter," I replied fervently, "although I know many consider it a peculiar interest for a young lady."

Mrs. Somerville exchanged an amused look with her son. "Oh, Miss Byron, we pay no mind to those sort of people."

"Mathematics in particular fascinates me, inspires me," I said. "It has done so for as long as I can remember. I would love to have a career like yours, and to make astonishing discoveries that we cannot yet imagine, and to have my name enshrined in memory with yours, Newton's, Euclid's —"

"You put my name in very illustrious company, and I'm not quite certain it belongs there. It is fame you seek?"

"Not at all. I've had a taste of fame and I don't care for it. I want to discover something, to illuminate something previously unknown, not for my sake, but to contribute to the advancement of science, to the sum of human knowledge. But as to fame —" I took a deep breath and plunged ahead. "If I cannot escape it, then I want it to rise from my own achievements, not my father's."

The torrent of words came to an abrupt end. Abashed, I studied my hands in my lap, heat rising in my cheeks. I had never confessed this secret desire to anyone, not even Dr. King, and I was under strict orders to tell him everything.

"It is an admirable goal, to wish to contribute to the advancement of science," said Mrs. Somerville kindly. "It is not, however, so often achieved as wished for, even in this age of wonders, when new discoveries and advancements seem to spring up overnight." She leaned forward, smiling warmly. "I admire you, Miss Byron, for your resolve, but do take care to enjoy the processes of investigation and experimentation as much as you do the discovery. I assure you, you will devote years to toil and only moments to shouting, 'Eureka!' "

I smiled, my heart full, joyful tears threatening. *She* admired *me.* She did not dismiss my longing for a career like her own as arrogance or folly. This was more encouragement than I had ever received from any of my tutors, who saw my studies only as a means to rein in my unbridled imagination.

"Thank you, Mrs. Somerville," I said, glowing with hope and gratitude. "I won't forget."

When Mr. Murray prompted us, we returned to my original question about her new book. As the title indicated, Mrs. Somerville believed that the different branches of natural science were not so disparate after all, but rather rose from the same fundamental wellspring of knowledge. "I intend for my book to demonstrate the astonishing tendency of modern scientific discoveries to simplify the laws of nature, and to unite these detached branches by certain general principles," she said. "Understanding that all sciences are essentially one rather than marking them off into distinct realms that share borders but no territory will, I think, increase our comprehension of them all in ways that we cannot yet imagine."

I nodded. "One cannot understand the branches if one does not first know that they are part of the same tree."

"Exactly so," she said, exchanging an approving glance with Mr. Murray.

"Intuitively I accept that the sciences are connected," I said, "but *how* are they connected? At the root, I assume, to extend our metaphor, but how do we observe this in practice? Or — can't we?"

"Indeed we can," said Mrs. Somerville. "It's not even very difficult. Simply choose one of the branches and trace it back to where it sprang from a limb, and follow the limb back to the trunk. There they all meet." I must have looked perplexed, because she smiled slightly and added, "I intend to make this process easier for my own readers by including in subsequent editions new data and discoveries that have emerged since the previous edition."

"And I expect there to be many editions," said Mr. Murray, and with genuine humility, Mrs. Somerville thanked him.

"I do hope you and Lady Byron will call on me at my home in Chelsea," she told me when we were obliged to part. "It's a rare pleasure to discuss mathematics with ladies who find the subject as fascinating as I do myself."

I thanked her profusely and promised we would call on her soon.

The following week — my mother thought it impolite to descend upon her sooner, though I had begged to — we visited Mrs. Somerville at the residence she shared with her husband at the Royal Hospital Chelsea, a splendid army pensioners' home established by Charles II and designed by the renowned architect Sir Christopher Wren. Her husband, Dr. William Somerville, was a physician there, and in time I learned that he was as kind, sympathetic, and generous as his wife. He encouraged Mrs. Somerville to pursue science and mathematics, editing her manuscripts, introducing her to prominent scientists he met through his medical and military connections, and obtaining books for her from the Royal Society, of which he was a member but from which she, as a woman, was excluded despite her accomplishments.

Mrs. Somerville welcomed us warmly into the home she shared with her husband, their two daughters, and often, if one included frequent visits, with Woronzow Greig, the eldest and only surviving child of her first marriage. The residence was simply but elegantly furnished, suggesting excellent taste, modest wealth, and a disinclination for excess, a true marriage of military order and womanly comfort. My private fears that my mother would decide that she liked Mrs. Somerville no better than Mr. Babbage were soon put to rest, for they soon discovered that they had much in common and became fast friends.

After that, my mother never objected when I asked if I might call on Mrs. Somerville, for she rightly concluded that our new friend would be a good influence, both for her understanding of mathematics and for her manner. She was in all things an excellent woman, the very model of serenity, decorum, and restraint, and I would do well to emulate her.

If my mother only knew how eager I was to

do precisely that, she might have alerted Dr. King that I was in danger of developing a new enthusiasm. How grateful I was, and still am today, that the wise, kindhearted Mrs. Somerville took me under her wing. She showed the greatest patience when I eagerly peppered her with questions about mathematics and astronomy, her favorite fields of study, as well as more sensitive topics, such as how to navigate the complicated world of London society, how to become a lady mathematician when there were so few of us, and how to get along better with my mother.

Recently my mother and I had entered one of our intermittent contentious phases, and unfortunately, her brief absence from London did not seem to be relieving the tension. A few days before, she had returned home to Fordhook because the new boarding school for poor boys she was setting up in Ealing Grove had reached a critical juncture. As always, founding a new school required the greatest portion of her attention, and when the doors opened it would require a great deal more of her money, too, for she had promised to pay all expenses for the first year of operation, estimated to be about one thousand pounds.

Education took her away from me, and education was the point of our most recent disagreement, namely, my growing dissatisfaction with the quality of my mathematics instruction. For all Dr. King's wisdom regarding medicine and morality, he was a physician, not a mathematician, and the difference was beginning to show. Recently, after I had asked him to clarify certain abstruse mathematical concepts, he had confessed to me that he did not grasp them well enough to explain them to me. "I regret that as a student at Cambridge, I rarely read any book that had not been assigned by my tutors," he admitted, "and this particular subject was never a part of my curriculum."

Before my mother left London, I had tried to convince her that I needed a more qualified mathematics tutor, and our argument continued through the post after she reached Fordhook. "Dr. King is an excellent tutor," my mother had written in reply to my most recent impassioned letter begging her to find someone else. "You need his moral guidance, and you make me suspicious when you try to cast it off."

Never once, not in person or through the post, had I suggested "casting off" Dr. King or his guidance. I did not demand that we abandon our long walks and moral lectures, even though they had become infrequent since I had come to London. I still intended to correspond with him regularly and to transcribe his moral precepts into the book my mother had given me. All I wanted, and all that I had specifically requested, was a new tutor in mathematics, preferably an actual mathematician. Back and forth letters flew between the increasingly frustrated daughter and the implacable, intractable mother, and soon I could no longer tell if my mother truly did not understand what I was asking for or if she was only pretending to misunderstand me out of sheer obstinance.

One afternoon, I called on Mrs. Somerville while still fuming from a letter that had arrived from my mother earlier that morning. "It's so difficult to make any progress when I cannot receive proper instruction," I fretted as Mrs. Somerville poured tea and offered me a fairy cake. "The program that sufficed when I was a fourteen-year-old girl languishing in a sickbed is simply not adequate now."

"You can always bring your mathematical questions to me," she replied mildly. "I'm sure your mother will help you find a more qualified tutor as soon as possible. In the meantime, never take what she has done for you for granted. She has always, unfailingly, encouraged you to learn. That is more than most girls will ever have."

"There should be schools for girls as there are for boys," I grumbled.

"There are some, but you have enjoyed private tutors at home, which many would argue is preferable to being sent away to be educated." Mrs. Somerville sighed softly. "I for one did not enjoy my year at school."

"A single year?"

"One utterly wretched year too many." Her voice took on a slight edge, and the strangeness of it riveted me. "When I was nine years old, I was sent to Miss Primrose's Boarding School in Musselburgh, near Edinburgh, southeast across the Firth of Forth from my home in Burntisland. A few days after I arrived, in an effort to correct my posture, although there was nothing whatsoever wrong with my spine, I was ordered to wear stiff stays with a steel busk in front over my petticoat. Over my dress, there were steel bands that drew my shoulders back until my shoulder blades touched. Then a steel rod with a half circle shaped to fit under my chin was fastened to the steel busk in my stays, to hold my head in a suitably elevated position. In this constrained state I and nearly all of the younger girls were expected to study and otherwise carry on."

"How dreadful," I exclaimed. "Thank goodness it was only for a year — but what a long year it must have been."

"The longest of my life," she said. "When I left, I felt like a wild animal escaped from a cage. My next foray in formal schooling came when I was thirteen, and it was a holiday in comparison. My mother had taken an apartment in Edinburgh for the winter, and she sent me to a writing school there. I learned to write a fair hand and studied the rudiments of mathematics. I learned to love reading there too, and it is well that I did, because I was essentially my own tutor after that. Back home in Burntisland, I studied French, and I taught myself some Latin and Greek. Of course, I was also obliged to master sewing, cooking, painting, and playing the pianoforte, the usual assortment of feminine accomplishments." She fell silent for a moment, lost in thought. "There was one person who approved of my intellectual interests, an uncle, a clergyman and an historian. He read Virgil with me, and taught me Latin, and always let me borrow books from his library."

"Was it your uncle who taught you mathematics?"

"No, not he. I suppose you could say that my drawing teacher introduced me to mathematics, but he certainly did not intend to." Mrs. Somerville smiled, amused by the memory. "We used to receive a monthly magazine at home, full of short stories, illustrations of ladies' gowns, riddles, and puzzles — you know the sort. One day I was leafing through an issue when I came upon an expression which at first glance I assumed was a simple arithmetic problem. When I examined it more carefully, however, I discovered something very curious, strange lines and symbols and x's and y's. I asked my younger brother's tutor what it meant, and I was told that it was an example of a kind of arithmetic called algebra. I was fascinated, but I could discover nothing on the subject in our family library."

"There was no one else you could ask?"

"No one," said Mrs. Somerville, but then she amended, "There was no one I *thought* I could ask. I suppose I could have pressed Henry's tutor for more information, but my parents would not have approved of my troubling him. Be that as it may, one day sometime later, as I was waiting for my drawing lesson to begin, I overheard my teacher talking to two ladies who had just finished a lesson, encouraging them to study Euclid in order to learn about perspective. He said that Euclid's *Elements* was essential not only for understanding perspective but also astronomy and all mechanical sciences."

"He's not wrong."

"Indeed not," replied Mrs. Somerville. "I memorized the author and title, and the next time I saw Henry's tutor, I begged him to help me acquire a copy of Euclid's *Elements*. He was a kind young man, and my longing must have moved him, for he secretly brought me an old school edition of the Euclid as well as Bonnycastle's *Algebra*."

"Why secretly?" I asked.

"Because I was only a girl." Her expression turned wistful. "My father firmly believed that a bit of reading, writing, and figuring was all that I would ever need, and he would never permit more, even if it did not interfere with my lessons in sewing, cooking, and the rest. He and my mother both worried that my health would suffer if I spent long hours poring over books, because at the time, it was believed that the strain of abstract thought would injure the tender female frame."

"How dreadful," I murmured, feeling exceedingly sorry for the young woman she had been. "But evidently you must have persuaded your parents to let you study."

"On the contrary, I never did. When my father discovered me reading Euclid, he forbade it, and when I persisted, studying in my bedchamber late at night, bothering no one, my parents removed all the candles so that I could no longer see my books." Her lips curved in a small, satisfied smile. "I found a way around this too. I memorized my texts during the day, reading surreptitiously between more ladylike pursuits, and I solved the equations in my head during the night."

My heart went out to the stubborn, clever little girl she had been, and I marveled at her diligence and resolve. I had always been encouraged to study and learn, and no one in my family had ever insisted that certain subjects were better suited for boys than for girls. I felt a sudden rush of gratitude for my mother, and a stab of shame that I had not understood how far she surpassed other parents in this regard.

"So you see, Miss Byron," said Mrs. Somerville, as if she could read my thoughts, "as displeased as you sometimes may be with your education and the qualifications of your tutors, compared to other young women, you have been indulged. That is not to say that you should not try to find the best instruction you can, because you should, but never take for granted your mother's encouragement and generosity. Where would you be without them?"

Without mathematics and science? In an asylum, I thought bleakly, utterly mad, clawing the walls and keening — but I craved Mrs. Somerville's good opinion too much to speak my secret fear aloud.

Chapter Seventeen:
The Quest of
Hidden Knowledge

May–October 1834

We were a study in contrasts, Mrs. Somerville and I, she with her steady calm and quiet confidence, I with my youthful exuberance, excitability, and anxieties. I'm sure I annoyed her sometimes when I disrupted the peaceful serenity of her home with my exhausting curiosity, but she never turned me away. As the summer passed, we became good friends, in the way of a mentor and a disciple. Her friendship, like Mr. Babbage's, led me into a vast new world so full of possibility and promise that it took my breath away. I'm not embarrassed to admit that I quite worshipped her.

Mrs. Somerville was too modest and selfless to talk about herself at great length, preferring to discuss scientific theories and mathematical concepts, especially her acquaintances' ongoing investigations and recent discoveries. Even so, as spring blossoms gave way to summer warmth, I learned how the intelligent young girl forbidden by her parents to study had gone on to become the greatest female mathematician and astronomer of our time — my words, not hers, for I have never heard her boast.

When she was my age, thirty-five years earlier, she, too, had been introduced into Society, but in Edinburgh rather than London. "I reveled in it," she told me, "all of it — the parties, the balls, attending the theatre and concerts, paying calls on friends, and, of course, the innocent flirtations."

"I think a woman can enjoy both mathematics and a fine country-dance," I said, remembering the sheet music Mr. Babbage had left on the table to prompt the Duke of Wellington to recall the Difference Engine whenever he attended a ball. "I certainly do."

"And why not? Music is quite mathematical, you know. I've often thought of music as the marriage of mathematics and poetry —"

My ordinarily poised mentor seemed to stumble over the word. She paused and studied me for a moment, as if judging its effect on me. It struck me then that she was one of the few people of my acquaintance who never asked me about my father or rhapsodized about his poetry, how meaningful they found it, how it had shaped them, how they would always associate certain poems with particular times or experiences in their own lives. I wondered why she had not. Perhaps she did not care for my father's poetry. Perhaps she refrained because of what I had said when we first met, that I would prefer to be known for my own accomplishments. Perhaps my mother had told her of her desire to rid me of any poetical impulses because of the dangerous Byron blood that flowed through my veins.

" 'The marriage of mathematics and poetry,' " I mused, determined to prove that I dared speak the word, that it held no power over me. "I don't believe I've ever heard a more apt description of music."

Mrs. Somerville smiled, her searching gaze grew relieved, and the tension of the moment passed.

On another occasion she told me about her first husband, Samuel Greig, whom she had married when she was twenty-four. He was an officer in the Russian navy when they met, but her parents, fearing he would take her to live in Russia and they would never see her again, consented to their marriage only after he was appointed the Russian consul in London. Within two years Mrs. Somerville bore him two sons — Woronzow Greig was the eldest; his younger brother was no longer living — but it was not motherhood that curtailed her studies. Even though Captain Greig had been well aware of her intellectual interests, after they married, he expected her to abandon mathematical pursuits and devote herself entirely to the duties of wife and mother. "He had a very low opinion of the capacity of our sex," she said, her piercing gaze turning regretful, "and had neither knowledge of, nor interest in, science of any kind."

"I cannot bear to think of a brilliant mind such as yours repeatedly stifled by men," I said, impassioned. "Fathers and husbands seem to be the bane of every intelligent woman's life."

Except my mother's, I realized suddenly. For all his faults, my father had never expected my mother to abandon her intellectual pursuits.

"Not all fathers and husbands deserve such censure," Mrs. Somerville said, almost as if she could read my thoughts. "Let us not forget that it was my uncle who encouraged me to learn Latin and history, and my mother who was absolutely opposed to it."

I nodded, conceding the point, but I felt a knot tightening in my stomach. I had thought that I should marry a gentleman who was interested in mathematics and science simply to improve the quality of our conversations, since we would be thrown together so often and would need to talk or go mad from boredom. It had never occurred to me that my future husband might forbid me to study.

When Mrs. Somerville told me that Captain Greig died three years after they married, my first feeling was relief, but I remembered to murmur condolences. She returned to Scotland with their two young sons and soon became well established in Edinburgh intellectual circles, befriending scientists, novelists, and statesmen. For the first time in her life, no one restricted her studies, and even in mourning, her intellect and imagination thrived.

Five years later, in 1812, she married Dr. William Somerville, her first cousin. "Dr. Somerville had read and traveled widely as an army doctor," she said, "and he approved of education for women."

"I would imagine that made all the difference in the world."

"Yes, Miss Byron. It made all the difference then, and still does today."

I nodded, understanding her unspoken warning. I would not forget it. How thankful I was that I had a fortune of my own, and therefore more choices. I did not hope to marry for love and passion — that dream had perished when Wills was lost to me — but I did long for friendship, companionship, and mutual respect. I could not imagine marrying any man who would demand that his bride relinquish something so essential to her very being as mathematics and science were to mine, but I would be a fool not to be watchful and wary.

That, I knew, could prove to be the most

important lesson Mrs. Somerville would ever teach me.

I spent many happy and enlightening hours in Mrs. Somerville's company. Chelsea was on the outskirts of London, quite remote, and sometimes if we attended a concert or lecture together, she would invite me to spend the night. In time I became quite good friends with her two daughters and her son Woronzow, who lived in Yorkshire and had recently become a barrister.

Mrs. Somerville was also very good friends with Mr. Babbage, of course, and as my mother was often disinclined to attend his soirées, Mrs. Somerville frequently offered to escort me. I enjoyed Mr. Babbage's soirées more than any other social gathering, and I had attended many of the finest in Society. Mr. Babbage was humorous and intelligent, with an insatiable intellectual curiosity that compelled him to investigate an astonishing variety of topics in every conceivable field of study. With a pleased, proud smile he indulged my repeated requests to examine the Difference Engine, both the demonstration model displayed in the special dustless room in his house and the full-scale version in progress, if that was the proper term for a project that had stalled indefinitely, in the workshop out back.

So fascinated was I by the magnificent machine, and so eager to understand all its mysteries, that I sometimes could be thoughtless of my dear mentor, taking advantage of her friendship with Mr. Babbage to call on him between soirées. By midsummer, I hardly ever visited Mrs. Somerville without nonchalantly suggesting that we drive out to Dorset Street to call on our mutual friend. One afternoon in early July, I tested her patience so much that she rebuked me, albeit gently, for behaving as if her friendship was valuable to me only inasmuch as it granted me access to him.

"That isn't so," I protested. "In fact, when I first met Mr. Babbage, I valued him as a friend mostly because I hoped he would introduce me to you!"

Mrs. Somerville laughed, and she told me that she understood and that I must forgive her for chastising me. I quickly assured her that there was nothing to forgive, but although we parted as cheerfully as ever, as I rode home to Mayfair, I had time to reflect and to regret. Mrs. Somerville had always been unfailingly kind and patient with me, even when I was at my most enthusiastic and vexing. If she felt slighted, then I had surely slighted her, although I had not meant to.

As soon as I reached home, I hurried to my mother's study, took up paper and pen, and dashed off a letter to my mentor.

Tuesday Evening, 8 July 1834

My Dear Mrs Somerville,

I am very much concerned that I must have seemed to you very presuming for always suggesting that we go to Dorset Street when I come to visit you, and I assure you I never meant to be so impudent. Nothing but my great interest in the Difference Engine could have made me so, I believe. But I think you must be fond enough of these sort of things to sympathize with my eagerness about them. I am afraid that when a machine, or a lecture, or anything of the kind, comes in my way, I have no regard for time, space, or any ordinary obstacles. This is the only excuse I can offer, and I regret that it is a poor one, but I trust you will always tell me whenever I encroach on your very great kindness.

Believe me ever,
Your sincerely obliged
A. Ada Byron

I spent an anxious few days awaiting her reply, and I felt faint with relief when she wrote to invite me to tea, saying nothing of the incident. Our friendship continued without interruption, but I was mindful for the first few weeks not to suggest that we call on Mr. Babbage. When we finally did ride out together to see him again, it was at Mrs. Somerville's suggestion.

By that time, the political winds had shifted once more, and Lord Melbourne had become prime minister.

I knew that my mother had been writing to her cousin, and that he never failed to respond promptly and cordially. My heart raced with the certainty that this could be Mr. Babbage's best hope, and I longed to be the agent of his triumph. "Mama, would you please speak to Lord Melbourne on Mr. Babbage's behalf?" I pleaded. "What good are family connections if we don't use them to help our friends? And it's not only Mr. Babbage I'm thinking of. Consider the benefit to the entire country, to commerce and science and industry, if his engine is finally completed!"

"I'm sure Lord Melbourne is besieged by enough petitioners already without me clamoring for his attention," my mother said. "I've told you, Ada, if I ever do beg a favor from my cousin, it will be for your sake or mine, and only because I have no other recourse."

I knew it would do no good to badger her, so I acquiesced.

As the Season drew to a close at summer's end, my mother announced her plans for us to travel in the north of England, where we would visit friends, explore the natural beauty of the countryside, and tour several newly constructed factories. My mother wanted to learn about recent advancements in industrial technology, as well as the condition of the workers, so she could better prepare the students of her industrial schools for the labor of the future. I thought this was an excellent idea, and I was curious to see how these machines — strong, hardworking, tirelessly productive — would compare to Mr. Babbage's elegant, ingenious Difference Engine.

We were both in good spirits as we set out for the Midlands, determinedly so, for we would be spending a great deal of time together in close quarters, and disagreements would make the carriage claustrophobic. My mother had brought some books on educational theory to read on the trip, and I had brought a few mathematics texts and the latest issue of the *Edinburgh Review,* which included a favorable article on Mr. Babbage's Difference Engine. I was not sure if the technical details would make sense to someone who had never seen the demonstration model in action, but if nothing else, I hoped the article would incite enough interest in the scientific community that the government would at last be induced to release his long-awaited funds.

Sometimes my mother and I took turns reading aloud from novels or the newspaper, but more often we dozed or admired the changing landscape through the windows.

One morning, as we rambled along the road from Bakewell to Buxton, we approached a man walking ahead of us. Even from a distance he seemed familiar to me, and as we overtook him, my mother gave a start. "Good heavens, that's Sir John Hobhouse."

I craned my neck to look back, and upon seeing his face, I knew my mother was right. "What would he be doing out here, I wonder," I mused as I watched him stride along with his walking stick in hand.

"Who knows?" said my mother dismissively. "Nothing good, I'm sure."

I frowned slightly, thinking of Lady Byron's kind, encouraging remarks about thinking for myself. "Should we offer him a ride?"

"Absolutely not." I must have looked surprised, and she would never want to seem ungenerous, for she quickly added, "We've left him too far behind and it would be inconvenient for the driver to stop here. Besides, he's probably out taking the air by choice. He can afford a carriage, if he wanted one."

Bewildered, I watched as she settled back against the seat, and then I again peered out the window at the spare figure swiftly receding behind us. I muffled a sigh, knowing it would do no good to argue.

Soon thereafter the road passed through the beautiful wooded grounds of a lovely estate, and I was entranced by the play of sunlight through the leaves, the sparkling rush of a swift creek beside the road, a herd of deer gracefully crossing a meadow. "What an exquisite place," I exclaimed. "Do we know the people who live here?"

"Of course we do," my mother replied, her own gaze riveted on the passing scenery. "This is Halnaby, the seat of the Milbanke baronets. Your grandfather was the sixth baronet, and his nephew, Sir John Peniston Milbanke, became the seventh upon his death."

"This estate was ours?"

"Not ours. My father's." A wistful shadow passed over her face. "Do you see that road, on the left? So many times, I could not guess how many, I rode my pony along it when I was a child." She paused. "Your father and I spent our honeymoon here."

"You did?" Little wonder she had never spoken of it to me.

"Yes, for three weeks in January of 1815. It looked quite different in winter than it does now in late summer, but it was still very beautiful, all shrouded in pure white snow and glistening with ice."

I waited, but she said nothing more, and when she pressed her lips together and inhaled sharply, I knew that she would not welcome questions from a curious daughter. We did not stop to call on our Milbanke relations, so I was left to wonder.

No other sites we passed prompted such revealing reminiscences from my mother, except when we stopped overnight at the homes of her friends along the way, but the cheerful memories they shared of their girlhood exploits never included my father. Onward we traveled, and as we drew closer to our destination, my thoughts turned from the past to the future, which seemed to be rushing forward to meet us with invigorating speed.

Nothing else I had ever seen, except, perhaps, the steam locomotive, emphasized that the future would be fast, powerful, and full of promise as did the factories my mother and I toured that summer. We observed ribbons being made with blurring speed in Coventry and spar being cut at Ashby-de-la-Zouch. In Derby we watched potters toiling at their wheels and women and girls painting chinaware. While I admired the machinery and marveled at how swiftly various goods were produced, my mother spoke to the workers as well as their masters, querying them about working conditions, wages, hours, and whether they were treated respectfully and courteously by their supervisors.

For me, the most fascinating stop on our tour was a cotton-spinning mill on the west bank of the river Derwent in Matlock Bath, Derbyshire. It was powered by the river, not by steam, and in that sense it harkened back to an earlier age, but it boasted a Jacquard loom, which, although it had been first demonstrated in France thirty years before, was still considered new and revolutionary technology. With astonishing swiftness and accuracy, these mechanical looms could weave patterns from simple to very complex, creating fabrics such as brocade, damask, and matelassé. The most elaborate designs, usually woven in fine silk, were nearly indistinguishable from a painting.

I could not say how long I stood and watched the looms at work, enthralled, examining them from one angle and then another, as close as our guide would allow me to approach. I learned that the various designs were created by varying the position of the warp threads, those that are first put lengthwise into the loom. For a plain weave, a raised thread would be followed by a lowered thread in a regular pattern across the desired width of the cloth. More complex weaves could be created by varying the pattern of raised and lowered warp threads — but more elaborate patterns required more time and more attention from the weavers. Silks featuring the most intricate designs, richly detailed images such as still lifes, landscapes, and even portraits, were very popular but tremendously expensive.

What made the Jacquard loom truly ingenious was that the raising and lowering of warp threads was controlled not by a pair of skillful, attentive weavers, but rather by a series of punched cards. Each card corresponded to a single row of the cloth, with holes punched through the card to indicate to a system of hooks and harness whether the warp thread in that particular location should be raised or lowered, and what color thread should be used. Thus patterns of astonishing complexity could be flawlessly woven in a fraction of the time a pair of human weavers could accomplish the task. Working a Jacquard loom, we were informed, a single weaver could create figured fabrics twenty-four times faster than two weavers working a traditional loom, creating roughly two feet of luxurious fabric every day.

Simple stiff paper, plain and ostensibly unremarkable, those punched cards were the key to the Jacquard loom's function. My mother was so impressed with them that she sketched one in her journal, while my gaze shifted from the sequence of punched cards to the flying lines of thread, to the exquisitely patterned fabric falling from the loom. The instructions for the weave were coded into the pattern of holes on the card, and thus the loom could carry them out without any person directly causing it to happen.

If punched cards could control a loom, why not another mechanical device, such as a calculating engine?

After that I could not think of the Jacquard loom without pondering what a similar system of punched cards could do for Mr. Babbage's Difference Engine. My swiftly dawning awareness of the potential for making extraordinary mathematical calculations — for any sort of logical calculation — set my imagination soaring.

My mother had mistakenly called the Difference Engine a "thinking machine," but this new machine I imagined, one capable of transcending mere mathematical calculations by employing a system of punched cards — perhaps it would be capable of rational thought, or something that looked very much like it.

If it could be designed, and if it could be built.

Our visit to the Midlands had been a revelation to me, and I could not wait to return to London and discuss my new insight with Mr. Babbage and Mrs. Somerville. But first we stopped in Buxton in Derbyshire to visit my mother's friend Lady Gosford, who had come to the spa town with her two daughters to take the waters. My mother decided that her health, too, would benefit from the geothermal springs of Saint Ann's Well, so she arranged lodgings for us and told us that we might remain a fortnight or more, depending upon how she responded to the cure.

While our mothers were off pursuing good

health and vitality, I passed the time with Lady Gosford's daughters, Annabella, who had been named after my mother, and Olivia. They were five and four years older than I, respectively, but I was enough like my mother that I took the lead. They were amiable and bright girls, but rather indolent, so when they spoke admiringly of my love of learning, I offered to tutor them in mathematics. I hoped that at least one of them would be inspired to take up mathematics as I had done. Annabella seemed to be the most likely candidate; Olivia preferred music, but that did not lower her in my esteem, because I loved music too.

I quite enjoyed teaching, and my friends were avid to learn, so when my mother decided it was time to resume our tour, we agreed to continue our lessons through the post.

I was quite surprised when my mother announced that our next destination was Doncaster, so that I could see the races. Just as she had sent me to see my first opera so that I could make an informed judgment, she wanted me to observe the famous racecourse "on principle," as she put it. "I abhor gambling," she said, "and I am indifferent to horses as long as they pull my carriage well, but want you to see for yourself how shamefully people disport themselves there. If I forbade you to go to the races, you would only become more curious and seek them out somehow. When you see them for what they are, they shall no longer tantalize you."

They never had tantalized me until my mother described them in such enticing terms, but I adored horses and my curiosity was piqued, so I was willing to defer our return to London a little while longer. Doncaster proved to be quite unlike anyplace I had visited before. The crowds were drunken and riotous, and my ears fairly burned from the shouted curses I overheard when a sure bet faded in the home stretch, but I found it new and exciting, and I was not at all repulsed. The horses were beautiful, magnificent, and I never tired of watching them run, and when a gentleman seated near us won fifty pounds, in my excitement I was tempted to ask my mother if I might place a bet. Fortunately I thought better of it, and I pretended to be shocked and dismayed by the boisterous antics of the gamblers, but I knew my mother's plan to make me dislike the races had failed utterly.

From Doncaster we returned to Fordhook, and over the last five miles I mentally composed a letter to Mr. Babbage, asking if I might call on him as soon as I could travel to London, for my tour of the industrial Midlands had inspired me with an idea for an adaptation to his Difference Engine.

At last we reached home, for I had come to think of Fordhook as home. I intended to get started on my letter right away, but my mother insisted that I unpack before I did anything else, and then I wanted to see Puff and check on my horses. By the time I returned indoors, my mother had sorted the post that had arrived in our absence, and there was a letter for me.

27 September 1834
Royal Hospital Chelsea

My Dear Miss Byron,
   With a sorrowful heart, I write to inform you of a tragedy that has struck our good friend Mr. Babbage. Yesterday afternoon, his daughter, Georgiana, passed away after a sudden illness. There are no words for this, the worst heartbreak a parent can suffer, and I know he will rely upon the consolation of friends to endure it.
   I regret that this letter will reach you just when you will have arrived home after a long journey. Please accept my apologies for diminishing the happiness of your homecoming, and extend my apologies to your most excellent mother as well.
                  I remain, as always, your friend,
                              Mary Somerville

CHAPTER EIGHTEEN:
WITH MY KNOWLEDGE GREW
THE THIRST OF KNOWLEDGE

October 1834–January 1835

Miss Georgiana Babbage was only seventeen when she perished, as shy as her father was confident, fair-haired, blue-eyed, sweet, and smiling. Although we were close in age, I did not know her well. She did not live with Mr. Babbage but with her paternal grandmother and two younger brothers on Devonshire Street, a ten-minute walk away, and since she was not yet out in Society she had only rarely attended her father's soirées. Still, I had always liked her, and I had hoped that we would become very good friends in time. Too late I wished that I had befriended her when I had had the chance rather than taking for granted that we had years and years ahead of us. But overwhelming every other feeling was sorrow for Mr. Babbage, and a deep, helpless regret that I could do nothing to ease his suffering.

My mother and I had received the news of Georgiana's death too late to attend the

448

funeral, but as soon as my mother could make arrangements, we traveled to London to pay our respects to her family.

The Dorset Street house, the setting for so many merry gatherings, was shrouded in the colors of mourning — black crepe on the front door and over the mirrors and above his daughter's portrait in the sitting room. Mr. Babbage's mother greeted us when we arrived, served us tea, and accepted our condolences with a heavy heart. She told us that she and Mr. Babbage's three sons — all the children that were left to him of the eight his wife had borne — were staying with him at present, but Herschel, the eldest, would likely return to his engineering apprenticeship soon, and she expected to take the two younger boys back home with her when she departed.

"We'll stay as long as he needs us, of course," she said, but she abruptly broke off when Mr. Babbage appeared in the doorway.

He was dressed in a black suit and armband, and when he greeted us his manners were as gracious as ever, but his eyes were red and his face was haggard and drawn, and his expression betrayed an unsettling air of bewilderment. He thanked us gruffly when we offered our condolences, but otherwise he diverted our few attempts to reminisce about Georgiana. We spoke instead of Mrs. Somerville's book, which I had read twice since Mr.

Murray had presented me with a copy in March and my mother had finished while we were in Buxton. A trace of his familiar animation returned while the subject was science, but not even that could distract him from his sorrow for long. On the way over, my mother and I had agreed that we should take care not to exhaust him, but just as I was beginning to worry that we were approaching that moment, my mother gave me a subtle signal that we should depart.

Mr. Babbage led us to the door, and just before we left, he said, "I've decided not to hold my regular weekly soirées for the time being."

"Of course, Mr. Babbage," said my mother, surprised. "I assumed you would not."

"But I would like you to call again soon," he quickly added, his gaze flicking from my mother to me. "I had some thoughts about the Difference Engine that I'd like to share with you, Miss Byron."

"I've had some as well," I told him. "Our industrial tours were most illuminating. I'll return whenever you're ready to receive me."

"Let it be soon," he said hoarsely. "Work is the only remedy for grief — work, toil, and time. I must think of something else or I'll —" His voice broke off and he shook his head, and I saw to my dismay that his eyes were shining with tears. "Call on me soon.

We have much to discuss and even more to do."

I bowed assent, and as my mother and I departed, my heart ached to think that we were leaving him alone with his pain. If he believed that work would distract him from his grief, I was determined to provide it.

I would have returned the next day if my mother had permitted, but my mother said that would be disrespectful and inconsiderate, and she insisted that I wait a week. When she finally decided I might go, she was feeling indisposed and could not accompany me, but since his mother would be present, she agreed that I might go alone.

Mrs. Babbage remained with us long enough to serve tea and to ask after my mother's health, but she soon excused herself and left us alone to discuss the Difference Engine. "I have decided, in honor of my beloved daughter, to devote myself to solving a difficult problem with the machine," Mr. Babbage told me, his gaze piercing and determined. "The arduous effort it requires shall occupy my thoughts and exhaust me enough that I shall be able to sleep at night. My inevitable success — for I shall not rest until I solve this problem — will be a fitting tribute to my Georgiana, who loyally believed me capable of anything."

I felt a pang of worry. "Are you not sleeping, Mr. Babbage?"

"Not well," he said curtly, dismissing that concern as unworthy of further discussion. "The problem I speak of resides not in the engine, but in the formulae. For certain calculations, the results become increasingly inaccurate as the creation of the table progresses, because some values have to be rounded off."

"Not just some numbers, but many," I said, nodding. "Every repeating decimal, in fact."

"Precisely. Certain numbers consist of an infinite number of decimals — one divided by three, for example — but it is impossible to create an engine with an infinite number of cogwheels." He leaned forward, impassioned. "What I must do is to find a way — some new device or adaptation — that would eliminate this persistent, compounding reduction in accuracy. I think — that is, I believe very strongly — that such a machine would also then be capable of far more than creating mathematical tables."

"It's an intriguing concept," I said, my excitement rising. "Perhaps I have an idea that may help you find that solution."

Eagerly I told him about the Jacquard loom — the speed, accuracy, and complexity of its production and the punch cards that controlled it. Mr. Babbage listened intently, nodding, and when I finished he told me that he had seen a Jacquard loom at work many years before but had not considered that its system of imparting instructions could be applied to a calculating machine. "I sense that it could work," he said, "but how to adapt it to the mechanisms of the Difference Engine, I cannot quite envision. But it could be possible."

"I'm relieved that you think so," I confessed. "I was afraid that I had overlooked some obvious fatal flaw that would oblige you to dismiss the idea out of hand."

"I would never dismiss any of your ideas out of hand," he protested. "On the contrary, Miss Byron, I marvel at your insight. Not one in a hundred thousand people would observe a loom at work and consider how its mechanism might improve a calculating engine. I'm quite astounded by the powers of your imagination."

"Thank you, Mr. Babbage," I said, warming to the praise. How unfamiliar and new was the inflection Mr. Babbage gave to that word, "imagination," which had always conveyed so much apprehension and warning when my mother spoke it. How unexpected and strange and somehow reassuring it was to hear imagination valued as much as intellect.

We chatted more about the Difference Engine, examining from one perspective and then another the problem of repeating decimals and compounding errors. I mused aloud that I could better understand the workings of the engine if I had illustrated plates or plans to study on my own, and he promised to have copies of both sent to me at Fordhook. In the meantime, he let me borrow several papers about steam engines he thought might interest me, and when I promised to return them as soon as I copied them over, he said, "Take all the time you require. I trust you implicitly, and I know my papers will be as safe in your care as they would be on my own bookshelves."

Mr. Babbage's praise lingered in my thoughts for several days afterward, and I found it very curious how much I cherished it. This was not a man who would stifle anyone's intellectual or imaginative pursuits, I realized, not even a woman's. He would celebrate her genius and encourage it to thrive.

One evening, as my mother helped me dress for a ball, I could not help reflecting upon what was meant to be the primary purpose for me to attend — to attract the interest of an eligible gentleman. My thoughts turned to my recent conversation with Mr. Babbage, and I mused aloud that he possessed many of the qualities I thought I would be wise to look for in a husband.

"Oh, Ada, no," my mother said, appalled. "You cannot think of marrying Mr. Babbage."

"I didn't say I wanted to marry him, only someone like him." But my instinctive, defensive reply jolted me with the realization that, unbeknownst even to myself, I had considered it.

"He is almost forty-four," my mother protested. "More than twice your age."

"Why should that matter? Girls my age marry older widowers all the time."

"Ada," she said firmly, taking me by the shoulders and fixing me with a steady look, "has Mr. Babbage spoken to you of marriage? Do you have an understanding with him?"

"Of course not," I replied, indignant. I had no right to take offense; I had made a secret engagement once before, and for all she knew, I might again. "We're friends, that's all — but I meant what I said, before you misinterpreted my innocent admiration. Mr. Babbage has many admirable qualities that I would like my future husband to have also. Courtesy, for one. Kindness. Intellectual curiosity. A passion for mathematics and science. The sincere belief in women's capabilities and genius. That's all that I meant."

"Ada," my mother said again, but her tone was softer. "I agree that Mr. Babbage has many virtues. However, I am very glad that he has not proposed to you, for you would have to refuse him."

"Why? Because of the difference in our ages?"

"You must marry someone of our own class," she said, bewildered, because of course

455

I ought to know this already. "Wealth is not enough. Your husband must be an aristocrat, ideally with a title more than a century old. These things matter. They always have and they always will." She released my shoulders and studied me as if she suspected I might be a changeling, and her real daughter, the dutiful, pious, serene child she should have been dressing for the ball that evening, was languishing in the land of fairy. "You're very lucky you're still regarded as eligible to marry at all. If certain stories from the past were to emerge —"

I felt a jolt of fear. "I'm not the same person I was last year. I've worked very hard to redeem myself in your eyes, and I wish you would believe me that I've changed, changed utterly."

The appraising look she gave me said more clearly than words that she could never be certain. She would worry that I might yet fall into irredeemable ruin until the day I was safely wed.

How grateful I was for friends and mentors who knew nothing of the scandal in my past, who never looked at me with apprehension, as if I were a wild beast that had not yet figured out that the lock on its cage was broken. I could not bear to disappoint them, especially Mr. Babbage and Mrs. Somerville, who respected my genius, held high expectations for me, and seemed to genuinely like me. Thus when Mrs. Somerville expressed misgivings that I was ignoring the requisite feminine accomplishments in favor of Euclid, I offered to sew her a new cap as soon as I finished the bonnet I was making for myself. And when Mr. Babbage, as promised, sent the illustrated plates and several pages of notes about the Difference Engine, not only did I write to thank him profusely before I allowed myself the pleasure of studying the pages, but I also wrote to Mrs. Somerville and asked her to thank him on my behalf the next time she saw him, in case my letter was delayed.

As the autumn days grew colder, I rode every day, savoring the brisk air, the brilliant colors of the foliage overhead, and the sweet melancholy of a once bright season fading into winter. Each afternoon I practiced my music, not only voice and guitar but also the harp, which especially captivated my interest in those days. I spent hours examining Mr. Babbage's illustrations and notes, and I studied mathematics with increasing delight, making swift progress thanks to Mrs. Somerville's gentle guidance, although Dr. King was still officially my tutor.

In mid-November, Mr. Babbage invited my mother and me to attend a small gathering at his home, the first he had hosted since his daughter's death. It would not be one of his famous soirées, he hastened to explain, even though it would take place on a Saturday, but something rather smaller and quieter. My mother had a prior commitment regarding her Ealing Grove school and could not attend, but she approved of my intellectual circle of friends, and since Mrs. Somerville would also be present, she agreed that I could attend if one of the Furies accompanied me. Of the three, only Miss Montgomery reluctantly admitted that she was free that evening, and since the alternative was to stay home, I resigned myself to her company.

Fortunately, soon after our arrival, Miss Montgomery struck up a lively conversation with Mrs. Babbage and quite forgot about me, so I was able to slip away and find Mr. Babbage, who had gathered with Mrs. Somerville, Mr. Dickens, Mr. Lyell, and a few others in the library. What a fascinating circle of friends I had acquired, I marveled, reflecting upon my lonely childhood, when my few playmates had been judiciously selected by my mother and had rarely been in my company. I could not help wondering, wistfully, how much happier I would have been if I had met them long ago.

My friends were discussing politics, not science or mathematics, but a frisson of tension in the air told me that the conversation could become quite animated, so I greeted everyone pleasantly, found myself a chair next to Mr. Dickens, quietly congratulated him for several excellent sketches and essays he had recently published, and settled in to watch the show.

Mr. Babbage could not keep to his chair, but bounded out of it and paced back and forth, agitated. "These rumors are diabolically confounding," he said, glowering. "I just want to know if he's in or out, and if he's out, who's going in?"

"Are we talking about sport?" I asked innocently.

A ripple of laughter went up from the others. "In a manner of speaking," said Mr. Lyell, grinning. I nodded politely but did not return his smile. I admired his scientific brilliance but did not like his lecherous leer, which he inflicted on any remotely attractive woman who crossed his path. He had married two years before, but wedlock had done nothing to cure him of this annoying habit.

"Politics, Miss Byron," Mrs. Somerville kindly clarified.

"Oh, I see. I prefer a horse race," I said lightly, mostly to amuse Mr. Babbage.

It worked, for he ceased pacing and smiled at me. "Politics and horse racing. There are times I do not know which involves the riskier gamble." A few chuckles rose, but as I glanced around the room, I glimpsed only somber, tense faces. "A rumor is circulating that earlier today Lord Melbourne resigned as prime minister at the request of the king."

"I had not heard that," I said, startled, but of course there was no reason I should have. My mother and Lord Melbourne corresponded, but they were not so close that he would have informed her of his resignation before telling his political colleagues.

"If Lord Wellington takes over as prime minister, this could be very good for you," Mr. Dickens reminded Mr. Babbage.

"Yes, and not only for me." Mr. Babbage resumed pacing, but he halted at the window and gazed outside, although night had fallen and I doubted he could see beyond his own reflection. "Lord Wellington is impressed with the Difference Engine, and he has told me himself that he believes it would be useful to the military. If he becomes prime minister, he could get the money flowing with a single word. When the Difference Engine proves itself, and I am confident it will, the government will be more amenable to funding other scientific research, other remarkable machines." He turned to face his guests, his eyes shining. "We could be on the verge of a second Industrial Revolution."

"So much depends upon one singular political appointment," said Mrs. Somerville.

"The duke is a war hero and a statesman," I said, looking to her and to Mr. Babbage for confirmation. "He served as prime minister before. Would he not be the most likely choice?"

"He would be, if not for Peel," said Mr. Babbage acidly.

I recognized the name, but I needed another moment to understand Mr. Babbage's sharp tone. Then I remembered: Sir Robert Peel had been the home secretary when Mr. Babbage first announced the invention of the Difference Engine, and Lord Peel had dismissed it as a foolish and potentially dangerous contraption, despite the endorsement Mr. Babbage had received from the Royal Society.

"Many believe that Peel has emerged as the new leader of the Tories," said Mr. Lyell, directing his explanation to me. I did not take offense. Not only was I the youngest person in the room; I was the only one asking questions, and no doubt I also looked the most bewildered.

"Yes, but Peel is abroad," said Mr. Dickens, "and perhaps he will stay there."

"If Peel becomes prime minister, he will kill my engine," said Mr. Babbage. "All the funding will disappear. He'll probably send me a bill for the funds already disbursed."

"Could he do that?" I asked.

"He wouldn't, Miss Byron." Mrs. Somerville hesitated. "At least, I don't believe he would. It's highly improbable."

"He wouldn't," said Mr. Lyell stoutly, and a chorus of reassuring assent filled the library, although Mr. Dickens said nothing, but only shook his head and frowned, skeptical. I

461

made an effort to add my voice to those encouraging Mr. Babbage, but I was sick with worry. The Difference Engine meant the world to me, and it was painful and outrageous to think that something as trivial as which gentleman would fill a political post, even the highest in the land below the sovereign, could determine its fate.

The following morning at breakfast, I asked my mother if she knew anything about the rumors swirling about Lord Melbourne, but she knew no more than Mr. Babbage did. Then, two days later, the story broke in the press: Lord Melbourne had indeed resigned, and Lord Wellington had taken over as prime minister. My joy was short-lived, however, for it soon came out that Lord Wellington actually had declined the post and had consented only to lead a caretaker government until a new prime minister could be appointed. Sir Robert Peel's supporters had already dispatched messengers to Italy to urge him to return to England with all speed.

The situation was still unsettled when I next visited Mr. Babbage with Mrs. Somerville not quite two weeks later. "My funding must come through while Lord Wellington is in charge or it will probably not come at all," he said, the strain evident in the furrow of his brow, the rough quality to his voice. I suspected he was still finding sleep elusive, and I worried for him.

I listened, increasingly apprehensive, as Mr. Babbage and Mrs. Somerville debated the reasons for the frustratingly sporadic nature of the support for his work. "Perhaps the world is simply not ready for a machine as revolutionary as the Difference Engine," she suggested.

"The world is never ready for any innovation," he grumbled. "The vast majority of people stubbornly cling to the past until people possessing foresight and a sense of adventure break a trail and bring them into the future."

"Perhaps your adventurers might be more successful if they tried to lead the people forward gently rather than dragging them against their will."

Mr. Babbage actually laughed. "A fair point, Mrs. Somerville, but I cannot overstate the urgency compelling me to complete my work. If I don't develop the Difference Engine, someone else will, if not here in Britain, then on the Continent. I don't think any of us want this new industrial revolution to belong to the French or to the Germans, allowing foreign nations to reap the first benefits of increased production and efficiency and obliging unlucky Englishmen to glean whatever we can from trips abroad."

Mrs. Somerville and I agreed that time was of the essence, but there was nothing we could do to compel Lord Wellington to make funding Mr. Babbage's work a priority within his caretaker government. And as the weeks passed, it seemed increasingly likely that Sir Robert Peel would assume the role of prime minister as soon as he returned to England.

In December, my nineteenth birthday came and went, marked by a heavy snowfall that kept me indoors with my harp, my books, and Mr. Babbage's notes and illustrations. Although we did not receive the news until the following morning, my birthday also marked the end of Lord Wellington's brief term as prime minister of the caretaker government and the first day of the government of the new prime minister, the Right Honorable Sir Robert Peel. Lord Wellington had become the leader of the House of Lords, and Lord Melbourne had succeeded him as leader of the opposition. My mother's cousin still possessed a great deal of influence and authority, but less than before, and I could not help but silently berate my mother for squandering her brief opportunity to appeal to him on Mr. Babbage's behalf.

Although the political storm was still thundering, the heavy snows passed and the roads were clear again in time for my mother and me to attend a dinner party at Mr. Babbage's home five days later. Mrs. Somerville would be there, and several other friends we had met at his soirées, and I might have been tempted to go alone on horseback or skis rather than miss it.

Mr. Babbage was animated and cheerful when he greeted us at the door, more so than he had been in weeks. I had expected to find him disgusted, outraged, or depressed about the ascendancy of Sir Robert Peel, and I surmised that he must have some other exciting news to share. He was fairly bursting with it by the time we had all gathered around the table, and he wasted no time in idle chat but got straight to the point. "I have made an important discovery," he declared. "I have fired the first salvo in what shall be a revolution of thought and technology."

I felt a thrill of excitement as the rest of us exchanged glances around the table. "What is it?" I asked. "Have you solved the problem of repeating decimals?"

"Not entirely, but I now know how I shall eventually solve it. It was, in fact, working upon that problem which opened up this new horizon to me."

"What horizon is that?" asked Mr. Dickens.

"I have conceived of an entirely new machine," said Mr. Babbage, his face alight with triumph. "It will far surpass anything I intended for the Difference Engine, solving equations that until now have been considered unsolvable. I call it the Analytical Engine."

I felt a curious surge of emotions, elation intermingled with astonishment. The Differ-

465

ence Engine was so magnificent, how could anything surpass it?

My mother deliberately sipped her water and set down her glass. "Mr. Babbage, do you mean to say that after all the time, effort, and expense you have invested into the Difference Engine, you now intend to abandon it and chase after a new invention?"

"Of course he doesn't mean that." I hesitated and turned a wary look upon Mr. Babbage, whose enthusiasm, I had learned, sometimes compelled him to ignore more pragmatic concerns. "You don't, do you?"

He shrugged and spread his hands. "That is my quandary. Do I continue to work on the Difference Engine, which has captivated my imagination for so many years, and has already come so close to completion? Or do I move on to the Analytical Engine, which I know will be the far superior machine?"

"You ought to complete the project you have already begun," said my mother. "You have already received grants for it, and you must have something to show for the investment if you ever hope to receive another."

His eyebrows rose. "*Another* grant? I hardly dare hope to receive the outstanding balance I'm still owed on the first."

"Lady Byron's caution is warranted," said Mrs. Somerville. "I cannot imagine that the chancellor of the exchequer would give you new funding for a second machine when you

466

haven't yet completed the first and they haven't reaped any of its promised rewards."

"I can hear the complaints already," said Mr. Lyell. "They will demand that you finish the Difference Engine to prove that you *can* finish something, and that your machine works as well as you said. Otherwise they will worry that they are throwing good money after bad."

Mr. Babbage nodded glumly, and I knew he had hoped that we would all enthusiastically urge him to throw himself headlong into this new project. "What precisely will your Analytical Engine do?" I asked. "How exactly is it different from the Difference Engine?"

"It will eliminate the problem of compounding inaccuracy, for one," he said. "Furthermore, as capable and efficient as the Difference Engine is, it is constrained by the necessity to reset the machine for each new set of calculations. All of those initial numbers must be arranged on the cogwheels by hand."

Suddenly, I understood — or thought I did. "Instead those instructions could be conveyed to the engine by another means," I declared. "Punched cards, as in the Jacquard loom!"

Mr. Babbage paused, wincing ever so slightly. "Punched cards could do it, perhaps, but my intention is to use a revolving drum with raised studs."

"Like a musical snuff box?" asked Mrs.

Somerville, intrigued, "or a *carillon à musique?*"

"Very much so," said Mr. Babbage, avoiding my gaze, or so it seemed to me. I felt strangely deflated, for I had hoped that he would modify the Difference Engine so that it would accept instructions from punched cards, increasing its capabilities immeasurably. Not only had he decided against that, but he intended to start all over with an entirely new machine, and he had no intention of incorporating my idea into the design.

The more I reflected, the more I became certain that Mr. Babbage was wrong to disregard my suggestion. Punched cards could be strung together in a virtually unlimited series, but a revolving cylinder would eventually begin to repeat itself. Even a cylinder with a circumference greater than it would be possible for Mr. Babbage's workshop to accommodate would eventually run out of room, and there the coded instructions would come to an abrupt halt — or rather, they would start over from the beginning.

But Mr. Babbage's enthusiasm was contagious, and as he described his Analytical Engine in more detail, not even my disappointment that he had disregarded my suggestion and my misgivings about the limits of revolving cylinders could suppress my excitement for the potential of his new machine. I wished I knew Sir Robert Peel well enough to go to him and personally plead Mr. Babbage's case. I wished I could borrow from my inheritance and fund his work myself, but my mother would never consent, and Mr. Babbage might be too proud to accept money from a friend.

Mr. Babbage was not far along enough in his plans to be able to describe the function of the Analytical Engine in precise detail, but his face seemed illuminated from within as he told us how he had felt when the first impressions of his discovery came to him, bit by bit, until the whole was revealed. "It is the same sensation of amazement and expectation one would feel when first apprehending the possibility of building a bridge from the known to the unknown," he said. "It felt as if I stood on a mountain, with peaks surrounding me on all sides. I gazed down into the valley below and found it shrouded in mist, but as I watched, the mists began to disperse, and I glimpsed a winding river. I could not follow its course, and yet I knew the river must eventually find an egress from the valley. Though it was concealed from view, I knew it must be there, and how to find it."

My heart warmed with happiness and pride to hear him describe his inspiration in such poetic terms, but I also felt a stirring of wistful recognition, for his words called to mind how I had felt in childhood when my imagination had first been captivated by Flyology. I wished again, as I had before, that I might discover my own Great Work, my own bridge from the known to the unknown.

By the time dessert was served, the general consensus among the guests was that Mr. Babbage absolutely must find a way to construct his marvelous Analytical Engine, but he should proceed with caution and respect when seeking funding for it. I knew him well enough even then to understand that this might prove to be a trifle difficult for him. He was a genial friend, a gracious host, and a courteous gentleman, but when he found himself thwarted by obstinate, bewildered bureaucrats who could not grasp the astounding significance of his inventions, he could be somewhat impatient, even caustic. Obviously he was less likely to get money out of the government coffers if he offended the men who disbursed it, but in a heated moment, he could forget that.

With Christmas swiftly approaching, it seemed unlikely that there would be any political developments either to help or to hinder Mr. Babbage's cause until the New Year. My mother and I settled in at Fordhook to celebrate the festive season with the Three Furies and a few other friends, one a married couple with a daughter, Agnes, who was close to my age. Agnes adored poetry and pressed her hand to her bosom dramatically each time she crossed the threshold of Fordhook and entered what she called "the sacred abode of Lord Byron," even though I told her this was a rented house and my father had never lived there. She also had the annoying habit of reciting certain verses from the third canto of *Childe Harold* whenever she came upon me alone.

"Did Agnes tell you she is engaged to be married?" my mother had asked me on their first day with us, pausing by my room to inspect me as I dressed for dinner.

"No, she did not," I said, glancing at the mirror, adjusting the ringlets framing my face. "She has scarcely stopped reciting poetry since she arrived, so unless the announcement could be made in rhyming couplets —"

"She's marrying a baronet," my mother interrupted. "He has a lovely estate in Shropshire and two thousand pounds."

"How nice. I hope they'll be very happy together."

"She's only two years older than yourself."

"Quite elderly, then."

"Ada —" My mother sighed and shook her head. "Come down to dinner. Our guests are waiting."

She did not bring the subject up again that evening, aside from toasting the bride-to-be at supper. Christmas passed pleasantly enough, and we welcomed the New Year merrily, and soon thereafter our guests departed. I resumed my customary routine of music and study, and I eagerly looked forward to my next trip to London to see what progress Mr. Babbage had made on the Analytical Engine. I was half-afraid that I would find the Difference Engine abandoned and shrouded in dust.

One afternoon a few days after Epiphany, I was writing to my friends Annabella and Olivia Gosford while my mother sat nearby, attending to her own correspondence. "Your Miss Bettencourt is betrothed," she remarked, her gaze fixed on a letter that had arrived that morning.

"She's not *my* Miss Bettencourt," I said, but my heart thumped. "To whom is she engaged?"

Sighing, she folded the page and set it aside. "The eldest son of the Duke of Rylance."

"Oh, yes. I met him." He was an excellent dancer, as I recalled, and exceedingly handsome. He loved horses, which had endeared him to me, but he had confessed himself to be "a right dullard" when it came to his studies, which disappointed. His title and the vast fortune he would inherit had rendered him the most eligible of all the young gentlemen in Society. "I rather liked him."

"If you had liked him more, you could have been a duchess."

With a twinge of jealousy that quite astonished me, I realized that one day Miss Bettencourt would outrank me. "Mama, he was never very interested in me, nor I in him."

"You could have made more of an effort to capture his interest."

"Mama, you know there are certain qualities I seek in a husband —"

"Yes, so you've said." My mother regarded me with an unsettling mix of sadness and apprehension. "You've had two Seasons. It's time you applied yourself to your duty to marry with the same fervor with which you study mathematics."

"But —" My mouth went dry, and I thought of Mrs. Somerville, or Mrs. Greig as she had been, commanded by her husband to relinquish mathematics and science for the duties of wife and mother. "I have not yet met anyone that I think will make me happy. I haven't met anyone I think I could love."

No one but Wills, and he was forever lost to me — and I could no longer ignore the bitter truth that he had let me go without much of a fight.

"Ada, it is your duty to marry and produce an heir," she said, more gently than she ever had before. "It will be your husband's duty as well."

"I know that, but there must be more to marriage than duty."

"Of course there is. You should marry

someone you respect, someone you trust to carry out that duty faithfully with you. Passion fades where once it burned brightly, but love, real love, can grow where only friendship was before." Her eyes were ineffably sad. "*I* married for love. *I* married the man I thought would make me happy. You know well what came of that."

I had come of it, I wanted to cry out, but I dared not. I could not bear it if she said aloud that my existence was poor recompense for her unhappy marriage.

CHAPTER NINETEEN:
I COULD NOT TAME
MY NATURE DOWN

January–May 1835

For as long as I could remember, I had been aware of my duty to marry and to produce an heir. This was expected of all young ladies of rank, but I felt the obligation more keenly than most because I was an only child, and my mother was an only child. There was no one else to fulfill this obligation for me if I refused.

As the beginning of my third Season approached, I felt more nervous and anxious than I had before my first. I'm not sure how long I had expected to get away with circulating in Society without soliciting a single proposal, but the end of the fun and frivolity loomed ominously before me, and a new determination seized my mother as she set about planning my wardrobe and arranging my social calendar. My irrational response was not to consider the young gentlemen I had already met and to weigh their virtues and flaws, or practice my dancing and witty remarks, but to study more intensely than ever before, as if I were desperate to cram as much learning into my fevered brain as I could before marriage brought my studies to a fatal end.

Dr. King, who had prescribed regular, diligent study as a cure for my overactive imagination, grew concerned that it was not having the calming effect on my nerves he had expected. "Indiscriminate reading will do you no good," he warned in a letter from Brighton. "Perhaps in a year's time you may explore a broader landscape of scientific topics, but for now you should focus on mathematics, especially Euclid, as well as Logic and Morals."

I dutifully agreed, even as my heart leapt with panic to think that in a year's time, I could be married, living with a husband I did not yet know in an unfamiliar house among strangers.

In late February, my mother and I traveled to London for the day, and while she arranged our lodgings for the Season, I called on Mrs. Somerville, hoping to escape my oppressive worries. Our conversation was pleasant and cheerful as she shared the news from Woronzow and her daughters, and as I described my recent progress in my studies. Then the conversation turned to Mr. Babbage and his two engines, and suddenly my thoughts flew to the enchanting Silver Lady displayed in his drawing room — beautiful, graceful, and a delight to behold, but unable to dance of her own free will, subject to the whims of her master and his inclination to depress the mechanism on her back or withhold his touch. Even when she was released from her frozen arabesque and allowed to dance, she was eternally constrained to a few square inches of tabletop, always the same pattern, always the same place —

Mrs. Somerville's gentle voice faded, drowned out by the surging of blood in my ears. I trembled and felt my heart palpitating, and as my throat constricted, a wave of nausea swept over me and beads of perspiration broke out on my brow and on the back of my neck. Dizzy, I clutched the armrests of my chair and tried to focus on Mrs. Somerville's voice as she urgently asked me if I was unwell. I remember that she helped me to the sofa, though I could barely stand, and then I was reclining on my back and Dr. Somerville was bent over me, peering intently into my eyes and holding his fingers to my wrist to measure my pulse.

Groggily I tried to sit up, and after I assured them that my head was clearing, Dr. Somerville arranged pillows behind my back to support me and Mrs. Somerville pressed a cup of tea into my hands. A servant had been sent to fetch my mother, and I was feeling quite restored by the time she swept into the room, her face pale, her lips compressed in a frown of worry.

"I'm quite all right now," I told them, rising a bit shakily from the sofa, but they were in firm agreement that I must be taken home to Fordhook immediately. My mother helped me into my wraps, and Dr. Somerville escorted me outside to the carriage, but not so quickly that I missed overhearing my mother and Mrs. Somerville discussing me in hushed, urgent tones.

"She may have exhausted herself from overwork," Mrs. Somerville told my mother. "Or it could be that life in London is too much for her. You know her best, but if I may, perhaps some quiet, restorative time at home would be better for her than the frenzy and stimulation of Town."

As my mother murmured agreement, my heart thumped with terror. I could not bear to abandon my studies, or to be banished from the intellectual encouragement I had enjoyed at Mrs. Somerville's and Mr. Babbage's homes. "I am quite well," I insisted as my mother joined me in the carriage, but all she would say was that she was glad to hear it and Dr. King would have the final word.

An examination was ordered forthwith, but Dr. King found nothing wrong with me, no trauma or fever, no recurrence of the terrible illness that had robbed me of the use of my limbs years before. "She may and should continue her studies," he pronounced, "but less vigorously than before. I believe idleness poses more danger to her than activity."

It was the best prescription I could have hoped for, but I knew my mother would not permit me to resume my activities in London unless Mrs. Somerville also concurred that it would not harm me. That very afternoon, I sent an impassioned appeal to my mentor and friend, first making light of my dizzy spell, and then imploring her not to cut me off from the intellectual activities that brought me so much good. "I am beginning to be alarmed, for I am afraid you mean to keep me in desperate tight order, and do you know I dare not disobey you for the world?" I wrote, my composure fracturing. "I cannot deny that I was shattered when I left you, but then I am for some unaccountable reason in a weak state, altogether now, and at this moment can hardly hold my pen from the shaking of my hand, though I cannot complain of being what people call *ill*."

I took a deep breath and refreshed my pen in the ink. Perhaps instead of denying that I was ill, which I was not doing particularly well, I ought to tell her I was quite well and getting better. "In a few weeks I daresay I shall be quite strong, particularly if I see a good deal of you," I wrote. "When I am weak, I am always so exceedingly terrified, at nobody knows what, that I can hardly help having an agitated look and manner, and this was the case when I left you. I do not know how I can ever repay or acknowledge all your kindness; unless by trying to be a very good little girl and showing that I profit by your excellent advice."

I could only hope that none of that "excellent advice" would include remonstrations that I should put away my books, languish in dullness at Fordhook, and miss the entire Season, as well as any new developments at 1 Dorset Street. I know Mrs. Somerville exchanged a few letters with my mother while I waited apprehensively for her to reply to mine, but my mother did not read them aloud to me, as we often did when one of us received a letter from a mutual acquaintance. In fact, my mother never acknowledged receiving any letters from the Somervilles, and if I had not glimpsed them on my mother's tray when her maid brought in the post, I would not have known about them.

This was enough to tell me that I was the subject of their conversation, and my anxious curiosity swelled until I could no longer bear it. I confess that one afternoon when my mother was off on business for her Ealing Grove school, I crept into her study and sorted through her papers until I found a letter in Mrs. Somerville's familiar script.

I had expected to find an analysis of my symptoms, perhaps accompanied by a course of treatment recommended by Dr. Somerville. What I discovered instead shocked and grieved me, not for my own sake, but for the Somervilles'. I knew that Mrs. Somerville had lost children, a son from her first marriage and a son and daughter from her second. What that letter revealed was that Margaret, the eldest child of her second marriage, had died at age ten, and that Mrs. Somerville blamed herself in part for her death. Margaret had been "a child of intelligence and acquirements far beyond her tender years," and so Mrs. Somerville, filled with maternal pride and devotion, had encouraged her to study mathematics and science, never restraining her hunger to learn even when it seemed insatiable. "I would not deny my precocious daughter as I had been denied," Mrs. Somerville wrote, "but when she fell ill of a brain-fever, I repented my leniency. For the rest of my life I will feel her loss more acutely, for I fear I had strained her young mind too much."

Anguished, I muffled a sob and returned the letter to the stack where I had found it. My heart broke for poor Mrs. Somerville, and for poor Margaret, too, and I understood then why my mentor feared that I would ruin my health with too much study. But although I felt a stirring of trepidation, I could not believe that too much study of mathematics could prove fatal, not even to a girl, certainly not to a girl like me. I was nine years older than Margaret had been when she perished, and presumably stronger. Furthermore, Mrs. Somerville had studied tenaciously as a young girl, memorizing textbooks by day and solving equations in her head by night. That was more grueling than anything I had ever attempted, and Mrs. Somerville had never suffered a single day for it.

I wished I could go to my mother and present a logical refutation of Mrs. Somerville's letter, but I dared not, as I had not been given permission to read it. All I could do was wait and hope that my mother would work out the flaws in Mrs. Somerville's reasoning just as I had, or that Mrs. Somerville herself would realize that the intensity of her emotions had swayed her usually infallible judgment.

I began to breathe a little easier, day by day, as no command to put away my books was forthcoming. In the middle of March I wrote to Mrs. Somerville again, a pleasant, cheerful letter in which I asked several questions about mathematics and astronomy, mostly to show her how well I was getting on. My hopes soared when she replied a few days later to say, after her customarily clear and informative responses to my queries, "I hope to see you in London soon. My daughters, Woronzow, and Mr. Babbage all send their kindest regards."

I rejoiced, for Mrs. Somerville would not give me false hopes. Surely this meant that she and my mother, and Dr. King, too, had agreed that I should not be exiled from London.

After that, I expected that any day my mother would instruct me to pack my things and prepare to travel — and she did, but her orders were not at all what I had anticipated. She would be going to Seaham for a few days, and then on to London, but I would be traveling to Brighton to partake of the restorative cure that my mother had always found so beneficial to her own health.

I balked at this, and my opposition grew when I was informed that Miss Frances Carr, easily the dullest and most disagreeable of the Furies, would be my traveling companion; but when my mother declared that for me the only road to London passed through Brighton, I acquiesced.

The fifty-mile journey to the seaside resort in Sussex took us two days by carriage and required an overnight stay at an inn along the way. The weather was blessedly fair, and since the carriage had a box both before and behind, I rode the greater part of the journey outside, not only to escape Miss Carr's oppressive presence, but also to lessen the discomfort of the carriage's disagreeable rocking and to enjoy the warm sunshine and fresh breezes.

The suite my mother had arranged for us at the Brunswick Hotel boasted lovely views of the sea and of the adjacent gardens, and after an invigorating walk along the beach and a delicious supper, I decided that a restful holiday to strengthen and inspirit me in preparation for the challenges of the upcoming Season was perhaps not the worst idea my mother had ever had. I rode every day, read novels, and studied mathematics — but not too vigorously, per Dr. King's orders, only when a question occurred to me as I strolled along the beaches listening to the crash of the surf and curiosity compelled me to look up the answer. Miss Carr chaperoned me to concerts and dances, and I discovered that she was not as sour and judgmental on her own as when the other two Furies were there to spur her on.

But although the days were pleasant and full of enjoyable distractions, my thoughts often turned to London — and more specifically, to the Difference Engine and its presumptive successor. Since I had come to Brighton I had heard from Mrs. Somerville infrequently and from Mr. Babbage not at all, and although I had been warned not to let myself become unduly agitated, I became increasingly curious and worried about the unresolved matter of funding, the progress of his plans for the Analytical Engine, and the state of the partially completed Difference

Engine. I fervently hoped that it was not sitting neglected in his workshop, and that if Mr. Babbage did not show it off to his guests anymore, that he at least remembered to send the maid out to give it a thorough dusting now and then.

On the fourth day of April, with the Season about to begin in earnest, I wrote to Mrs. Somerville, hoping that she would tell my mother how wonderfully restored I seemed. First, I offered a brief, lighthearted account of our long, arduous carriage journey, and then, composing my thoughts before setting pen to paper, I turned to the subject of my health.

As for myself, I am much stronger. I have been taking what has always been to me the finest of all medicines — horse exercise; & if I am to believe your daughters' own account of their feelings on this tender subject, I am afraid I shall excite in them hatred, & malice, & envy, & all manner of bad passions, when I say that I generally ride in the riding school everyday, and — best of all — leap to my heart's content. I assure you I think there is no pleasure in way of exercise equal to that of feeling one's horse flying under one. It is even better than waltzing.

I am very well able now to read Mathematics, provided I do not go on too long at a time, & as I have made up my mind not to care at present about making much progress, but to take it very quietly & as much as possible merely for the sake of improvement to my own mind at the time, I think I am less likely to be immoderate.

I wrote a little more about the weather, and about a few interesting people I had met, and I concluded with a cheerful invitation for Mrs. Somerville and her daughters to join me and Miss Carr in Brighton. "It is not too late either now," I wrote, "so pray take it into consideration." I invited them in all sincerity, for it would have been lovely to spend time together there, but the remark was also calculated to show that I was not overeager to leave. It seemed to me that happiness and contentment would suggest that I was fully restored to good health, whereas any disgruntled urgency to leave Brighton would be taken as a sign that I had not yet achieved the peace of mind everyone thought I needed.

Whether my letter convinced Mrs. Somerville, or Miss Carr sent favorable reports of my progress, or my mother realized it would be very difficult for me to partake of the Season from more than fifty miles away, I will never know, but at last my mother summoned me to London. By the middle of April, I was happily settled into my rooms at the house my mother had taken for us at 10 Wimpole Street in Marylebone, a delightfully short half-mile walk to Mr. Babbage's house. An invitation to his next soirée was waiting for me when I arrived, and I could barely contain my elation as my mother and I crossed the threshold of the now familiar Georgian house, where friends greeted us warmly and interesting new acquaintances were met. Mr. Babbage and I had much catching up to do, and we both expressed great satisfaction at seeing each other in good health and fine spirits. I was relieved to hear that he had not abandoned work on the Difference Engine but had continued to tinker with it, as well as he could with his obstinate engineer off sulking somewhere. "I've entertained several new ideas for the Analytical Engine," he told me, promising to show me his latest drawings the next time I called. He had nothing to report about his long-delayed funding.

"I suppose that could be considered good news," I remarked. "At least Sir Robert Peel has not canceled your grants."

"Only because he has not thought of it yet, I'm sure," said Mr. Babbage. "He's been too busy dealing with his failure to win a majority in the House of Commons to bother with me. If he cannot even control his own party, how can he expect to lead a nation?"

"Or to properly fund scientific research for the public good?"

"Exactly so."

"Political winds are ever shifting," I reminded him. "They did not blow your way last winter, but perhaps soon they shall."

I had never claimed to possess the gift of prophecy, but my words soon proved to be curiously prescient. Unbeknownst to us, that same evening Sir Robert Peel's Tories concluded that his dismal showing in the January elections had rendered it impossible for him to govern. The Whigs returned to power, and two days after Mr. Babbage's soirée, Lord Melbourne was once again prime minister.

When I read the story in the newspaper, I gasped aloud. "Mama —"

"No, Ada," she replied calmly, sipping her coffee. She had already read the paper, and she had prepared her response before I knew I would be asking the question. "I shall not trouble my cousin about Mr. Babbage's funding."

Her refusal did not surprise me, but I'd had to try. It was my duty to Mr. Babbage and to science. I consoled myself with the awareness that circumstances had turned in Mr. Babbage's favor despite my mother's refusal to use our family connections on his behalf. Simply having the scornful Sir Robert Peel out of office was no small triumph.

Although my devotion to helping Mr. Babbage realize his dream had not diminished, I was mindful of the other duty that had brought me to London that spring. More anxious and yet more determined than I had been in my first two Seasons, I dressed for balls as if I were donning armor for battle, a reluctant soldier in the war upon spinsterhood. I was a bit taken aback to discover how many of the young gentlemen I had flirted with had become engaged to other young ladies since I had last seen them, and it was disconcerting to note how many fresh, bright, pretty young ladies clad in pure white dresses were making their first court curtseys to the king and queen.

I do not mean to suggest that the Season was all drudgery and toil. I enjoyed concerts and dances, where the enchanting music swept all other concerns from my mind, but I preferred smaller gatherings, especially those at Mr. Babbage's and Mrs. Somerville's homes. I had become very good friends with Martha Somerville, who was close to my age, and her sister, Mary, two years younger, and of course I previously mentioned Woronzow Greig, the eldest son of the family, who was already becoming the steadfast confidant I would trust and depend upon later in life.

One evening in the last week of April, the Somerville family invited me and my mother to a dinner party. The spring twilight was so lovely that after supper we all went out to wander the parklike grounds of the Royal Hospital. My mother walked ahead with Dr.

and Mrs. Somerville, and the two sisters were laughing and chatting with a cousin visiting from Edinburgh. Other guests were dispersed here and there in pairs and small groups, and I found myself strolling beside Woronzow.

He started to speak, then hesitated, then tried again. "Ada, I've been thinking."

"Oh, dear. Perhaps you shouldn't. That can lead to trouble."

He grinned and ducked his head. He never quite knew what to make of my jokes. "I have a friend —"

"That's not true," I protested. "You have many."

"I have one friend in particular," he said emphatically, "that I think you would like to know."

I understood the implication. "I'm listening."

"His name is William, Lord King, eighth Baron of Ockham," Woronzow said. "We met as students at Trinity College, and we've been friends ever since."

"I know a *Dr.* William King, and a King William." And a William Turner, I thought, but could not say. "How is it that I have never met William, Lord King?"

"He has been abroad until recently." As the light faded with the sunset, Woronzow offered me his arm. Lampposts lined the walking paths, but the flickering gaslight only faintly illuminated our way. "After Cambridge, he went overseas to pursue a career in the diplomatic service. As you would expect, he is very well traveled, and he most recently served in Greece as secretary to Lord Nugent, governor of the Ionian Islands."

"What would compel him to give up a prestigious post in such a beautiful part of the world?"

"An unhappy impetus, I'm afraid. A little more than two years ago, his father passed away quite suddenly. William was obliged to return to England to take on the title and responsibilities as the eighth Lord King." Woronzow gave my hand a little squeeze where it rested in the crook of his arm. "I think you and Lord King would be exceptionally well suited. His accomplishments speak for themselves, and he's as well read as he is well traveled, conscientious, and intelligent. He's particularly interested in science, engineering, and philosophy. I believe he inherited his interest in the latter from his father. He published John Locke's *Life and Letters.*"

"Did he indeed? My mother would approve."

"Lord King has many other virtues that would impress your mother even more." His tone conveyed volumes; he knew my mother would be difficult to please, and he would not have bothered mentioning his friend if he considered Lord King in any way below the mark. "I confess I've taken the liberty of telling him about you."

"Oh, dear." I kept my voice light, but I felt a nervous fluttering in my chest. "I shudder to think what you might have said."

"Only good things," he assured me. "I have only good things to say."

"In that case, if we ever do meet, he will never recognize me."

Woronzow halted. "Would you like me to introduce you?"

I needed only a moment to consider. "I would be delighted to meet any good friend of yours," I said, "but I cannot allow you to play matchmaker under false pretenses."

"What do you mean?"

"I would like very much to tell you —" I took a breath to steel myself. "I cannot deceive you, or have you even unwittingly deceive a friend. May I have your promise that what I tell you now, you will share with no one?"

His brow furrowed in concern, but he managed a reassuring smile. "Ada, as a barrister, I'm entrusted with important secrets every day. You have my solemn promise that I shall never betray yours."

I inclined my head to indicate that we should walk somewhat apart from the others, and when I was sure they would not overhear us, I quietly and straightforwardly told Woronzow about my affair with Wills. I omitted the most sordid details, and I did not divulge how much I had loved him, but I did not conceal that we had been intimate and that I had intended to elope with him.

I could barely bring myself to look at Woronzow afterward, but to my relief, he looked shaken, but not disgusted or horrified. "Forgive me this impertinent question," he said. "Think of me as a lawyer now, and not as your friend. Am I correct to understand that your liaison was . . . unconsummated?"

"Yes." Then I remembered my mother's distinction between virginity and purity, and honesty compelled me to add, "But only just."

"You need say nothing more." Woronzow regarded me with the same compassion and understanding that I had seen so often in his mother's face. "This man was older than you, and in a position of authority. He took advantage of you."

"No," I said firmly, shaking my head. "I will not foist the blame upon him. I was perfectly willing. It was I who packed a bag and went to him."

"You don't want to condemn him, and I understand that, but that does not change the fact that you were only seventeen years old, and rather sheltered, from what you've told me. He was an adult, and he should have known better."

I blinked away tears. Woronzow was stating

the facts but not the truth. It pained me to hear of my love for Wills dismissed as girlish infatuation, and worse yet, his love for me as something sordid and criminal. "My mother says that I am ruined."

"With all due respect to your mother, non-sense."

I was so startled that I laughed. I had never heard anyone dismiss my mother's judgment so easily.

"Ada, I have been one of Lord King's closest friends for many years, and I can tell you with utmost certainty that this affair, as you call it, did not progress far enough that it would cause him any concern." Glancing over his shoulder at the sound of laughter, he lowered his voice as his sisters and cousin wandered our way. "It in no way discourages me from recommending you to him. In fact, your honesty only increases my esteem for you."

I regarded him with no small measure of disbelief. "Knowing what you know, you would still want to introduce us?"

"Do you still want to meet him?"

"Yes, of course."

Woronzow smiled and promised to arrange for us to meet as soon as possible, and I promised not to get engaged to anyone else in the meantime. We strolled on, and when the party reunited, I said nothing of our conversation to my mother. If I did eventually meet William, Lord King, and found him ghastly, I did not want her to know he existed.

In early May, my mother accepted an invitation for us to visit the family of her friend Sir George Philips at their estate in Warwickshire about ninety miles northwest of our London residence. His father, the first Baronet Philips, had earned a fortune in the textile industry and had constructed a magnificent new country house to reflect his successes. Weston House had been completed only two years before, and a veritable stone fortress indeed it seemed to me as I glimpsed it through the windows of our carriage, with its numerous round turrets, tall pinnacles topped by stone finials, and massive columns flanking the front entrance.

Both the elder and the younger George Philips had invited other friends for the week, and so there were many guests whom my mother and I did not know. One of the first to whom the younger George introduced us was his good friend William, Lord King.

I was so startled by the name that I could barely murmur a reply. Lord King was tall, with a strong, lean build and broad shoulders, hooded brown eyes that were both piercing and ineffably kind, wavy light brown hair, and a cleft chin. Woronzow had neglected to mention how handsome his friend was, and when Lord King smiled somewhat shyly down upon me as we were introduced, I felt unmistakable delight and anticipation.

"I believe we have a mutual friend," Lord King said to me at dinner, for we had been seated next to each other, an arrangement too fortuitous to be dismissed as coincidence.

"Yes, two, in fact, Sir George and his son," I said, feigning innocence as I inclined my head to indicate our two hosts.

Lord King colored slightly. "Of course, but I was referring to Mr. Woronzow Greig."

"Oh, really? Do you know Mr. Greig?"

"Yes, we've been great friends ever since our Cambridge days." Now he looked endearingly confounded. "I beg your pardon, Miss Byron, but he led me to believe that he had spoken to you about me."

I took pity on him. "He has, Lord King. I confess I've been teasing you."

"Ah, yes. He warned me that you might." He smiled, and I found myself smiling back. "He also told me that if I wanted you to speak to me, I had only to ask you about Mr. Babbage's Difference Engine and you would go on at length."

"He said that, did he?"

"He did. Don't tell him I told you." When he smiled at me, I was struck by the way his earnest, attentive manner made him seem even more handsome than upon first glance. "So? Have you seen this remarkable engine everyone is talking about?"

Naturally I had much to say on that subject,

and Lord King impressed me with his thoughtful, intelligent questions, which I did my best to answer. The conversation eventually turned to other subjects; architecture in particular fascinated him, and he shared several intriguing stories of his travels in the Near East. It was a thoroughly enjoyable dinner, and I could not help noticing that my mother looked on with great interest from her place near the head of the table.

Whether by chance or by design, Lord King and I found ourselves together often during the three days of our visit. He asked me about my mathematical studies and my music, and we discovered a mutual love of horses. In turn I learned quite a lot about him — the taciturn nature that concealed a scholarly mind; his fluency in Greek, French, Italian, and Spanish; his political aspirations, which he seemed more than capable of achieving; and his keen interest in applying new scientific discoveries to farming and animal husbandry. He was Woronzow's age, which meant that he was nearly eleven years older than I. He revered Mrs. Somerville, whom he had known since he and Woronzow had met at university, and he denounced it as "an outrage and a travesty" that the Royal Society proudly celebrated — and tacitly laid claim to — her scientific accomplishments by displaying her bust by Chantrey in their Great Hall, and yet would not allow her to become a member or use their library because she was a woman.

I think it was this passionate denunciation of the injustice done to my friend that transformed my growing interest into warm admiration.

Too soon our visit came to an end. As my mother and I prepared to depart, Lord King asked if he might write to me, and I consented. "I hope to see you again soon," he said as he helped me into the carriage. "Perhaps even before a letter would reach you."

"We'll be in Town for the Season," my mother assured him, and he bowed his thanks.

As we rode back to London, my mother remarked that Lord King had impressed her with his sincere interest in her industrial schools and her philosophy of progressive education. "He does not readily draw others into conversation," she acknowledged, "but I would not call him taciturn, because once he warms to a topic, he can be quite engaging." That was the worst criticism she leveled at him, which spoke volumes in his favor.

Unbeknownst to him, or to me, while I had been otherwise occupied with Lord King, my mother had busied herself making quiet inquiries of Lady Philips and other friends. Everyone she had spoken to at the party praised him as a sensible, rational gentleman who respected tradition and disdained frivolities. He owned two estates: his impressive ancestral seat of Ockham Park in Surrey, and Ashley Combe, a smaller but more picturesque estate at Porlock in Somerset, which boasted splendid views of the Somersetshire coast. He also owned a residence in the most fashionable neighborhood in London, 12 Saint James's Square. His title had been created in 1725, comfortably older than the minimum age of a century my mother required, and his family commanded prestige, political influence, and immense wealth.

"I hope you like him," my mother said, shaking her head at my foolishness if I did not, "because he certainly seems to like you, and you could not do better."

"I do like him," I admitted. What I did not say was that he excited my imagination the way no other gentleman I had met since Wills had done, and I thought that in time I could perhaps come to love him.

As soon as we settled back in at 10 Wimpole Street, I began to watch for a letter from Lord King, but before any arrived, I met him at a party in Whitehall. His obvious delight at seeing me warmed my heart, and although we were not seated next to each other at dinner, we spent nearly every other moment of the party together, enough so that I have no doubt we attracted speculation.

Lord King was somewhat reserved, as both my mother and I had noticed, but my teasing, playful manner drew him out as it had at Weston House, and soon we were conversing like old friends. I told him of my love for singing and playing the harp, and how I secretly hoped that one day I would be as renowned for my music as I expected to be for mathematics. He told me of the great pleasure he derived from improving his estates, not merely chatting with the gardener and architect and watching their men at work, but drawing up plans, removing trees, and building stone walls himself. I suspected, but was not bold enough to say, that this hardy labor out of doors surely accounted for his vigor, his well-muscled arms and back, and the hint of gold in his light brown hair.

He told me that he had three sisters and a younger brother, and he confided that he and his mother were not on cordial terms, and that his relationship with his sister Emily and his brother, Locke, had ever been contentious. In turn I confided to him that my mother could be didactic, overbearing, and impossible to please, and yet I had an irrepressible compulsion to try. More hesitantly, I told him how I had struggled all my life as the child of the great poet Lord Byron, an unwilling celebrity from the day of my birth, and that I longed to know more about my father even as I feared what I might discover.

"Please don't tell anyone," I added at a sudden flash of terror that in the morning I would be greeted with a newspaper headline screeching, "Byron's Daughter Laments Poet's Legacy."

"I would never divulge any of your secrets, Miss Byron," he said, shocked by the very idea. He took my hand, hesitated, and said, "I wonder if you could ask your mother if I might speak to her tomorrow afternoon."

"I will," I said, a tremor in my voice. "I know she plans to be in to receive callers, but I'll write to you all the same after I speak with her."

He smiled warmly, holding my gaze, and I felt again the delicious, happy, disconcerting flutter in my midsection that only one other man had ever evoked in me. I was stunned by the sudden realization that perhaps I dared hope for more from marriage than a union with a steadfast partner committed to the mutual duty of producing heirs.

As the party drew to a close, Lord King and I parted on the glad expectation of meeting again soon. Almost immediately afterward, my mother came looking for me, and she no doubt discerned from my bright eyes and flushed cheeks that something of great significance had happened. She promptly summoned our carriage, and as soon as we were seated within, I told her that Lord King wished to speak with her the following afternoon.

"Of course I'll be in," she said, a little breathlessly. "If I had plans, I would cancel them. As soon as we get home, you must write to him and say I will be happy to receive him at two o'clock."

"He may only wish to speak to you about educating the poor," I cautioned her. I confess that part of me, overwhelmed by the speed and suddenness of the apparently imminent change of my fate, hoped that this was true.

"Don't be ridiculous. He's coming to ask for your hand in marriage." My mother's face was flushed with elation. "This is wonderful, simply wonderful. How lucky it is that Lord King has been abroad all these years, or he would surely already be married."

"And how fortunate," I retorted sharply, "that, if his father had to die, he arranged it perfectly so that his son would be obliged to return to England precisely when I would be seeking a husband."

"Ada! What a dreadful thing to say." She studied me intently. "I assumed that you would welcome his proposal. Was I mistaken?"

"Of course not," I said, contrite. "If tomorrow Lord King asks to marry me . . . I will accept."

He arrived promptly at two o'clock the following afternoon, and by half past, it was decided.

I would marry Lord King.

CHAPTER TWENTY:
LINKS GRACE AND HARMONY
IN HAPPIEST CHAIN

June 1835

An astute observer would note that I had known Lord King less than a fortnight. One might expect a young lady to feel alarmed and overwhelmed by such a swift progression from introduction to acquaintance to betrothal, but I felt swept away on a wave of excitement and relief. Lord King seemed the ideal husband for a mathematical young lady such as myself, and since he was evidently fond of me and I liked him very much, we had every expectation of happiness. And now that the decision had been made, I felt as if I had been struggling up the steep slopes of Mont Blanc for two years and had at last reached the summit. At last I knew that I would not disappoint my mother by failing in my foremost duty. I would not be condemned to the miserable fate of the Three Furies, forever lingering in the shadows of other people's happiness. And, best of all, Lord King would not expect me to abandon my mathematics once I became his wife — in fact, he would be surprised and disappointed if I did.

Lord King had spoken to my mother alone in her study while I was supposed to be sitting demurely in the garden, innocently unaware of what transpired inside. Instead I had paced, imagining the many different directions their conversation might take, and only after Lord King had joined me in the garden, my mother on his arm, both of them smiling, had my lingering worries fled. With my mother looking on approvingly, Lord King had taken my hand in his and had knelt before me, and when he proposed, I had joyfully accepted.

We embraced, and he gave me a chaste kiss on the cheek, but his lips lingered close to my mouth, trembling with anticipation. I felt it too, and I smiled up at him with happy tears in my eyes. I think we both forgot about my mother standing a few paces away until she cleared her throat and said, "Perhaps we should discuss a date for the wedding?"

Lord King readily agreed, and so the three of us sat down on adjacent benches, my mother took her diary from her pocket, and we considered the options. My mother and Lord King agreed that since there was no impediment, financial or otherwise, to our marriage, a long engagement was neither necessary nor advisable. "I am happy to wed

Miss Byron at the earliest possible opportunity," Lord King said, his eyes shining with affection as he took my hand, kissed it, and pressed it to his heart. I was too overcome with happiness to reply, but I knew he understood all I could not say.

My mother paged through her diary. "What about the eighth of July?"

My heart gave a little jump. "That's little more than a month away," I said, my voice sounding very small and meek. "Will we have enough time to prepare?"

"Of course, my dear," said my mother, so affectionate and solicitous that I was quite taken aback. "A small family wedding is a relatively simple affair. We'll spare no expense, and it will be done exactly as we wish."

"If the eighth of July is the earliest it can be arranged, I can wait until then," Lord King declared. I could not have asked for a more ardent fiancé.

"July eighth it is," said my mother, writing in her diary. She underlined something for emphasis, but when she glanced up from the page, her expression became more serious. "Lord King, I do hope we might beg a favor from you."

"Name it. You're giving me your only daughter. I'm happy to give you anything you ask."

"All I want is your silence."

He blinked at her and threw me a puzzled

glance before returning his gaze to my mother. "My silence?"

"For as long as it is worthwhile to maintain it." My mother looked to me for confirmation, and I gave her the barest of nods. "My daughter has been an object of popular fascination from the moment of her birth because she is the daughter of Lord Byron. Neither of us wishes for her wedding — the most sacred, intimate event in a young woman's life — to become a public spectacle."

"Nor do I," said Lord King. "I'll say nothing, and I'll swear my family to secrecy."

My mother regarded him gravely.

Lord King's eyebrows rose. "Oh, I see. You wish me to keep this secret from my family as well."

"Yes, for as long as possible." My mother sighed and made a graceful gesture signifying resignation in the face of the inevitable. "The truth will come out eventually, but until then, we would prefer to enjoy our mutual happiness in peace and privacy."

Lord King assured us that he would not breathe a word of our engagement until my mother gave him leave to do so. He added, wryly, "Please let it be before the day of the wedding or my family will never forgive me."

I laughed, but my mother did not even smile. "We should be so fortunate," she said. "Some caterer or florist's assistant will likely divulge the secret well before then."

My mother invited Lord King to return later that evening to dine with us, but he declined regretfully, explaining that he had to return to Ashley Combe at once, to evaluate what refurbishments would be necessary to make it a suitable place for our honeymoon. "Good-bye, darling," he said in parting, the first time he had ever used an endearment to address me. The tenderness of his expression moved me.

The next day I received an ardent letter from Lord King, so warm and affectionate that I could scarcely keep from smiling as I read it. The next day another letter came, and I laughed in sheer wonder that he could be so in love with me already. In my reply, I mentioned that I planned to visit Mrs. Somerville on the first day of June; in his next letter he said that he had planned to be in London that day, and he suggested meeting me in Chelsea and driving me home after my visit. He added that he had not told Woronzow about our engagement even though our mutual friend deserved the credit for it. "That is how faithfully I keep my vows," he wrote, signing himself, "Yours with the most devoted affection and respect, King."

Eagerly I replied to give my consent, and then I awaited the first day of June with great anticipation. My visit with Mrs. Somerville, Mary, and Martha was as delightful as ever, but it was all I could do to keep my happy secret from bursting from my lips. When Lord King arrived to drive me home in his carriage, Mrs. Somerville looked askance at us both, but she had known Lord King for years and trusted him not to lead me into scandal, even if she did not entirely trust me to avoid accidentally blundering into it.

We were all merriment and good cheer as we made our farewells to the Somervilles, but once Lord King had helped me into the carriage, seated himself beside me, and rapped to signal the driver to commence, we fell into an awkward silence. Even though the hood of the barouche was drawn back so we could bask in the warm summer sunshine, for the first time we were essentially alone, and for all our mutual admiration and blossoming affection, we were still strangers. William seemed to realize this at the same time I did, and when I sensed him withdrawing into his customary reserve, I decided that it was up to me to set the course for how we would carry on together.

As the carriage took us down the sun-dappled Royal Hospital Road, I drew upon two of my favorite subjects, music and horses, in hopes of putting him at ease. I described the new piece I was learning for the harp, Beethoven's "Six Variations on a Swiss Song," which I could not wait to play for him. I told him about my favorite horse, Tam O'Shanter, and how I looked forward to exploring the grounds of Ashley Combe on horseback with my bridegroom leading the way. At first Lord King only listened, earnest and attentive, but by the time the carriage reached the banks of the Thames, his reserve had melted, and he was chatting with me as easily and frankly as he had during our visit to Weston House.

He took my hand, and when we reached a secluded spot, he glanced around to be sure we were unobserved before kissing me tenderly on the mouth. I sighed and lifted my face to his to claim another kiss, and he responded with ardor and passion, until for a moment I think we both quite forgot that we could be seen by anyone we passed.

After seeing me home, Lord King stayed long enough to give his regards to my mother, then raced back to Ashley Combe. In the days that followed, letters flew between us, his imbued with love and anticipation, mine with happiness and increasing affection. Enthusiastically he described his efforts to prepare his Somerset estate for our honeymoon, "to make this hermitage (for it is little more) less impossible in its appearance, & to make it not unworthy of your presence. The scenery is the only thing that can so entitle it, for within doors it is of the most humble description and it is in the state which most homes are which have not been inhabited for fifteen years, & even then only temporarily & with long intervals."

"You make my future home sound thoroughly rustic and abandoned," I teased in my reply. "If you think to discourage me from marrying you, or at least from marrying you so soon, you will have to do better than that. I would be happy to spend our honeymoon in the most humble cottage, or even in the stables in the hayloft, as long as we are together, although I confess I hope for a proper bed and strong walls to shut out the world."

Although I honestly had not meant to be suggestive, his next letter revealed that my words had inflamed his ardor, and even I laughed at my inadvertent innuendo, my own arousal heightened. Even so, not knowing who else might see my letter — my mother, perhaps, before I had a chance to post it — and thinking that perhaps like most men he preferred an innocent bride, I phrased my response more carefully, affectionate but measured, as if I were only vaguely aware of the pleasure that a man and woman could give to each other.

His reply suggested that perhaps I had been too restrained, for a new note of worry infused it. "I look upon our future happiness as too excessive to be enjoyed otherwise than in a dream," he confessed, "as too splendid and too overcoming for a reality. I am only rescued from this delusion by reflecting upon your own sincerity and nobleness of character." A slight alteration in the pressure of his pen revealed his emotion when he added, "I hope to present myself at your home this coming Friday and to be assured from your own lips that you do not repent of having made me the happiest of men."

I cared for him too much to toy with his feelings, so as soon as I finished reading his letter, I composed a reassuring reply. "Your letter has been an unexpected happiness to me this morning," I wrote, "but I cannot allow you even to mention such as thing as my 'repenting' of anything that has passed between us. I do not know when I have been in so calm and peaceful and, I hope I may add with truth, so grateful a state of mind, as I have been since you made me the happiest of women."

He wrote back wryly to say that he envied me my sense of peace and calm, for his thoughts were a tangle of "excitement and an absence of mind," which nonetheless delighted him.

As Lord King made ready Ashley Combe, my mother and I prepared my trousseau, which involved a great many dressmakers' fittings and visits to the finest shops in London. One evening, as my mother and I sat together in the library, I writing a letter to Lord King and she perusing the bills, she looked up from the slips of paper and remarked, "The expenditures for your wedding now equal all that I have spent on the Ealing Grove school this year. Only in a mother's arithmetic could one's own daughter equal eighty other children."

Her tone was light, but nonetheless, I hastened to acknowledge my indebtedness and gratitude and to thank her for her generosity. It occurred to me to point out that soon I would be someone else's burden, but I held back the words, suspecting that she did not look forward to relinquishing her authority over me.

As often as he could, Lord King came to London to attend to matters of business, and he never failed to visit me and my mother. On 19 June, after one of these visits, he wrote earnestly to my mother to ask if she would now grant him leave to inform his family, in strictest confidence, about our upcoming nuptials, for his mother and his uncle, especially, would surely feel slighted if he neglected them any longer. My mother consented, and she confided to me that she was rather surprised we had managed to keep the news out of the papers so long, for she had observed shopkeepers' assistants staring at us and whispering together from the moment we began assembling my trousseau.

I remained reluctant for our forthcoming wedding to be announced before I was ready to accept the onslaught of attention it would inevitably provoke, but I agreed that it was high time Lord King's family was informed. The next day, I confided in Mrs. Somerville, but I begged her not to tell Woronzow, Martha, and Mary. "Your friends would want to share in your happiness," she protested mildly.

"Of course they would," I replied, "and I'll let you know as soon as the news may be imparted to the rest of the family. But our wish at this moment is to keep everything as quiet as possible."

She smiled understandingly and agreed, as I had known she would, but there were others about whom I was not so sure. Since I had come out in Society, I had seen two of William's sisters, Hester and Charlotte, here and there without knowing I would one day be engaged to their brother. To interested observers, it must have seemed curious that a warm friendship had blossomed between us apparently overnight, for one day we merely exchanged polite nods at parties and the next we were smiling, arm in arm, whispering in corners. I was delighted that at last my longing for siblings was going to be fulfilled.

Whether our conduct raised suspicions, or shopgirls gossiped, or one of the intimate friends to whom my mother divulged the news did not keep her confidence, I can only speculate, but by the last week of June, letters of congratulations were trickling in to

Fordhook and 10 Wimpole Street. A rather astonishing number of these letters, most of which were addressed to my mother, congratulated her on marrying me off and expressed astonishment that I had captured the heart of so good a man. "Do they believe I've been seeking a bridegroom at Newgate Prison?" I said, indignant. "Why shouldn't a good man want to marry me?"

My mother regarded me from beneath raised brows as if she hardly knew where to begin.

After I shared the news with Mrs. Somerville, the very next person I had confided in was Mr. Babbage. He was overjoyed, and tears filled his eyes, and although we did not usually embrace, on that occasion he held me by the shoulders and kissed me on both cheeks. With a pang of sorrow, I realized that he was probably thinking of his own Georgiana and wishing that he could have danced at her wedding and toasted the happy couple, a proud father entrusting his beloved girl to a worthy gentleman.

One humid afternoon when the promise of rain hung heavy in the air, Mr. Babbage paid me an unexpected visit. My mother did not usually receive callers at that hour and she happened to be out, but I showed him into the drawing room, where cross breezes through the open windows offered some relief from the heat, and I offered him a cool glass of cider. He accepted with his thanks, but his manner was unusually agitated and I wished I had something stronger to serve him.

"My dear Miss Byron —" He stopped, regarded me grimly, and tried again. "Do you know of the Contessa Teresa Guiccioli?"

"Only by name," I said, taken aback. "I believe she knew my father when he was in Ravenna, before he made his final journey to Greece."

"I see. Well, perhaps you may have guessed that she knew your father very well, very intimately." In case I missed the point, he added, "She was his last mistress, before his death, and by all accounts the one he loved best." I must have flinched, because he quickly said, "My apologies. I regret the indelicacy of this subject."

I took a deep, steadying breath. "It's all right. I know you must have good reason for bringing it up." I clasped my hands together in my lap and waited, preparing myself for whatever would come next.

"Contessa Guiccioli is presently in England," he said. "She has come on a pilgrimage to visit the most significant locales of Lord Byron's life. She has already toured Newstead Abbey and has placed a wreath on his grave at Hucknall Torkard."

"I see," I said, dismayed. "My father never lived here or at Fordhook, so I suppose I needn't fear her knocking upon my door and demanding a tour and souvenirs." Another thought struck me. "Is it possible that our paths might cross in Society?"

"She has been making the rounds since she arrived in London," he said carefully, "but you travel in different circles, and I, myself, would never invite you to the same dinner party. However, some of our acquaintances are not so conscientious."

"And still others would relish the thought of bringing us together in the same room to see what might unfold." I drew in a breath and pressed my hand to my heart. "Oh, goodness. How fortunate it is that my mother is at Fordhook. Perhaps I can contrive to keep her there. Do you know how long the countess intends to stay in London?"

"I don't know, but there is another matter of concern." He winced and rubbed his jaw, stalling for time. "She has long wanted to meet you, and she's heard rumors of your impending marriage, and — Miss Byron, I regret to say that she plans to attend the wedding."

"Is she mad?" I cried, bounding to my feet. "What could she be thinking? My mother will be there!"

"I know, I know." He held up his palms in a calming gesture as I paced. "I told her that this is a terrible idea and I urged her to reconsider, but she is resolute. She wants nothing more than to meet the daughter of Byron."

"Well, I don't want to meet her," I said hotly, dropping back into my chair. "Especially not on my wedding day. And never when my mother is present. What a dreadful creature this contessa must be, to want to flaunt her affair with my father in his widow's face."

"She's actually quite charming," said Mr. Babbage, a trifle dreamily. "Petite and quite voluptuous, with lovely auburn hair and an enticing manner. She has already acquired many admirers here in London —"

"I sincerely hope you are not one of them."

"No, no, not I," he quickly replied.

I gave him a sharp look, and he shrugged, all wide-eyed innocence. "What am I to do?" I lamented. "I can't have her there. It's going to be a very small affair in the drawing room at Fordhook, with only family in attendance."

"She believes otherwise," said Mr. Babbage, and for the first time, a small, satisfied smile played in the corners of his mouth. "She thinks that she will lose herself in the crowd of well-wishers and observe you unnoticed. It's a reasonable assumption, I suppose, that the daughter of Byron would have a very grand and very public wedding ceremony."

As his smile grew, I became increasingly suspicious. "Is it possible that she was somehow guided to this assumption?"

He shrugged and feigned ignorance — I was certain it was feigned. "I wouldn't want to speculate, but I believe she is under the impression that you and Lord King are going to marry on July eighth before a large assembly at Saint George's Church in Hanover Square."

"She has the date right —"

"But only the date." Mr. Babbage regarded me with affectionate sympathy. "My dear Miss Byron, I wouldn't have burdened you with this nonsense but for the fear that you might run into her at some dance or dinner. The thought of you being caught unaware by the irrepressible contessa, swept up in an embrace of lace, perfume, and swift, effusive, dialectal Italian —" He shook his head. "I simply could not allow that to happen."

I thanked him fervently, my imagination spilling over with the appalling scenes that might have unfolded if I had not been forewarned. Now I needed only to prevent the correct location from leaking to the press — and keep my mother from learning that *la contessa* was in England. My wedding was little more than a week away. Surely I could forestall disaster a few days more.

That was what I told myself as I escorted Mr. Babbage to the door and hurried off for paper and pen to write to Lord King and warn him about our determined would-be guest.

A few days later, my mother returned to London, her work with the Ealing Grove school set aside for the moment so that she could assist me with some last-minute details in Town before taking me home to Fordhook for the wedding. The moment she crossed the threshold, her expression told me that she bore a heavy burden of worry. At once I assumed that she had heard about the contessa, and I was in the midst of choosing words that would best comfort her when she asked me to join her in her study.

I had done nothing wrong, so her abrupt tone did not trouble me for my own sake as I obediently followed her down the hall and sank into my usual chair facing her desk. My mother seated herself behind it and studied me over the mahogany expanse for a long moment in silence, all regal grace. "After much careful thought and prayer," she said, "I have decided that you must inform Lord King of your imprudence with Mr. Turner."

My heart plummeted so swiftly that I thought I would be sick. "You can't mean it."

"I most sincerely do."

"But . . . why? You have always said it must remain a secret, that no one must know —"

"I am motivated by a stern sense of justice and right," my mother interrupted, her expression stony. "Secrets were kept from me before my marriage, truths that, if revealed to me in time, would have changed the course of my life. I cannot perpetrate that same injustice upon anyone, particularly not a gentleman as good and honest as Lord King."

My vision blurred with tears. "You have said that no one would marry me if —"

"If you and Lord King marry, you must marry into truth."

If we marry, she said. If. The room seemed to spin slowly to the right, and I closed my eyes, fighting back nausea. "I cannot tell him," I choked out. "I cannot." I pictured myself standing before him in shame, the sordid tale tumbling from my lips, the warmth fading from his smile, disappointment and disgust clouding his eyes, the face I already cherished turning away from me in cold contempt. "Please don't make me do this. What can I say to convince you that this is a terrible mistake?"

"The mistake was yours, when you heedlessly ran off in the night to your tutor," my mother snapped. More calmly, she added, "You should tell him yourself, to show proper remorse and penitence, but if you cannot do that, you could write him a letter."

"I cannot do either."

"Then I shall write to him."

"Good God, no," I exclaimed. I had read the characters she had written about me from the time I was a small child. I knew how she described me in letters to her friends. My mother's condemning account of my indiscretion would ruin any chance I might have of obtaining Lord King's forgiveness.

My mother interlaced her fingers and rested them on her desk. "You won't tell him, you won't write to him, you say I shall not write to him. What is the alternative?"

My mind raced. "Woronzow," I said at last, defeated. "He knows, and he is Lord King's closest friend. He would do this for me, if you insist that it must be done."

"Woronzow Greig knows of your disgrace?"

"Yes," I said brittlely, tempted to declare that he knew, and he did not consider me ruined. "I told him before he introduced me to Lord King."

"So you admit you understood, even then, that you should be honest about your indiscretion."

I felt weak, utterly drained of hope. "Woronzow should be the one to tell him," I said dully. With great effort, I hauled myself out of the chair and walked unsteadily to the door.

"Where do you think you're going?"

"To write to Woronzow," I said, biting out each word.

My letter was brief because he already knew the tale. All I did was tersely report my mother's orders to inform Lord King.

I signed the letter, sealed it, and sent it on its way — and then there was nothing to do but wait. I scarcely spoke to my mother all that day and the next, but listlessly wandered the rooms, gazing out windows, picking up books and setting them down unread. Although before my mother had returned from Fordhook I had been happily bustling about, attending to last-minute wedding preparations and ticking tasks off my list, after posting my letter, I abandoned my work. Why prepare for a wedding that might not happen?

Three days after my mother's staggering decree, Woronzow called. My mother was upstairs indisposed, so I seized his hand and pulled him into the sitting room. I felt faint; blood rushed in my ears; I groped for the edge of the sofa and nearly collapsed upon it. "What did he say?" I murmured, my throat constricting, bracing myself for the worst.

Woronzow sat beside me and took my hand. "Lord King knows everything," he said gently, "and he remains most anxious for the marriage."

A sob escaped my throat, and I fell into my friend's embrace, weeping. I realized then that Lord King must have truly loved me.

And then, amid my relief and gratitude, I discovered a tiny, cold ember of rage. My mother had been willing to jeopardize all my hopes and happiness because of some lingering resentment about her own marriage, some hatred she still clung to although my father had been cold in his grave eleven years.

Or was there more to it? Could she not bear to see me happily married to a good, kind, forgiving man, since she had not enjoyed such happiness? Did she really envy her disgraced, unworthy daughter enough to snatch away the good fortune that she thought I did not deserve?

Soon she could no longer command me, I thought bitterly as I dried my tears. Soon I would no longer be Ada Byron, daughter of Lady Byron, but Lady King, beloved wife of William, Lord King, eighth Baron of Ockham, and my mother's pawn no longer.

CHAPTER TWENTY-ONE: ON WITH THE DANCE! LET JOY BE UNCONFINED

June–September 1835

To be fair, my mother was not wrong.

I question her methods, and I suspect her motives, but she was not wrong to discourage me from marrying Lord King with a guilty secret poised to drive a wedge between us. If he had broken off our engagement after learning my secret, I never would have forgiven her, but in hindsight, I see that it was better that he knew before we married. If the truth had come out later, it could have poisoned our marriage or led to our divorce. Instead I had learned that my bridegroom was an eminently just, reasonable, and forgiving man, and he learned that I was imperfect but striving for goodness. We had faced our first test and had passed it. Was it not better that way?

Eventually, I decided that it was, but I did not come to this conclusion until much later. At the time, I burned with resentment and counted the days until I could marry Lord

King and escape my judgmental, imperious, domineering mother once and for all.

But I could not be free of her quite yet. The marriage settlement still had to be negotiated, and once my mother was certain that the wedding would proceed, she promptly summoned her lawyers and got down to business.

Because there were substantial sums of money and large properties to consider, my settlement would be more complicated than most. My mother did not discover until then that Lord King was not as exceptionally wealthy as we had thought; although he owned two impressive estates and a house in London and had excellent prospects of rising in politics, in comparison to other peers he enjoyed only modest wealth, for his estates had to support several members of his extended family. My mother resolved to compensate for this relative deficiency and to use her significant resources to promote his career.

When my grandparents had negotiated my mother's marriage settlement with my father, they had provided sixteen thousand pounds "for the issue of the marriage," and these funds essentially became my dowry. My mother contributed an additional fourteen thousand pounds of her own, which meant that upon marrying me, Lord King would receive the staggering sum of thirty thousand pounds, along with the near certainty of inheriting the considerable Wentworth estate sometime in the distant future. Astounded by her generosity, Lord King immediately directed his lawyers to accept the arrangement, as soon as he and my mother agreed upon my pin money.

I still cannot think of this part of the settlement without resentment, gritting my teeth at the injustice and humiliation of their meager provision for me. Because, of course, as a mere woman, a wife, I would never own any of that wealth and property, though it would descend from my mother. Instead, as my husband, Lord King would control every penny and every square inch of land. I would receive an annual income, my "pin money," which I was to use for my own expenses, such as clothing and other feminine necessities.

My mother and Lord King quickly settled upon the sum of three hundred pounds per annum, which they both agreed would be more than sufficient for my needs. "It is what I received when I married your father," my mother said when I objected to the paltry sum.

"Yes," I retorted, "twenty years ago. Three hundred pounds will not be enough when you consider the cost of books, and ball gowns, and —"

"In that case," she interrupted, "you will simply have to ask Lord King for more as your needs require. He has already proven to be generous. I'm sure he will deny you no reasonable request."

He probably would not, but I resented the very concept of pin money, of the obligation to go to him, head bowed in submission, and humbly petition him to pay my debts. It was evident that marriage would not bring me the independence I craved but would simply transfer me from my mother's control to my husband's. I could only trust that after marriage I would live under a more benevolent regime.

With the settlement drawn up, signed, and witnessed, there came a mad scramble to finish the preparations for the wedding, the honeymoon, and my first months of married life. Lord King worked from dawn to dusk at Ashley Combe, taking care of last-minute repairs and furnishing the rooms. At Fordhook and 10 Wimpole Street, the trickle of letters of congratulations and good wishes swelled into a stream, signifying that the word was out. And then, a week before the wedding, my heart thumped when I discovered my own name in the "Saturday Night" column of *The Examiner:*

It is said that the Hon. Miss Byron, "Ada, sole daughter of my house and race," is about to be united in marriage to Lord King. The bride will be twenty in next December; his lordship was thirty in February last.

I inhaled deeply, relieved that it said little that was not already public knowledge. I steeled myself before searching the other morning papers, but although I found a nearly verbatim announcement in *The Morning Post,* neither the location of the ceremony nor the date was revealed.

"There was only a slight notice of our wedding in the papers today," I wrote to Lord King later that afternoon, "nothing that need annoy us, although they did misquote *Childe Harold,* which I imagine will vex my late father's legions of fanatical readers. May they bury the editors in letters of complaint." I knew the third canto by heart, of course, having heard it recited to me more times than I could possibly count.

Lord King and I had exchanged several letters since Woronzow had played the solicitor between us, but neither of us mentioned my past indiscretions. Twice I hesitantly mentioned how grateful I was for his forgiveness, but since he never addressed those remarks in his replies, I concluded that we were never to speak of the matter again.

A few days before the wedding, my mother and I returned to Fordhook with all my wedding accoutrements and my trousseau. That same afternoon Lord King's family joined us there, including the brother and sister he did not get along with and his chilly, distant mother. She was equally cool to me and my mother, but I promised myself I would do all I could to bring William and his estranged relations together. A few of my mother's friends and some of my own completed our retinue, which was small, exactly as I wished. My mother had been obliged to obtain a special license from the archbishop of Canterbury so that Lord King and I could be wed in the drawing room at Fordhook, but we all agreed that our solitude was well worth the inconvenience.

Despite the friction among the Kings, and the barely contained astonishment at my "unlikely match" among my mother's friends, we were a merry company. At least most of us were, most of the time. At supper that first night, when Lord King's uncle innocently asked my mother if my nuptials resembled her own wedding to Lord Byron, she gave him a stony look and said, "Except for the small size of the gathering, and the fact that my daughter will be married in a drawing room, there is no resemblance whatsoever." The poor old gentleman had no idea what he had said to offend her, and my mother did not acknowledge his flustered apologies.

On the morning of Wednesday, 8 July, I woke early, excited and happy for the day to begin. My gown was the same confection of white tulle and silk I had worn for my presentation at court, with some alterations to make the style fashionably *au courant,* and I wore a long, elegant veil instead of the hat trimmed in ostrich feathers. Lady Gosford's daughter Olivia was my maid of honor, radiant in a dress of rose satin, and my dear bridegroom was wonderfully handsome in his blue silk jacket, snug trousers, and embroidered waistcoat.

I was so overcome by blissful excitement that I scarcely remember processing into the drawing room and joining Lord King before the minister. The brief ceremony was over before I knew it. There were prayers and exhortations, and we recited our vows and kissed, and then we were man and wife, lord and lady. A joyful throng of friends and family surrounded us, offering us embraces, congratulations, and good wishes in abundance. My mother looked as if she might swoon from happiness — and relief, too, no doubt, that it had all come off as planned. I was astonished and touched to glimpse tears in her eyes, for they were so rarely found there.

As we all filed into the dining room to enjoy a delicious wedding luncheon, I suddenly thought of Contessa Teresa Guiccioli, wandering forlornly through the empty, echoing nave of Saint George's Church in Hanover Square, wondering where everyone had gotten to. How grateful I was to Mr. Babbage for diverting her so that she would not spoil our happy day!

After luncheon, William and I — for I would call him William now, and he would call me Ada — departed Fordhook amid another flurry of embraces and good wishes. I had intended to bid farewell to my mother last of all, but when the moment came, she was standing at the back of the crowd chatting with Lady Gosford, the only two of all the company with their eyes turned anywhere but upon the bride and groom. Concealing my disappointment, I gave my parting kiss to Olivia instead.

"Well, Lady King?" William inquired when we were settled in the carriage, taking my hand, "did you have a good morning?"

"The most wonderful morning of my life," said I, delighted to hear my new name on his lips.

We first went to Ockham Park, William's family seat in Surrey about thirty miles southwest of Fordhook, so that I could meet the servants and tour the magnificent estate of which I was now mistress. As our carriage approached the elegant, brown-and-red brick Italianate mansion, I glimpsed a hipped, plain-tiled roof partially obscured by parapets, a striking front entrance with pilaster piers, and several bays. Although I could not see them all, William said there were fourteen bays in total, seven on one side of the two-story residence, and seven on the other.

William also told me that Ockham Park had been built nearly two hundred years earlier as a manor house, but when Peter King, the lord chancellor and first Baron King, had purchased it nearly one hundred years later, he had altered it according to plans by Nicholas Hawksmoor, the famous architect of the English Baroque style. "My father completed the next significant renovation only five years ago," William told me as I peered eagerly through the carriage window at my new home. "It was he who extended the house and fashioned it in the Italian style." He put one arm around my shoulders, and with his other hand, he indicated where the additions had been made, and also where the orangery, stables, and kitchen wing could be found. He himself had supervised construction of the lone tower beyond the house, barely visible through the tall cypress trees and hedgerows lining the drive.

As we drew closer and the carriage slowed, I saw that the servants were lined up outside the front entrance waiting to greet us. I was somewhat nervous, wondering how they would accept their new mistress, but everyone was kind and smiling, except for one footman, who gaped and stammered when we were introduced. I smiled kindly, assuming that he was either exceptionally shy or a new hire, but I later learned that he was a great lover of poetry, and he had been as excitable as a nervous colt from the moment he learned that his master was to wed the daughter of the great Lord Byron. It was then that I learned that even though I was now styled Lady King, I would always be "Ada!" of the third canto, sole daughter of my father's house and heart, to those who worshipped my father's memory.

My husband — how strange and wonderful it felt to think of him that way! — escorted me across the threshold. My first glance took in a spacious hall that opened into grand yet comfortable rooms, as lovely and as beautifully furnished as any place I had ever called home, with the exception of Kirkby Mallory, which to my loyal heart had no equal.

Home, I marveled. No longer would I be moved from one rented dwelling to another at my mother's whim. At last I had a place I could truly call my own home, and what a wonderful place it was.

Delighted, I seized William's hand. "Give me the grand tour, lord husband," I demanded, tugging his arm and pulling him down the hallway after me. Laughing, he obeyed, and although we did not visit every room that day, we at least paused in the doorway and glanced inside most of them. I claimed one particularly pleasant, sunny room on the first floor as my study, and further down the hall in the conservatory, I sighed over the lovely pianoforte. A moment later, when William directed my attention to the opposite corner, I cried for joy to behold a beautiful harp, intricately carved and perfectly tuned, his wedding gift to me.

"You're going to have a very difficult time persuading me to ever leave this room," I told him as I plucked arpeggios, luxuriating in the sonorous tone.

"Oh, indeed?" William said, eyebrows rising. "Do you think so?"

"I know so."

With a playful growl, he swept me up into his arms, and as I laughed and shrieked with delight, he carried me off to another room, in which I was to spend even more pleasurable hours than the conservatory.

William proved to be an eager, generous lover, and perhaps because he knew that I was no innocent, timid child, he did not restrain his ardor. Our lovemaking was passionate or playful as the mood took us, and if I did not feel the same dizzying rush of ecstasy as I had in Wills's arms, William brought me to such heights of pleasure that even from the first, I trusted our passion would become even richer and more fulfilling with time.

Perhaps because we passed so much time enjoying the pleasures of the marital bed, a week proved insufficient for me to explore every room of that lovely residence and each of the nearly five thousand acres of the surrounding estate. But our honeymoon cottage beckoned, and so on my seventh day as Lady King, we departed for Ashley Combe, about one hundred seventy miles to the west in Somerset, on the Bristol Channel.

At that time the journey was formidable, requiring several long, uncomfortable, and exhausting days in a carriage, with overnight stays at inns along the way, but newlywed bliss and anticipation sustained us. William amused me by describing the history or significant geologic features of places along our route, and we also passed the time simply holding hands and enjoying companionable silence. As we ventured westward, we seemed to leave civilization behind, as the towns became smaller and more widely scattered, the wilderness we passed through denser and more vast.

The last village we passed through was called Porlock, tucked into the rows of hills along the coast between the town of Minehead — which had nothing to do with any mine, as William told me, but was a corruption of the Welsh word *mynydd,* or "mountain" — and the picturesque but rugged Valley of the Rocks. I confess that I clutched William's arm anxiously when the carriage passed through Porlock and turned onto a rough, narrow track that climbed precariously up the west side of the valley, rocking and creaking up the steep slope. When we reached the top and I beheld Porlock Common, a blessedly flat, windswept plain covered in gorse and grass, I heaved a sigh of relief so profound that William laughed and kissed my cheek.

"The worst is behind us," he assured me, taking my hand. "This marks the edge of our estate. Look there and tell me what you think."

He inclined his head to the window, and I edged closer and peered outside — and drew in a slow breath, awestruck by the stunning view of the wide Bristol Channel, the rolling, forested hills of Exmoor to the south, the green shores of Wales to the north. "This vista is worth the precipitous climb," I said, an easier assertion to make now that the steep slope was behind us.

But my apprehensions returned as the road crossed the plateau and plunged into a dense forest. After the carriage descended a gentle slope, it wound through a series of sharp, heart-stopping turns as it began a steep descent to the sea. The road followed alongside a rushing stream, which cascaded over split boulders and tumbled rocks that looked alarmingly bare of moss and soil, as if they had only recently fallen from the hillside. Just when I was tempted to tell William that I would walk the rest of the way regardless of the distance, the carriage turned onto a level, relatively smooth path and halted before a gate.

"We're almost there," William reassured me as the coachman jumped down, opened the gate, led the horses through, and closed the gate behind us before resuming his seat. We moved on through a deep, tranquil wood, the stillness broken only by the sound of the horses' hooves on the level earthen trail, the rustling of the leaves high overhead as the wind moved through the boughs, the twittering of songbirds, and the cascading rush of the stream, which I could no longer see but guessed to be not far away.

We turned a corner and came upon a clearing, and there, seemingly built upon a deep ledge cut into the hillside, was a three-story stone house, elegantly rustic, as if it had grown out of the natural rock and had been perfected by an artisan's hand. It was surrounded by stone terraces filled with lush cedar, bay, cork, and oak trees, which lightly tossed their branches in the gentle winds, benevolently shading the house from the bright sunshine.

"You said it was a cork-burner's cottage," I gasped, my eyes fixed on the enchanting residence.

William smiled. "It was, once."

"That's like calling Saint James's Palace a scullery maid's house because one happens to live there," I scolded, my smile betraying my delight. Admiring the irregular structure, so unlike the symmetrical order of Ockham Park, as well as the elaborate arches and patterned brickwork, I almost could have believed myself back on the shores of Lac Léman, or in Switzerland in the foothills of Mont Blanc.

"I'm constructing a clock tower over there," William said, waving to indicate a location on the hillside; I craned my neck but saw no sign of it. "I'm also building a water garden in a shady spot in the heights above it, which will be fed by a nearby lake. I might have to cut some irrigation channels — not quite sure yet. We'll see."

"I thought you were removing a few trees and plastering walls," I said as the carriage halted before the front door, and a man and a woman, likely a housekeeper and a footman, hurried out and stood ready to welcome us. "This is a major architectural project."

"It's a labor of love," he said, bounding down from the carriage and holding out his hand to help me descend. "Another gift for my beautiful bride."

Tears of joy sprang into my eyes. I had never felt more adored, more wanted, more loved.

After we met the few servants, William offered me his arm and led me on a tour of the residence. Inside all was spacious and airy, with the scent of new plaster and paint lingering faintly in the air, but the diamond-paned windows were open to welcome the freshening breeze and after a moment I did not notice the odor. The rooms were comfortably and handsomely furnished in dark woods, wools, and leather, with a minimum of adornment and clutter, which I thought suited the natural setting very well.

The bedchamber we would share was on the second story at the back of the house, secluded and quiet, overlooking a lush flower garden. With the windows flung open to welcome the soft, cool air, I heard a stream burbling merrily somewhere unseen but not too distant, perhaps sweeping down the hillside to join the larger stream that followed the road.

The dining room and the drawing room on the first floor were bright and sunny and boasted breathtaking views of the Bristol Channel, and down the hall in the room beneath our bedchamber, I discovered a large library that would have been a credit to any gracious home in London. Perusing the shelves, I discovered fine editions of works by the greatest writers and philosophers of England and of the world, including the *Essay Concerning Human Understanding* by William's ancestor John Locke; numerous historical novels of Sir Walter Scott; and several volumes of poetry by Samuel Taylor Coleridge, who had written his fantastical poem

Kubla Khan at Withycombe Farm near Culbone, the parish church for William's estate. Perhaps I should say only that Mr. Coleridge had *begun* the poem there, for as he had written afterward, a hapless visitor from Porlock had rapped upon his door when he was in the midst of feverish composition. When he had returned to his desk after the interruption, he had discovered that his poetical inspiration had faded, and "with the exception of some eight or ten scattered lines and images, all the rest had passed away like the image on the surface of a stream into which a stone has been cast."

"A poet ought to be able to expect uninterrupted solitude in which to write in such a remote place as this," I was musing aloud to William just as my gaze fell upon several leather-bound volumes given pride of place upon their own shelf in the center of one long wall of bookcases. I drew closer, and with a pang of something — surprise or wariness, or an unsettling mixture of both — I discovered the finest editions of my father's poetry, what surely must have been every poem he had ever written.

"I did not know you were such a devoted reader of Lord Byron," I said, keeping my voice light. "You rarely speak of his work."

He put an arm around my shoulders and gave me a rueful, sidelong smile. "You always seem reluctant to discuss it."

"Only because I've read so little of it," I admitted. "A few years ago, when I had just turned fifteen, my mother read aloud to me selections from some of his works, but she grew agitated when I asked for more, and it was always understood that I was never to read them on my own."

"You and I shall have a different understanding." William turned me so that together we took in the entire room with all of its literary treasures. "You're welcome to read any book you find here, including, and especially, your father's poetry."

I thanked him with a kiss, and I selected a beautifully bound edition of *Don Juan* to read later.

Never before had I been offered unrestricted access to my father's work, and once I began to indulge in his sublime imagery, his provocative humor, his wicked satire, my appetite for his poetry became insatiable. After *Don Juan* I turned to *The Prisoner of Chillon,* in remembrance of my sojourn at Lac Léman, and then to a volume of beautiful lyric poems.

I confess I found some of my father's verses unsettling, and not only because all of his poetry carried an air of the forbidden, as I knew my mother would disapprove of my devouring it in such great portions. A strange apprehension stirred in me as I read how the hero of *Manfred,* tormented by the memory of an unnamed "half-maddening sin," confesses to the Witch of the Alps his love for the deceased Astarte, who

> was like me in lineaments — her eyes,
> Her hair, her features, all, to the very tone
> Even of her voice, they said were like to
> mine.

This anguish of passion he wrote of, this love that burned and seethed and tormented, was nothing like what I felt for William, and it both intrigued and frightened me. I confess there were moments when I hastily closed a book upon verses that provoked dark and curious imaginings, only to return to them later, feeling somehow as if I were trespassing upon my parents' fraught and fractious history in a way I could not quite define.

Although the library offered innumerable diversions, the sublime beauty and dramatic vistas of the hillsides and forests always beckoned. Exulting in my freedom, every day I explored the natural wonders of the estate, sometimes setting off on foot along narrow, winding trails through the densest part of the wood, feeling like a woodland fairy as I made my way through dense stands of ash, birch, hazel, and oak and slipped past thickets of bramble and whortleberry. I collected samples of velvety lichen and rare, vivid yellow reindeer moss, and I delighted in glimpses of deer, fox, badger, and pheasant as well as the music of the ubiquitous songbirds.

Often I rode off alone on the back of a Forester mare, ranging over dales, valleys, moors, and downs, up into the hills or down along the shore. Sometimes William accompanied me, but often he was occupied with the business of the estate, so he would see me off with a kiss in the morning and welcome me back with another in the afternoon. On other occasions, while he and his small team of workers built stone walls or cleared underbrush for the water garden, I would spread a soft blanket beneath a nearby tree and recline in the shade, writing letters, reading poetry, or studying mathematics, glancing up from my books and papers now and then to note the men's progress and to admire my husband, who would pause to catch his breath, wipe his brow, and grin cheerfully back at me.

I confess I fell in love with Ashley Combe even more swiftly than I had with its master.

As isolated and rugged as the estate was, my rapturous letters to friends and family extolling its tranquility and sublime beauty proved too alluring, and we had been there less than a fortnight before we welcomed our first visitors. Dr. and Mrs. King stayed three days with us, which offered them ample opportunity to admire Ashley Combe and to scrutinize me — preparing a report for my mother, no doubt.

On the eve of their departure, Mrs. King took me aside and warned me that my mother was seriously ill, her tone and look reproving me for my selfish absence. A panic of guilt and worry seized me, and as soon as I could speak to William alone, I tearfully told him what Mrs. King had reported. My anxiety subsided somewhat when he reminded me that in her letters, which came nearly every day and were invariably cheerful, my mother had complained of only mild symptoms and nothing new, nothing she had not complained about for years.

"If Lady Byron's condition was as dire as Mrs. King claims," William said, "she would have told us herself, for she never shies away from such admissions, or she would have been too frail to write at all."

Somewhat reassured, I did my best not to worry, but as our honeymoon drew to a close, the joy of Ashley Combe diminished beneath the urgent pressure to return to Fordhook and see for myself that my mother was not languishing on her deathbed.

I wrote to assure her we were on our way, but on the morning of our departure, I received a letter informing us that she would not be at Fordhook to receive us and would visit us at Ockham upon our return instead. Bewildered, I decided to take that as a good sign that she was recovering, although I was beginning to suspect that Mrs. King had exaggerated, who knew why. Perhaps upon seeing me and William together, she decided that I was inordinately happy and ought to be brought down to earth. She had certainly accomplished that.

The journey back to Ockham Park was as long and rugged as our westward travels had been, but William's affectionate companionship and my anticipation for my new harp helped to keep me in good spirits despite the close quarters and the jolting of the carriage wheels. We had barely settled in when my mother arrived for her promised visit, and not only was her health quite satisfactory, but she was in astonishingly good spirits. She was obviously delighted to have acquired such a perfect son-in-law, and her approval of William somehow had raised me in her esteem as well. Whereas once she had dreaded my ruin and suspected latent madness thanks to my bad Byron blood, suddenly all her misgivings had vanished and she was as affectionate to me as if I had ever been the good, pious, dutiful, and brilliant daughter she had always wanted.

"I have discovered," she confided as we strolled arm in arm through the lovely gardens of Ockham Park, "that in consequence of your marriage, I am become amiable, affable, and all sorts of pretty epithets, in the opinion of those people who never thought me so before."

"It's wonderful to see you so happy," I ventured, not wanting to admit to being one of those people.

My mother remained with us only a few days, but from Fordhook and London and wherever else she traveled afterward, she sent us frequent letters, praising William, expressing her joy in our marriage, and addressing me with fond endearments that she had never before employed. "Dear little canary bird," she cooed in a note included with a gift of sheet music, "may your new cage be gladdened by the notes of your voice and harp."

"Which is meant to be the cage," I asked William archly, "Ockham Park or marriage itself?"

"Don't be unkind," he said, smiling to take the sting out of his rebuke. "She doesn't mean to imply that you're a prisoner, only that you're protected and cared for."

"Of course that's what she means," I said, forcing a smile, although I would have preferred to let out an exasperated sigh. William, I had learned, revered my "formidable and accomplished" mother and nearly always took her part whenever I found fault. In fact, their mutual admiration was so fervent and strong that I often felt somewhat set apart, as if William were my mother's son and I her daughter-in-law. But regardless of my own feelings about canaries and cages and the various metaphors they implied, my mother's phrasing commenced what would become our playful practice of addressing one another with ornithological nicknames — "Bird," "Thrush," or "Avis" for me; "Cock" or "Crow" for William, the latter for his piercing eyes; and "Hen" for my mother.

We had ample opportunity to apply our new fond nicknames, for having suddenly found myself the mistress of a grand estate with not the faintest idea of how to run a household, I wrote to my mother often with questions posed in every mood from contentment to curiosity and on through apprehension and frantic alarm. My mother never failed to reply with calm, deliberate authority, advising me on hiring servants, managing staff, arranging dinner parties, and hosting houseguests. Other subjects I did not ask her about, but for which she offered suggestions anyway, included when I should call on William's sisters, including Emily, the one with whom he did not get along; how I should show proper respect and deference to my mother-in-law while firmly preventing her from getting the upper hand; which books and verses to review when I studied the Scriptures; what concoctions I should drink each morning to ensure good health; and other topics, more than I would have thought there was ink enough in the world to transcribe.

I had to laugh ruefully when I remembered my bitter reflections in those last days before my marriage, that soon my mother would no longer command me. I no longer lived beneath her roof, but as I scrambled to learn how to be a wife and the mistress of a household, I found myself deferring to her experience and superior knowledge more than ever.

Then, in the third week of September, I discovered a new reason to seek my mother's counsel, one I had anticipated with great hope and joy ever since my wedding night.

I was expecting a child.

CHAPTER TWENTY-TWO:
ALL WHO JOY WOULD WIN
MUST SHARE IT

September 1835–May 1836

Although I thought I might burst with eagerness to divulge my happy secret, I waited until I was certain before I told William. "My sweet, beloved wife," he exclaimed, embracing me tenderly. "I thought you had made me the happiest of men when you agreed to marry me, but now — oh, Ada, my darling, my jubilance knows no bounds."

Next I wrote to my mother, smiling as I imagined her response when she read the joyous news. For as long as I could remember, she had impressed upon me my sacred duty to provide heirs, not only to my husband but also to her, to the Wentworth and Milbanke families. How thrilled she had been when I had taken the first essential step toward fulfilling that duty by marrying William. How elated she would surely be when she learned that I was with child!

A few days later, her reply came in the post from Southampton, where she was staying in a rented cottage by the sea with one of the Furies, Miss Montgomery. Eagerly I opened the letter, expecting to bask in her happiness and praise, and feeling a twinge of glee when I thought of how the spiteful Miss Montgomery would have been obliged to express at least grudging delight when my mother had shared my happy news.

Dearest Ada,

If what you surmise be true, you must expect to feel very uncomfortable for a few weeks — perhaps depressed, but if you remember this, the misfortune which would otherwise appear real, will seem to you the mere results of physical causes. You must take great care of that back of yours, and it will be difficult for you to do so in company without occasioning the sort of remarks that would be particularly unpleasant as people are very ready to suppose this cause.

The less known to others the better till it cannot be concealed.

I read on, disbelieving, as she turned the subject to her most recent illness, which seemed to be abating as she had been able to eat a little porridge that morning, and Miss Montgomery's current illness, which was not as serious as my mother's although she complained twice as often and thrice as loudly.

I had never been able to interest myself in their rivalry of infirmity, and on that day I found it especially irritating. Where were her congratulations and good wishes? Where was her pride in my duty fulfilled, at least imminently so? Where was her gratification in learning that in a few months' time, she would cuddle her first grandchild? Where, for that matter, were the endearing nicknames I had come to expect in her salutations, instead of the terse "Ada"? At least I was still "Dearest," but she wrote that even to people I knew she disliked, so it brought me no comfort. Nor did her chilly reluctance to accept my news as something confirmed rather than surmised, or her gloomy predictions of depression and back pain.

"I simply don't understand her," I grumbled to William as we enjoyed a late, private supper in our dining room, the windows open to the cool evening air, which carried a crisp hint of autumn. "How difficult would it have been for her to write, 'My dearest daughter, how happy you have made me with your wonderful news. I cannot wait to kiss my darling grandchild. I hope you are feeling well, and I trust that you are resting and eating as you should. Your blissfully contented and infinitely proud mother,' et cetera?"

"I'm sure that's what she meant."

"There's nothing in her letter to suggest that."

He sighed and cut his roast duck into tiny pieces. "Perhaps she's so eager for a grandchild that she would prefer not to get her hopes up until the doctor has confirmed your condition. Also, she's probably worried about you, about your health and your upcoming ordeal. I am too. Whatever you're interpreting as abrupt and cold is probably intended to be rational and calming."

Incredulous, I set down my fork and fixed him with a level gaze. "You always take her part. I think you adore my mother so much that if not for the aforementioned necessity of producing heirs, you would have preferred to marry her instead of me."

His dark, piercing eyes met mine for a moment, but he took his time chewing, swallowing, and sipping his claret. "I understand that ladies in a delicate condition are subject to curious and often exasperating moods," he said, unperturbed. "Keeping that in mind, I will forgive you that wholly inappropriate remark, which does not become you."

I gaped at him, astounded to hear him sounding like a baritone version of my mother. They were in perfect agreement on almost everything, especially when I was concerned. Little wonder they got along so well. I briefly, irritably wondered if I should have instead married someone my mother disliked, someone more inclined to take my side, but I loved William dearly and shoved those disloyal thoughts aside.

Striving for the rational calm William had displayed, I waited a day before responding to my mother's letter. Before I took pen in hand, I decided to assume that my husband was correct and that my mother's restraint resulted from disbelief that I was truly with child. Leaving unspoken my disappointment that she had not received my good news with the elation I might have expected, I informed her that I would soon be examined by the King family physician, whom I expected to confirm my diagnosis. In the meantime, the more intense symptoms I had experienced since my last letter, unrelenting nausea in particular, certainly seemed to point to one happy cause. I underlined "happy," hoping she would eventually see it as such.

A letter soon came from the cottage in Southampton, but the tone was decidedly one of resignation, not joy. "I think from what you tell me of the fastidiousness of your stomach, that your fate is decided," my mother wrote. "I have kept my mind in a state of perfect neutrality on the subject. If it is appointed for you to undertake the responsibilities of a Mother, I cannot doubt that they will conduce to your personal welfare, if rightly discharged. I fancy too that your husband will like to have a child to play with."

It was cheering to see that she had come around to the idea that some happiness might result from my condition, even if it was only that it pleased her to imagine William playing peekaboo with a smiling cherub. I was tempted to dash off a caustic note deriding her "perfect neutrality" and reminding her that producing an heir was the entire point of my marriage, or so she had always taught me, but since William and I intended to visit her in Southampton the following week, provoking her seemed unlikely to bring me any lasting satisfaction.

Instead I wrote to William's mother and his three sisters, and in the days that followed, I received three warm and happy replies. From Emily I heard nothing, but Hester's delight more than made up for her eldest sister's silence. "I shall come and care for you in your confinement," she promised, "or come afterward to help you recover from your ordeal, or both, or neither, as you prefer. I pray you are well and I hope the babe resembles you and not my ugly brother (and you may tell him I said so for he will know I am only teasing)."

I doubted very much that William had told my mother of my disappointment, for it might have sounded like a reprimand, perish the thought, but by the end of September, her letters suggested that she was gradually accepting the idea of my pregnancy. That was fortunate indeed, as her grandchild was coming in May whether she liked it or not. As for me, I was happy and excited, for the most part, although I did suffer occasional bouts of trepidation, like any other expectant mother.

The date of our visit approached, and as William and I traveled about seventy-five miles south of London to the Hampshire coast, I prepared myself to find my mother in any mood from indifference to outrage. Yet when we arrived at her cottage, she greeted us with warm embraces and solicitously asked me how I was feeling. "Come inside, Ada," she scolded as if I had been standing shoeless and hatless in a snowstorm. She guided me inside to a comfortable armchair, which I did not really want because I had been sitting for hours, but I was too surprised to refuse.

She told us that Miss Montgomery had left the previous day to visit a niece in Swindon, a development I silently cheered, for it dramatically improved the forecast for our visit. We settled in to catch up on all the family news, and when my mother's tone remained resolutely pleasant, I relaxed my vigilance and began to enjoy the views of the Channel and the sunshine spilling through the windows.

"I have canceled my plans to go to Greece,"

my mother announced at supper that evening, a simple affair with plain, wholesome food that comforted my unsettled tummy.

"Didn't you want to inspect your estates?" William asked, and I realized with a jolt that he knew much more about her plans than I did. A few months before, she had spoken vaguely about going to Europe after the wedding, but she had not decided between Malta, Euboea, or Switzerland, where she hoped to learn more about the Hofwyl method of education. That was the last I had heard on the subject, but apparently she had kept William better informed.

"My cousin Edward Noel is serving as my agent there, and he keeps everything in good order. Besides," she said, reaching for my hand, "if I went, I almost certainly could not return in time for the introduction of your young gentleman into the family circle. I would not miss that for the world."

"When the time comes," I confessed, astonished but grateful, "I'll feel better knowing you're near."

"As will I, but we'll make sure you're attended by the finest doctors." She smiled fondly at us both. "How handsome and intelligent the child of such parents shall be. He is sure to delight all who see him."

" 'He'?" William echoed, smiling. " 'Him'?"

"Yes, you see, I've determined that I shall have a grandson." Squeezing my hand, she gave me an appraising look, and my first instinct was to promise that I would certainly give it my best attempt. "Have you settled upon names?"

William and I exchanged glances, and I carefully said, "We've considered a few, but we still have several months to decide."

"Byron, perhaps," said my mother, as if it had only just occurred to her. "The name could not otherwise be preserved."

"That's the very name I would prefer if we have a boy." William and I had considered it but had regretfully abandoned it, assuming my mother would strongly object. "Anne Isabella for a girl, although we shall call her Annabella, like her namesake."

"Very fine names indeed," said my mother, glowing. To William she added, "I'm sure I have you to thank for this honor."

"On the contrary," he said, "it was Ada's idea."

My mother smiled and nodded, but she did not seem convinced.

As the days passed, I began to wonder, somewhat irritably, why my mother would not prefer to name my firstborn after William, for the mutual admiration between my mother and my husband, so evident in their letters, now swelled and spilled over like bread dough left to rise in an undersized bowl.

Recently William had decided to emulate

my mother by opening an industrial school in the town of Ockham modeled after hers in Ealing Grove. He had toured the school near Fordhook shortly after we had returned from our honeymoon, and for the next fortnight letters had flown between my husband and my mother as he queried her about educational philosophies and pedagogy. When he had announced his intentions, I had been proud of him, and pleased to know that I had married a generous man who cared about his tenants and the working poor. Before long, however, my misgivings had grown as their correspondence had consumed increasingly more of the leisure hours William had once spent with me.

In selecting an appropriate building, appointing a headmaster, hiring teachers, and establishing a curriculum, he had put himself entirely under my mother's direction. He would have been foolish not to benefit from her experience when she had so willingly offered her help; but even so, I wished he had sought my opinion now and then too, for I could have offered useful suggestions, especially about the mathematics curriculum. I felt excluded, as if I had been sent upstairs to the nursery with my governess while the adults discussed important matters in the library.

William was almost eleven years older than I, and my mother was only thirteen years older than he, so I supposed it was only natural that they would share certain opinions and interests that I did not. And yet I found it vexing when he went from consulting my mother about founding a school to soliciting her advice about managing his estates, his farms, his tenants, and many other matters. I was only nineteen, but I was Lady King, his wife, and a rather clever and well-read person besides, and I longed for him to care as much for my opinion as he did for my mother's.

After four days with us in Southampton, William returned to Ockham to practice maneuvers with the Surrey Militia, one of his favorite obligations of his role as lord, while I remained with my mother. It was the first time William and I were parted in the three months of our marriage, and I missed him terribly. I distracted myself with reading, studying mathematics, exchanging letters with Mrs. Somerville and Fanny Smith, and taking long, leisurely walks through the village and along the shore.

Despite these pleasant distractions, I was lonely without William. I wrote to him every day, but he rarely responded. My mother reminded me that he was busy with the militia and likely had few opportunities to take pen in hand, but knowing how he had written so frequently to my mother even when he had been occupied with the business of his estates, I could not help feeling abandoned. "If I could only impart to you how happy it makes the poor Bird to receive your letters, long or short, you would be quite happy," I wrote him forlornly in the second week of October. "The poor Birdie feels grateful even for a few lines from her dear Crow."

I grew restless for news, not only from home but also from London. "I wonder how Mr. Babbage is getting along with his engines," I mused one day, disconsolate, after my mother sorted the post and found nothing for me. I had not seen or heard from Mr. Babbage since before my wedding. How I missed his cheerful company and fascinating conversations. I fervently hoped I would be able to attend at least a few more of his delightful soirées before my delicate condition became noticeable and it would be unseemly for me to appear in mixed company.

One sunny morning I arranged for the use of a horse and went riding for an hour and a half, but when I returned to the cottage, happily fatigued and breathless, I found my mother pacing fretfully in the sitting room. "You must be more cautious," she scolded me as I removed my hat and gloves. "Excessive activity could cause you to lose the baby."

"Excessive inactivity could cause me to lose my mind," I retorted lightly, refusing to let her spoil my good mood. "The baby is still so tiny, Mama. There's very little that can harm it."

"That's no excuse to be reckless."

Reluctantly I agreed not to ride at any pace swifter than a walk while upon the unfamiliar horses at Southampton, but I refused to promise that I would not ride at all while I still could.

No sooner had we reached accord on that issue than my mother raised objections to my long walks. "Exercise is hazardous in your condition," she declared, and when I came down with a slight cold, she cited that as evidence that I should spend most of my day reclining with my feet up. Her constant vigilance almost made me nostalgic for her indifference.

On the last day of my visit, I was packing my bags in my bedchamber when my mother entered, carrying a pasteboard box. "I wondered if you might have room for this," she said, her expression serene and inscrutable.

"It would take up a lot of room, so it depends what it is," I teased, but when she held it out to me without a word, I set down the petticoat I had been folding, accepted the box, and lifted the lid. Inside was an inkstand of gleaming silver and ebony, about twice as long as it was wide and deep, with two inkwells and caps, a shaker for sand, and a drawer for quills and wipers. Although it had evidently been carefully cleaned and polished by a loving hand, it showed signs of frequent use, and I knew at once that it had been my father's.

When I glanced up from this treasure to turn a quizzical look upon my mother, she folded her hands at her waist and met my gaze calmly. "It was Lord Byron's," she said. "Your aunt Augusta received it shortly after his death, and earlier this year she gave it to me, as a token of her thanks for assistance I offered to her daughter Medora —" She made an impatient gesture to indicate that we would not discuss that now. "I think it would look very well in your new study at Ockham Park, if you would like to have it."

"Of course I would," I breathed, setting the box upon the bed and carefully removing the inkstand so I could examine it more closely. I possessed so few mementos of my father — the small emerald ring, the locket with his dark brown curl, and little else. To think that he had dipped his pen in this inkwell as he composed a great poem — the first cantos of *Childe Harold* perhaps, or earlier works, poems he had written before his exile to the Continent. He had surely used it to write letters too — to court my mother, to plan with his publisher, to beg for news of me.

"Take good care of it," my mother said, turning to the door.

"Of course," I said. "I shall cherish it."

Her departing nod and almost impercep-tible frown told me that she did not want me to cherish it too much. It was a relic not only of my father but also of her husband, who had hurt her deeply. All my life she had interpreted any interest in or affection for him as tacit approval of his behavior. She required me — not only me, but everyone of her acquaintance — to choose a side.

On a cool, rain-swept morning in mid-October, I departed for Ockham, and upon my arrival William welcomed me so affectionately, and with such tender concern for my health and for our child, that I entirely forgave him for not writing as often as he should have.

"Do you think we might go to London sometime soon?" I asked him later that night, after I had put him in a particularly amenable mood. "I miss Mr. Babbage and Mrs. Somerville, and I believe my brain is atrophying from the lack of intellectual stimulation. If my mother's phrenologist friends examined my head, I've no doubt they would find new bumps and dips in all the wrong places."

William laughed, for although he would never admit this to my revered mother, he shared my skepticism of phrenology. "I don't know when I could get away," he said. "I have much to do around Ockham before I return to Ashley Combe."

"You're going back?"

"Of course, darling." He kissed me. "Our

honeymoon is over but the improvements go on."

"Shall I go with you?"

"I'd love to have you with me, Birdie, but you shouldn't hazard the rough journey in your condition."

"I was in this condition when we traveled home from our honeymoon," I pointed out, concealing a sting of annoyance behind a teasing smile.

"True enough, but we didn't know about the little hatchling then." Gently William rested his hand upon my abdomen, which had scarcely begun to swell. "And considering that the alternative would have been to leave you in that remote place throughout your confinement until you and the child were strong enough to travel, we really had no choice."

I knew I would never persuade him to let me accompany him to Ashley Combe, but I still held out hope for London. "Darling, I need company and intellectual activity. You don't want me to become a dull little wife, do you?"

"You could never be dull." He kissed me again and regarded me with fond amusement. "Why don't you invite Mr. Babbage and Mrs. Somerville to visit us here?"

My spirits rose. "May I?"

"Certainly. Invite Woronzow and his sisters, too, for that matter. Have them all come at once and make a party of it, or arrange separate visits so you'll always have someone here."

Promptly after breakfast the next morning, I sent invitations and commenced anxiously awaiting their replies. Mrs. Somerville wrote back within a few days to say that she and her daughters would love to visit me as soon as they could possibly arrange it, perhaps in late October. Woronzow, too, accepted, and after a few letters back and forth we fixed a date for Saturday, 28 November. Soon after that Mr. Babbage wrote to say that he was heartily glad for the invitation, and he thought he could come out to Surrey in early December.

When it was all said and done and the dates were recorded in my diary, my happiness dimmed somewhat, for although I had pleasant visits to look forward to, the first was nearly a fortnight away, and I missed my absent friends no less than before.

I knew my mother and my husband would agree that I should fill my days with useful work and study. I had many duties as the mistress of Ockham Park, of course, and I was still learning what they were. I resumed my mathematical correspondence with Mrs. Somerville, determined to progress as much as I could before the arrival of my hatchling interrupted my studies indefinitely — but not, I prayed, forever. I read mathematics every day, focusing on trigonometry and cubic and biquadratic equations and working through Dionysius Lardner's *Analytical Treatise on Plane and Spherical Trigonometry*. I also sang with my voice master and played the harp for at least an hour each morning and afternoon, often more, finding joy and solace in the music.

As the autumn days passed, and at my mother's and husband's urging rather than from any wish of my own, I sat for my portrait with the celebrated artist Mrs. Margaret Carpenter, who had studied at the Royal Academy and had won several medals from the Society of Arts. I should say that I *stood* for my portrait, for I posed at the bottom of the staircase in our grand hall, as if I had swept down from my boudoir on my way to a ball. I wore an elegant gown of ivory silk with a claret overskirt trimmed in gold, with a wide, open neckline and full sleeves gathered at the elbow, and my hair was styled in an elegant chignon with a bandeau of silver filigree and diamonds encircling my head. I had wanted to wear it slightly longer on the sides to make my face appear more narrow, but Mrs. Carpenter insisted that I style my hair up and away from my face. I had also wanted to wear my peeress's robes, but my mother discouraged me from doing so, arguing that they would obscure my slender figure, age me by at least a decade, and look overly formal. "Furthermore, you have never appeared in them publicly," she had written. "If you were painted in them, one could accuse you of desiring too eagerly a Coronation, which smacks of disloyalty to the present King and Queen."

I certainly would not want my portrait to provoke accusations of treason, so I wore the ivory silk gown instead, which had been a particular favorite of mine ever since William had told me I looked exquisitely lovely in it. Even if he had not told me, the way his face lit up with eager desire when he beheld me in it told me all I needed to know.

When Mrs. Carpenter invited me to see her preliminary sketches, I knew that the ivory silk gown had been the right choice. She had captured the graceful draping of the fabric on my figure to perfection, and I knew she would make the colors so luminous and real that an observer would almost expect to hear the rustle of silk. My hair looked elegant, my neck long and graceful, so I admitted that I had been wise to heed Mrs. Carpenter's recommendation in that regard too. The only element I regretted — and this was the fault of Nature, not the artist — was my bold chin, but I had never been one to gaze into the looking glass mournfully and fret about my looks. I was too relieved that I had not turned out as plain as Miss Chaloner had predicted.

I did not know it then, but this was not the

only portrait, or perhaps even the most important one, that would occupy my thoughts in the last months of 1835.

In the first week of December, William left for Ashley Combe to supervise work on the clock tower and the water gardens, and rather than have me spend my birthday alone, it was decided that I should stay with my mother at Fordhook. I missed William, but it was strangely pleasant to return home as a married woman, and stranger still that I considered Fordhook another home, after stubbornly refusing to do so throughout my youth. Better still, Fordhook was close enough to London that I was able to visit Town and call on Mrs. Somerville and her daughters, and to attend one of Mr. Babbage's soirées.

"Married life agrees with you, Lady King," said Mr. Babbage when we met in his drawing room. "I've never seen you more radiant."

I smiled, for although I had not shared my news with anyone outside of the family, and my voluminous dress hid what little evidence there was, his knowing look told me that he had guessed my secret. "Thank you, Mr. Babbage. I have come to agree with married life."

"Are you still studying mathematics and science, or do your duties as mistress of Ockham Park consume all of your waking hours?"

I felt a pang of loss when I recalled how

many hours I had once been able to devote to my studies, how many delightful evenings I had spent in that very room discussing new scientific discoveries and mechanical wonders. "Matrimony has by no means lessened my taste for those pursuits," I said, "nor my determination to carry them on, although it has necessarily diminished the time I have to devote to them."

He nodded sympathetically, and I felt a wistful ache when I considered how, in a few months' time, motherhood would greedily consume even more of those hours. Then it occurred to me that Mrs. Somerville had managed to balance motherhood and mathematics, so such a thing was evidently not impossible. Mrs. Somerville was so generous that I had no doubt she would be willing to guide me through this new and uncharted landscape.

Shortly after my twentieth birthday William and I reunited at Ockham Park and merrily prepared to celebrate our first Christmas together. "Is it not strange to think that last year at this time we had not even met?" I said as we crossed paths in the foyer, where I was supervising the servants as they decorated the hall and he was bringing in evergreen boughs to adorn the mantelpieces. "Yet here we are now, with the festive season approaching, husband and wife, with a child on the way."

"It's astonishing to contemplate how much can happen in a year," he agreed, craning his neck to kiss me over an armload of fragrant greenery.

We had invited my mother to join us, as well as William's mother and siblings, but my mother was indisposed again and planned to spend Christmas in Brighton with Miss Carr. Of the Kings, only his sisters Hester and Charlotte would be joining us, so I invited Mr. Babbage and the Somerville family as well, and to my delight, they readily accepted. Soon after these invitations were confirmed, William informed me that he and my mother had also arranged for Dr. King to stay with us for a few days before Christmas, but not for the holiday itself. I found the timing curious but not objectionable, as I had always liked Dr. King. Perhaps my mother and husband simply wanted him to confirm that I was healthy and that the baby was growing well.

On the twentieth of December, Dr. King arrived, and although the air was frosty and a thin layer of icy snow covered the grounds, the paths were clear enough for us to walk and converse as we had done so often at Fordhook. He queried me about my moods, which had never been more contented, and my concerns about impending motherhood, of which I had several, certainly, but nothing that struck me as unusual or extreme. "I'm very pleased to find you so well," Dr. King said heartily as we turned back toward the house, but I thought I detected a note of wariness in his voice. It puzzled me, but I surmised that I had turned out to be a better wife than he and his wife — especially his wife — had expected, and he wondered why.

The following afternoon, a gray and blustery day, when each gust of wind carried the scent of approaching snow, I was seated by the fireplace poring over an especially complex chapter of Lardner's *Trigonometry* when William appeared in the doorway of my study. "Hello, darling," he said. "Your mother's Christmas present has just been delivered. Would you like to come down and see it?"

He smiled, but his expression was guarded. "What is it?" I asked, setting the heavy book aside and pulling myself up out of my chair.

"You'll see," he said, offering me his arm.

I took it, hiding my sudden apprehension. Dr. King's wariness, my husband's evasiveness — something was afoot, and I suspected everyone in the household but I knew what it was.

William escorted me to the drawing room, where Dr. King was supervising two footmen as they pried open a large rectangular crate. "Easy, now," William warned as they removed the lid and carefully withdrew a thin, flat object wrapped in protective muslin.

As the two footmen slowly unwound the wrappings, I released William's arm and drew closer. The dimensions of the object steadily became more apparent, and before long I was able to see that they concealed a painting. The last of the muslin was drawn away until only a draping of green velvet covered canvas and frame. Suddenly I thought I smelled faint tobacco smoke and heard the distinctive *click* of billiard balls, but it was only a memory from the distant past, beckoning me home to Kirkby Mallory.

I halted before the painting, which the two servants held waist high between them, their glances shifting from Lord King to me and back again.

"Shall I see what my mother has sent me?" I asked the room, and when no one replied, I glanced over my shoulder to William and raised my eyebrows in inquiry. He nodded.

Rising on tiptoe, I removed the green velvet curtain and stepped back. Before me was a portrait of a man, a strikingly handsome man with a strong jaw and a cleft chin and a full, sensuous mouth. He had a thin, neat, tapered mustache and dark hair, most of which was concealed beneath a turban with a braided silk tassel that fell to his shoulders, the native headdress of some foreign land. He held a ceremonial sword, and his eyes were dark and expressive, his face in partial profile as he looked off to his right — and suddenly I imagined this portrait hanging above the mantelpiece next to the sketch Mrs. Anderson had made of me, and the two faces, so similar in the eyes and the hair and the chin and the jaw, the two faces gazing at each other —

"Ada?"

I tore my gaze away from my father's portrait and found William at my side, his brow furrowed, his hand outstretched, his expression apprehensive. My gaze traveled from him to Dr. King, and I suddenly understood why he had been summoned to Ockham Park: They all feared how I would react when I beheld my father's visage for the first time. My mother and Dr. King must have told William what an excitable child I had been, prone to manias and hysterical illnesses. One could only imagine what I would do when the portrait was so dramatically unveiled — I might swoon, or burst into frantic sobs, or suffer an onset of my former paralytic illness.

This was a test, and only by appearing perfectly calm and rational would I pass it.

Even as my mind raced to determine the appropriate response, I realized that Dr. King would report every detail of my reaction to my mother, whose conflicted, contradictory feelings about her husband I must consider. I must show enough feeling and gratitude to prove that I respected and appreciated the significance of the gift, and yet not too much emotion, which would indicate that my father's romantic image had made me forget his crimes against my mother. I must honor his genius while condemning his wickedness. It was a fine line to tread, but with my mother, it always had been.

"What a remarkable portrait," I said, when I could speak. Turning to Dr. King, I inquired, "Is it a good likeness?"

"Very much so," he replied, drawing nearer.

"And his costume?"

"Albanian." Dr. King indicated the turban and the sword. "Lord Byron acquired it while on his Grand Tour of the Mediterranean in 1809. The artist is Thomas Phillips, and it has been said that this is one of the very few portraits of himself that Lord Byron approved."

"It's excellent work." It seemed safe to praise the artistry without reflecting upon the character of the subject. "The rich texture of the fabrics, the play of light and shadow, Lord Byron's expression — it's masterfully accomplished. If I'm not mistaken, my grandparents displayed this portrait in Kirkby Mallory years ago."

"Indeed," said Dr. King. "Your grandmother bequeathed it to you, with the stipulation that you should not receive it until your twenty-first birthday. However, since you are now married, your mother decided that you should have it."

"How generous of her, how very kind." To William I added, "Where do you think we should display it, darling? We must hang it before my mother's next visit so that she will know how much we appreciate her gift."

As William proposed a few suitable locations, I watched from the corner of my eye as Dr. King looked on approvingly, smiling slightly with satisfaction and nodding. Apparently my well-chosen words had hit the mark. I had passed the test so well that they did not realize that I knew I had been tested, or that it vexed me to have been tested. They saw only a sensible amount of appreciation and interest. They had no idea the profound, powerful emotions the portrait evoked in me, the strange sense of kinship and recognition, the wistful longing and deep ache of loss, the inexplicable love, the barely perceptible stirring of anger — directed toward whom or what, I could not say.

His mission fulfilled, Dr. King departed the following day, but soon thereafter, the Somervilles, Mr. Babbage, and Hester, Charlotte, and their mother arrived to celebrate the holidays with us. We enjoyed a joyful, festive Christmas and rang in the New Year merrily, with songs and games, delicious food and drink, fond reminiscences of holidays past, and grand hopes and expectations for the year to come. It was the merriest festive season I could remember.

I was sorry to bid our guests farewell in January, but I kept myself busy throughout the winter studying mathematics, corresponding with friends, and preparing my little one's nursery and layette. At the end of April, William and I moved to our home at Saint James's Square for my confinement, and remembering how my mother had canceled her trip abroad rather than miss her grandchild's arrival, William wrote to invite her to join us at home to await the imminent event. If she preferred to remain at Fordhook, he offered to send a messenger racing with the news as soon as my trials began.

"I was very glad to hear from King," my mother wrote to me in reply, "and both his invitation and his offer were kindly received, but pray tell him that I do not wish to have a nocturnal announcement of the *first act* of your performance. I would much rather be notified during the coda than the prelude."

"I would not have asked, but she said she would not miss it for the world," said William, bewildered, when I read her letter aloud.

I smiled to hide my disappointment. "Perhaps, like so many other things, attending the birth of a grandchild is an experience better enjoyed in theory than in practice."

"I'll send word to her early anyway," William resolved. "Regardless of what she says now, when the moment comes, she may wish to be at your side."

I raised my eyebrows at him, astonished that he would do otherwise than obey her explicit command. I was curious to see what would come of it.

When the moment came at last, I was too engrossed in my travail to know or to care when William notified my mother, but it was my dear sister-in-law Hester who held my hand and wiped my brow when my child entered the world on 12 May 1836, his arrival coinciding with an eclipse of the sun. Afterward, as I held my precious babe in my arms, with William kneeling at my bedside, kissing me and beaming with pride upon his son and heir, we agreed that this celestial event was a portent of the glorious, happy future awaiting him, awaiting us all.

CHAPTER TWENTY-THREE: DAYS STEAL ON US AND STEAL FROM US

May 1836–August 1839

William and I christened our son Byron King, and we were as besotted with him as any two parents ever were of their firstborn. Though my mother had been ambivalent about my pregnancy and disinterested in the birth, when she met her grandchild three days after he entered the world, she was immediately smitten. His dark eyes, plump cheeks, and tiny cries so enchanted her that she wrote an amusing character about him to share with her friends, predicting that he would be in youth an athletic prodigy, as a man indifferent to the opinion of Society, and in maturity a respected professor of philosophy. As for me, I so passionately adored the perfect little creature he already was that I gave no thought to who and what he might be five, ten, or twenty years in the future. All I wanted was to hold my beautiful child and love him better than I had been loved.

In early spring, my mother had volunteered

to find a suitable nurse for her grandchild, one who would be firm yet kind, devoted yet not indulgent, energetic but calm, and intelligent enough to keep one step ahead of a boy who was surely predestined to be very clever. "Do you require a wet nurse?" my mother had asked me by letter in March.

I was planning to nurse the child myself, as my mother and other ladies had told me that this would help me regain my figure more quickly. "Any qualified baby nurse would do," I wrote to my mother.

"Would an older woman be objectionable?" she had asked next. I had replied that on the contrary, someone more experienced would be most welcome, as long as she was spry.

"I have found the perfect nurse," my mother told me as she held her grandson for the first time. "She can start tomorrow, if that is satisfactory."

"Should I not meet her first?" I asked. "I don't mean to question your judgment, but —"

"You have met her, although you might not remember her." My mother's voice was light and high, the tone one instinctively adopts when one holds a newborn, even when one is speaking to someone else. "Her name is Mrs. Grimes, and she was your own nurse. Do you remember? It was so many years ago. She left our service to care for a sister, I believe."

My heart cinched. Of course I remembered

Mrs. Grimes, though I had not seen her in more than fifteen years. I studied my mother, waiting for more, but she was entirely absorbed in cuddling Byron, and she did not notice my penetrating looks. I could never forget Mrs. Grimes, the devoted nurse who had cared for me so tenderly and tirelessly when I was afflicted with chicken pox.

"I do remember Mrs. Grimes," I said evenly. "I can think of no one I would trust more to care for my son. How did you convince her to accept the post?"

I meant to convey my astonishment that Mrs. Grimes would hazard employment with our family a second time after my mother had peremptorily discharged her in the middle of a promised two-year engagement, but when my mother glanced up from sweet Byron, she regarded me with what seemed to be genuine puzzlement. "I told her you needed her, and she immediately accepted," she said. "I remember her as a kindly, good woman, and very competent as a nurse, except for her tendency to spoil you."

"I don't remember any spoiling."

She laughed lightly. "Well, of course you wouldn't, would you?"

I held back a rebuke, reluctant to give her any reason to second-guess her decision, so urgent was my longing to see my beloved nurse again. Nor did I wish to give my mother any reason to leave in a huff, not when she was so unabashedly eager to pour out upon my son the unconditional love and affection she had always denied me.

The next morning when Mrs. Grimes arrived, I nearly threw myself into her arms, and we clung to each other, laughing and crying as if we had both gone quite mad. Her hair had become entirely gray, and her once reassuringly sturdy frame had been whittled down to a more slender and stooped figure, but her kind, wise eyes were the same, as were her voice and her smile. "You've grown into the strong, lovely young woman I always knew you would be, darling Ada," she murmured in my ear, and I basked in her praise, fresh tears springing into my eyes. When I introduced her to my son, she picked him up with such strong, assured grace that I knew he would be well loved and protected in her care.

With Mrs. Grimes's help, I steadily became accustomed to the duties of motherhood, but I often gratefully acquiesced when she urged me to rest while she minded the baby. I had come through my travail fairly well as these things go, but I remained exhausted and sore for more than a fortnight after Byron's birth, and the leechings and cuppings my mother ordered my doctor to administer did nothing to restore my vitality. By the end of June, however, I was ready to receive visitors, and one of the first was Mr. Babbage.

He had brought a gift for my son, a soft toy horse he enjoyed gnawing on — Byron, not Mr. Babbage — and a set of building blocks for when he was a little older, finely sanded and stained until the wood shone like satin. Mr. Babbage unwittingly brought me a gift too, and not only the news from London's intellectual circles, which I had craved. "I've improved the design of my Analytical Engine significantly since last we spoke," he said. "I've concluded that using a revolving cylinder to communicate instructions will be too limiting, so I've decided to employ punched cards instead."

I was so delighted that I laughed aloud. "I had hoped you would come around eventually. Is this decision in honor of my handsome young heir?"

"Not at all," he said, smiling. "It's in recognition of the superior wisdom of his mother."

Soon after Mr. Babbage's visit, my mother left for Brighton to pursue a cure for her ongoing infirmity, whose vague and ever-changing symptoms had stymied Dr. King. My mother had become quite frustrated with his inability to diagnose her, and even more so with his tentative suggestions that perhaps her illness was all in her head, so unbeknownst to him, she had begun consulting other physicians. In my worry for her I had quite forgotten my own weakened condition, and up until the day my mother departed for Brighton, I overexerted myself tending her and fussing over the baby until Hester and Mrs. Grimes joined forces to compel me to rest.

Rest came more easily when we withdrew to Ockham Park in the middle of July. Hester amused me with cheerful conversation as she pushed me in a bath chair around the gardens, and when I wasn't nursing Byron or smiling upon him and William as they played together, he was in Mrs. Grimes's watchful care, so I could always rest comfortably knowing he was well looked after. As exhausted as I was, I was also completely happy. I had honored my duty to give my mother and husband an heir. My childhood longing for a sister and a happy home had at last been fulfilled. For the first time in my life, I felt as if I had satisfied everyone's expectations for me, and I intended to enjoy it as long as it lasted.

By the end of July I was walking quite well on my own, steady and strong, and I felt more vigorous every day. By mid-August, Hester and I were exploring the estate on horseback, and by the end of the month, I had progressed to jumping.

"I feel entirely recovered," I told William happily one afternoon when he came upon Hester and me in the stables brushing our horses.

"You look glorious," he said, seizing me around the waist and kissing me full on the mouth. I kissed him back, my blood racing from the exhilarating ride.

"Honestly, you two," protested Hester, laughing. "Can you not at least wait until you're alone?"

With one last, quick kiss, we broke off our embrace, but William's hand lingered on my shoulder and I anticipated joyful abandon in his arms later that night. I had told him that I would prefer not to have another child until Byron was two years old, so we chose our times carefully, although it was not easy to resist our mutual ardor. I was still nursing, which I had heard would offer some measure of protection. I fervently hoped such feminine wisdom was not a myth.

By late August, Byron had become quite a little darling, bright and strong, and at just shy of four months of age, he had developed an experimental disposition. He was attracted to motion more than color, and to discordant noises more than pleasant sounds. One day, while Hester held him on her lap in the drawing room, he made a great study of her necklace, moving the chain into one position and then another, observing the patterns with serious attention, especially when the necklace shifted after he lifted his chubby little hands away.

"Little Byron is going to grow up to be a

scientist or a mathematician like his mother," Hester declared. I smiled, but my heart sank to hear myself referred to as either, since domestic cares had made it nearly impossible for me to delve into my intellectual pursuits. Every month I vowed to resume my studies as soon as Byron was a little older, but one by one the days came and went, every hour filled with more immediate distractions, while my books and papers remained untouched.

By late autumn I realized that my studies would be deferred even longer, for despite my intentions to delay enlarging the family, I discovered that I was again with child. William was thrilled, and I, too, was happy, but I will not pretend that I felt no misgivings. I wanted more children, certainly, but not quite so soon.

With new resolve I set aside all frivolous distractions and resumed my studies, determined to progress as far as I could before my thoughts and arms were again occupied by a precious infant. Geometry and trigonometry appealed to me most at that time, and thinking that I could better comprehend certain complex topics if I had physical models to examine, I asked Mrs. Somerville to order some for me anonymously. I was still Lord Byron's daughter, still an unwilling object of fascination before the public, and I did not care to have my purchases trumpeted in the press. My kind mentor readily agreed to make the arrangements, and in December, shortly after my twenty-first birthday, she also presented me with a wonderful gift of a telescope so that I might study the heavens from the towers of Ockham Park on clear, cold winter nights.

All that winter and through the spring I divided my attention between raising Byron, preparing for the arrival of his younger sibling, attending to my duties as Lady King, and studying mathematics and astronomy. One might wonder where my duties to Lord King appeared on this list, and if I were not neglecting him by including those among my obligations as mistress of Ockham. In truth, William was preoccupied with concerns of his own at that time, the usual duties of his lordship as well as the newer responsibilities of establishing his industrial school. What little time he had left over he devoted to young Byron and to the never-ending improvements of his estates, building towers, adding gardens, digging tunnels to the back doors of the residence so that the arrival of delivery carts did not spoil the views. William and I loved each other no less than before, but we could not reside within the private, romantic seclusion we had enjoyed at Ashley Combe indefinitely, not with the responsibilities of family and the cares of the world ever encroaching. To me it felt as if William and I still stood side by side, hands clasped and fingers intertwined, but with a slightly greater distance between us. As long as we did not let go, and still faced the same direction, I would not worry.

Byron celebrated his first birthday in May of 1837. As my mother had predicted soon after his birth, he had become a happy, vigorous, active little boy, crawling everywhere with remarkable speed and such confidence and daring that we were constantly on alert lest he cheerfully scramble into danger. He could stand if he clung to an outstretched hand or supported himself on furniture, and one of his favorite pastimes was to open and shut cupboards, studying the workings of the hinge and latch, much to the amusement of his observers. He loved to roll a ball on the floor away from himself, then crawl swiftly in pursuit, laughing and crowing like a hound after a fox. My only concern, and it troubled me only now and then because he was clearly a bright and attentive child, was that he had not yet spoken a word. Mrs. Grimes assured me that he understood nearly everything that was said to him, and that he would find his voice in time. "One day you will be unable to keep him from chattering about anything and everything," she predicted, smiling, "and you will look back on these days fondly and wish they would return."

I cannot imagine how I would have managed without Mrs. Grimes, her assured presence in the nursery, her wisdom borne of experience. Never could I forget how my mother had wronged her, and I could only hope that my gratitude and Byron's adoration would remedy the injuries of the past.

Our little family withdrew to the enchanting solitude of Ashley Combe in June, and it was there that we received the news that King William IV had died after a lengthy illness. Although he had sired ten illegitimate children with his longtime mistress before he married, Queen Adelaide had borne him only two daughters, who had died very young, and so he had no direct heirs. The heir presumptive was his favorite niece, Princess Alexandrina Victoria, the daughter of his younger brother, Edward Augustus, and his brother's German-born wife, the Duchess of Kent.

It was well-known that King William had disliked his scheming sister-in-law, and rumor had it that he had worried that he might die before Princess Victoria came of age, leaving the kingdom in the Duchess of Kent's control as regent. Through either divine grace or sheer strength of his own will, he survived almost a month past Princess Victoria's eighteenth birthday. The nation seemed to breathe a collective sigh of relief that there would be no regency, and my mother told me that Lord Melbourne and his political friends were greatly satisfied when the young queen cast off her strong-willed mother's control. "Lord Melbourne remains Queen Victoria's closest advisor," my mother wrote to me from Fordhook, a simple phrase that implied so much more than it stated. My mother had long deferred seeking her cousin's patronage, but I knew then that she would not abstain forever.

Political intrigue compelled only mild interest from me then, for the time of my confinement was swiftly approaching. We returned to London in the first week of September, and it was there in our home in Saint James's Square that I gave birth to a daughter on 22 September. William and I both had expected a second son, and I am ashamed now to admit that we were both somewhat disappointed even though our little girl was healthy, beautiful, sweet-tempered, and otherwise perfect in every way.

I had scarcely begun to recover from my ordeal when I was struck down by a dreadful illness. I did not have a name for it then, but I have since learned that it must have been cholera. The devastating illness was well-known and feared in India, and epidemics had swept close to Europe before, but always they had retreated before laying waste to England. A few years before, however, the disease had finally breached our country's defenses, and I was caught up in the final throes of an epidemic that had peaked in London earlier in the decade. I shudder from horror when I remember my suffering in the months I lay in my sickbed — the persistent, debilitating dizziness, the violent vomiting and unrelenting diarrhea, the terrifying fevers and raging thirst. I nearly died — I was expected to die — and if not for the care of my mother's physician, Dr. Herbert Mayo, I very likely would have. I honestly have no idea how I survived. At the time, it did not seem possible.

It was not until late winter of 1838 that I emerged from danger, but the disease had wrecked and wasted my body, leaving me emaciated and feeble even when it seemed likely that I would live. By springtime I had steadily gained both weight and strength, but I remained quite ill.

I observed then with sad resignation two unhappily enduring consequences of my illness.

The first — it shames me to admit this — was that I did not feel as close to Annabella as I did to Byron. Within a week of her birth she had been taken from my arms for her own safety when my symptoms first came upon me, and the risk remained for months afterward. When the danger of contagion passed, I was simply too weak to care for her. She wanted for nothing, as Mrs. Grimes, Hester, and William looked after her with a greater measure of love and attentiveness to make up for what I was powerless to offer, but we lost those precious early days when I should have been easing her passage into the world, bathing her in the warm light of maternal love and affection, weaving unbreakable ties between our two hearts. In the years since, I have tried to compensate for all I could not do in her first months, but I know I often failed her, and even today I feel a lingering estrangement.

The second unhappy consequence may have come about another way, at another time, even if I had not fallen ill.

I have said that I was expected to die. William had no reason to doubt this, for by every sign and every measure, my sufferings appeared fatal. Devastated, William began to mourn me before I died, and to steel himself for life without me as the grieving father of two motherless children. I believe he began to detach his heart from mine in late December, when my death seemed imminent, so that he was not pulled into the grave after me. I do not blame him for this; he had to protect himself so that he could remain strong for our children's sake. But I lived, and the heartstrings he had severed to save himself from fatal grief were never mended. He loved me still, but dared not risk loving me too deeply. After that I felt as if we still stood side by side, facing the same direction, but instead of clasping hands, we stood with only our fingertips touching.

By March I was feeling much improved, but William was often away from Ockham on business in London or off supervising construction at Ashley Combe, so he was not there to see flesh returning to my frame and color to my cheeks. I wrote to him almost every day, cheerful accounts of playtime with Annabella and Byron, leaving unwritten the pang of grief I felt when, at seemingly arbitrary moments, our daughter shied away from me and reached for Mrs. Grimes. "Byron is exceedingly mischievous, & more independent than ever," I told William instead. "The baby grows more beautiful than ever. I wonder how she will strike you after this absence."

I also wondered how I would strike him, but I left that unwritten too.

Visits from friends were rare, because everyone worried about exhausting me, but amusing, interesting letters came in droves, and I was grateful for every page. Mr. Dickens visited several times and kindly sat at my bedside and read aloud to me the latter chapters of his delightful *Pickwick Papers,* as I had read the first few before my illness and had thoroughly enjoyed them. My convalescence persisted so long that he was able to read me the entirety of his next major work, *Oliver Twist,* as well.

Mr. Babbage, too, offered me a welcome diversion by sending me a copy of his most recent book, the second edition of *The Ninth Bridgewater Treatise,* an intriguing work of natural theology in which he discussed ostensible contradictions between science and religion. I found it fascinating and quite illuminating, but I had no doubt that he would stir up outrage among the clergy and the masses for his assertion that the book of Genesis was not meant to be interpreted literally as a geologic history of the Earth. I thanked him kindly for his gift and sent him one in turn, a folding umbrella to shield himself from the inundation of pious outrage sure to come.

In April I departed Ockham with the children and Mrs. Grimes, and William left Ashley Combe with his plans and drawings, and we reunited in London at 12 Saint James's Square. I was very glad to see William, for I had missed him, and his embraces, terribly. We had been reunited less than two months when, in late June, we received astonishing, wonderful news. In the Coronation Honors in the celebration of the accession of Victoria to the throne, William, the eighth Lord King, was elevated to the rank of earl, for a peerage had been created for him.

There was no question but that Lord Melbourne had brought about this honor in acknowledgment of our kinship. In gratitude, William searched my mother's family tree for an appropriate title and soon chose the earldom of Lovelace. At first my mother had suggested that he select Byron, but that would have created untold confusion for our son when he inherited the title, and a seventh Lord Byron already existed. Then William discovered among my mother's ancestors a Lord Lovelace of Hurley, whose line had become extinct, and he thought it would be right and proper to revive the name. Thus he became William King, first Earl of Lovelace. I would thenceforth be known as Ada Byron King, Countess of Lovelace. Our son became Byron King, Viscount Ockham, and our daughter Lady Annabella.

As a countess, I now outranked my mother and would take precedence over her in all formal and semiformal occasions. It was an astonishing notion, but if she had in any way objected, I doubt very much that William's peerage would have been created. Although my mother never declared herself the agent of our good fortune, I did not doubt that she had finally made use of the familial connection she had patiently refrained from exploiting for so many years. At last I understood why she had refused to appeal to her cousin on Mr. Babbage's behalf. She had nurtured much greater ambitions all along.

But as Lord Melbourne giveth, Lord Melbourne taketh away. I did not learn this until several years later, but as one branch of my family prospered, another had been reduced to poverty. A few months before my mother's cousin arranged for William to become the Earl of Lovelace, he had eliminated the three hundred pounds my aunt Augusta received per annum in recognition for her past service as a lady-in-waiting to Queen Caroline, and he also abolished the pension she and her husband, Colonel Leigh, had been awarded many years before. These emoluments were their only source of income not mortgaged to the extreme, and thus with a few strokes of the pen, they had become paupers.

I was aware that Colonel Leigh had wronged the prince regent in the past, and I hoped that Lord Melbourne had leveled this devastating blow for just cause rather than personal enmity. I prayed that my mother had nothing to do with it. But again, I was not in touch with my aunt Augusta anymore, for my mother had forbade her to contact me. Thus I did not learn of the Leigh family's pecuniary sufferings until years afterward, or I could not have enjoyed William's preferment without some remorse.

Soon after Queen Victoria's coronation, William and I attended a ball at Buckingham Palace. I wore a gown of emerald silk brocade, which suited my fair skin and dark hair and evoked satisfactory compliments from my husband. Lady Byron had assured me that we would not be presented to the queen but would only pass by to make our bow and curtsey. This we did, in a lengthy procession of others who had been raised in the Coronation Honors, but when William and I took our turn, the queen made a little gesture implying that she wished me to go up to her. I thought that I must have misunderstood her, for there was no reason why I should have been distinguished out of that illustrious company.

"Go up to the queen," William urged through clenched teeth, barely moving his lips. "Why would you keep her waiting?"

Startled, I promptly obeyed, ignoring the sudden tremulous fluttering in my chest. The queen looked serene, regal, and very pretty, with glossy dark hair and alabaster skin, but also very young. As I drew near she graciously held out her hand to me, which fortunately I had enough presence of mind to take. She spoke only very briefly, but it was very kind of her to take any notice of me at all, and soon I curtseyed again and backed away to resume my place at William's side.

There were other balls that summer, and dances, parties, and evenings at the opera, but I preferred Mr. Babbage's soirées and small dinner parties at Mrs. Somerville's. My intellectual friends kept me apprised of all the most fascinating exhibits and demonstrations in London, such as the model of the new electrical telegraph at Exeter Hall, experiments in mesmerism at University College Hospital, and displays of exotic animals at the Surrey Zoological Gardens. I reveled in the certainty that every day I could go out to observe a new scientific marvel and never exhaust the possibilities.

In August, as the Season drew to a close, we escaped the suffocating heat of the city by withdrawing to Ashley Combe. My expectation of enjoying the tranquility of nature was shattered, however, by our young viscount and lady, who had entered a period of naughtiness unprecedented in our family. Even now my head aches remembering the impudent retorts, the raucous antics, the bickering and whining, and the perpetual disobedience. Mrs. Grimes simply could not manage them on her own, and I cannot fault her for that, as the children were simply impossible.

"If I had behaved so badly, my governess would have tied bags around my hands and locked me in the closet," I muttered through clenched teeth as we tried to wrestle the hooligans through their baths. "And my mother would have fled to a spa and I would not have seen her for months."

"Why, Lady Lovelace, I never did such a dreadful thing," exclaimed Mrs. Grimes, forgetting to hold tight to Annabella in her shock. The young miss squirmed away and darted out of reach, jeering.

"Not you," I said, scrubbing behind Byron's ears as he howled that I was murdering him.

"One of those who came after you."

She sank back onto her heels, stricken. "You were locked in a closet?"

"Yes, many times," I said shortly. "I survived."

But there were many days I did not think I would survive motherhood. It can well be imagined, then, how I felt back at Ockham Park on the eve of my twenty-third birthday when I realized that I was again expecting a child.

William was thrilled. "A boy this time," he declared, kissing me. "I'm certain of it."

"I'll do my very best," I said wearily, but I had to smile at his happiness and at the warm enthusiasm of his kisses.

William was happier yet on the second day of July 1839 when I gave birth to a robust baby boy with a strong voice and a thick shock of dark hair that bore a startling resemblance to my father's. "You have given me another fine son," he declared at my bedside, smiling tenderly upon our boy as he slept peacefully in my arms. "I trust you will soon give me back the graceful, slender girl I married."

Though I sat up in bed supported by soft pillows and covered in quilts, I stiffened from a sudden chill. Suddenly, inexplicably, my thoughts flew to Wills, who had loved me and desired me when I was a plump, clumsy girl of sixteen, still recovering from illness and certain that I would never be pretty. I felt a crushing weight of disappointment so sharp that tears sprang into my eyes, but I blinked them away, unwilling to spoil my son's first day with recriminations for his father.

We christened him Ralph Gordon, and from the first he was a darling, content to snuggle up to me and nurse blissfully while his elder brother and sister shrieked and snatched away each other's toys. At two weeks, I swear he smiled at me as I sang him a lullaby, and when he was able to sit up on his own, he would clutch a toy, wave it in the air, and crow for joy as if he thought life could never be more perfect. Or he would sit on my lap while his brother and sister tore a path of destruction through the nursery, regarding them with calm bewilderment as if he could not fathom why they did not find a better way to occupy themselves.

If Ralph had not been such a sweet angel of a boy, I think I would have gone quite mad.

My feelings shamed me. I had fulfilled my life's most important duty by marrying and giving my family not one but three healthy heirs. Should I not have been happier than ever before in my life? Should I not have been so besotted with my darling children that I needed nothing else? But I had learned so little of mothering from my own mother. I wanted so badly to love and care for my children as I had always wished I had been, but I felt uncertain and inadequate.

My sinking certainty that I was not up to the task seemed confirmed one summer afternoon when Annabella was confined to her bed, afflicted with some simple childhood ailment. To ease her symptoms, I gave her some calomel, a mercury purgative prescribed by the doctor. She swallowed it down like a good girl, but almost immediately she began vomiting so violently that I thought she would turn herself inside out.

"Mrs. Grimes," I shouted, alarmed. "Come at once!"

Within moments she hurried into the nursery, and quickly assessing the scene, she promptly took over, easing Annabella into a more comfortable position, holding her hair back, positioning the basin in her lap where she could better retch into it. "What happened to bring this on?" Mrs. Grimes asked, breathless and bewildered.

"Nothing," I said, tears in my eyes. "I simply gave her the medicine as the doctor ordered —"

"How much did you give her?"

I told her, and her eyes widened in horror. "Send for the doctor at once," she exclaimed.

I obeyed, and the doctor came within the hour, and soon thereafter he informed me that I had given my helpless daughter more than twice the proper dose. As he swiftly administered an antidote, I sank into a chair, faint from shock. I had poisoned my daughter. How could I have made such a stupid mistake?

Later, when the danger had passed and the doctor was packing his satchel, he scolded me and ordered me to follow his instructions more carefully next time. William was adamant that there would not be a next time. "Perhaps administering medicines is a task better entrusted to Mrs. Grimes," he said, but although his phrasing was mild enough, his expression made it clear that this was no mere suggestion.

In the days that followed, I overheard the servants murmuring about how Lady King had almost done in Miss Annabella, and thank goodness Mrs. Grimes had prevented a murder. My incompetence as a mother confirmed, I became hesitant even to cross the threshold of the nursery, and I deferred more often to Mrs. Grimes's superior wisdom and skill. Thus, instead of acquiring greater confidence and proficiency as I grew into the role, I stepped away from it, plagued by uncertainty, terrified that I might unwittingly do my children some injury for which there was no remedy.

As the children grew, time seemed to distort, for although the days stretched endlessly from the moment I dragged myself wearily from bed until I dropped exhausted into it at night, the months seemed to pass with astonishing swiftness, accumulating relentlessly, leaving me wondering where the time had gone and why I had so little to show for its passage.

I loved my children dearly, I loved my husband, I was grateful for our wealth and position — and yet I felt as constrained and restricted and subjected to the dictatorial whims of others as I ever had.

Once upon a time, a little girl named Ada had dreamed of flight. She had called the new science she invented Flyology, she had designed wings to carry her through the skies, and she had believed that through the power of mathematics and science and imagination, she would one day fly above the patchwork countryside of England delivering packages for her absent mother, or soar to the top of Mont Blanc to observe the Alps as no one had ever done before.

I wondered what had become of that audacious girl, and if I could find her again.

CHAPTER TWENTY-FOUR: RUMOURS STRANGE, AND OF UNHOLY NATURE, ARE ABROAD

September 1839–February 1841

By the autumn of 1839, I had resolved to resume my mathematical studies in earnest. At first I toiled on my own as I had done intermittently for the past few years, but by November I realized that in order to make steady progress, I required a tutor, a distinguished mathematician and scientist to guide me.

I realized, too, that unless I had sufficient time to study, the best tutor in the world would avail me nothing. I needed to be relieved of some of my maternal duties, even if this meant hiring another governess to assist Mrs. Grimes.

I had come to this conclusion after dining with Mrs. Somerville one evening, and in a private moment when she asked me why I seemed so harried and tense, I poured out my heart to her. "Annabella is an intolerable torment," I lamented. "I cannot endure her constant noise! The chatter, chatter, chatter to herself is incessant and prevents me from thinking, much less carrying on any occupation."

Mrs. Somerville smiled sympathetically. "Some little girls do enjoy conversation more than others."

"If it were conversation, I would not mind it so much, but she just talks and talks without waiting for a reply. I don't think she even cares if anyone hears her, as long as she can hear herself. She is constantly plaguing and interrupting me." Close to tears, I reached out to touch Mrs. Somerville's arm imploringly. "You have accomplished so much. How did you manage it when your children were young? How were you able to be both a mathematician and a mother?"

"You forget that for many years, I couldn't," she said, regarding me with frank sympathy. "My first husband discouraged me, and I rarely read anything mathematical except in stolen moments. It was not until after I returned to Edinburgh as a widow that I found a circle of like-minded friends to encourage me."

"I have the friends," I said, patting her arm to indicate that she was foremost among them. "What I lack is time."

"It seems to me that Lord Lovelace is very like Dr. Somerville in his support for women's education. Perhaps if you explain to him how the current arrangement is untenable, he'll offer to help."

I had to laugh at the idea of William changing nappies and wiping dirty faces so that I would be free to study, but he could certainly afford to hire someone who would. Thus I concluded that I needed a governess for the children as well as a tutor for myself. The only other alternative was to wait until the children were much older before I resumed my studies, but I truly feared I might go mad in the meantime.

Although I was a countess, I could never afford these expenses on the pittance of pin money I was granted each year, so I was obliged to swallow my pride and petition William to pay the costs. At first he was reluctant, but I persisted, noting that he could have paid for an entire year's wages for a tutor and a governess for a fraction of the cost of one of the tunnels he had recently completed at Ashley Combe — and I circumspectly reminded him that the money for those improvements had come from my mother, who had always wished me to continue my studies. Eventually he agreed.

Next I turned to the task of finding a tutor. While my mother inquired among various intellectual acquaintances she had met through her work in education, I consulted Mr. Babbage. "I have quite made up my mind to have some instruction next year in Town," I explained in my letter, "but the difficulty is to find the tutor. I have a peculiar way of learning, and I think it must be a peculiar person to teach me successfully. I believe I have the power of going just as far as I like in such pursuits, where there is so very decided a taste, I should almost say a passion, as I have for mathematics."

I heard nothing for so long that I suspected my letter had gone astray, but before I could send another, Mr. Babbage replied with apologies for the delay, explaining that he had been traveling and upon his return had become preoccupied with the Analytical Engine. "I have just arrived at an improvement which will throw back my drawings a full six months unless I succeed in carrying out some new views which may shorten my labor," he wrote. "I think your taste for Mathematics is so decided that it ought not to be checked. I have been making inquiries but cannot find at present anyone at all to recommend to assist you. I will however not forget the search."

My mother had no better luck, so I resigned myself to a long wait, and in the meantime, I hired a second governess to assist Mrs. Grimes and continued to study on my own.

Occasionally I encountered a particular concept in trigonometry or calculus that drew my thoughts back to Mr. Babbage's Difference Engine, as well as his Analytical Engine, which as far as I knew still existed only on paper and in its inventor's remarkable mind. Some deep instinct told me that both machines were capable of far more complex calculations than Mr. Babbage had mentioned yet.

"Have you ever seen a game, or rather puzzle, called Solitaire?" I wrote to him on a frigid afternoon in mid-February 1840. "There is an octagonal board, like the enclosed drawing, with thirty-seven holes in the positions I have marked. Thirty-six small pegs are inserted, filling in all the holes but one, and the remaining pegs must hop over, capture, and remove one another as in Draughts. The object is to leave only one peg on the board, but people may try thousands of times and not succeed. I have mastered the puzzle by trial and observation, but I want to know if the problem admits of being put into a mathematical Formula. There must be a definite principle, a compound of numerical and geometrical properties, on which the solution depends, and which can be put into symbolic language."

If it could be put into symbolic language, could it not be put into an engine? Mr. Babbage's guests were enthralled by the Silver Lady as she danced. What, I wondered, would they make of a machine that could play a game or solve a logic puzzle?

When I contemplated Mr. Babbage's Difference Engine and its successor, and all that

I believed they could accomplish, I felt as if I looked through an immeasurable vista, and though I could see nothing but vague and cloudy uncertainty in the foreground, I fancied that I discerned a very bright light a good way farther on, and this made me worry less about the cloudiness and obscurity nearer to me.

I supposed such thoughts were dangerously poetical, which was probably why I did not share them with anyone but Mr. Babbage.

My search for a tutor continued throughout the winter and into the spring, until at last, in early summer, the renowned mathematician and logistician Augustus De Morgan accepted the challenge. Like my father, my husband, Woronzow Greig, and Mr. Babbage, he, too, had studied at Trinity College at Cambridge, and he and Mr. Babbage were quite good friends. Mr. De Morgan was even better acquainted with my mother, for he had married Miss Sophia Frend, who had been one of her closest and most trusted friends for longer than I could remember. Most of our instruction took place through correspondence, a system of learning I was quite accustomed to, but we also met once a fortnight to discuss concepts, problem-solving techniques, and complex theories more easily imparted in person than through the post.

With Mr. De Morgan's guidance, I made

great progress through differential and integral calculus, with such astonishing speed that he worried that I was studying too vigorously, and that it might prove injurious to my health. With unfortunate timing, I did happen to fall ill in late July, and he promptly wrote to my mother and to William expressing his concern that my constitution might not be robust enough to endure the study of mathematics. When they assured him that he was quite mistaken, he reminded them that he, not they, was the expert in this matter, and that he was deeply worried about my "voracious attack" on mathematics. A lady should sit demurely and take instruction respectfully, he wrote, but I questioned him relentlessly, wanting to understand not only *how* something functioned as it did, but *why.*

"I feel bound to tell you," he wrote to my mother, "that the power of thinking on these matters which Lady L. has always shown from the beginning of my correspondence with her, has been something so utterly out of the common way for any beginner, man or woman, that this power must be duly considered by her friends with reference to the question whether they should urge or check her obvious determination to try not only to reach but to get beyond the present bound of knowledge."

In other words, I should strive to master only what was already known. I must not under any circumstances attempt to discover something new.

The questions I asked, Mr. De Morgan patiently explained, were simply not appropriate for any woman to ponder, not even Mary Somerville, whose books he used in his teaching. The sixteenth-century mathematician Maria Agnesi, who had been appointed to the University of Bologna by Pope Benedict XIV, might have been — *might* have been — one remarkable exception, but otherwise such advanced studies were dangerous to the fragile female form. "No other female mathematician throughout history had wrestled with difficulties and shown a man's strength in getting over them," he explained. "The reason is obvious: The very great tension of mind which they require is beyond the strength of a woman's physical power of application."

I was not present when my mother read Mr. De Morgan's missive, but when she showed it to me afterward, I could well imagine her bristling as she discovered his opinion of women's intellectual limitations. When William received his copy, he burst into laughter, which I overheard from another room and wondered at; when he found me in my study afterward, he handed me the letter and declared that Mr. De Morgan might know mathematics, but he obviously did not know me. He and my mother were in confident agreement that, as always, mathematics was a steadying influence upon me, indeed, that it was my salvation. They both promised to respond to Mr. De Morgan with firm assurances that my studies should proceed at whatever pace I chose, and since he continued on as my tutor, they evidently persuaded him.

I suppose I make him sound like an odious, pedantic person, and one might wonder why I would want him to remain as my tutor if he lived in fear that I would collapse beneath the weight of too much laborious cogitation. On the contrary, he was a very good instructor, and when I wasn't worrying about his worry, I learned a great deal from him. I had never felt more intellectually satisfied in all my life.

Fortunately, the conflict was more or less resolved before my mother departed for France in August, where she had been compelled to go on a matter of great urgency regarding my cousin Medora.

Elizabeth Medora Leigh, as I have mentioned before, was the fourth eldest of my aunt Augusta's seven children. I scarcely knew her, or any of my cousins, since my mother had vigilantly shielded me from their family, going so far as to forbid my aunt Augusta to approach me in Society after I came out. I had heard almost nothing of my Leigh cousins since shortly before my mother and I had embarked on our tour of the

Continent, when my mother had permitted Augusta's eldest daughter, Georgiana, and her husband, Henry Trevanion, to take up residence at Bifrons in our absence. Georgiana had been expecting her first child, and Medora had joined her sister and brother-in-law in our former home to attend to Georgiana in her confinement.

That time was now ten years past, but throughout the spring and summer of 1840, my mother's letters hinted at trouble within the Leigh family, ominous glimpses of scandals and conflicts that she had apparently been drawn into after receiving a letter from Medora's lawyer in July. Medora was living in France in poverty and precarious health, and her lawyer begged my mother to help relieve her suffering.

I knew my mother had made some arrangements to provide for Medora — what, precisely, I had not known — but eventually she had determined that she must go to France and see for herself how her niece was faring.

A few days before her departure, my mother had written to me to say that she wanted to see her grandchildren before she sailed. Since she was very busy packing and preparing for her trip, she could not spare time to come to Ockham Park, so we must go to her at Fordhook. Dutifully I packed our bags and loaded the three children, their nurses, and myself into a carriage and made the twenty-mile journey north to my former home, enduring the children's howls of complaint at being confined and jostled for so long.

Naturally they transformed into darling little angels the moment they crossed the threshold of their grandmother's house and ran into her welcoming embrace, which gave me, Mrs. Grimes, and her new assistant, Mrs. Green, a blessed moment to catch our breath and wipe our brows. While we settled ourselves and the children into our rooms, my mother kept the children happily occupied, and I even found a moment to rest in my old bedchamber.

I did not suspect any other purpose for my mother's summons until, after the children went to bed, she invited me to join her in the drawing room for a glass of claret and a chat. "I'm sure you believe I am acting upon a whim in going to France," she said, raising her glass to her lips.

"Not at all," I replied. "You canceled your plans to go abroad after my wedding and never rescheduled. To me this holiday doesn't seem impulsive, but long overdue."

"This is no holiday, but rather a rescue mission." She hesitated, grimacing, and instinctively I braced myself for whatever would come next. "God willing this story will never make it into the papers, but in case it does, I want you to be forewarned."

The trouble had begun long ago, she told

me, when fifteen-year-old Medora had gone to live with Georgiana and Henry at Bifrons. Henry, a man of questionable character and judgment, had never been considered a good match for Georgiana, and he proved his unworthiness a few months later when the formerly innocent Medora was discovered to be pregnant. A clergyman and his wife, friends of the family, learned the distressing secret, which they reported to George Anson Byron, whom my mother had entrusted with her affairs while we were abroad. With her approval, Lord Byron arranged for Henry and Medora to be sent abroad, and after Medora gave birth in Calais, the infant was placed in the care of a local doctor and Medora was sent home to her mother, who remained utterly ignorant of what had transpired.

"The baby arrived earlier than expected," my mother added, "and caught me unprepared. As soon as word reached me, I tried to discover his whereabouts, but my searches were fruitless."

"Were you sure the child was still living?" I asked tentatively.

"No, not at all. Under such circumstances, I fear it was far more likely that he perished soon after he was born. I suppose I'll never know."

Meanwhile my aunt Augusta was preparing for Medora to come out in Society, unaware that she had resumed relations with her brother-in-law, this time beneath her mother's own roof. When she became pregnant a second time, Medora confessed the whole truth to her mother, who became frantic, not only for her daughter's sake, but because she feared Colonel Leigh would murder Henry. Quickly she arranged to send Medora, Georgiana, and Henry away to Bath, but distance proved no deterrent to Colonel Leigh, who erupted in a violent rage and stormed off to Bath to retrieve his ruined daughter. To keep her out of Henry's clutches, instead of bringing her home, he placed her in a home for wayward girls near Regent's Park. The matron, a strict, watchful woman, kept Medora virtually imprisoned in her house, where before long she delivered a stillborn child. Within a fortnight Henry discovered her whereabouts, contrived to liberate her, and fled with her to the Continent, abandoning Georgiana and their three children.

"For two years they lived in Normandy, calling themselves Monsieur and Mademoiselle Aubin," my mother said. "They pretended to be brother and sister."

"They had eloped," I said, bewildered. "At that point, why pretend to be brother and sister instead of husband and wife?"

She gave a little shrug. "You should not expect rational behavior from impulsive and irrational people. In any event, the ruse, such

616

as it was, lasted only as long as their money did. In desperation, Henry tried unsuccessfully to wring an income out of some sympathetic relatives, while Medora converted to Catholicism and contemplated leaving him to become a nun."

I could not help it; I laughed. "I'm sorry. It's not funny."

"No, it isn't," she said, a trifle sharply. "As ridiculous as it was, her plan had no chance of success, for soon she was expecting another child. She gave birth to a daughter in May of 1834, whom she called Marie, and they settled into something resembling family life in Brittany. That lasted until Henry sold his marriage settlement for eight thousand pounds, grew tired of Medora, and brought a new mistress into the household. Medora was forced to become their servant or be put out into the street."

"How dreadful," I gasped. "The whole sad, sordid tale — and the poor little girl. None of this was her fault."

"No, indeed. After a time, Medora did leave Henry, unable to bear the degradation any longer. She and her daughter are presently living in Tours, utterly destitute, and now her lawyer informs me that Medora is dangerously ill." My mother sighed and sipped her claret. "Now you understand why I must go and see what I can do for them."

"Why does this task fall to you?" I asked.

"It is good of you, of course, but why does my aunt Augusta not provide for her?"

"Mrs. Leigh can barely provide for herself and her other children." My mother hesitated. "And I understand that she and Medora are fiercely estranged. Medora prefers me."

I thought I detected a tiny note of satisfaction in her voice, but I hoped I was mistaken. "Of course you must go to her," I declared. "How fortunate she is to have such a generous aunt! Please let me know how William and I might help too."

"Of course, although I wish William might be spared knowledge of this shameful chapter in your family history." She frowned and fell silent for a moment, brooding. "There is more to it, something I hesitate to tell you."

I managed a small, tremulous laugh. "After all that you've already told me, if you hesitate to say more, I hesitate to hear it."

She gave me a searching look. "Perhaps you're right."

"No, do go on," I urged. "I didn't mean you shouldn't tell me, only that —"

"Another time, perhaps. I think we've had enough wretchedness and heartbreak for one evening."

I nodded acquiescence, and I could not have said whether I was more disappointed or relieved that she did not continue.

My mother did not pick up the thread of her story during the few days we remained at

Fordhook, and soon after I took the children home, she departed for France. At the end of August, she wrote to tell me that she had found Medora and Marie in Tours and had convinced her niece to entrust herself and her daughter to her care. Taking up her alias anew and masquerading as a widow, Medora agreed to accompany my mother to Fontainebleau, where my mother arranged for comfortable lodgings and proceeded to scrutinize all the letters my aunt Augusta had sent Medora throughout her ordeal.

Medora had some hope of an income, my mother soon reported, a deed that my aunt had written up in 1839 to provide three thousand pounds for Marie upon my aunt's death. If Medora could sell this deed, she and Marie could live modestly off the interest — but it would be no small feat to wrest the deed from Augusta's control.

My mother did not say so, but I was certain she intended to lead the charge.

As summer flared and faded into autumn, my thoughts churned ceaselessly, turning first upon mathematics and science — electricity, magnetism, and mesmerism particularly interested me — and then upon my mother and her story of Medora's sad history, and then back again, and forth, and back. I pored over my mother's letters with the same intensity with which I studied calculus, for although she complained of various illnesses of the lungs and heart, she sounded inexplicably content, as if caring for Medora and Marie had given her new purpose. "I am particularly happy at present," she wrote to William, but of course he shared his letter with me, as she must have known he would. "Feelings that have long lain, like buried forests, beneath the moss of years, are called forth and seem to give happiness to one for whom I have something like a Mother's affection. I must not attempt to justify the affection I feel for her. Other sentiments strengthened by a decided resemblance have endeared her to me and made her my adopted child."

"How delightful that her maternal feelings have shaken off their moss and sprung to life at last," I said tightly, thrusting the letter back at William.

"Don't be jealous, darling," he replied, folding it carefully and tucking it into a pocket. "Medora needs all the love and maternal affection she can get."

And I did not? I almost blurted, but I hated to seem selfish and petulant.

I decided that I did not need my mother and Medora and the whole ugly drama of her ruin and redemption; I had my studies, I had my horses, and thankfully, I had my health. I had not felt so full of energy since before I had the cholera, since before I was married, as if electricity surged through my body, fueling my thoughts, my intuitive leaps, my comprehension. Sometimes due to over-work I experienced strange physical symptoms, such as the swelling of my face or tingling in my limbs, but without fail they troubled me for only a little while before fading. Despite those annoyances, I felt wonderfully altered as to courage. I was afraid of absolutely nothing. I had never been so bold and full of nerve at any time in my life.

Before long my mother complained that my letters sounded as if I had been seized by a mania, but I dismissed that with a laugh, since she could do nothing about it, as the English Channel separated us and she could neither take my books away nor lock me in a closet to keep me from them. My mother had never understood my peculiar vivacity, and how could she, given her own serene nature and her nearly perpetual invalidism? She had always been suspicious of anything she had not herself experienced.

From her lodgings at 24 Rue de Rivoli in Paris, she urged me to write to Dr. King or to be examined by my physician, Dr. Locock. She encouraged me to spend time away from my books in the company of friends, but William was often away at Ashley Combe, and even when his Birdie and Chicks joined him there, he was often called back to Ockham or to London on business. Recently Lord Melbourne had appointed him to the distinguished office of lord lieutenant of Surrey, a splendid honor that accorded him many new responsibilities, as well as certain delightful privileges, including a life ticket to drive through Constitution Hill. He was busier than ever, preoccupied with other duties, just as my mother was, toiling in Paris with my troubled cousin over the matter of the deed.

As for Mrs. Somerville, she and Dr. Somerville had moved to Italy for his health, much to my sorrow, as I worried about him and missed her dreadfully. Mr. Dickens, who had married shortly before my son Byron was born, was now the father of three young children and the author of two more wonderful stories, *Nicholas Nickleby* and *The Old Curiosity Shop,* so preoccupied with family and writing that he hardly had time to pause and take a deep breath, much less visit me as often as I would have liked. Even Babbage was gone from me that September, for the Italian mathematician Giovanni Plana had invited him to attend a conference of illustrious scientists in Turin.

Mr. Babbage had been invited the previous year but had declined, explaining that he was too busy working on his Analytical Engine to go abroad, but in spring the persistent Signor Plana had written again, and this time his letter revealed such depth of understanding of the Analytical Engine and its potential that Mr. Babbage was persuaded to go. I was thrilled for him because the conference would allow him to introduce his work to many important and influential men of science, and perhaps — if he did not take umbrage at some ignorant remark and blister the ears of his fellow scientists with a string of caustic retorts — he might garner enough support for his work that the funding he so badly needed might finally come through.

Hester came and stayed with me at Ockham Park whenever she could, but without my intellectual friends, I often felt isolated and alone. In the last months of the year, when winter settled heavily upon the countryside — unusually, bitterly cold, driven by a strong, relentless east wind — I declared it "Mathematical weather," perfect for settling into a comfortable armchair by the blazing hearth and studying, solving equations, and contributing to a new project, my Mathematical Scrapbook. The children were less content to be confined indoors, and they became absolute terrors, Byron in particular. He tormented Annabella with such terrifying tales that Mrs. Grimes and I could not coax her to sleep alone in her own bed at night but were obliged to tuck her in beside me. Even then nightmares would jolt her awake, her cries of terror making sure that no one else in the household slept well either.

I confess that this incident made me briefly wonder if I had erred by not constraining my children's imaginations as my mother had mine. From the time they were old enough to understand, I had allowed their nurses to indulge them in fairy tales and adventure stories, and both William and I read aloud to them often ourselves. Many of my happiest moments as a mother were spent wandering through the woods and gardens entertaining my children with stories of the natural world and the land of fairy, as Miss Thorne and I had done so long ago. If I had not cultivated Byron's imagination, he would not have been able to torment his sister so, but even so, I refused to regret my choice.

In early January I was rather startled to receive a gift from Medora, a pincushion she had sewn herself, brilliant red needlework and gold braid upon a dark black background. I perceived the colors as emblematic of her life: the dark fabric her dreary and hopeless past, the red and gold a mixture of bright anticipation about her future. "Will you thank Medora for me?" I wrote to my mother. "Tell her it is ready for use as soon as I want a fresh pin." After admiring the taste and neatness of the workmanship, I added, "I quite revere and adore the Hen's whole conduct and feelings respecting this singular and apparently unfortunate being. It well paints your whole principle and character."

I sincerely meant it. Medora and her daughter were desperate, and among all her relations only my mother had gone to help them, despite the many other demands upon her time and generosity. That was something I should admire and emulate, not spitefully regard as the misplacement of affection that ought to be mine.

In her next letter, my mother invited me and William to come to Paris, where she and her charges had taken up residence at 22 Place Vendôme. I dithered, reluctant to leave my studies, but my mother persisted, and so we settled upon early April, when William would have no Parliament or business in Town due to the Easter holiday.

The day after my mother's letter arrived, William and I attended a soirée at the home of Mr. Babbage, who had long since returned from Turin, triumphant and hopeful. He had been received as a distinguished inventor and scientist by the illustrious gathering of learned men from around the world, and their respect and admiration for his Analytical Engine both gratified and encouraged him. And yet I detected a hint of resignation in his manner, and as soon as we had a moment to ourselves, I gently inquired about it.

"I have been forced to confront a melancholy truth," he admitted. "I see now that it is highly unlikely that I shall ever be able to afford to build the Analytical Engine."

"Oh, Mr. Babbage, no," I exclaimed. "You can't believe that."

"I do, my dear. My own personal wealth, though by no means insignificant, is simply inadequate to the task." He seemed remarkably calm for a man who had concluded that his life's work would never be realized. "Consider, Lady Lovelace, that the Analytical Engine would require the manufacture of tens of thousands of parts all made to my exact specifications by a skilled engineer whom I can barely persuade to answer my letters. These parts must be assembled in an intricate arrangement within precise tolerances in a frame fifteen feet high, six feet wide, and roughly twenty feet long."

As I imagined it, my heart sank with dismay. "That's nearly the size of a locomotive."

"A small one, yes, and my Analytical Engine would require nearly as much steam as a locomotive to operate. An objective view of these facts leads me to conclude, not that it *cannot* be done, but that it *shall* not be done." He inhaled deeply, squared his shoulders, and managed a smile. "And yet I will persevere, with no less dedication than before, for I still have reason to hope."

"I'm glad to hear it," I said. "And this reason is?"

"My work was very well received in Turin," he said. "It is possible that one of the eminent scientists I met there will publish a lengthy and detailed study of my engine, which would confirm its importance to science, commerce, and industry here at home. That could provide me with the evidence I need to convince our government to issue me another grant."

"I wish you much success." His confidence emboldened me to say to him something I had contemplated throughout that cold and bleak winter. "If I may say so, Mr. Babbage, it occurs to me that at some future time — it might be within three or four years, or it might be many years hence — my mind and mathematical capabilities may be employed to some of your purposes and plans. If so, if ever I could be worthy of or capable of such service, you need only command me."

"Thank you, Lady Lovelace," he said. "I'm gratified by your generous offer, and you may be certain I won't forget it."

After that, I waited in daily expectation of an invitation to assist him in his work.

In late February, our family moved from Ockham Park to our residence at Saint James's Square, which William had spent the winter remodeling and was now wonderfully improved. I was in my study writing invitations for a party, at which we would reveal the delightful renovations to our friends, when a letter arrived from Paris.

"My dearest Ada," my mother wrote, "you may recall that when we last met, on the eve of my departure, I intimated that there was more to Medora's troubling history than you knew, a darker, more disturbing secret that I could not bring myself to reveal. Now that you are coming to Paris to meet her, I believe the time has come to tell you all."

My heart thudded, and for a moment I shut my eyes and let my hands fall to my lap, still clutching the letter, which I now dreaded to read.

And yet I knew I had no choice. Steeling myself, I opened my eyes and read on.

"The young woman you know as your cousin," my mother wrote, "is in fact your half sister, your father's child by his half sister, Augusta."

CHAPTER TWENTY-FIVE:
IT WERE THE DEADLIEST SIN
TO LOVE AS WE HAVE LOVED

February–May 1841

Reeling, my revulsion and shock swiftly rising with every line, I read on as my mother described what she had learned of the peculiar, twisted, sordid relations between my father and my aunt that had led to Medora's birth in 1814, eight and a half months before my parents married.

Of course, I thought with each new abhorrent revelation, of course. So many curious matters that had bewildered me all my life suddenly made sense — my mother's burning enmity for my aunt, my grandparents' antipathy for my father, the opaque green curtain they had placed before my father's portrait before packing it away, the "facts utterly unknown" that had compelled the Separation and had made reconciliation impossible. Then, too, there were the strangely unsettling verses that had troubled me when I first delved deeply into my father's poetry at Ashley Combe. It was fallacy to believe that all poetry was autobiographical, but my father had been known to draw upon his own life and experiences when composing his greatest works. Now certain characters, motifs, and phrases leapt out at me like accusing witnesses. I understood at last why so many of my father's poems after 1814 alluded to the anguish of forbidden love, to the torment of shameful secrets, to incest.

Incest. The word resonated in my mind until I grew faint, my ears ringing, my heart pounding, as the truth gradually sank in, though I shrank from it.

I sat for nearly an hour alone in my study, the letter resting on my lap, staring straight ahead at nothing, my emotions swinging from outrage to revulsion to resignation to despair. I knew I had to tell William. I dreaded it, but I knew the task would become only more difficult with delay.

I found him alone in the library, frowning thoughtfully at a heavy volume of property law. "From my mother," I said, handing him the letter and settling myself gingerly upon the sofa to wait while he read, feeling strangely bruised and exhausted. "I read it with no surprise."

His face steadily drained of color and took on a stony cast as he absorbed my mother's revelations. "I cannot believe it," he said at last, shaking his head, setting the letter on the desk and pushing it away as if the sight of it sickened him. "I never would have imagined it."

"I imagined it," I said softly, realizing the truth of my words only as I spoke them. "It is exactly what I anticipated would eventually be revealed, as shocking as it all is."

"You imagined *this*?" exclaimed William. "How?"

I shook my head; I did not entirely understand it myself. "I have so long suspected that this, or something very similar, had occurred in my most miserable and unhappy family that the admission of it is neither new nor startling."

He shook his head, disbelieving. "And your mother is certain that Colonel Leigh has no idea Medora is not his child?"

"So she says," I said, gesturing to the letter. "I'm inclined to believe so. He has accepted her as his daughter all her life."

"I suppose the fact that he has not murdered Mrs. Leigh is proof enough of his ignorance."

"In these circumstances, ignorance may be bliss." I felt tears gathering, but I blinked them away. "It is a most strange and dreadful history, and I can hardly bear to contemplate it."

Quickly William joined me on the sofa and took my hands. "The shame falls upon your father and his sister and upon them alone," he said firmly. "You and your mother aren't complicit in their sin. You are blameless."

"My poor mother," I said, feeling faint again. "To think of her all those years ago, such a young girl, purity and innocence itself, suddenly plunged into the midst of the greatest depths of depravity and betrayal — why, subjecting her to that is almost more dreadful than the sin itself!"

"How well she has borne the burden of this secret all these years, in brave silence and dignity."

I murmured agreement, but I doubted that she had been entirely silent. My grandparents and my mother's lawyer had known; of this I was certain. Who else knew? My aunt Augusta, clearly. My cousin — my sister — Medora, very likely. My mother's deeply loyal friends — many of them surely knew, and their seething hatred for my father suddenly took on new facets I had not perceived before. No wonder they had regarded me with suspicion and mistrust all my life, waiting for me to tumble headlong into sin. I carried the bad Byron blood. My corruption was inevitable.

I had proven them wrong, all of them. I was more Milbanke than Byron. I had to be. The alternative was unthinkable.

I needed a day to reflect before I could reply, but I knew my mother would be anxiously awaiting my response, so I eventually secluded myself in my study, took pen in hand, and allowed my thoughts to spill upon the page.

Dearest Mama,

I am not in the least astonished. In fact, you merely confirm what I have for years and years felt scarcely a doubt about, but should have considered it most improper for me to hint to you that I in any way suspected.

I therefore learn the fact with no surprise. I have always expected to hear it some time or other; and I only feel now upon it as I have long done, that the state of mind in both parties in which only such a monstrosity could have originated, is indeed appalling.

I trust that my most unhappy and unfortunate parent is now freed from his shocking and I must think willful defiance of law, nature, reason, and instinct. From all I can gather respecting him, I believe that even his worst crimes originated more in *defiance,* than in love of the *crime* — in short, a good principle, the love of the exercise of free will, carried to a fearful and distorted extent. I trust it has been so, for I think it is a shade more easily retrievable than the absolute depravity which loves the crime for its own sake.

When I reflect on my own natural defiance of law, of everything imposed, I sometimes tremble. But for my excellent understanding (for which I thank heaven and you for your wise cultivation of it), I should not have been one whit better or happier than my unhappy parent. I might not have committed exactly the same crimes, but I should have been just as bad in some line or other. I may well tremble, when I think on all I might have inherited!

As I wrote, it became ever more apparent to me that I resembled my father in ways I had never realized. This frightening truth so upset me that I was obliged to set down my pen and take deep breaths to keep from breaking into sobs. If my mother had not carefully trained me in logic and reason, and had not vigorously commanded me to control my imagination, I might have committed sins as grave as my father's. I nearly had, with William Turner.

"If my poor Father had but possessed a little of my real philosophical turn!" I lamented to my mother when I continued my letter. "Nothing else, depend upon it, can ever keep that sort of character in order. Neither circumstances, nor conscience, nor impulses." And yet, as distraught as I was, I remained hopeful that I — and Medora too — could overcome whatever sinister elements we had inherited from our father and lead good, useful lives. "Believe me, dearest

Mama, to be your Hopeful Bird," I wrote. "Yes — I must hope well even for Mrs. L, whom I feel is more inherently wicked than my father ever was."

Now I understood why my mother had kept my aunt Augusta away from me, and I was thankful. Medora and Georgiana had certainly not fared well beneath her influence, and I shuddered to think how she might have corrupted me.

When I received my mother's reply a few days later, I was surprised and disappointed to see that her greatest concern was not to comfort me in the aftermath of her devastating revelations, but to insist that, whatever suspicions I might have had about my father and my aunt, she had done absolutely nothing to sow seeds of doubts in me. "I know not, dearest Ada, what I ever said to you that could even suggest the idea of vice on Mrs. Leigh's part," she wrote. "Of her want of veracity and artfulness I have spoken. When you alluded to poems in which there was a remote reference to the fact, I have always avoided discussing them. It is, however, another proof added to many in my experience that the truth always makes itself felt, at least to persons of a certain kind of intellect, by means which are neither tangible nor imaginable." She added that she had always endeavored to leave my father's "aberrations sufficiently indistinct" whenever she spoke of him to me, so that I might still be able to contemplate his memory with respect and gratification. Her friends had considered this refusal to condemn him before me a weakness on her part, she noted, but she had no regrets. Now that all was revealed, "I will hope that the true charity which replaces the imaginary feeling is better for you and, if he knows it, more acceptable to him in his purified state."

I contemplated her words in bewilderment and uncertainty. Although she had never explicitly declared in my presence that she despised my wicked father, she had made it known in a thousand silent ways, and I had never doubted it. As to when I had first begun to suspect an illicit affair between my father and my aunt, I could not recall the precise moment or circumstance that first suggested it to me, although I certainly knew of several that had confirmed and strengthened this impression in all the years since. This I carefully explained to my mother in my reply, adding, "I should tell you that I did not suspect the daughter as being the result of it."

William and I had discussed this after the initial shock had faded and we could consider the facts more rationally. My aunt Augusta had been married at the time of Medora's conception, so how could she know with any degree of certainty which of her two lovers had fathered her child? My mother seemed absolutely certain that Medora was my half sister, but William and I agreed that it could never be proven, and that the violent, ill-tempered Colonel Leigh must never be given reason to doubt.

This question of uncertainty I delicately placed before my mother, and then I posed another, one that had been troubling me since the beginning. "I should like sometime to know how you came to suspect something so monstrous," I wrote. "The natural intimacy and familiarity of a Brother and Sister certainly could not suggest it to any but a very depraved and vicious mind, which yours assuredly was not. I cannot help fancying that my father himself must have given you some very clear hints of this. He enjoyed taunting you with his crimes."

"All my life I have wanted a sibling," I said ruefully to William as I sealed the letter, "and now my mother will accuse me of wanting to deny my sister."

"Under the circumstances, it is perfectly understandable why you should want to," said William shortly. His respect and reverence for my mother had long bordered on worship, but recently he had taken to wondering aloud why she had chosen to reveal such dreadful secrets to the benefit of absolutely no one, and why now.

I could only speculate, and none of the

answers I came up with reflected well upon her.

Regardless of how we felt about my mother, her motives, and the troubled young woman she insisted was my half sister, we were obliged to meet Medora. Our plans to travel to Paris in the first week of April proceeded apace, but in late March, William came down with influenza. Although he was soon out of danger, by the first day of April, it was evident that he would not be well enough to make the journey.

"I dread the thought of traveling without you," I told him as I sat on the edge of his bed, applying a cool cloth to his brow to soothe his fever.

"Then don't go," he said hoarsely, interrupted by a fit of coughing. "I fail to see how meeting her will benefit you."

"Perhaps meeting *me* will benefit *her*," I said, knowing that I would make the journey despite my misgivings. No excuse short of fatal illness would have satisfied my mother — and I will confess that I had become curious to meet Medora, as one is perversely compelled to push a thumb into a bruise to discover just how badly it hurts.

I enjoyed the sea voyage across the Channel, wishing only that it could have lasted longer, both to prolong my enjoyment and to delay my arrival in Paris. When I finally arrived at the door of 22 Place Vendôme, I was fatigued from my travels and somewhat wary, which may have contributed to the confusion I felt when my mother welcomed me with open arms and kisses upon both cheeks, beaming so cheerfully that I almost did not recognize her. Bewildering me further was the absence of any sign of Medora and Marie, whom I assumed were residing with her. When I delicately inquired, my mother explained that she had settled them in an apartment in a different wing of the house, so that neither would be forced upon the other, nor would Medora encounter any of my mother's visitors unless she had been specifically invited to meet them.

"Would you like to meet her?" my mother asked, studying me expectantly.

The only possible answer was yes, so I nodded, and my mother sent a maid hurrying off to fetch Medora and Marie. In the meantime she led me to a sitting room on the second floor overlooking the street, beautifully furnished in gold and white damask with watercolor landscapes of the French countryside on the walls and vases of fresh flowers everywhere. We seated ourselves, and a moment later, a tall, slender, dark-haired woman entered holding the hand of a little girl who looked to be about six years old, her brown eyes solemn, her chestnut hair held back from a sweet, heart-shaped face by a broad white ribbon and bow. Fixing her solemn gaze upon me, the little girl snatched her hand away from her mother, who made no attempt to reclaim it.

"Come here, my dears," my mother beckoned. Marie hurried to her and climbed up on her lap, while Medora glided sedately after her and took the armchair closest to me. My mother introduced us and we exchanged the usual perfunctory remarks, all the while fixing each other with unabashedly appraising looks. Medora was strikingly pretty, with bold features and a complexion reminiscent of Spanish gentility, and although my mother had gone on at length about her poor health, she seemed as alert and strong as anyone in the bloom of youth, albeit a trifle too thin.

Medora politely inquired after William and the children, and after she and my mother tutted sympathetically about his influenza and nodded approvingly at my accounts of the children's recent accomplishments, the conversation turned to my journey, my first impressions of Paris, the sights my mother and Medora were eager to show me, and what dresses I had brought and what I might want to have made up for me while I was there. Marie sang a pretty song for us in French, and when I praised her exquisite accent, Medora blushed slightly and admitted that her daughter spoke perfect French, but not a word of English.

My mother and Medora must have arranged a discreet signal between them, for soon thereafter Medora begged us to excuse her and led Marie away, ostensibly to rest before dinner.

When they were gone, my mother turned to me, eyes shining. "Well? What do you make of her?"

"She seems very nice," I said, noncommittally. "I'm glad to see her so well. I thought you said she was quite ill."

"She is — consumption, I believe — but she has steadily improved ever since I brought her out of that hovel in Tours." My mother's mouth tightened at the memory. "But did you not see the resemblance to your father? Even if you had not known the truth, I think you would have guessed it the moment you set eyes on her."

Briefly I wondered if that was another reason my mother had kept us apart for so many years. "I think she favors Colonel Leigh," I said carefully, knowing that she would interpret my words as she saw fit no matter what I said or failed to say. "She certainly has his height. I think she resembles my father no more than any niece would resemble an uncle."

"Nonsense," my mother said, astonished. "She looks more like your father than you do."

"Do you think so?" I inquired, deliberately leaning forward and resting my very Byronic chin on my hand.

"Perhaps not so much in the face as in her movement and manners. Medora has his bearing, his piercing looks, his particular way of turning his head when he hears a sudden noise."

"I wouldn't know."

"I suppose not." My mother's gaze lingered on the door through which Medora and Marie had departed, a faint, fond smile on her lips. It faded as she turned to face me. "You asked how I first learned about your father's affair with his sister. Mrs. Leigh herself confessed the truth to me, but that was not until much later. The signs were present all around me from the moment I first met your father, but I was too innocent, too trusting, too very much in love to interpret them correctly."

Then, in a steady voice that only rarely betrayed a quaver of emotion, my mother told me of their courtship and marriage, my father's strange outbursts and erratic behavior, the unsettling clues in his poetry that I myself had discovered — much, but not all, of the fraught history with which I opened this narrative.

It was a great deal to take in, and after my mother finished, I sat still and silent, my thoughts in a tangle, my head aching, and my heart too. Even if I doubted my mother's evidence — which was circumstantial, though emotionally damning — I could not doubt that my father had committed incest if my aunt herself had admitted it. But that did not prove that Medora was my father's child.

In the days that followed, it became evident that my mother wanted me to think of Medora as my sister, even in the absence of proof, and I decided that it would be ungenerous of me not to try. As I learned more of her tragic tale, my sympathies were more deeply provoked, and as we spent more time together, I came to like her quite a lot. Still, there was a grasping shrewdness about her that I found distasteful, and though I tried, I could never think of her as more than my cousin. Hester felt like a sister, but Medora did not. Perhaps, unbeknownst even to myself, the cogs and wheels of my mind had been turning, calculating the infinite difference of how Medora had betrayed Georgiana, and I had decided that she was not the sort of sister I wanted.

I was happier when my mother and I were alone together, just the two of us, with Medora out of sight and as far out of mind as I could put her. My mother would take me to the theatre or on long, pleasant strolls along the Champs-Élysées, companions drawn closer by our shared secrets. She bought me lovely new gowns in the Parisian style, and after William recovered from his illness and joined us, she arranged for us to be presented at the French court. William was courteous and kind to Medora on the few occasions when we were brought together at my mother's home, but one night as we were undressing for bed after a long day, he wearily reminded me that we would not be able to receive her openly at home, not because of her parentage, but because of her moral lapses.

"We needn't worry about that," I said, taken aback. "Surely Medora realizes that she can never return to England. Here in France she can live in some comfort and respectability as the widow Madame Aubin. In England she is known and the scandal would be too outrageous. She would be shunned, and anyone who took her in would be ruined with her."

"Let us hope your mother remembers that," he replied curtly.

I studied him for a moment before he put out the light and darkness engulfed us. I was tempted to ask him if he regretted marrying the daughter of the great poet Lord Byron, the only tie that bound him up in this tangle of familial discord and impropriety, but I was afraid of the answer.

Chapter Twenty-Six:
Longings Sublime,
and Aspirations High

May 1841–February 1843

In late May, William and I returned to England exhausted and disconcerted. We reunited with our children at Ockham Park and soon settled the family in our London residence, where we picked up the threads of our lives, which Medora had unraveled and tangled with a careless wave of her hand. William returned to his improvements to the estates and, with less enthusiasm, to his political career. I returned to my maternal duties, my social engagements, and my mathematical studies.

But always in the back of my mind was the hard, bitter knowledge of my father's sins. At odd moments throughout the day I found myself brooding over my bad Byron blood, and when the children misbehaved, I imagined it flowing through their veins as well. I now recognized my father in his most tormented poetic dramatis personae — Manfred and Childe Harold, Selim and Don Juan —

and I wondered how I could have missed the signs of his own anguish so vividly drawn in his characters' struggles and distress.

I had told my mother that I believed my father had sinned with his half sister not because he loved the sin, but because he reveled in defying convention, in rebelling against Society, in flouting the rules that bound ordinary people. That same tendency had compelled and tormented me all my life, but when I reflected upon the shattered hearts and ruined lives my father had left in his wake, I resolved that I would not follow after him. If it was my nature to be defiant, then I would harness that power to defy my fate. I would save myself and redeem my lost father.

I resolved to become as great a mathematician as my father had been a poet, so that I could in some way compensate for his misused genius. If he had passed on to me any portion of that genius, I would use it to bring out great truths and principles. I felt very strongly that he had bequeathed this task to me, and I felt a surge of confidence and satisfaction when I thought that I was performing a sacred, redemptive duty on his behalf.

So I resolved, such was my ambition, but I was thwarted almost before I could begin by my longtime adversary, illness. None of my old, trusted remedies brought me any relief this time, so I searched for new treatments, finding some relief in mesmerism and, under the advice of Dr. Locock, in laudanum. Even now I smile when I recall the soft bliss those precious drops bestowed upon me, the warm, enveloping sense of comfort, the cessation of pain and care. Sometimes the treatments upset my stomach or made it difficult to focus on my studies, but when the medicine held me in its embrace, I did not care.

Laudanum certainly softened the frustration, anxiety, and jealousy I experienced when my mother returned from Paris, not alone, but with Medora and Marie in tow. "I have come to think of her as an adopted daughter," my mother had written to me before they set sail, and she asked if my sister and niece might stay with us until she found them a suitable residence. William was greatly displeased, but he was too good a man to refuse shelter to any relative, even if we could not determine the precise nature of the relationship. Even so, he insisted that Medora come to us in the guise of the widowed Madame Aubin.

We kept their arrival as quiet as we could, but Medora was baffled and insulted by our desire for secrecy, and she made her displeasure known with scowls and acid remarks. My mother had not warned me about this aspect of my half sister's character. My heart went out to the poor child, Marie, who had never set foot in her native country and spoke not a word of the language, and for her sake I was willing to let them remain with us as long as they liked. Nonetheless, I felt great relief when my mother found a large, elegant home for them at Moore Place, an estate in Esher about seven miles northeast of Ockham Park. To my astonishment, my mother moved in with them, explaining that someone was needed to keep the peace between the mother and daughter, who, as it turned out, absolutely despised each other. Over time, Medora's spitefulness and constant complaints became too much for my mother, so she arranged for Marie to live with trusted friends, a pair of doting spinster sisters who saw to her education, while she herself fled home to Fordhook.

Moore Place remained Medora's home and the military headquarters for their vengeful campaign against my aunt Augusta, who remained at a distance, linked to her resentful daughter only by post. With my mother's staunch support, Medora had filed suit against her mother for the deed, but it was not until the following May that the matter was finally resolved. On the day my aunt would have been brought before the court, she surrendered the document, and at last Medora had her source of income in hand. Perversely, instead of thanking my mother for all that had been done on her behalf, Medora complained that the three thousand pounds she stood to earn from the deed would not suffice. She had wanted a trial because she had wanted to expose her mother's ill treatment of her before the public.

Now she would be prevented from making the public denunciation, which she apparently did not care would have tarnished my mother, and me, and William by association. Bitterly disappointed, Medora turned on my mother full of rage and spite, shocking her with the violence and fury of her invective. "No one has treated me so vilely since I lived with your father," my mother told me shakily when I hurried to Fordhook in response to her urgent summons. "I never should have accepted her expressions of confidence and affection. I will endeavor to forget them. It is enough for me that I know I was her friend and guardian. I have never asked for anything in return."

She had not needed to ask, I realized, for Medora had willingly given what my mother had wanted most: the means to exact revenge against Augusta. I finally understood that my mother's generosity had never been prompted by kindness and mercy, but by vengeance. It was little wonder that a scheme born of contempt and anger had ended badly for everyone involved.

"Your mother should have left the wretched woman in Paris," William grumbled, and I heartily agreed. Although she had won her suit, Medora refused to leave England until she had the justice — and the additional funds from her mother — she argued were rightfully hers. My mother wanted nothing more to do with her, so I felt as if I had no choice but to intervene in her place. Eventually I convinced Medora to return to France with a French maid as her companion, whom I hired and whose wages William paid. The sacrifice would be well worth it. We would all breathe easier with Medora on the other side of the Channel.

At last, in July, I was able to write to my mother with good news. "I have no doubt that Medora's ship sailed last night," I announced. "Today would be beautiful for the passage. There's a good strong wind to speed her to the opposite shore, the very thing we all desire. I am glad for all of us that this business is concluded. The last half hour I spent with her yesterday evening, she subjected me to a discourse on the bitterness of dependence, and she threatened to throw herself at the first man she might persuade to marry her. May she find more happiness with this scheme than the last."

With tremendous relief, I turned my attention to Hester, whom I truly thought of as a sister, and who was much more deserving of a champion in her time of need. She had fallen in love with Sir George William Craufurd of Burgh Hall, the third baronet and the rector of Scremby, Lincolnshire, a bachelor forty-five years of age. They wanted to marry, but William was adamantly opposed, and for the most ridiculous of reasons: Sir George was unfortunately very stout, and my husband had an irrational hatred of fat. He was always first to let me know when I had put on weight, which hurt my feelings even though I could not deny that his caustic remarks encouraged me to remain slim. Still, his prejudice seemed a very stupid reason to forbid his sister to marry a man who was kind and adored her and had excellent prospects. I promised Hester to do all I could to make William see reason, but secretly I feared that I had little power to influence him. Once, years ago, I had felt that we were united, standing side by side, hands clasped, our faces turned toward the same distant horizon. Now it seemed that we stood at an angle, our backs slightly turned upon each other, my hands holding a book, his arms folded across his chest. It was not only for Hester's sake that I worried about the growing distance between us.

When I was not advocating for Hester, I filled my hours with mathematics and science and with renewed interest in music, as well as a new passion for the theatre. My love for music and drama rose to such heights that William began to complain that I had come under the influence of a violent mania, and he feared that I would abandon mathematics and science for what he considered more frivolous pursuits. I vehemently disagreed with his evaluation of the arts, and his use of the irksome term "mania," so long a favorite of my mother and Dr. King, exasperated me. I had no intention of allowing any new pursuit to eclipse the guiding passions of my life, so my increasingly intractable husband had no need to worry. Even so, I was obliged to write him a great many letters assuring him of this truth before he would accept it.

How could I even contemplate relinquishing science and mathematics when so many new, thrilling discoveries and inventions were announced almost every day? There was the fascinating electrical telegraph, of course, which I had first seen on exhibit at Exeter Hall, which sent messages to distant regions with nearly the speed of thought. The rapidly expanding steam railway system, with its awe-inspiring, thunderous, powerful locomotives, carried passengers to more places more swiftly than ever before, making travel easier and more comfortable even as it became more exciting. Not everyone shared my opinion. Whereas I considered the railway a grand and marvelous invention, my dear friend Mr. Dickens saw it as a menace bringing terror and destruction in its wake, and as it spread throughout the formerly serene countryside, he began referring to it grimly as a "triumphant monster."

But even the ingenious steam locomotive faced the possibility of being surpassed by newer technology when the Samuda brothers introduced the "traction piping" railway based on the principle of atmospheric propulsion, employing a system of vacuums, tubes, pistons, and pumps to propel rail carriages along the track at an astonishing twenty-files miles per hour. Its advantages over the steam locomotive, including its superior performance when traversing slopes, impressed me greatly, and the ride itself was so thrilling that I took not one but two trips at the public demonstration.

Discoveries from the natural world were as astonishing as these technological marvels. Mr. Babbage's friend Charles Darwin had returned from a five-year voyage around the world, studying geology and natural history, making remarkable observations and collecting astonishing samples. At Mr. Babbage's soirées, he spoke of a theory he was developing based upon his observations, something he called "natural selection." I found it fascinating and utterly revolutionary, but privately Mr. Babbage and I agreed that when he published his results, scores of detractors would surely denounce him as a heretic.

Perhaps even more intriguing to me were Michael Faraday's experiments in electricity and magnetism. We would eventually become very good friends, as my growing fascination with electricity compelled me to re-create some of his experiments, but he confessed to me that he was not very interested in mathematics, and so he could not express the same interest in my work as I did in his. I used to tease him mercilessly about that, to our mutual enjoyment.

Mr. Faraday and I were to disagree cordially regarding the enchantment of mathematics, for as ever, it held me in its thrall. Once, as I reflected upon the curious transformations many formulae could undergo, I suddenly found them strangely reminiscent of the stories Miss Thorne had told me long ago. "I am often reminded of certain sprites and fairies one reads of," I mused in a letter to Mr. De Morgan, "who are at one's elbows in one shape now, and the next minute in a form most dissimilar; and uncommonly deceptive, troublesome, and tantalizing are the mathematical sprites and fairies sometimes; like the types I have found for them in the world of Fiction." Sadly, my tutor was no more amused by my fanciful talk than my mother would have been.

Even when I did not speak of fairies, Mr. De Morgan was sometimes discomfited by subjects that fascinated me. All that summer I had been deeply engrossed in the study of imaginary numbers, mathematical curiosities such as the square root of a negative number. Such creatures were neither positive nor negative, but something different altogether, and although they behaved somewhat differently than ordinary numbers, they could still be manipulated according to the simplest rules of arithmetic. They reminded me of fairies who had emerged from their supernatural realm to flit about an English garden, something not of this world that dwelt among us for a time before disappearing again.

My contemplation of imaginary numbers, the complex equations they yielded, and the new form of two-dimensional geometry these equations created led me to wonder if this could not be extended further, into a geometry of three dimensions, and that again to a further extension into some unknown region, and so on, ad infinitum. When I posed this matter to Mr. De Morgan, he replied rather curtly that he had already struggled with this question and had gotten nowhere with it. Implicit in his statement was that if a solution had eluded a man of his intellect, no solution existed, but secretly I disagreed, and I continued to ponder the matter on my own.

It was a summer of wonders for me, but my mathematical and scientific revelry halted, or at least paused for a somber moment, at the end of August. Earlier that month, Lord Melbourne had received a vote of no confidence in Parliament, and on 30 August, he submitted his resignation. The Tory government returned to power, and Sir Robert Peel once again became prime minister. I felt sympathy for my mother's cousin, whom I imagined must have been very disappointed by the outcome of the vote, but I felt no regret for my own family's sake, for Lord Melbourne had already done so much for us that I expected nothing more. For Mr. Babbage, however, I was apprehensive, as I knew he would consider Sir Robert Peel's elevation as another strike against his engines.

The next time we met, I was relieved to find Mr. Babbage nonetheless in good spirits. "I still have a few irons in the fire," he assured me, and at his regular soirée the following week, I discovered the most important of them: The Duke of Wellington and Prince Albert, Queen Victoria's husband, were in attendance. Prince Albert's vast intellect was well-known, and my heart was full of happiness and hope as I observed Mr. Babbage at his most courteous and engaging as he escorted his honored guests to the drawing room to view the Silver Lady, and on to the exhibition room to observe the demonstration model of the Difference Engine, and then out back to his workshop to examine the partially complete full-size version and his plans and notes for the Analytical Engine. Perhaps this interview would at last bring Mr. Babbage the funding he and his engines so deserved and so badly needed.

In October, another promising development raised my hopes even higher. Signore Luigi Federico Menabrea, a professor of mechanics and construction at the University of Turin whom Mr. Babbage had met at the conference of Italian scientists two years before, published a treatise on the Analytical Engine in the renowned Swiss journal *Bibliothèque Universelle de Genève.* William and I attended the dinner party Mr. Babbage hosted to celebrate the publication, and his dearest friends raised one toast after another in his honor, congratulating him and declaring that surely the British government would now take notice of his work. "Your biggest problem will be adding on another room to your workshop to accommodate the Analytical Engine," Mr. Faraday remarked.

"I was thinking that instead I would remove the wall between the drawing room and the dining room and construct it right here," Mr. Babbage quipped, and we all burst out laughing. It was a merry evening, full of hope and expectation, bright with promise. William and I returned home that night contemplating how the country would be transformed by his marvelous machine, and for the first time, it seemed much more than fanciful speculation.

Soon thereafter, Mr. Babbage wrote me with delightful news: The Duke of Wellington and Prince Albert had learned about the treatise. The approbation of the scientific community coupled with their own observations of Mr. Babbage's work convinced them to arrange a meeting between Mr. Babbage and Prime Minister Peel.

"This is his chance," I exulted, fairly dancing into William's study and giving him the letter. "He has the support of the prince and the duke. If he can convince the prime minister — why, construction on the Analytical Engine could begin within days! It could be completed within a year!"

"Babbage should take care to be on his best behavior," William said, scanning the letter. "This is not an ideal time to petition Peel for anything. I've seen him recently, and it's obvious that he's exhausted and burdened with care. The people are struggling, not just in the cities but in the villages and on the farms as well. With widespread hunger and rioting to sort out, I cannot imagine that a very expensive machine would be high on his list of priorities, especially since he's not particularly fond of Mr. Babbage."

"Mr. Babbage understands that everything depends upon winning over the prime minister," I said, but even as I spoke, doubt crept in. "Surely he'll use the utmost tact and respect. He can be so warm and engaging and congenial when he wants to."

I left unsaid what William already knew:

When Mr. Babbage did *not* want to, he could be sullen and querulous, turning against him people who otherwise would have become his steadfast friends.

As the hours ticked by on Friday, 11 November, I imagined what Mr. Babbage was doing as he prepared for the meeting. Now he is in his study organizing his papers, I thought at eleven o'clock; and now he is fortifying himself with a hearty luncheon, I thought at noon. At one o'clock I imagined him climbing into a carriage and riding off to the prime minister's offices, and then, too anxious to focus on anything else, I paced in my study, hoping and praying that all would go well. It was all I could do not to hurry over to 1 Dorset Street, invite myself into his sitting room, and await his return.

My first indication that the meeting had not gone as I'd hoped came that evening at dinner, when a guest, my friend Charles Wheatstone, an inventor and physicist who had helped create the first practical application of the telegraph in Europe, mentioned that he had seen Mr. Babbage walking in Westminster in the late afternoon. "He was striding along quite purposefully," Mr. Wheatstone said, "scowling and giving way to no one, his face a thundercloud."

I threw a stricken look to William, who sighed heavily and covered his eyes with his hand.

My worry grew as another day passed with no word from Mr. Babbage. We heard other rumors from mutual friends that the interview had been a disaster, but I held out hope until I received his letter, a nearly minute-by-minute account of the meeting that confirmed my worst fears.

Inexplicably, Mr. Babbage had approached the entire discussion as if it were a confrontation, apparently believing that the object was to browbeat the prime minister into submission rather than to rationally and pleasantly persuade him. Instead of clearly and succinctly explaining the difference between his two engines and describing their practical benefits, he spoke of how the jealousy and personal malice of certain men in the government had thwarted him. While he had emphasized that the Analytical Engine was superior to the Difference Engine, he failed to make the case for funding a new project when the Difference Engine had not yet been completed.

When he had heard enough, the prime minister had interrupted him with the pointed observation that by his own admission, Mr. Babbage had rendered the Difference Engine useless by inventing a better machine. Babbage had fixed him with a hard stare. "I consider myself to have been treated with great injustice by the Government. But as you are of a different opinion, I cannot help myself." With that, he rose, bade the prime minister a curt good day, and abruptly left the room.

Mr. Babbage's letter rendered me entirely speechless, so I could not prepare William for what it said, but only handed him the letter and collapsed into the nearest chair. "Babbage is a fool," he said when he finished reading. "He did absolutely nothing to ingratiate himself with the most powerful man in Britain, and the only one who could have given him precisely what he needs."

"Why did he have to be so defensive and ill-tempered?" I lamented. "And this is his own account of the meeting. I shudder to imagine Sir Robert Peel's version."

Sighing, William folded the letter and handed it back to me. "I regret to say this, but your Mr. Babbage just spoiled his last and best chance to secure funding."

I thought of the full-scale Difference Engine gathering dust in his workshop, his notes and sketches for the Analytical Engine yellowing with age, the ink fading, the edges curling, and I wanted to weep. "Perhaps, unless — William, have you ever considered seeking the post of prime minister?"

William uttered a strangled laugh. "Never. Good Lord, Ada, that is not the answer."

"Would you consider it?"

"Not unless the queen herself personally asked me. Perhaps not even then. Darling, a man who would strive to become prime minister simply to fund his friend's scientific projects would never deserve the post."

"I suppose not," I said, disconsolate. "I hardly know what to say to him. I'm sure he needs encouragement at this moment, but I'm so exasperated that all I can think of to do is to seize him by the shoulders and give him a good shake. If the meeting had been with Lord Melbourne, I'm certain Mr. Babbage would have been congenial and clever."

"He is his own worst enemy," said William, and I could not disagree. If Mr. Babbage was ever going to complete either of his engines, he would require a great deal of help from steadfast friends capable of advancing his interests far better than he himself could.

Soon thereafter, we withdrew to Ockham Park for the Christmas holidays, so I was spared an uncomfortable encounter with Mr. Babbage. I did write him a sympathetic, encouraging letter, and I had William and Hester read it over before I sent it, to make sure that I had not allowed a single note of recrimination to creep in. I was so profoundly disappointed that I frequently had to remind myself that it was not *my* funding that had been cut, not *my* engines that would not be constructed. I was merely a very interested onlooker and friend. Mr. Babbage owed me no apology for what he had done, but as his friend I did owe him my loyalty and support.

Two days after my twenty-seventh birthday, a letter came from Charles Wheatstone wishing me felicitations and inquiring if he might call on me at my earliest convenience regarding a matter of utmost scientific interest. I wrote back inviting him to call, and by the time he arrived the following week, I was brimming over with curiosity.

Mr. Wheatstone was a small, quiet man about two years older than William, with a round face, thinning blond hair, and bright blue eyes. He had grown up in Gloucester as the son of a music seller, and most of his early experiments and inventions had involved musical instruments. He had been the first to recognize that sound traveled as invisible waves. He was quite reserved in public, but an eager and attentive conversationalist in smaller groups. We had become friends through our mutual love of music, and we could talk happily for hours about the science of sound and the relationship between music and mathematics.

"Have you seen our friend Mr. Babbage recently?" I asked after William and I had shown him his bedchamber and we had settled in the library to await supper.

"Not since that afternoon in Westminster," Mr. Wheatstone replied. "However, the matter that prompted my request to visit you does concern him."

Somehow I had known it would. "I'm

happy to help him however I can."

"Do you know Richard Taylor's *Scientific Memoirs*?" he asked. "It's a rather new publication, dedicated to printing translations of the most significant scientific papers published in foreign journals."

"Yes, I've read it, on occasion."

"Mr. Taylor has engaged me to solicit pieces for his journal," he said. "Menabrea's treatise on Mr. Babbage's Analytical Engine is exactly the sort of work he wants to publish. Knowing that you are not only perfectly fluent in French, but also that you're second only to Mr. Babbage in understanding the Analytical Engine, I concluded that you are the most qualified person to translate it into English."

"My goodness," I said, a bit breathless.

"Lady Lovelace, if you accept, you would have my gratitude, as well as Mr. Taylor's, but you would also be providing a great service to Mr. Babbage," he said earnestly. "Many of our countrymen who might support funding his work if they understood it cannot read Menabrea's excellent treatise. If a version in English is provided to them, it could influence a great many people in his favor."

"Of course I'll do it," I declared. How could I possibly decline, when I had been longing for an opportunity such as this for so long? "I'm flattered that you thought of me."

"Yours was the first and only name I considered."

"A testament to your keen insight as an editor," I teased. "Give me all the particulars, when you need the manuscript and so on, and I'll commence work immediately." I glanced at William, who gratified me with a proud smile. "Or perhaps I shall wait until after supper."

I waited a trifle longer than that, but as soon as Mr. Wheatstone departed, I set myself to the task. Although Signor Menabrea's prose was usually clear and eloquent, I did not want to simply provide a flat, word-for-word translation, but rather to capture the poetry of Signor Menabrea's explanations, and to add clarity where he had left obscurity. I certainly do not mean to slight the original author, but Mr. Wheatstone was quite correct to say that only Mr. Babbage knew more about the Analytical Engine than I, and there were certain technical details that consequently I understood better than did Signor Menabrea.

I set my work aside somewhat reluctantly for the Christmas holidays, and, of course, my usual duties as wife, mother, and countess prevented me from working as steadily as I might have wished, but by February I had composed a faithful, poetic, and polished translation of Menabrea's treatise. I was quite proud of the result, and when I traveled to London to deliver the manuscript to Mr.

Wheatstone, I encouraged him to let me know if he ever again required my services.

It was a bittersweet moment when I departed the offices — my task complete, my arms empty, my heart full. I could not wait for the translation to be published, and I dared to think that someday I might look back upon this moment as the beginning of a true mathematical career. I would be an author, I realized, and I could not suppress a smile at the thought. I wondered if my father had felt this same glow of expectation when he learned that his first poem would be published.

I stayed overnight at Saint James's Square rather than returning immediately to Ockham Park — and what a blissful night it was, my first taste of peace and quiet and blessed solitude in years. The following afternoon I called on Mr. Babbage, after sending a servant to inquire if he would be receiving visitors. He had been ill, I had heard, but inconveniently rather than seriously, and so he had not hosted an evening soirée or gone out in Society for weeks. He had no idea that I had been working on the translation for Taylor's *Scientific Memoirs,* and I was looking forward to surprising him with the news, and with a copy of Signor Menabrea's treatise in English, written in my finest hand.

I found Mr. Babbage hoarse and a bit pale, but cheerful and very pleased to see me. He offered me tea in his drawing room, and we caught up on all the news since the previous autumn. Neither of us mentioned his unfortunate meeting with Sir Robert Peel.

"I have a surprise for you," I told him, smiling as I handed him the paper-wrapped parcel I had brought along, and which until then he had politely pretended not to notice. "I have been a busy little mathematical fairy all winter, or perhaps I should say *une petite fée très occupée,* flitting about and making magic with my pen."

"What is this?" he said, removing the manuscript from its wrappings. As he leafed through the pages, a smile of wonder and delight slowly lit up his face. "Why, Lady Lovelace, this is astonishing. But I must ask, did you write this up for me alone? It appears ready for publication."

"It is not for you alone. It is for anyone wise enough to purchase the issue of *Taylor's Scientific Memoirs* in which it shall appear." I explained to him about Mr. Wheatstone's assignment, modestly adding that I had been his first choice as translator.

"Of course you would be. Who better than yourself?" Then his brow furrowed in puzzlement. "But, Lady Lovelace, rather than translating Menabrea's piece, why did you not instead write an original paper, since this is a subject with which you are so intimately acquainted?"

"Because —" I hesitated. "Because that is not what Mr. Wheatstone requested, and I confess the idea never occurred to me."

"I see." Mr. Babbage frowned, thoughtful. "Then perhaps you might consider adding some notes of your own to the work."

"What sort of notes?"

"Your own observations, of course. Notes illuminating aspects of the Analytical Engine that Menabrea left obscure, as well as those details that have been supplanted by the alterations I've made to the design in the meantime." He regarded me expectantly. "I think that would be a most welcome addition to the translation, don't you?"

"I agree," I managed to say, "but don't you think —"

I broke off, embarrassed to give voice to my doubts. Except for Mary Somerville, who was an extraordinary exception, women almost never published papers in respected scientific journals. When women did write on scientific subjects, it was to make the discoveries and ideas of men of science understandable to ladies with an interest in science, but no expertise. Mr. Babbage was suggesting something entirely different — an original scientific paper written for an audience of scientific men.

It was unimaginable — and yet it was precisely the sort of original scientific work I had longed to do since I was a little girl dreaming of Flyology, the Great Work that would advance human understanding and enshrine my name among those of the greatest scientists, philosophers, and mathematicians of my generation.

"Lady Lovelace?" Mr. Babbage prompted.

"I think it's a brilliant notion," I declared, smiling, "and I believe I'm the ideal person to attempt it."

CHAPTER TWENTY-SEVEN:
WHAT IS WRIT, IS WRIT

February–August 1843

My first task was to write to Mr. Wheatstone and inform him of the proposed changes to my manuscript. He and Mr. Taylor readily agreed to wait to publish the translation until I could compose my notes.

My second task was to obtain copies of Mr. Babbage's notes and sketches for the Analytical Engine. I had examined them before, but he had altered the design in the meantime, and I would need to refer to them too often in the weeks ahead to rely upon memory alone. Mr. Babbage promptly supplied everything I requested, thousands of pages of drawings and descriptions. He seemed almost as eager as I was for the project to begin.

My third task was to set aside notes, sketches, plans, papers, and translation so that I could prepare for a very happy event — Hester's marriage to Sir George Craufurd. I will not claim credit for persuading William to give the match his blessing, although I had staunchly taken George's part whenever the question arose. Instead I think that George, by conducting himself with honor and integrity every day, convinced William that he would be a devoted, faithful, loving husband to Hester. A brother would have to have a heart of stone to forbid a marriage that seemed so certain to bring love, joy, and comfort to a cherished sister, and although William and I were not as close as we once had been, I knew better than anyone that he had a loving heart.

They were wed at Ockham Park on 15 February, a sunny, clear, and frigid day, but the bride was so radiant, the groom so jovial, and the company so merry that we scarcely noticed the cold. We kept warm with dancing, and by drinking spiced cider and mulled wine, and I confess I shed tears of joy when Byron, Annabella, and Ralph, adorably splendid in their wedding finery, kissed their auntie Hester good-bye just before her new husband assisted her into a gleaming black carriage and they set off for their honeymoon through a gentle fall of snow.

As soon as the wedding festivities concluded, I commenced work on my notes in earnest. From the moment I took up my pen, I knew that two challenges in particular confronted me: how to explain clearly the purpose and function of a machine as complex as the Analytical Engine, which frankly was rather difficult for even the most brilliant scientific minds to understand; and how to convince my readers that it mattered, that it was an even more important technological development than the railroad or the Jacquard loom.

I soon realized that I could not accomplish this by simply presenting facts and figures, straightforward and linear, because facts alone could never adequately explain something that had never before been imagined. To convey what a true marvel the Analytical Engine was, I would have to delve into the metaphysical — dare I say the poetical.

And so I threw myself into the work, beginning with what I considered the most essential and most difficult aspects to explain: how the Analytical Engine differed from the Difference Engine (as well as the simpler calculating machine Pascal had created years before), how the Analytical Engine functioned, and what it was capable of doing. It was capable not only of tabulating the results of one particular function, I emphasized, but of developing and tabulating any function whatsoever. In fact, this ingenious machine could act upon any information that could be represented symbolically, not only numbers. "Supposing that the fundamental relations of pitched sounds in the science of harmony and of musical composition were susceptible of such expression and adaptations," I wrote, drawing upon one of my favorite subjects, music, to illustrate this point. "The engine might compose elaborate and scientific pieces of music of any degree of complexity or extent."

I described the Analytical Engine in great detail, aiming for clarity and simplicity but also completeness, especially in a long section in which I explained how useful it would be, how it would offer untold practical benefits. My pragmatic readers might agree that the Analytical Engine was a marvel of technology, but they would remain reluctant to pay for it if they thought it was no more than an object of curiosity. They would never support funding a project that would turn out to be no more than a very expensive and far less charming Silver Lady.

Well aware of how strange and unfamiliar the Analytical Engine would seem to readers who had never seen it, who had not spent years observing it and contemplating it as I had, I endeavored to compare the unknown to the familiar:

The distinctive characteristic of the Analytical Engine, and that which has rendered it possible to endow mechanism with such extensive faculties as bid fair to make this engine the executive right-hand of abstract algebra, is the introduction into it of the principle which Jacquard devised for regulating, by means of punched cards, the most complicated patterns in the fabrication of brocaded stuffs. It is in this that the distinction between the two engines lies. Nothing of the sort exists in the Difference Engine. We may say most aptly that the Analytical Engine weaves algebraical patterns just as the Jacquard-loom weaves flowers and leaves.

There was much more to say on this opening subject, of course, and I said it. As I wrote, I found myself understanding the Analytical Engine even better than I had before, discovering new facets that had eluded my imagination until then. I realized that it could provide two types of results, numerical and symbolic, and thus would be capable of generating not only numbers, but entirely new operations. Wonder and excitement fueled my writing, and when at last the draft was complete to my satisfaction, I titled this portion "Note A," sent it off to Mr. Babbage for review, and commenced with bolstered confidence and undiminished enthusiasm my work upon Note B.

The next day, the second of July, Mr. Babbage sent me a most gratifying reply. "If you are as fastidious about the acts of your friendship as you are about those of your pen, I much fear I shall equally lose your friendship and your Notes," he wrote, a comic lamentation. "I am very reluctant to return your admirable and philosophic Note A. Pray do not alter it. All this was impossible for you to know by intuition and the more I read your notes the more surprised I am at them and regret not having earlier explored so rich a vein of the noblest metal."

Warmed by his praise, and relieved to know that I was proceeding as I should, I toiled away diligently and contentedly, likening myself to a mathematical fairy weaving magic with numbers and words. Throughout July the work offered me respite and distraction from unpleasant developments elsewhere in my life, the bane of persistent illness and the worrisome news from France, where Medora continued to plague and harass us through the post. All this — or most of it, anyway — I was able to put aside as I worked through Notes B, C, D, E, and F, which described in minute detail the mechanical functions and processes of the Analytical Engine.

By that time it had become apparent that my Notes were going to be much longer than the translation of Signor Menabrea's original treatise, perhaps more than twice as long. "Never mind that," Mr. Babbage urged me in a brief letter. "You have not included a single extraneous phrase yet, in my opinion. Use precisely as many words as you need to do justice to your subject, no less and no more."

Heartened, I wrote "Note G" at the top of a fresh sheet of paper and carried on.

In this Note, which I presumed would be the last, I wanted to offer several practical examples of how the Analytical Engine had transcended the bounds of arithmetic the moment punched cards were introduced to the design. Because of that feature, not only the mental and the material, but also the theoretical and the practical in mathematics could be brought into more intimate and effective connection than had ever been possible with any previous machine.

If my readers could understand this, they could not doubt that the Analytical Engine was too important, too revolutionary, to let it remain merely a brilliant but unrealized idea, merely ink on a page.

Of the examples I included, I was most satisfied with my explanation of how the Analytical Engine would generate Bernoulli numbers, an endless sequence of rational numbers that figure significantly in certain functions and formulae. I decided to create an algorithm that the Analytical Engine could employ to generate these numbers easily, quickly, and flawlessly as they tumbled off in an irregular fashion to infinity. This, I knew, would impress my scientific readers more than any other example, due to the complexity of the sequence of operations that must be performed. No other calculating machine in existence could accomplish this feat without human intervention throughout the process. This example would prove that the Analytical Engine was superior and unique.

Naturally, composing this algorithm was easier said than done. "I am doggedly attacking and sifting to the very bottom all the ways of deducing the Bernoulli numbers," I wrote to Babbage one afternoon. "In the manner that I am grappling with this subject, and connecting it with others, I shall be some days upon it." Then, reflecting upon how adept I had become at this subject I had studied so long, I quipped, "It is perhaps well for the world that my line and ambition is the mathematical, and that I have not taken it into my head, or lived in time and circumstances calculated to put it into my head, to deal with the sword, poison, and intrigue, in the place of x, y, or z."

As I struggled with this complex and elusive algorithm, I confess there were moments when I doubted I would succeed. "I am in much dismay at having got into so amazing a quagmire and botheration with these numbers," I lamented, setting the whole mess aside for a moment to vent my frustration in another letter to Mr. Babbage. But I did not despair, and eventually I was able to neatly resolve the last remaining puzzles.

How exhilarated I felt when the algorithm was complete! I was so thrilled with the accomplishment that I could almost forget my exhaustion, and yet, as I read over Note G, I realized that I must add a caveat or two, lest I raise expectations that the Analytical Engine in all its magnificence could not fulfill. Although I had promised nothing I was not absolutely certain the machine could do, I knew the more skeptical readers in my audience would assume I exaggerated its capabilities unless I also devoted a few lines to what it could *not* do.

And so I returned to the beginning of Note G and added a word of caution. "It is desirable to guard against the possibility of exaggerated ideas that might arise as to the powers of the Analytical Engine," I noted. "In considering any new subject, there is frequently a tendency, first, to *overrate* what we find to be already interesting or remarkable; and, secondly, by a sort of natural reaction, to *undervalue* the true state of the case, when we do discover that our notions have surpassed those that were really tenable."

I could think of no more polite and cordial way to plead with my readers to keep an open mind. Then I remembered my mother's reaction when she had observed the demonstration model of the Difference Engine, how she had referred to it as a "thinking machine." It would be disingenuous of me, in my enthusiasm, to lead anyone to believe that the Analytical Engine could "think" any more than its predecessor could. And so another caveat: "The Analytical Engine has no pretensions whatever to *originate* any thing," I emphasized. "It can do whatever we *know how to order it* to perform. It can follow analysis; but it has no power of anticipating any analytical relations or truths."

With that Note G was complete.

But of course, I was far from finished. Throughout the spring and summer I had sent Mr. Babbage my work in progress, received his comments, and revised my Notes accordingly. Our exchange was humorous, delightful, illuminating, and occasionally infuriating. Sometimes he sent me praise and useful comments, and we bantered teasingly back and forth about how I was like a fairy using my magic in his service. Then, on other occasions, I confess I sent him snappish, indignant letters complaining about changes he had made to my writing. "I am much annoyed at your having altered my Note," I wrote in mid-July. "You know I am always willing to make any required alterations myself, but that I cannot endure another person to meddle with my sentences."

Then, less than a week later, I became furious with him after he confessed that he had somehow misplaced several important pages of the manuscript, obliging me to redo work that had been tedious and difficult to create in the first place. "I have always fancied that you were a little harum-scarum and inaccurate now and then about the exact order and arrangement of sheets, pages, and paragraphs, et cetera," I huffed, thoroughly exasperated. "Witness that paragraph which you so carelessly pasted over! I suppose that I must set to work to write something *better,* if I can, as a substitute. The same precisely I could not recall. I think I should be able in a couple of days to do something. However I should be deucedly inclined to *swear at you,* I will allow."

I did not swear at him, though, and he replied with such abashed apologies that I quickly forgave him. It would have been my own undoing not to, for our collaboration was proceeding so well — aside from the aforementioned incidents and a few others involving his careless substitution of a previous version of a table for one that had been properly revised — that I cannot think how I would have fared without him.

The more I worked upon my Notes, the prouder I became. I began to refer to them as my firstborn mathematical child and expressed hopes that other younger siblings might follow it. "I cannot refrain from expressing my amazement at my own child," I wrote to Mr. Babbage as my revised Notes were going into proofs. "The pithy and vigorous nature of the style seems to me to be most striking; and there is at times a half-satirical and humorous dryness, which would I suspect make me a most formidable reviewer. I am quite thunderstruck at the *power* of the writing. It is especially unlike a woman's style surely; but neither can I compare it with any man's exactly."

I was particularly sensitive to the question of whether the author's voice — my voice — would be perceived as masculine or feminine, because I knew this would influence how the information and analysis I offered would be measured. While I bristled at the unfairness of it all, I was reluctant to reveal that the author of the Notes was a woman, because that might diminish the value of the work in the minds of more prejudiced readers.

"Although I don't wish to proclaim who has written it, I have to sign it somehow," I worried aloud to William one sultry, humid evening as we walked together through the woods around Ockham Park, seeking relief from the oppressive heat as the sun declined to the horizon. "It's necessary, if only to distinguish my work from Menabrea's. Then, too, I wish to individualize my work, so that anything else I may produce in the years to come can be identified as work of the author of the Notes."

William smiled. "You're not so proud of your work that the thought of 'Translated with Notes by Ada Byron King, Countess of Lovelace,' appearing on the title page holds no appeal for you?"

"Perhaps a bit," I confessed, "but then — don't you see? — suddenly attention would be riveted by the fact that this work was produced by Lord Byron's daughter. People will regard it as a curiosity, as they have always regarded me. I want my work to be judged on its own merits, and I want nothing to distract from the significance of the Analytical Engine. If that were to happen, all my toil would be for nothing."

"To think that all this time, I've believed that you sought fame," he teased.

"Fame for my work, perhaps," I conceded. "As long as my work is respected, I don't care if any but my closest friends and family are aware that I'm the author of it. I think I prefer a more anonymous sort of fame, if that isn't an oxymoron."

"Anonymous fame," William mused. "Sounds much better than the usual sort. Why don't you use your initials, then? A.A.L., for Augusta Ada Lovelace."

I mulled it over, imagining how it would appear on the printed page. "Yes. Yes, I think that would be the very thing."

With that fraught issue resolved, I began to look forward with increasing excitement and anticipation to the publication of the translation and Notes, which collectively had come to be called the Memoir, in the fashion of the time. This could indeed be my magnum opus,

I thought, or better yet, the first of many Great Works of mathematics and science, the one that launched me into a career as impressive and enduring as Mary Somerville's. She was a far more brilliant mathematician than I would ever be, but that did not mean I could not shine just as brightly in my own sky.

In writing the Memoir, I had discovered something astonishing about myself — that my genius resided in my ability to synthesize abstract ideas, to marry the intellect and the imagination into a new kind of insight. That was why I understood the capabilities of the Analytical Engine even better than its inventor did. That was why I had never been able to repudiate my father, despite the ominous warnings about the bad Byron blood that had been drummed into my consciousness since childhood. All my life I had been told that I must choose between my mother or my father, the intellect or the imagination. Now I knew that I was nothing without both.

Despite searing headaches and debilitating ailments of the stomach, through fatigue and pain, I labored over the final proofs with zealous joy, mindful of my swiftly approaching completion date. Mr. Taylor and his co-editor, William Francis, were eager to publish the Memoir, its featured article, in time for the next meeting of the British Association for the Advancement of Science in September. Convinced that I would find no more opportune moment to bring my first scientific child into the world, I was determined to have it ready.

My proofreading was more than halfway complete when my work was interrupted by an urgent request from Mr. Babbage. He had written a stern, forthright, third-person account of his grievances with the government, establishing point by point his criticism of the manner in which various officials and departments had handled the development and funding of his engines. "Please review this statement and return to me with comments, if you have any, with all speed," he requested in an accompanying note, his curtness emphasizing his great haste.

I regretted taking time away from the proofs, but Mr. Babbage had always put my requests for reviews before all other obligations, and I felt that I must respond in kind. Fortunately, the document was not particularly long or complex, although the strident tone occasionally made me wince, a fact I noted in the margins. I returned the statement to him that same afternoon, along with a note recommending caution and wishing him well.

Mr. Babbage's request cost me very little time, and soon thereafter, I finished proofreading the Memoir and arranged for it to be safely delivered to the offices of *Taylor's Scientific Memoirs.* A strange melancholy settled upon me then, for I felt both exultant and bereft. I looked forward to the forthcoming publication, of course, and after that, I expected the ensuing accolades to lead to more assignments for A.A.L., but until then, the empty hours stretched ahead of me, waiting to be filled.

My first priority was my patient family, whom I had neglected in my preoccupation with the Memoir. I visited my mother at Fordhook for a few days, and then William and I took the children to Ashley Combe, a journey that had become delightfully swift and easy since the Great Western Railway had opened a branch line to Bridgwater in 1841. The blessed peace and solitude of our Somerset estate was a welcome remedy for my exhaustion and strain, and after I had enjoyed a good rest, I joined my husband and children in romps through the gardens, long walks along the seashore, and exhilarating horseback rides through the forest.

In the first week of August, we returned home to Ockham Park refreshed and happy, but my contentment was spoiled soon after we crossed the threshold. A letter from Mr. Babbage awaited me, and in the first of many angry, indignant lines, he inexplicably urged me to withdraw the Memoir from *Taylor's Scientific Memoirs.*

Dumbfounded, I read on, but his request made absolutely no sense even after I had read the letter a second time. His outrage had something to do with the diatribe against the government he had asked me to review in July, something about how Mr. Francis had refused to run it unsigned and had the audacity to suggest that it appear as a separate pamphlet. "In consideration of our long-standing friendship," Mr. Babbage thundered, "I trust you will respond to this insult by informing the Editors that you forbid them to publish the Memoir."

Aghast, I stared at the letter in disbelief. How could he even think of canceling the Memoir when it might finally win him the financial support he desperately needed? How could he ask me to withdraw my Great Work from publication after I had toiled over it for so long and when I had such high hopes for how it might establish me as a mathematician? I felt as if I had been thrown into the midst of a fierce argument and had been forced to choose a side before I could even discover the cause of their discord.

Strangely, there was no letter from the journal offices, and so, my heart thudding with apprehension, I wrote to Mr. Wheatstone, Mr. Taylor, and Mr. Francis. I assured them that I had no intention of pulling the Memoir but that I must know what on earth could have prompted Mr. Babbage to make such an astonishing demand.

They replied immediately, because time was

of the essence, and the story they told was as bewildering and outrageous as it was unexpected. Unbeknownst to me, Mr. Babbage had submitted his statement to the editors with instructions to publish it as a preface to my translation and notes. Mr. Francis had been reluctant to comply, since the statement was unsigned, and would therefore suggest that I was its author. Mr. Taylor should have ruled on the matter, but he was abroad, so Mr. Babbage had sent Charles Lyell as his representative to negotiate with Mr. Francis and Mr. Wheatstone. They offered several options, all of which advised publishing the statement separately from my Memoir and making it clear that I had not written it. Mr. Wheatstone even generously offered to sign the statement if Mr. Babbage would not put his name to it. All of these options Mr. Babbage refused.

Shocked and furious, I insisted that they must not publish Mr. Babbage's statement with my Memoir, and that under no circumstances should his diatribe be attributed to me. "I cannot believe him," I told William, who seemed angry and indignant but not surprised. "Why would he do this to me? Why would he do this to himself? Is his hatred for Sir Robert Peel truly that much greater than his desire to see the Analytical Engine built?"

"His stubbornness and pride have always been his undoing," said William. "You are absolutely right to stand up to him."

My feelings of betrayal and outrage so overwhelmed me that I took a day to reflect and compose myself before writing to Mr. Babbage. Even then, I could not contain my anger. "No power should induce me to lend myself to any of your quarrels, or to become in any way the medium through which you express them," I declared. "I shall myself communicate directly with the editors on the subject, as I do not choose to commit a dishonorable breach of engagement, even to promote your advantage, and in this case, it would be neither for your advantage nor my own to withdraw the Memoir from publication." I told him that I intended to write to him again, very strongly and very soon, regarding "some points in which I consider you mistake your own interests," but that I would not do so until it was clear how the matter would ultimately be resolved. "Be assured that I am your best friend," I wrote, impassioned, "but that I never can or will support you in acting on principles which I conceive to be not only wrong in themselves, but suicidal."

Mr. Babbage's reply was immediately forthcoming. He was furious, and he accused me of betraying him, and he condemned me in the harshest of terms. I was quite certain that he would never forgive me, and my heart ached with sorrow and regret.

The next day I wrote to my mother to apologize for not writing since we had returned from Ashley Combe, blaming the recent unpleasantness for my neglect. "I have been harassed and pressed in a most perplexing manner by Mr. Babbage's conduct," I wrote, still stinging from his angry rebuke. "We are, in fact, *at issue*. I am sorry to have to come to the conclusion that he is one of the most impracticable, selfish, and intemperate persons I have ever met. I do not anticipate an absolute alienation between us, but there must ever be a degree of coolness and reserve, I believe, in the future."

A week went by, and with each passing day my regret grew that Mr. Babbage and I should part company on such angry terms after all we had accomplished together. I believed in his genius, and I believed that his engines would accomplish everything he had promised and then some, but he seemed perpetually determined to sabotage himself just as he approached his goal.

He was too proud, I knew, to approach me with apologies. If we were to reconcile, I would have to petition him. It was unfair and ridiculous that I should be obliged to do so; he had wronged me, not the other way around, and although I *wanted* his friendship, he *needed* mine. My translation and notes would be published regardless of his objections, and so whatever advancement to my career was destined to result from it, that would be mine regardless of whether Mr. Babbage and I were estranged. But for his part, it seemed very clear to me that unless a caring friend intervened, he would continue to churn furiously in place without progressing forward, like a cart stuck in deep mud.

I had invested too much time and passion in Mr. Babbage's engines to simply throw my hands in the air, stride away, and leave him to grow old and bitter among his unrealized dreams. I wanted to see the Analytical Engine built for his sake, and for Britain's, and yes, for my own. But above all, I cherished his friendship too dearly not to try to salvage it.

On Monday, the fourteenth of August, I composed what turned out to be a sincere, impassioned, sixteen-page letter in which I broached the possibility of mending our ties, while also clearly and firmly establishing the terms according to which I would agree to work with him in the future.

I began cordially by informing him about the progress of the Notes through the publication process, how the difficult work with the printers was happily concluded, and how I was well satisfied with the Memoir. I then turned to his last letter, the one that had wounded me so deeply. "Your note is such as demands a very full reply from me," I said carefully, "the writer being so old and so esteemed a friend, and one whose genius I not only so highly appreciate myself, but wish to see fairly appreciated by others." Still, I could not continue without saying that the less notice I took of that letter, the better, "as it was only worthy to be thrown aside with a smile of contempt."

I told him that I understood that I had disappointed him by not withdrawing the Memoir from publication, and that he remained deeply hurt. I explained why my sense of duty, honor, and obligation — not only to him, but also to the editors — would not have permitted me to do otherwise. I hoped in time he would understand.

"I must now come to a practical question respecting the future," I told him. "Your affairs have been, and are, deeply occupying both myself and Lord Lovelace. Our thoughts as well as our conversation have been earnest upon them. And the result is that I have plans for you, which I shall either develop, or else throw my energies, my time, and my pen into the service of some other department of truth and science, according to your reply. I give to you the first choice and offer of my services and my intellect. I do beseech you therefore, deeply and seriously, to ponder the question of whether you can subscribe to my conditions."

Having forewarned him, I presented my ultimatum: First, if I were to continue working with him, he must leave all practical matters to me, especially when it came to relations with other people. I did not mention Sir Robert Peel by name, but he was foremost in my thoughts.

Second, when I required Mr. Babbage's intellectual assistance and supervision, he must focus his whole and undivided attention upon the matter at hand, and he must be more attentive, organized, and careful in our future collaborations than he had been during the writing of the Notes.

Third, he would place me in charge of managing the business enterprise of the Analytical Engine, in which capacity I would develop plans for funding and constructing it, subject to the approval of a board of friends and colleagues of his own choosing.

Each of these conditions I elaborated upon in great detail, but my tone was unfailingly earnest, never pedantic or demanding, or so I thought. I brought the letter to a close fondly, with a few remarks about the Bernoulli numbers and an invitation to visit us at Saint James's Square as well as at Ockham Park, where we planned to be later that month. I hoped to show him how easily we could resume our friendship, as easily as picking up the threads of an interrupted conversation.

And yet at the very end, I turned wistful. "I wonder," I wrote, "if you will choose to retain the lady-fairy in your service or not."

It was now for Mr. Babbage to decide.

Chapter Twenty-Eight:
Go, Little Book,
from This My Solitude

August–September 1843

The next morning I woke with an ache in my heart and the heavy weight of melancholy on my shoulders, but I needed a moment to remember the cause. It pained me to think that I might no longer be welcome at 1 Dorset Street, and that I would play no part in bringing Mr. Babbage's plans for the Analytical Engine to fruition. Even more dispiriting was the worry that without my help, neither of his engines would ever be constructed.

My only hope was that his desire to prove to the world that his Analytical Engine was everything he had always promised would overcome his pride, and he would agree to reconcile.

I went about my usual morning routine subdued and anxious, reminding myself that I should not expect a reply so soon. Finally I could bear the silence no longer, and I decided that if he would not write to me, at least I could still write to him. I took pen in hand and composed a short note about certain revisions I had made to the proofs after our disagreement. "You will have had my long letter this morning," I concluded. "Perhaps you will not choose to have anything more to do with me. But I hope for the best, and so I simply write to you as if nothing had passed."

I sent the letter off, and paced around the garden disconsolately, and returned to my study to write to my mother. "I am uncertain as yet how the Babbage business will end," I told her. "He has written unkindly to me. For many reasons, however, I still desire to work upon his subjects and affairs if I can do so with any reasonable prospect of peace. I have written to him therefore, very explicitly; stating my own conditions, without which I positively refuse to take any further part in conjunction with him, upon any subject whatever."

I paused there, struck by sudden misgivings. Perhaps I had presented my ultimatum too forcefully. Perhaps I should have sought reconciliation first, and then, when we were friends again, told him, face-to-face and as cheerfully as possible, how I expected our future collaborations to be conducted. But it was too late now to change a single word.

"If he does consent to what I propose," I continued my letter, "I shall probably be enabled to keep him out of much hot water;

and to bring his engine to consummation. All I have seen of him and his habits the last three months, makes me scarcely anticipate it ever will be, unless someone really exercises a strong coercive influence over him."

I wanted that someone to be myself, but that was entirely up to him. How helpless and distressed I felt knowing that my future as a scientist and mathematician depended entirely upon the decisions of someone other than myself!

By late morning the post had been delivered, but I was deeply grieved to find no letter from Mr. Babbage. By the early afternoon I had quite worn myself out from pacing and worry, and I had almost decided to write to Mr. Babbage again, when the maid announced that the cause of all my consternation was awaiting me in the drawing room.

My heart leapt, and swiftly I descended the stairs and met him. "Good afternoon, Mr. Babbage," I greeted him, smiling, although my hopes dimmed slightly at the sight of his furrowed brow. "How pleasant it is to see you."

I invited him to sit, and requested tea, and for a few minutes we chatted a bit guardedly about our children and mutual friends. Mr. Babbage was the first to broach the contentious subject that had divided us. "I understand your reasons for refusing to withdraw the Memoir, and I respect them," he said, "although I confess I do not agree."

"I respect your disagreement," I said, managing a smile.

"As to your conditions for our continued collaboration —" He shook his head and frowned, and my heart plummeted. "I cannot possibly agree to them. You are my interpreter, Lady Lovelace, not my master. The Analytical Engine is my masterpiece, my magnum opus. I could not possibly place it entirely under your control — or anyone else's, for that matter."

My heart thudded, and for a moment I could scarcely breathe. "I understand," I said, my voice quiet but steady.

"If you would, however, consider withdrawing your conditions . . ." His voice trailed off, and he raised his eyebrows in a question.

For the briefest of moments, I was tempted. Then I remembered the great many times Mr. Babbage had compromised his own best interests at the very moment they seemed poised on the verge of fulfillment. How could I plunge back into that morass of aggravation, bewilderment, and frustration? I could not bear to devote years of my life to work that he seemed perversely determined to ruin, again and again and again.

"I regret with my whole heart that I cannot," I told him.

He tried to smile, but grimaced instead. "I understand. I had expected as much." He inhaled deeply and gazed off to his right, drumming his fingers on the arm of his chair. "Well. So be it. I do hope, however, that we shall remain friends."

"I should be devastated if we did not," I replied, impassioned.

After that, there was nothing more to say. Mr. Babbage rose, thanked me for receiving him, and departed, leaving me to wonder sadly when we would meet again.

Thankfully, he did not oblige me to wait and worry long. In the first week of September, he sent me a cheerful note accepting my invitation to visit us at Ashley Combe, an invitation I had assumed he had long since disregarded. Eagerly I replied, and a few notes flew back and forth between us as we tried to fix a date, a task that Mr. Babbage's busy schedule and numerous obligations made very difficult.

Eventually Mr. Babbage determined that if he waited until he was free, he would never visit at all. "My Dear Lady Lovelace," he wrote on 9 September, "I find it quite in vain to wait until I have leisure, so I have resolved that I will leave all other things undone and set out for Ashley, taking with me papers enough to enable me to forget this world and all its troubles and if possible its multitudinous Charlatans — everything, in short, but the Enchantress of Numbers."

Enchantress of Numbers, I thought,

warmed by the endearment. If he could think of me as such, perhaps there was hope for our future collaboration after all.

Soon thereafter, in mid-September, my translation and notes were published in *Taylor's Scientific Memoirs* under the title "Sketch of the Analytical Engine Invented by Charles Babbage, Esq." Even now I am gratified to recall how warmly my Memoir was initially received by the mathematic and scientific community. My friends were impressed with my work and showered me in congratulations and praise. Mr. De Morgan wrote to declare it very fine work and to express his great pride in my accomplishment. From Italy, Mary Somerville sent an even more wonderful letter of congratulations, praising me so warmly that tears came to my eyes, and assuring me that she had no doubt this was only the first triumph of what was sure to be a long and illustrious career. My mother sent me a lovely letter of congratulations along with a basket of beautiful flowers and vegetables from the Fordhook gardens. William was exceedingly proud of me, and even the children understood, in their fashion, that their mother had done something extraordinary.

I was thrilled and grateful, but my joy was tarnished by my diminished hopes that the Analytical Engine, which I had introduced to the world with such poetic insight and scientific understanding, would ever be constructed.

Within a few weeks, Mr. Babbage's critique of the government was published anonymously in the *Philosophical Magazine,* another journal edited by Mr. Taylor and Mr. Francis. It attracted almost no notice whatsoever.

I had sent my first scientific child out into the world, and nothing remained but to see how it would flourish. "This engagement has been in some respects arduous and troublesome," I had written modestly to Robert Noel in early August, "and it will probably bring me in but little return of reputation or fame (which were indeed no part of my motive when I undertook it): for there is more of a quiet patient labour and industry in it, than of brilliancy or attractiveness. I have plenty of imagination and eloquence for when the right time shall come. Meanwhile I wish to build upon strong foundations of logic, industry, and real study and training. But I am glad to have got launched, in however humble and dry a form."

It should come as no surprise that despite the modest expectations I expressed in that letter, I fervently hoped that great things would swiftly follow the publication of my Great Work. William knew this, as did my mother, Mary Somerville, Hester, and Woronzow. We all waited, brimming over with anticipation for the public acclaim and accolades that would set me upon the mathematical and scientific career that had been my heart's desire for so many years.

I waited, and hoped, to no avail.

Although my work had met with interest and approval in the immediate aftermath of its publication, curiosity quickly arose regarding the identity of its author, and before long it came out that A.A.L. was in fact Ada Byron King, Countess of Lovelace. As soon as it became well-known that the Memoir had been written by a woman, its perceived value as a scientific work precipitously declined. If a woman had written it, these men of science concluded, it could not be as important as they had first believed. The reasoning could not be as sound if it had come from a female mind, the subject not as significant if it had been entrusted to feminine hands.

The acclaim, modest to begin with, quickly faded to a whisper, and then fell silent.

CHAPTER TWENTY-NINE: WHAT DEEP WOUNDS EVER CLOSED WITHOUT A SCAR?

1844–1850

The years passed as all years do, in happiness and heartbreak, sunlight and shadow.

Mr. Babbage and I remained friends — very good friends — but he never completely forgave me for siding with the publishers against him, as he saw it. Even after I humbled myself and went before him, offering to be simply the high priestess of his Analytical Engine, and to serve my apprenticeship faithfully before I fancied myself worthy to venture a step higher, he kept me at a distance. Eventually there came a time when I knew no more about his plans for his engines than any other acquaintance who attended his soirées. Considering that I remained only second to himself in understanding the Analytical Engine, and in some respects I knew it better, the pain this exclusion caused me was so acute it was almost as if I were mourning a death.

I believe this profound sense of loss contributed to a sudden, precipitous decline in my health. I was unwell even before Mr. Babbage broke with me, the exhaustion and strain of writing having weakened me over the summer, but suddenly I became afflicted with frightening seizures, difficulty breathing, and strange sensations about the eyes and head. Dr. Locock prescribed exercise and laudanum, until I was taking at least a few drops every day. His treatments brought me some respite from my sufferings, although they never cured whatever ailment it was that caused them. My mother mistrusted laudanum and urged me to try bleedings and a rest cure at Brighton instead, but laudanum offered me euphoria, while leeches and cuppings merely exhausted me.

Mercifully, I was bedridden for only a short time, but my convalescence under Dr. Locock's care stretched on for years. In this time, having concluded that there was nothing left to improve at Ockham Park, William moved our family to East Horsley Park, a lovely two-story residence about four miles to the south. It was designed by Sir Charles Barry, the renowned architect who had built the new Palace of Westminster, but William was determined to improve upon his work. We had scarcely settled in when William resolved that we should have a new residence in London as well, so we moved from Saint James's Square to a temporary residence at

Grosvenor Place, and then to another at Great Cumberland Street, until Mr. Babbage helped us find a suitable residence at 6 Great Cumberland Place, several blocks from Marble Arch and Hyde Park. Fortunately, William thought Ashley Combe had not yet reached perfection, or he might have decided to part with that beloved estate too. I doubt very much that he could ever be content to reside anywhere that was not constantly under construction.

The relentless packing and unpacking and shifting about afforded me little time for work or study, so my mother offered to take responsibility for the children's education so that I could devote myself to a profession. At first I demurred, not only because I would miss my children, for all their naughtiness, but also because I could not settle on any particular vocation. The interest I felt in one subject or another was a faint glimmer compared to the bright fiery sun of the Analytical Engine, and so I flitted from one branch of mathematics or science to another, like a hapless, distractible fairy. My mother pointed out that if I did not have to worry about the children, I would be better able to discern what profession most appealed to me, and so with William's blessing, I finally consented. Ralph was young enough to remain at home with a governess, but Anna-bella was sent to my mother at Esher, and

Byron was entrusted to the care of Dr. and Mrs. King in Brighton. Annabella did not want to live with her grandmother and she passionately disliked her new governess, but eventually she resigned herself to her circumstances. As for Byron, he found Dr. King's perpetual sermonizing annoying to the extreme, and since William felt the same way, he soon entrusted Byron to my mother's cousin Charles Noel, who managed her Leicestershire estates at Peckleton.

With the children sorted, I had no more excuses not to devote myself to a profession, but neither that nor my improving health was what finally compelled me to rediscover my passion for mathematics and science.

I had remained a faithful protégée of Mrs. Somerville even after she and her husband had moved to Italy, and I continued to correspond with her and follow her work with great admiration. By that time, her marvelous book *On the Connexion of the Physical Sciences* had gone through numerous editions, and in each one she included new information and discoveries that had surfaced since the previous version. In the sixth edition, she noted that her tables providing measurements of the motion of the planet Uranus were already "defective," probably because the planet had been discovered too recently for accurate measurements to have been taken. Or, she mused, the apparent discrepancies could be the result of "disturbances from some unseen planet revolving about the sun beyond the present boundaries of our system. If, after a lapse of years, the tables formed from a combination of numerous observations should be still inadequate to represent the motions of Uranus, the discrepancies may reveal the existence, nay, even the mass and orbit, of a body placed forever beyond the sphere of vision."

A few years later, inspired by Mrs. Somerville's remark, the English astronomer John Adams searched the heavens for that hypothetical planet beyond Uranus that could be affecting its orbit — and discovered Neptune.

Mrs. Somerville confided to me that she was grateful that Mr. Adams had proven her hypothesis, but she regretted that the discovery was not her own. "If I had possessed originality or genius, I might have found the new planet myself," she wrote.

I was so astonished that I immediately replied to insist that I knew of no one who possessed more of both qualities than herself, but in her next letter, she firmly yet sadly disagreed. "I am conscious that I have never made a discovery myself, that I have no originality," she wrote. "I have perseverance and intelligence, but no genius." Later, she added that she suspected that this "spark from heaven is not granted to our sex. Whether higher powers may be allotted to us in another existence God knows, but original genius — in science at least — is hopeless in this world."

Those words of defeat and resignation, coming from the woman I admired more than any other, dismayed me beyond measure. If she believed she had no genius, no originality, then what hope was there for the rest of us? What hope was there for me?

I agonized over her conclusion and ultimately formed one of my own: I could not agree with her. She possessed true genius, even if she was too modest to recognize it. She was a woman. Therefore, God did not deny the essential spark of genius to our sex.

I resolved then that with my own work I would prove it.

Mathematics, calculating engines, and music all held their attractions for me, but the one that proved the most irresistible was a new science — no, not Flyology — but something I called a calculus of the nervous system. I was fascinated by the mysterious means by which thoughts emerged from the brain, and sensations from the nerves, and I wondered if this could be expressed in a mathematical model. I hoped, and in fact anticipated, that I could one day understand cerebral phenomena so well that I could put them into mathematical equations, laws for the mutual actions of the molecules of the brain. I saw no reason why mathematicians could not comprehend cerebral matter as easily as they did stellar and planetary matters and movements, if we inspected it from the proper perspective. The question of how to conduct the practical experiments required to get the exact phenomena I wished to examine provided an obstacle, but I happily embraced the challenge.

Even as I delved into this new calculus of the nervous system, another more seductive diversion enticed my attention away from my studies. I had always loved horses, and at certain occasions in my youth I had tasted the excitement of racing, but in these years gambling became an absolute passion with me. At first it was a simple pleasure, and then a guilty one, and then I tried to turn it into a subject for scientific study. If it had been possible to derive a mathematical formula to successfully predict the outcome of the Doncaster races, I would have earned riches beyond my wildest imaginings, but horses are capricious forces of nature, not dice or cards. Eventually my gambling became a dangerous habit, one I tried unsuccessfully to conceal from William and my mother as I backed the wrong horses again and again and tumbled deeper into debt. My pittance of pin money could not even begin to pay off my losses, so I borrowed from my mother, claiming that I needed the funds for books and fine gowns for court. She grew suspicious, but that was not enough to deter me, because although I knew I would not be able to deceive her much longer, I always expected to recoup all of my losses in the next race.

My inevitable confession was deferred by other concerns that plagued my mother in those years. My half sister (or cousin) Medora did not disappear quietly after she collected Marie from the spinster sisters and set sail for France with her daughter, her deed, her French maid, and her maid's husband. Instead, although she had hurled invective at my mother at their last meeting, she continued to write and appeal for money. On one occasion, she brazenly compelled poor little Marie, then nine years old, to write on her behalf, piteously describing how ill and impoverished her mama had become, and how she longed to hear from her former advocate. My mother sent a little money in response to each request, and finally one remarkably generous payment of one thousand francs with the understanding that it would be the very last, but not even that was enough for Medora. She and her entourage continued to live well beyond their means, traipsing from one luxurious hotel to another, one step ahead of their creditors, convincing the hoteliers that her aunt, the wealthy widow of Lord Byron, would cover their expenses. Before long my mother would be obliged to pay the bills and to instruct the hoteliers not to extend any more credit.

Eventually legal action loomed. I was obliged to go to the French embassy to sort out the tangled web of lies and deceptions, and the same lawyers who had negotiated my parents' Separation negotiated a settlement. The unscrupulous French maid and her husband were paid off and sent packing, little Marie was placed in a convent in Saint-Germain to be educated, and Medora, alone, settled into a *pension* in Saint-Germain-en-Laye. Her letters abruptly halted, and it was only much later that we learned what had become of her. Apparently solitude and simplicity had compelled her to change her life, for she took a job working at *la pension,* where she met one of the boarders, a soldier named Jean-Louis Taillefer. When his term of service was complete, they married, she bore him a son, he adopted Marie, and they settled on a farm in southern France.

A year and a day after her marriage, Medora died, some said of cholera, others of smallpox. To the brief will she had written on her deathbed, she had added, "I also declare here that I forgive my mother and all those who have so cruelly persecuted me, as I hope myself to be forgiven."

I could only assume that she included me and my mother in her list of persecutors. Even so, I felt bittersweet relief that she had redeemed herself in the end, and genuine sorrow that she had not lived to enjoy her newfound happiness.

Around that time another death struck our family a far more devastating blow, one that grieved me so much that even now I cannot think of it without pausing to catch my breath and to blink away tears.

My sister-in-law Hester, who had always been so good and kind to me, had moved with her darling husband, Charles, to Italy for his health. There she gave birth to a son, but her time with her baby boy was all too short. She died soon afterward, leaving us bereft and heartbroken. My poor daughter, Annabella, was distraught from grief, for she had particularly adored her aunt Hester.

Hester had been the sister I had always longed for, and I mourned her deeply. In my grief I turned to William, but he was too overcome with his own sorrow to offer me the comfort I needed. I wish that we could have come together in our time of mutual loss, and lessened the burden of our grief by sharing it, but William and I had drifted further apart with each passing year, until we only infrequently spent any time together. It was not deliberate, at least not at first, but with the children scattered, the compelling purpose of family unity no longer required us to live together unless we chose to, and often I preferred one residence for matters of taste or convenience and William was occupied with improvements or business at another.

I think — in fact, I am certain of it — that even then, the chasm separating us might have remained an easily overstepped fissure if not for William's determination that Byron should go to sea. William had spoken of enlisting our eldest child in the Royal Navy for years, insisting that the discipline would strengthen his character and rid him of his irritating, childish habits. "He is too young," I protested every time William dragged the idea out for a good airing, but as the months passed and Byron became more fractious with his tutors and more sullen, obstinate, and unpleasant at home, I found my resistance wavering. Still, I raised every reasonable objection I could think of — he was too young, life at sea was too dangerous, he would not see his siblings for years, and they would lose all sense of family connection. One by one William parried my thrusts by listing the many benefits Byron would attain through military service, until I was quite worn down and disarmed.

And so in the summer of 1849, thirteen-year-old Byron went off rather reluctantly to sea, and the rest of the Lovelace family withdrew to Ashley Combe to distract ourselves from missing him. I worried constantly for the first fortnight he was gone, expecting every day to receive word that his ship had gone down with all hands, but a body could not long endure such constant fear and vigilance. Eventually my worries hardened into a stone that sank deep into the pool of my mind — always present, never forgotten, but no longer set directly before me, blocking all else from view.

It may seem contradictory, but through the disillusionment, the discord, and the disappointments, William and I remained fond of each other. In fact, I venture to say that we loved each other very much. We encouraged each other in our separate pursuits, we made each other laugh, and each would staunchly defend the other from unjust criticism from the children and any attack from beyond the family circle. And so when William proposed that we tour the North of England together in the lovely late summer and early autumn of 1850, I readily agreed.

"Perhaps it's time we accepted Colonel Wildman's invitation to visit him at Newstead Abbey," he said, almost as an afterthought. "He's been asking us to visit since the day we married, and Nottinghamshire would be on the route."

My heart seemed to stop for a moment. I took a deep breath, ignored a brief flash of worry at the thought of my mother's reaction, and told William I thought that was an excellent idea.

We planned an itinerary, wrote to friends we hoped to visit along the way, and packed our bags for an extended journey. We departed East Horsley Park at the end of August, heading first to Knebworth House in Hertfordshire, the home of our friend the writer Sir Edward Bulwer-Lytton. From there we moved on to Thrumpton Hall, the residence of my father's successor, Lord George Anson Byron, and his family, about eight miles from Nottingham, where we enjoyed a pleasant family reunion.

During our first dinner together, William remarked that we intended to visit Newstead Abbey later in our tour, although it was the nearest of our remaining stops. "It would be more convenient to go there from here," he acknowledged, "but Colonel Wildman is not home to receive us, so he suggested September instead."

Lord Byron's eyebrows rose as he turned a quizzical look upon me. "Does your mother know?"

"Of course," I said, feigning innocence. "We sent her a copy of our itinerary before we departed, and we've each written her several letters since."

"And she does not object?" Lady Byron asked.

"Why should she object?" asked William.

"Lord Lovelace, don't be coy," scolded Lady Byron, smiling.

"Newstead Abbey may no longer belong to the Byron family, but it is an important part of Lady Lovelace's heritage, and she ought to see it," said William. "Colonel Wildman has been inviting us to visit since we were married, and it's well past time we accepted."

"If we neglected the colonel this time too, while visiting so many other families, he would surely feel slighted," I said. "He would be quite right not to forgive us."

"I wholeheartedly agree with the visit and the intentions." Attempting to restore the jovial mood, Lord Byron added, "However, I suspect Lord Lovelace's true purpose is to study Colonel Wildman's improvements to the estate and compare them to his own efforts, and perhaps borrow a few ideas. Is that not so, Lord Lovelace?"

"I should have known better than to think I could keep my ulterior motives hidden from you," said William with forced humor. "That is, in fact, the only reason I intend to drag Lady Lovelace back to Nottinghamshire so soon after we will have left it."

We all smiled, some of us more tentatively than others.

"Of course you must go to Newstead Abbey," Lady Byron said to me. "You should have gone long ago. But all teasing aside, do take care how you describe your visit to your mother."

I nodded. She was kind to warn me, but I already knew my mother would be upset if I praised my father's former estate too highly, just as she took it as a personal insult if I admired his poetry, his portrait, his inkstand, or anything else that was from him or of him.

After a few days with Lord Byron's family, we continued on to Lea Hurst in Derbyshire, and then to Yorkshire, where we visited the second Earl of Zetland, Thomas Dundas, and his wife, Sophia, at Aske Hall. We had become friends through our mutual enjoyment of horse racing — my enjoyment, rather, not William's — for they owned my favorite horse, Voltigeur, one of the great champions of the day. From there William and I continued on to the Cumberland lakes, where we admired the breathtaking scenery, relaxed on the serene shores of clear waters, and enjoyed many delightful, strenuous rambles in the forests and fells. In this romantic place we discovered anew our old affection and desire, and I almost wished that we could remain forever, but instead I resolved to carry our rekindled passion home with us, and not to allow the distractions and duties of ordinary life to divide us again.

Then our journey turned south and east, as we set out for the Byron ancestral seat of Newstead Abbey.

CHAPTER THIRTY:
A NOBLE WRECK
IN RUINOUS PERFECTION

September 1850

My mother had rarely spoken of the Byron ancestral estate secluded deep within Sherwood Forest, except perhaps once or twice in reproving asides to rebuke my father for the careless, spendthrift ways that had obliged him to sell it to pay off excessive debts and save himself from poverty. Even so, it was too well-known, and too important to my heritage, for me to have learned nothing of its history along the way.

Newstead Abbey had begun life as an Anglican priory, founded by King Henry II around 1170 as part of his penance for the murder of Saint Thomas of Canterbury. In 1540, during the Dissolution of the Monasteries, King Henry VIII granted the original building and the surrounding lands to my ancestor, Sir John Byron of Colwick, who converted it to a country house. Through the years, his heirs expanded the house and improved the grounds until the estate came to my father's great-uncle, William Byron, the fifth Baron Byron, in 1736. He was known as "the Wicked Lord," and "the Devil Byron," two interesting sobriquets to find on one's family tree, to say the least.

By all accounts, he earned those names. He was violent and erratic and, according to some, quite mad. He lived to excess, adding Gothic follies to the estate and transforming the abbey into a stately and elegant home, but he also built a miniature castle in the forest, where he threw lavish parties and wild orgies, and he constructed two forts near a lake, where he staged naval battles complete with a live cannon to lend them an air of authenticity.

That marked him as eccentric; he was called wicked beginning in 1765 after he killed his cousin at a London tavern, running him through the stomach with his sword after a drunken argument over whose estate was more flush with game. He was tried for murder, but due to a quirk of the law, he was found guilty only of manslaughter and was commanded to pay a modest fine. Afterward, he had the sword he had used to kill his cousin mounted on his bedroom wall.

On another occasion, during another argument, William Byron shot his coachman dead, heaved the corpse into the coach over his wife's lap, took up the reins, and drove on. It was little wonder that his wife, Elizabeth, left him after this, but he unconcernedly took one of the maids as his mistress and required everyone to call her "Lady Betty."

Newstead Abbey might have survived his tenure as lord if his son and heir, also called William, had not defied him to elope with his beautiful cousin Juliana. The Wicked Lord had objected to the marriage on the grounds that he needed his son to marry a wealthy heiress in order to rescue the family from his own massive debts, and also because he believed they were too closely related and their children would be prone to madness, and clearly there was enough of that in the bloodline already. Outraged and vengeful, he resolved to despoil the beautiful estate so that his defiant son would inherit nothing but debt and ruins. He hacked down acres of ancient forest, slaughtered more than two thousand deer, pillaged once fertile fields, let ponds grow stagnant, and allowed the magnificent abbey to fall to pieces.

In the end, his vicious destruction of his ancestral estate was all for nothing, for he did not get the revenge he sought. He son died in 1776, and his grandson eighteen years later. Thus, upon the Wicked Lord's own death four years later, his legacy of madness and ruination, as well as the title of Lord Byron, fell unexpectedly to his ten-year-old grand-nephew, George Gordon, my father.

Newstead Abbey was leased to another baron until my father came of age, at which time he came to live in the derelict residence, despite the nearly caved-in roof and the rain-soaked paper left to rot on the walls. He promptly commenced the badly needed and very expensive renovations, and he tried to raise a mortgage so that he could afford them, but he was never able to manage it, and on the advice of lawyers and friends, he reluctantly decided to sell his ancient family home. For several years, one prospective sale after another fell through, but in 1818, when I was little more than two years old and living contentedly with my grandparents at Kirkby Mallory, oblivious to my father's struggles, he finally sold the estate for ninety-five thousand pounds to Colonel Thomas Wildman, who had been an admirer and sympathetic friend since they were schoolboys together at Harrow. In his more than three decades as master of Newstead Abbey, Colonel Wildman had invested a fortune in restoring it to its former glory, painstakingly preserving significant artifacts from my father's time there in tribute to the great poet.

William and I drove through the front gates of Newstead Abbey on the evening of Saturday, the seventh of September, crossing through the restored forest, rounding a corner, and glimpsing in the distance a clear, bright lake and the ruins of the Wicked

Lord's fortresses on opposite shores. And then, in the autumn twilight, I caught sight of Newstead Abbey itself, rising above the lake and reflected in its waters. It seemed to be split in two — one half a stately baronial hall, strong, whole, and resplendent; the second half the derelict ruins of the abbey, many of its stones evidently appropriated to restore the first.

The coach halted at the front entrance, where Colonel Wildman waited to welcome us, footmen standing ready nearby to assist us with our luggage. "Welcome to Newstead Abbey at long last, Lady Lovelace, Lord Lovelace," he said as we descended. "While you're here, and ever after, you must think of this as your own home."

"Thank you very much," I murmured, overcome with apprehension and anxiety, which had been steadily rising since we passed through the front gates. I felt the strange, unsettling sensation that I had been there before, as if I were observing my ancestral seat through my forebears' eyes. To my relief, I realized that I merely recognized it from its appearance in *Don Juan,* for my father had written it into the poem as Norman Abbey, the Amundevilles' country house.

Colonel Wildman was a slender, athletic man, as befitted an accomplished officer, of slightly more than average height, with tousled dark hair, a small mustache, and a minuscule beard that was little more than a vertical tuft of hair beneath his lower lip. "You must be famished and exhausted after your long journey," he said as he led us through the tall, arched front entrance. "Dinner is nearly ready, and I promise we won't keep you up too late afterward. We'll reserve the tour for tomorrow."

I could only nod as I gazed around the grand foyer in awe and inexplicable sadness. It was magnificently appointed with portraits and tapestries, dark wood and white plaster-work, illuminated by brilliant candelabra, but by my unhappy mood, I might have stumbled into a dark, foreboding cavern.

Just then, a small, brown-haired, apple-cheeked woman in a modest dark blue gown with gigot sleeves and a white lace fichu swept into the room. "Lord and Lady Love-lace," she said, smiling warmly, extending her hand as she crossed the room to join us. "My apologies for not being here to greet you, but I was detained by some last-minute excite-ment in the kitchen. It's all sorted now, so please do come in and restore yourselves with some good Nottingham food and drink."

She was so warm and merry that my spirits began to lift, and I sighed in relief as I took William's arm and Colonel and Mrs. Wild-man showed us to the dining room. To my surprise, this was, in fact, the abbey's Great

Hall, which was larger than ours at East Horsley Park and superior in comfort. It had a medieval character, with heraldic devices and armor adorning the paneled walls; a tall, peaked ceiling with dark beams and braces; an ornate oak screen framing the entrance; a massive fireplace in the center of one long wall; tall windows set back in alcoves that reached nearly to the ceiling on the wall opposite; and a minstrels' gallery, where I imagined I glimpsed the shadow of a bard strumming a lute, but it was only a trick of the light.

Mere moments after we walked in, another couple entered the hall from a doorway at the far end of the room. The Wildmans introduced us to their other guests, the Hamilton Greys, and we all sat down to table together.

The meal was excellent, exactly what I needed: wholesome, nourishing, and flavorful rather than fussy and heavy. Colonel Wildman entertained us with stories of his extensive renovations to the estate, some comical, others harrowing, but all bearing witness to his love for Newstead Abbey, his admiration for my father, and his devotion to his memory.

After supper, the men withdrew, but sensing my exhaustion, Mrs. Wildman kindly offered to show me to my room, which was on the second floor, dark with oak wainscoting and opening above the old cloister to the east, overlooking a Gothic fountain. Alone, I prepared for bed almost soundlessly, feeling as if I had entered a shrine, not only to my father, but also to his poetic heroes, like Childe Harold and Don Juan, and to other Byrons long past — the Wicked Lord and the first Lord Byron and all the others before and between.

It was a haunted room, filled with shades and memories, and though the bed was soft and warm, it was only with great difficulty that I drifted into restless sleep.

The next day, Colonel Wildman devoted himself to showing us around the estate, beginning with the interior of the abbey and then, after luncheon, leading us around the gardens and the grounds nearest the house. He courteously tried to draw me into conversation, but I felt too melancholic to reply except in brief murmurs. Fortunately William carried his share of the conversation and mine, too, and as I walked along quietly a few paces behind them, they discussed the colonel's renovations as only two devotees of that particular sport could. I was gratified to see that the baronial hall had been restored with taste and feeling, and that relics of my father and other ancestors had been respectfully preserved. I admired the stately, well-lit gallery and a cloister that formed a library, and I could see that the many rooms had been furnished with both comfort and elegance in mind — and yet none of the loveliness I observed could dispel my sense of desolation, as if I were walking through my family's tomb.

"The colonel's renovations are solid work, of excellent quality," William remarked to me when we were briefly alone before dressing for dinner. "Our bedchambers, however —" He glanced around, shaking his head. "They're far too gloomy and want better light. The arrangement of the house is too complicated, and the grounds are too encumbered with trees. Clearing them out would improve the views tremendously."

I murmured polite replies, but except for the gloomy bedchambers, I had not disliked any of the features my husband found objectionable. My problems with Newstead Abbey were of an entirely different nature.

Later that evening, after supper, I found myself again unable to sleep, so I dutifully wrote a letter to my mother, knowing that she would be expecting, and perhaps dreading, an account of my first impression of my father's former home. "We came here yesterday," I began.

I have not yet been over the whole, but it is grandly monastic, and everything speaks of the past history of the place and of the Byrons, for centuries. The repairs and restorations are most admirably done, and certainly no Byron could have afforded to do such justice to this antique and historical residence.

I feel as if, however, it ought to belong to *me;* and I am altogether horribly low and melancholy. All is like death round one; and I seem to be in the Mausoleum of my race. What is the good of living, when thus all passes away and leaves only cold stone behind it? There is no life here, but cold dreary death only, and everywhere — The death of everything that was!

I am glad to see the home of my ancestors, but I shall not be sorry to escape from the grave. I see my *own* future continuing visibly around me. They *were*! I *am,* but shall not be. Alas! Well, so it is, and will be, world without end.

We ought to have been happy, rich, and great. But one thing after another has sent us to the four winds of Heaven. The Civil Wars destroyed the estates and fortune, which were immense till the Roundheads seized it all. Only a very small part was restored to the Byrons afterwards.

They tell such tales here of "the Wicked Lord" as he was called commonly; — my father's predecessor and great-uncle, the one who killed his cousin.

I have not yet seen my father's rooms. No one is here but the Hamilton Greys, and we are perfectly quiet.

Only I feel as if I had become a stone monument myself. I am petrifying fast.

The following day, the colonel showed us my father's bedroom, which had been preserved unchanged, so that he might have walked out only moments before; afterward, he and Mrs. Wildman escorted us around the more distant parts of the grounds. We walked for hours through the enchanting forest, and the sunshine, the green foliage dancing in the breeze overhead, and the cheerful yellow gorse brightening the landscape did much to soothe my troubled spirits. The lakes were wonderfully soft and deep and clear, but the waters were forbiddingly cold.

The colonel again gallantly endeavored to engage me in conversation, and he had evidently studied for the occasion, for he introduced several topics of scientific interest. I was touched that he had gone to such lengths to prepare, and I tried to chat cordially with him, but I could not shake off my sorrowful mood despite the natural beauty all around us. At dinner I was no better, and as the men withdrew, I observed Colonel Wildman speaking earnestly to William, and William making what seemed to be apologies in return. I felt deeply embarrassed, for no hosts could have been kinder or more agreeable than the Wildmans had been, and they were surely concerned that I seemed to be having a miserable time.

I resolved to do better.

On Monday, the six of us rode out together to Annesley, the former home of Mary Chaworth, the granddaughter of the man whom the Wicked Lord had murdered. As a boy my father had adored her, but although they played together and were as close as siblings, his love for her was unrequited, and eventually she married another, breaking my father's young heart. Annesley, too, was strangely familiar to me, for my father had drawn it into his poem "The Dream." Mrs. Chaworth-Musters, as she became after her marriage, had died eight years before, so we met with her daughter instead. After we departed, the Wildmans assured us that she was strikingly like her mother, lovely, gentle, and well mannered.

"Perhaps you should avoid mentioning this excursion when you next write to your mother," William suggested in an undertone as we returned to the coach afterward.

"Excellent advice," I murmured back. "I intend to follow it."

From Annesley we rode out to Hucknall Torkard to pay our respects at my father's grave.

I expected to feel profound sorrow and regret upon viewing his tomb for the first time. What I did not expect, and what overwhelmed and moved me, was the sense of peace and love I felt near my father's final resting place. The family vault itself was in no way beautiful or profound, and yet standing there surrounded by the memorials to my father and so many other Byrons, I felt a strange sensation of welcome, of acceptance, of reconciliation. I said nothing to my husband, but I could imagine no better place for my own eternal rest than here, beside my father.

I was quiet and pensive as we returned to Newstead Abbey, but it was a different silence than before, contemplative rather than mournful, although I suppose the distinction was imperceptible to anyone else.

On the morning of 10 September, I rose early and decided to stroll through the gardens, cool and fragrant in the mist. I inhaled deeply, taking in grass and earth and late-summer blossoms, and I imagined my father here as a young man full of hope and impatience and ambition, breathing in and breathing out, grinning as he envisioned how magnificent the estate he had inherited would be after he restored it to its former glory.

I smiled too, wistful, as I turned away from the garden and plunged into a thick grove of ancient trees. This was called the Devil's Wood, planted by the Wicked Lord and strewn with statues of fauns and satyrs. This forest alone he had spared from the axe and the torch, and it had become dark and overgrown, and the colonel had told me that my father had loved to explore it. I followed the path to the fishpond, soothed by the music of songbirds flitting through the boughs above as I imagined placing my soft boots into my father's own footprints, long since erased by wind and rain and time.

I had heard that in the center of the wood grew an unusual elm tree, two trunks springing from the same root. I recognized it from a distance and carefully made my way off the path and through the underbrush until I reached it. Side by side the two trunks stretched upward to the sky, separate but unified, their branches growing, intertwining, to form a single leafy green canopy. I lay my hand upon the tree and walked around it, the bark rough against my palm, searching for another memorial my father was said to have left behind. Then I saw it, and my heart ached with regret and compassion. Here, on a farewell visit to their ancestral estate before it was sold, my father and my aunt Augusta had carved their names into the bark, uniting them in the seclusion of the wood as they never could be out in the world.

I traced the letters with my fingertips and wished my father and my aunt had been granted more peace and happiness than they had known in life. There was still hope for Augusta, but to me it seemed but a faint, flickering light, too easily extinguished.

I lay my cheek against the tree for a moment, a gesture of farewell, and then I retraced my steps until I found the narrow path back to the gardens. I had almost reached the fishpond when a shadow shifted in front of me. I gasped and halted in my tracks as the shadow solidified into the figure of a man.

"Lady Lovelace?" said Colonel Wildman, emerging into a shaft of light that broke through the boughs overhead. "Are you lost?"

"No, not at all," I said, relieved. "Merely exploring. I was on my way back to the house."

"Shall I accompany you?"

"Please do."

He offered me his arm, and I took it. We strolled along in silence for a while, but whenever the path narrowed, I was obliged to release his arm so we could walk single file. The darkness thinned, more sunlight broke through, and then we emerged into the gardens. The morning sun had burned off the mist, and trees and flowers and hedgerows appeared before us in harmonious order.

"Lady Lovelace," said Colonel Wildman, "forgive me, but I must speak. Are you displeased with the changes I've made to Newstead Abbey?"

"Not at all," I said, surprised. "Everything has been wonderfully restored. No Byron could have done better. I even wrote to tell my mother so."

My praise seemed to please him, and yet his brow was furrowed, his expression pensive. "Then may I ask why you have been so silent and unhappy during your stay? Have we done something, or failed to do something?"

"Oh, dear me, no," I exclaimed, dismayed. "You and Mrs. Wildman have been lovely and gracious hosts. I beg you to forgive my reticence, but I have been overwhelmed by the feelings this extraordinary place evokes in me. If I had come here as a child, if I had always known it, I'm sure I would not feel so, so —" I inhaled deeply to steady myself. "So disconcerted, so much at home and yet so much a stranger. I confess that the sadness and loss I feel upon seeing so many memorials to my father, a father I don't even remember, have quite overwhelmed me." My voice quavered, and I struggled to compose myself. "Then, too, I have felt oppressed by the necessity to keep my feelings hidden."

"Lady Byron is not here to observe you," he said gently. "You don't have to pretend you feel nothing for your father, not here."

I managed a shaky laugh. "It has become a habit."

"Perhaps it's time you broke it. Come." He offered me his arm again. "Let's stroll around the garden for a while. I think you've had enough stories about Lord Byron. Let me tell you about George Gordon, the boy he was, the boy I knew."

As we walked, he shared with me his own memories of my father, as well as confidences my father had shared with him — his difficult childhood with an unreliable mother given to violent tempers, his shame and disgust for his deformed foot, his early passion for literature, his love for the Scottish Highlands, his initial academic struggles at Harrow, his outrage at the horrid treatment he received there.

For the rest of our visit, Colonel Wildman generously reminisced for me, until for the first time in my life I felt that I knew my father — not the poet who had astonished the world with his genius, not the husband who had wronged my mother, but the boy he was and the man he became. And with every story the colonel told, Newstead Abbey became more dear to me.

When the time came for William and me to continue our tour, I was truly sorry to go, but I was heartened by Colonel Wildman's assurance that I was welcome to return anytime. I hoped I would soon.

I had been so overwhelmed by all that I had observed and discovered at Newstead Abbey that I had not found time to write to my mother since I had had recorded my first gloomy impressions on our second night there. It was not until a week after sending that letter that I was able to write another, from Radbourne in Derbyshire.

Yours of the 14th received this morning. We came here last evening after a most delightful and successful tour of three days to see all the Beauties of Derbyshire. A completely nomadic life suits me wonderfully.

My first and very melancholy impressions at Newstead gradually changed to quite an affection for the place before I left it. I began to feel as if it were an old home, and I left it with regret and reluctance, and feel that I must go back to it before a year is over.

Colonel Wildman is a man of talent, feeling, and good taste. There is no profession in him, but he acts and lives in devotion to my father and my race. He knew my father only in his very young days, Col W's profession as a Soldier entirely withdrawing him afterwards.

It has been the salvation of Newstead, that he has had it. No one else in the world would have resuscitated it, and all its best reminiscences, as he has done. And no Byron could have afforded even to preserve the edifice from actually tumbling down. The outlay requisite has been enormous.

There is an old prophecy that the place was to pass out of the family when it did, and which further adds that it is to come back in the present generation!

Altogether it is an epoch in my life, my visit there. I have lost my monumental and desolate feeling respecting it. It seemed like descending into the grave, but I have had a resurrection. I do love the venerable old place and all my wicked forefathers!

After Radbourne, William and I parted company for a few days, as he went off to Lincolnshire to learn about the latest advances in agriculture and animal husbandry, and I returned to Lord and Lady Zetland at Aske Hall in Yorkshire. The Zetlands had invited me to accompany them to Doncaster, where their horse Voltigeur would compete against Flying Dutchman for the Doncaster Cup, the most illustrious of all races. William missed the first day of the tournament, so he did not see Voltigeur sail to a first-place finish in his early race, but he joined us the next day in time to cheer on Voltigeur as he challenged Flying Dutchman, who was said to have no equal.

William was fortunate indeed that he had come, for together we witnessed history. How thrilling it was to see Voltigeur speeding down the homestretch and crossing the finish line ahead of all challengers, including the invincible Flying Dutchman! It was the greatest triumph ever in racing, a magnificent struggle between these two greatest of champions, like single combat between two gallant knights of olden times. How delighted I was to have witnessed what would surely go down in history as the greatest of all races!

We returned to Aske Hall exultant in victory, especially our hosts, who were justifiably proud of their champion. Eventually, however, I noticed that William's joviality seemed somewhat forced, but I attributed that to his displeasure to see me gambling more than I should have. I had won handsomely, so he had no cause to complain, and so I put it out of my thoughts.

The next day when we were alone after breakfast, I discovered the real cause of his displeasure. "I hesitate to show you this," he said, frowning, as he handed me a letter. "Your mother sent it to me first, with a letter instructing me to give it to you after I had read it."

"Oh, dear. What now?" I muttered, but I unfolded the letter and began to read.

Even from my mother's pen, it was an astonishing diatribe, a vicious rebuke for entertaining mythical ideas about my father spread by "the partisans of Byron" among whom I had been living. "They consider me as having taken a hostile position towards him," she wrote. "You must not be infected with an error resulting from their ignorance and his mystifications. I was his best friend, not only in feeling, but in fact, after the

Separation, and saved him from involving himself in what would have injured his private character and reputation still further."

I knew the injurious act she alluded to, for I had heard her boast to her friends that she had saved my father from eloping with my aunt Augusta, which would have ruined him utterly. She never explained exactly how she had accomplished this, at least not in my hearing, and I was not quite sure that she had prevented anything. If my father had truly intended to elope with his sister, why had he not taken her along when he went into exile?

My mother continued on in the same shrilly furious manner, defending herself, condemning my father's wicked friends for deceiving me, condemning me for being deceived. Then, in a breathtaking maneuver that I can only imagine was meant to frighten me into submission, she threatened to cut off all contact with my children if I chose to remain friends with those who despised and maligned her. "It would be better for my grandchildren not to have known me," she declared, "if they are allowed to adopt the unfounded popular notion of my having abandoned my husband from want of devotedness and entire sympathy — or if they suppose me to have been under the influence, at any time, of cold, calculating, and unforgiving feelings."

On and on she went — or so she might have

done, except she reached the end of the page and had to conclude, which she did with the curt invitation, "Write to me what you think and feel openly."

Of course she did not mean that; she never did. She did not want to know what I truly thought and felt unless my views perfectly aligned with her own; she did not want to hear me speak unless my words expressed perfect adoration of her perfection. She could not permit anyone to perceive any fault in her, or rather, she could not accept that she possessed any faults. My father, for all of his mistakes and bad choices, at least had been willing to acknowledge that he was a flawed human being, striving for goodness and greatness, but too often falling short of the sublime ideal.

I would have given anything for my mother to have possessed an ounce of such insight and humility.

I hardly knew how to respond to her letter. How could one address such an astonishing array of baffling accusations? And the threats to withdraw her love, attention, and support from my children if I did not repent my defiance — what sort of grandmother would do such a thing?

The same sort of woman she had always been, I realized, from the moment she had carried me away from my father and had insisted that I repudiate him. She could have

737

brought me up to view him with compassion-
ate understanding, regretting his sins but loving the good in him. I had had to learn that
on my own — with the help of kind, honest
people she now wanted me to renounce.

But I was no longer a little girl she could
order her proxies to lock in a closet.

I took a day to compose my thoughts, to
reflect upon all that had passed between us.
Then I responded, as kindly and respectfully
as I knew how.

I feel some difficulty in replying to your
enclosure of yesterday — because it seems
to me as if addressed to a Phantom of
something that does not exist.

No feeling or opinion respecting my father's moral character, or your relations
toward him could be altered by my visit to
Newstead, or by any tone assumed by any
parties whatever.

I am confident, however, that no tone of
the kind you conceive exists with the Wildmans. One may feel the deepest interest in
persons and characters whom one cannot
(morally speaking) admire.

Nothing passed while I was there which
could, directly or indirectly, bear the slightest relation to his matrimonial history, or to
any of the indefensible points of his life. I
am persuaded that there is nothing of the
Partisan about Col. Wildman, and if all my

father's friends had been of Col. Wildman's sort it would have been well for him. But after school days they lost sight of each other.

Mrs. Leigh and her children are no favorites at Newstead. Indeed it is some years since she has been there. I heard a good deal about that.

So far from having a mythical veneration for my father, I cannot (to adhere only to personal considerations) forget his conduct as regards my own self.

I write this all off hand and in a hurry. Probably I shall write again and more fully on the subject.

That would be entirely up to my mother, and how she responded to my refusal to cower before her threats, to accept as right what was so obviously wrong.

With her own words and deeds, she had finally freed me of the tether of mythical veneration of either of my parents. I had built my own wings, and with them I would soar to the stars.

EPILOGUE:
HOPES WHICH
WILL NOT DECEIVE

September–December 1850

I had defied my mother by standing fast for what I believed to be true — and I had lived to tell the tale. In the weeks that followed, my mother fired back a few more angry, self-righteous letters, I responded with sincere concern and love, and eventually she yielded. That is not to say that she admitted wrongdoing or apologized, but she ceased condemning me, and she did not abandon her grandchildren.

That was victory enough for me.

In hindsight, I realized that my rebellion had begun long ago — not in my childhood defiance of rules and restrictions, but in my embrace of the imagination, my gradual rejection of the notion that I must suppress it, deny it, if I hoped to escape a fatal descent into madness. All along it had been the vain struggle to purge myself of imagination that had almost destroyed me, not my bad Byron blood, not some inherent wickedness.

I think that all my life, in small ways and great, I had tried to bring together the intellect and the imagination, sensing that they were not two separate faculties, but two halves of the same genius. Both intellect and imagination had inspired my childhood pursuit of Flyology, and both had been essential to my understanding of the Analytical Engine as I wrote my Notes. After the ill-fated publication of the Memoir, as I struggled to find a new vocation, to devote myself to another Great Work, I had argued with my mother about the imprudence — in fact, the impossibility — of renouncing the imagination entirely and forever. "You will not concede me philosophical poetry," I had written to her angrily after she had tried to discourage me from studying music, poetry, and philosophy. "Invert the order! Will you give me poetical philosophy, poetical science?"

Poetical science, I resolved, would be my new vocation, and I was filled with excitement and anticipation as I awaited the discovery of where this would lead me in the years to come.

With fortuitous timing that seemed to me evidence that I was embarking upon the right path, another celebration of a great and glorious future of science and wonder was coming to London. This Great Exhibition of the Works of Industry of All Nations, opening in

May, was meant to demonstrate to the entire world Great Britain's role at the forefront of industrial accomplishment and innovation. It would present to an eager audience, expected to run into the millions over the course of its six months, the greatest discoveries and artifacts of industry and culture. The Great Exhibition promised to be a magnificent display of technology, art, science, and commerce, honoring the achievements of the past while offering thrilling glimpses of our hopes and aspirations for the future.

Mr. Babbage had been eager to participate in the management of what was certain to be a glorious event, but his ongoing disputes with certain powerful men in government had led to his exclusion from the organizing committee. He was bitterly disappointed, but he found some consolation in writing a book about the Great Exhibition, which, as he pointed out, would continue to intrigue and inform readers long after the exhibition closed in October 1851.

As a part of his research, he interviewed many potential exhibitors, including William, who intended to display the innovative process he had developed for brickmaking. Mr. Babbage also studied plans for the various construction projects under way on the exhibition grounds in Hyde Park, especially the Crystal Palace, an enormous structure of glass and cast iron that already was being touted as an architectural marvel even though it was only partially completed.

In late December, Mr. Babbage invited me to accompany him on a tour of the construction site with Sir James South, a mutual friend and member of the organizing committee. "Be sure to wear thick stockings and sturdy shoes," Mr. Babbage instructed. "There are many potential hazards underfoot, and delicate lady's slippers are no match for them."

I immediately accepted the invitation, although I was quite unwell and had been for several weeks. My complaints were vague and various, but the most persistent were abdominal pains — sometimes sharp, sometimes a dull ache — and bleeding when I was not expecting my menses. Laudanum offered me some relief from the pains, but as always, it did nothing to cure whatever caused them. When the glow of the drops faded, the torment returned, sometimes more intensely than before. Dr. Locock was baffled; he and William suggested that perhaps it was all in my head. I knew they were wrong, but how did one prove that one felt pain?

But on that December day, my interest in the Great Exhibition compelled me to ignore my discomfort and ride out to Hyde Park with Mr. Babbage. I bundled up in my warmest dress and heaviest wool coat and hood to ward off the cold, and fortunately the winds were calm, the sun pale but valiant, and only a few flakes of snow drifted lazily down upon us when we arrived at the construction site. It fairly swarmed with workers carrying all manner of tools and iron pieces back and forth. Mr. Babbage promptly spotted Sir James South in the crowd and offered me his arm, and together we carefully made our way to his side.

It was a fascinating tour, and as our courteous guide showed us around and described the enormous palace of glass that would emerge from the present chaos, a veritable cathedral to science and industry rising in the heart of London, I could imagine it sparkling like a jewel, casting beams of enlightenment that would reflect around the world. In this chamber would be the display of scientific instruments — microscopes, barometers, the telegraph, and every other imaginable device. Here would be a demonstration of steelmaking, and there a reaping machine sent all the way from the United States. And there, given pride of place, would be the Jacquard loom, which offered not only beautifully woven fabric, but inspiration as well.

From time to time I caught Mr. Babbage's eye, and from his rueful half smile, I could tell that he was thinking, as I was, that the most astonishing invention of our age would not be celebrated here, for it was back in

Marylebone in Mr. Babbage's workshop, represented by thousands of pages of notes and drawings, and one all too quickly forgotten Memoir.

It was profoundly unfair that Mr. Babbage would not be represented at an exhibition meant to celebrate the very best of industrial achievement and innovation.

At the end of the tour, Sir James South bade us farewell, and Mr. Babbage and I walked the long way around the construction site to take one last look at the busy scene before we returned to the carriage. "It seems to me that in such a vast space, they ought to be able to find room to display the demonstration model of your Difference Engine," I told Mr. Babbage as he assisted me aboard.

Shaking his head, he climbed in after me and seated himself. "There's room enough for the entire Analytical Engine, if they cared enough to show it. Of course, that would require them to care enough to have it built."

"If they only knew what it was and what it could do," I said, impassioned, "if they truly understood, they would spare no expense."

"The men who pay the bills don't understand, and the men who understand don't have the resources," said Mr. Babbage. "I'm beginning to agree with our dear friend Mrs. Somerville, that perhaps the world is not ready for my engines."

I reached out to him, took his hand, and

squeezed it. "One day it shall be," I told him emphatically. "Your engine shall be built, and all of our disappointment will be nothing but a fleeting memory."

He nodded and thanked me, and in an undertone that I was not sure I was meant to hear, he added that he sincerely hoped I was right.

I was sure that I was. I had to be. A magnificent invention such as Mr. Babbage's Analytical Engine could never be entirely forgotten once the idea of it was set free into the world. It might be neglected, perhaps for years, but eventually its time would come, and it would thrive.

As for me, I often feel that my time is running out, and that I will not live to see the Analytical Engine constructed. I will not marvel as it transforms the world; I will not enjoy a sense of proud vindication when my own Great Work is finally respected and hailed as prophetic. But I daresay I will not be forgotten. This narrative will survive me, as will my Notes, and when Mr. Charles Babbage finally realizes his magnificent dream, my contributions also will be celebrated. But whether this will be next year or many decades from now, even with the combined powers of my intellect and my imagination I cannot know for certain. I can only hope.

Ours was a false dawn, a soft, brilliant glow that swiftly faded, but eventually day would